A Modicum of Truth

Justice #2

SUZAN HARDEN

A Modicum of Truth
ISBN: 978-1-938745-59-1
Copyright 2018 by Suzan Harden
All rights reserved
Ingramspark Special Edition: June 2019

Published by Angry Sheep Publishing
Findlay, Ohio
Cover by For the Muse Designs
Interior Design by QA Productions

For more information or to join her mailing list, visit Suzan's website at www.suzanharden.com

To Professor Helen Jenkins of South Texas College of Law and Author Mercedes Lackey, two ladies who don't realize how much they've influenced me.

Prologue

It is said Balance arose from the primal nothingness of Chaos. As She divided land and sea and air, stars and sun and moon, animals and fish and birds, She realized She had no one with which to share Her new world. So She divided Herself and created Light. When He beheld the beauty of Balance for the first time, He gave a name to what He felt. And Love was born from Them.

However, Love grew jealous of the bond between Balance and Light. She also divided Herself and released Conflict into the world. But Conflict knew no boundaries. Love begged Him to prove His affection for Her. In Her envious spite, She whispered that if all things were gone, She would be His forever. So to seal Love's affection, Conflict laid waste to the world Balance had wrought.

Balance and Light were appalled by what Love and Conflict had done. They banished the Two and swore never to be together again as Themselves. To amend the damage of Conflict, Balance and Light became Mother and Father. Their second offspring was Child, who healed and cared for the decimated earth, repairing the destruction wrought by Conflict.

But when She was done with Her task, Child searched for something else to do. She took after Mother in Her urge to create. With Her clay, Child formed little statues of Mother and Father. But they did not move as the other creatures Balance had made. She asked Mother how She was created. Fearing for the world after the destruction Love had initiated out of Her jealousy, Mother refused to tell the truth so She gave Child a different word.

Child went back to Her little statues and whispered the word She'd been given. Hearing the word, "Life", the human race took its first breath.

Love couldn't survive alone with Conflict, so She snuck back into the world and beheld Child's new creations. While Love was delighted with Child's new beings, Her ancient envy infected them.

Angered by Love's abandonment, Conflict followed Her and discovered Her new obsession. He took His loneliness and rage out on the humans. But rather than harm them directly, He took a lesson from Love's manipulations. Conflict murmured falsehoods, urging the humans to hurt, or even kill, one another, which they did easily and without remorse because of Love's envy.

When Light discovered Conflict's malevolence towards mankind, He sought to counter the damage by showing them Truth.

- The First Book of Light, Verses III thru IX

Chapter 1

I brushed past High Brother Luc's personal attendant Istaqa and laid the scroll I carried on the chief priest of Light's desk. "The pardon arrived. It's official. I've been given leave to go south with you."

While Istaqa stood in the doorway of the high brother's office and harrumphed in disgust, Luc took his time chewing whatever was in his mouth. The orange-warm items on his plate had bites missing. A surreptitious sniff of the room revealed sweet pumpkin bread and eggs coated in Cantish hot sauce. My empty stomach grumbled its delight of both aromas.

Luc swallowed and regarded me. "Istaqa, the Chief Justice won't leave until you feed her. Also, please bring her another pot of tea. And Anthea—"

I resisted the urge to sigh. Luc was determined to hold me to my oath at his predecessor's funeral to do a better job as Orrin's chief justice. I faced his attendant and bowed. "My apologies for my rudeness, Istaqa."

The man's second harrumph was slightly less disgusted than the first. He pivoted smartly on his heel and marched from the office.

"Sorry," I muttered.

"I'm impressed you remembered his name," Luc remarked.

"You made a point of addressing him by it." I glared at Luc.

"But there was a whole three heartbeats between me saying it, and you apologizing." He grinned. "It doesn't say much for Balance's vaunted memory training."

I called the high brother a Cantish name that questioned his parentage, though mine was far more scandalous than his. Especially since I'd recently learned his predecessor at the Temple of Light, High Brother Kam, was my maternal grandfather.

Scandalous since members of the Temple of Light took a vow of chastity. As did members of my own order.

Not that our vows had ever stopped Luc or I from indulging.

Luc broke into laughter. "I know you're excited about regaining your freedom—"

"I'm hoping to see an old friend and discover she's all right," I said primly. And I truly did hope the Reverend Mother's fears that something had happened to Justice Elizabeth were unfounded. She was the only priestess who showed me a modicum of kindness after I attempted to give myself sight.

"—but you need to scale down the enthusiasm," Luc finished as if I hadn't spoken. "Things are tenuous enough with Mother Bianca and Father Jerrod."

I winced as I sat in a visitor's chair. The two temple seats had sent letters of protest to the queen when they learned she planned to pardon me for my illegal execution of her cousin, Samael DiRoy. The priestess and priest seemed to forget I did it because DiRoy summoned demons in order to seize the throne. The Twelve only knew what else the little idiot had planned before I cut off his head.

And if I hadn't killed him to break the summoning spell, everyone in Orrin would be dead, and the demons would have spread across the world.

My relationship with Bianca and Jerrod wasn't helped by the fact I made them look like fools when the plots and schemes of Gerd, the former High Sister of Love, came to light.

Balance help me, I couldn't even consider Gerd my mother anymore even though the traitorous bitch had given birth to me. When she was caught attempting to sell a demon grimoire along with children for immoral uses, her actions left me feeling less than charitable toward her. Plotting with the Assassins Guild to kill me was the proverbial last straw.

I shook my head and sighed. "I imprisoned Jerrod so he would be blameless for my actions. He'll forgive me eventually." I hoped. My methods to expose the traitors within Orrin's Twelve Temples were questionable, but I hadn't known who I could trust or how deep the conspiracy went.

At best, I should have been reprimanded and removed from my post by my own order's Reverend Mother. At worst, the assassins could have succeeded in killing both Luc and me.

He picked up the scroll and perused it. "Have you had any word concerning Gerd's trial?"

I shook my head again at the mention of her. I definitely hadn't drunk enough tea before the courier arrived with the queen's pardon to deal with any thoughts of her. I snatched Luc's mug and took a gulp. The overly sweet tea made me want to retch.

He eyed me over the edge of the scroll. "You spit that back in my cup, and I'll throw you in the gaol myself."

I forced the mouthful down my throat and made a face at him while I set down the cup. "That's nearly pure honey. How can you stand drinking it?"

He slapped my hand as I reached for a slice of bread. "Serves you right for stealing someone else's tea. And it has medicine in it to increase my blood flow. The honey masks the taste."

I tried not to stare at his stump propped on a padded stool. The stump where his left foot and ankle had been a month ago. Guilt squirmed in my mind. Luc had been abducted because Gerd had started the rumor we were having an affair. I should have been amused how her spiteful gossip led everyone in the city to believe we *weren't* having an affair after she was arrested for treason.

Unfortunately, the renegades she dealt with, and who believed her rumor, decided to hold Luc hostage against me and my office. Then they sent me proof they imprisoned him.

"Stop it," Luc ordered.

"What?" I said, trying to act innocent.

"I can't stand that kicked puppy expression you get when you look at me."

"It's my fault it didn't occur to me the bitch was selling demon artifacts."

He didn't have to question which bitch I referred to. He gulped his tea before he spoke. "And it's my fault I didn't realize that imposter Mat, Micah, whatever his birth name was, wasn't a true brother of Light," he growled.

"It's both of your faults that we are short-staffed at the moment." Istaqa set a tray in front me before he turned to Luc. "And once again, High Brother, I must protest. A woman as a member of the order of Light is highly inappropriate."

I gratefully sipped my plain black Jing tea, enjoying the fact I wasn't the one being lectured for once. My own staff dished out more than enough.

Luc sighed and leaned back in his chair. "What did Sister Shi Hua do this time?"

"She still insists on bathing with the men!"

I stifled a laugh at the attendant's mortified tone. Unlike the order of Light in Issura, their counterpart in the Jing Empire allowed both men and women to serve as clergy. In addition to admiring the sister's more than capable skills, I personally liked Shi Hua. It had been my recommendation the Jing priestess assist Luc while our own Reverend Father of Light audited all the temples of his order in Issura for additional imposters.

Luc appeared calm, even to my peculiar sight as he regarded his aide, but I could feel his irritation prickle along my psyche. "We do not have a separate facility for her. Not to mention she's used to joint accommodations in her homeland."

Istaqa's coloring creeped from orange to red. "This could turn into a scandal."

Luc crossed his arms. "Are you planning on sending her down to the public bath house? Because that *would* cause a scandal. It says my staff can't keep their vows, or their libidos, in check when we have a guest."

"B-b-but—" Istaqa turned to me for help.

I quickly shoved a huge bite of eggs rolled in flatbread into my mouth and gave him an innocent look. I'd done a great many ill-conceived things in my thirty-one winters, but I wasn't about to jump into the middle of this argument.

"There is no 'but' here, Istaqa," Luc ground out. "If neither you nor the rest of the staff can behave yourselves around Sister Shi Hua, I'll be happy to send the lot of you back to Standora for reassignment. And that's after she finishes kicking your asses."

The assistant's visage shaded from red to crimson. I wasn't sure if it was Luc's threat to send him back the main temple at the capital or that Luc reprimanded him in my presence.

Or maybe it was the fact that Shi Hua probably could take on the entire priesthood, wardens, and staff of the Orrin Temple of Light and win.

"Yes, High Brother." Once again, Istaqa pivoted on his boot heel and stomped out of Luc's office. This time, he slammed the heavy oak door for good measure.

I finished chewing and swallowed. "Trouble?"

"Nothing you didn't start," Luc snapped.

His bad mood stung. "I was trying to help you when I recommended Shi Hua. With that damn audit and—" I shrugged. There was no judicious way to point out between the imposter who'd murdered the real Brother Mat, Kam's death during the battle to regain control of the Temple of Love, and Luc's own injury, the junior-most priest at Light, poor Brother Jeremy, had been run ragged until both the Issuran and Jing Reverend Fathers of Light agreed to Shi Hua's temporary transfer.

With my prodding and assistance from both nations' Reverend Mothers of Balance.

"I know. I'm sorry." Luc poured more tea into his mug and added a healthy dollop of honey. "With the current investigation into the infiltration—"

"Yes?" I prompted.

"This cannot leave my office."

I raised an eyebrow. *And how do you plan to stop Istaqa? He's listening outside your door, you know.*

Luc sipped his tea before he grinned. *By using silent speech so he can't hear a blessed word.* He quickly sobered. *They found another infiltrator at the Temple of Light in Multnomah.*

A chill rippled across my skin. Part of me had hoped our situation here in Orrin was an isolated incident. *But that's in Pagonia.*

And Tandor is on the border with Cant.

Tandor. Our sister city to the south. All evidence pointed to our problems coming from there, but if Issura's northern neighbor also had been compromised . . .

But our imposter was born on the island of New Thenos, I countered.

And that's on the other side of the continent. I agree with Shi Hua. With the demon incidents here and in Jing, we may have stumbled across a worldwide conspiracy. It's not a coincidence so many Light Temples have been compromised. Discreet messages have gone out to our counterparts in other lands. Very quietly.

I couldn't suppress my shiver. Such a plot would explain why someone had hired the Assassins Guild to kill me. Thanks to my inept attempt to gain human eyesight, I was the only one who could see demons, regardless of their spells and shapechanging.

And once again, it made me wonder why Shi Hua was at the top of the wishlist of the Assassins Guild's mysterious client. I was beginning to think it wasn't because she was a distance speaker of incredible power.

"You're worried about leaving Jeremy and Shi Hua here alone," I said, giving Istaqa something to gossip about.

"I'm more worried about my staff doing something incredibly idiotic," he started, using a variation of one of my favorite words. "Especially when it comes to our visiting sister."

"This is what happens when they demand chastity from our orders," I grumbled. "I could have Gina guard her in the bathing room here if you want. Or she could use the facilities at Balance."

"Or I could petition the Issuran Reverend Father of Light to amend our order's criteria and allow the admission of women."

I stared at Luc. "Do you think he'd actually consider such a proposal?"

Luc shrugged. "We may not have a choice. Not if there are more infiltrators like Micah. It all depends on what we find in Tandor when we ride down for the audit."

"And in the meantime?"

He grinned. "I'm looking forward to watching our visitor from Jing wipe the cobblestones with anyone idiotic enough to lay an improper finger on her."

Chapter 2

Later the same morning, court lasted less than a candlemark. My new protégé, Justice Yanaba, banged the hilt of her sword to end the day's session. For the last week, I'd observed her demeanor and knowledge. I'd also acted as her truthspeller in my own court to give poor, overworked Brother Jeremy a break.

Port trade and petty crime usually picked up at the end of winter once it was safe to cross the Peaceful Sea. But even with the Sea Peoples fleet still in port thanks to another series of storms, the city of Orrin's mood remained subdued. With the recent murders of a priest and priestess plus fourteen wardens, no one wanted to break the brittle peace. Not even the foreign sailors looking to spend their bonuses.

The unease was part grief and part fear. The murders were unprecedented. Add in the fact that during the course of our investigation and rescue of Luc, Brother Jeremy had killed a demon in the ancient escape tunnels dug beneath the city walls, and everyone was jumping at shadows.

Lately, the docket had been very light, mainly consisting of the settlement of the estates of the dead and the city peacekeepers caught taking bribes in the midst of the recent chaos. It didn't help the citizens' fear when word got out that the imposter priest Mat had died under my truthspell rather than submit to my questioning.

Over the last month, I stared at my bedchamber ceiling and wondered if Balance was simply allowing me to catch my breath before a worse crisis occurred.

My chief warden Little Bear approached my chair to the side of the podium as people filed quietly out of the Temple courtroom. "Chief Justice?"

He rarely hesitated, and even more rarely used my full formal title, which forced my undivided attention. "Yes?"

"I'm about to have a meeting with the rest of the Balance wardens."

I waited, trying to swallow my impatience.

"We request your presence, Chief Justice."

His words made my clerks Donella and Leilani hesitate as they gathered the day's paperwork. Even Yanaba tilted her head in my direction. To say Little Bear's request was unusual would be like saying I loved Jing black tea. From the stiff posture of Warden Tyra by the court's double doors, something had crawled up the temple guards' collective asses, and they weren't happy confronting me about it.

I faced Little Bear again. "May I ask why?"

His face shifted to deep orange. "I'd rather not say in a public space, Chief Justice."

Serious enough to warrant a very private conference. With the recent spate of murders, the corruption of Love, and the imposter priest caught within Light, I'd normally be far more cautious. But if one of my wardens belonged to the renegades and wanted to slit my throat, they could have done that when I bunked with them over the week the Reverend Mother of Balance reviewed my investigation of the murders and the problems at Love.

The old biddy had co-opted my quarters out of spite rather than share the guest rooms on the second floor with her entourage. Privately, I thought she kicked me out of my own bed out of sheer laziness rather than climb the stairs herself.

No. The more likely answer regarding the Reverend Mother's behavior had to do with her admission she knew about mine and Luc's affair. A subtle punishment since dragging us back to the capital for trial would cause even more scandal.

I nodded to Little Bear. "Very well then." I followed him to the temple's main receiving room. Tyra brought up the rear. Inside, the other ten wardens waited, standing.

Along with Orrin's magistrate, Malven DiCook. He and I hadn't gotten along when I was first assigned here, but over the last month, we had come to respect each other's abilities.

I cocked my head. "Since when do you need trickery to visit during the midday meal, Magistrate?"

"I wish your Deborah's wonderful cooking was the reason for my presence." He hooked his thumbs in his belt, which meant he was disturbed by something. "I didn't think it was wise to announce this in public."

A chill crawled up my spine. "Announce what?"

"One of my peacekeepers was found dead in his home when he didn't appear for his shift this morning. His wife and children were dead as well. We have reason to believe they were poisoned. I came to ask for your insight into the matter."

I didn't need to read his thoughts to know what he feared. The members of the Assassins Guild sometimes used poison on their victims.

Or on themselves when they were caught.

Unfortunately, my temple was technically in charge of any murder investigation, but this was one of his people.

I nodded and turned to Little Bear. "Was this the only matter to be discussed?"

"No, Lady Justice." My chief warden's countenance was grim. "But it has taken priority for this hour." As if to mark his words, the stones beneath my feet thrummed as the temple bells rang First Afternoon.

I met the eyes of two of the junior wardens. "Noko, Daniel, you're with me." I faced DiCook again. "How far is the home?"

"Two side streets from Government Gate."

Government Gate was the main entrance into Orrin from the National Road. In other words, not far from Government House, which hosted the bureaucracy that kept the city running, including the magistrate's office. Far too close to the peacekeeper's main facility for Malven's comfort.

"May I bring Justice Yanaba with me?"

He scratched his beard. "I suppose. I didn't think I'd be dealing with my third justice during my term. I also didn't think the Reverend Mother of Balance would reassign you so soon."

"Reassign me? What the demon are you blathering about?"

He shrugged. "You made no secret you don't want to be here in Orrin during the funerals last month."

I suppressed my wince. I'd been a little too honest during my eulogy of Warden Aglaia.

"I figured with the queen pardoning you, you'd request reassignment," DiCook finished.

I blinked. "How did you find out about my pardon? It only arrived this morning."

DiCook shrugged. "Not too much is secret in Orrin these days." He grinned. "Especially when a couple of temple seats are pissed at both you and the queen, and they want everyone in the duchy to know."

I scanned the faces of my wardens. "Is my potential reassignment one of the items you wanted to discuss?"

"Yes, Chief Justice," eleven of them chorused.

"And arrangements for your absence while you're in Tandor, m'lady," Little Bear added.

"I see." From the other wardens' expressions, Little Bear's paranoia had spread through our temple since the two attempts on my life by the Assassins Guild in the last month. Three, if one counted the demon their unknown employer unleashed. I nodded curtly. "I promise we will discuss these matters when we return from the magistrate's excursion. Warden Noko, if you would gather Justice Yanaba for me."

Little Bear appeared as if he would argue my choices, but Tyra nudged him with her elbow. Luc had been the one to originally lecture me about trusting my own wardens, instead of treating him like one. It seemed my chief warden also had a problem with trust and letting go of old habits. Since he, the court clerks, and my personal attendant hid my predecessor's senility and kept the temple running before my assignment here, I could understand his need for control.

But I couldn't let his pride or mine act as a detriment to our respective duties.

"All right." I clapped my hands together. "Everyone at the evening meal tonight in the common room. We'll bar the gates and doors. Is that satisfactory?"

Little Bear looked askance at me. "You want all the staff involved, Chief Justice?"

"Might as well," I said. "Considering Sivan and Nathan were poisoned the same time I was, it'd be best if all the staff were prepared for contingencies, not just the wardens. Don't you think?"

We both knew I wasn't really asking his opinion. When his ears heated, I wasn't sure if it was due to me overriding him or how close he came to losing Sivan. Why they didn't make their arrangement formal was beyond me. But the staffs for Balance and Light often adhered to the priestly restrictions regarding chastity and celibacy even though they weren't required for support staff.

And more than once I considered dragging Istaqa to the Temple of Love. I had no doubt Sister Dragonfly would find a way to loosen up Luc's tightly wound assistant.

"Very well, Chief Justice," Little Bear acknowledged stiffly.

Noko entered with Yanaba on her arm. "You requested my presence, Chief Justice," my protégé said. Then she curtsied.

Curtsied.

I crossed my arms. "You were one of those girls who sucked up to the teaching sisters in Standora, weren't you?"

"At least, I'm not imitating the Reverend Mother's lack of manners," she said primly.

Gina slapped a hand over her mouth to stifle her giggles, Tyra grinned broadly, and Little Bear looked skyward, no doubt praying for patience. The rest of the wardens stiffened, waiting to see what my reaction would be.

However, DiCook laughed outright. "I amend my original concerns, Anthea. I think Justice Yanaba and I are going to get along very well while you're gone."

"As long as you realize she's here to spy for the Reverend Mother," I shot back.

Yanaba sniffed. "Yes, I am here to monitor Orrin for our blessed mother. That's because I know better than to place a temple seat in the gaol without cause."

DiCook laughed even louder. "I'd be pleased to escort you, Lady Justice."

She inclined her head in his direction. "Very well, Magistrate."

It took him a moment to realize he needed to go to her. Unlike me, she was totally blind.

As a proper justice should be, said a little voice in the back of my mind.

Yanaba and DiCook headed out the door. I started after them when Little Bear grabbed my arm.

He dropped his hand to his side as soon as he realized what he'd done. "You do realize she wants the Balance seat here in Orrin," he said under his breath.

I sighed as I watched her retreating robes. "If I had a choice in the matter, she could have it. But the Reverend Mother has made it quite clear I'm not leaving the city anytime soon." I crossed my arms and glared at the assembled wardens.

"Except to visit Tandor," Tyra said, a sad look on her face.

"That's a different matter," I snapped.

Gina folded her arms to match my stance. "Which is why the Reverend Mother is concerned you will try to get yourself killed during your trip to Tandor."

"I'm not—" The realization my warden baited me kicked me in the head, and I abandoned my defensiveness. "We will discuss this tonight over the evening meal," I bit out as I dropped my arms to my sides. I pivoted on my heel and stalked out of the receiving room. After three steps, Noko and Daniel scurried to follow me.

Chapter 3

Per usual for the last month, people on the streets stopped and stared as I left the Temple of Balance. When they thought I was safely out of hearing range, the whispers started.

The gossip had been bad after I'd been sentenced to Orrin's Balance seat as opposed to assigned, even though I'd been Orrin's acting justice since Chief Justice Penelope's death a little over a year ago. It didn't matter I had stopped a member of the royal family from seizing the throne through demons. But since then, a demon had been discovered and destroyed inside the Jing Embassy, and Brother Jeremy of Light had killed another one in the tunnel system beneath the city. All of this happened in less than a year, two of the occurrences within the city walls. And I was involved in every single incident.

After the shock of the renegade infiltration of Love and Light had worn off and the initial grief of the murders started to dissipate, the rumors shifted the blame to the Red Justice for bringing demons back to Issura.

Part of me wanted to scream at the civilians for their complacent and lackadaisical attitude. As long as someone else solved their problems, they acted like spoiled, ungrateful children. It almost made me want to summon a demon horde since they were already accusing me of it.

Almost.

I shivered at the awful thought and shoved it back into a dark hole at the back of my mind. Demons would simply eat me if I did summon them. After they found a more complacent pawn in order to remain in our dimension, that was.

But my experience of actually handling a demon grimoire scared the water out of me. I'd lose far more than my life if I'd given in to the temptations the evil tome had murmured in my head when I touched it.

Noko marched at my side, Daniel at my back, as we followed DiCook and Yanaba. A little envy rose in my heart while the magistrate and the justice walked arm in arm.

Before I was condemned to Orrin, I often walked about the city by myself when the Reverend Mother added it to my circuit after Penelope's death. After two attempts on my life by the Assassins Guild in the span of a week, well, three if one counted the attempted stabbing that killed my grandfather Kam, neither the peacekeepers nor the other temples, much less my own wardens, would let me attend the privy by myself. Forget strolling up Bakers Street for a treat.

Once we passed Government House, DiCook turned right onto a quiet side street. He guided Yanaba through a left turn. The tiny avenue held small, but well-appointed, two-story buildings, the kind that held a storefront at street level and the family quarters above.

DiCook stopped at a shop and knocked on the door. It opened, and he led Yanaba inside. He didn't want an obvious guard outside the storefront. That would have invited speculation from the neighbors, which meant he was far more worried than he had let on at the temple.

However, the appearance of Yanaba and me at the shop would elicit the same questions.

"What kind of establishment is this?" I whispered to Noko as we approached.

"The sign says the proprietor is a seamstress," my warden whispered back.

Noko shifted so she was in front of me. The door opened and a peacekeeper opened the door just wide enough for us to slip through.

He bobbed his head. "Warden Noko, Lady Justice, Warden Daniel."

I was impressed he knew everyone's names. His politeness was another re-minder of my poor behavior over the last year.

"I must apologize for my forgetfulness, Peacekeeper. What is your name?"

"Jaime, m'lady." His head bobbed again because he didn't have enough room to execute the proper bow he obviously intended.

"This way, Justices," DiCook called for my benefit.

I steeled myself as I followed him and Yanaba. The sickly sweet smell of death and bitter almonds tainted the air. Two corpses sat slumped over a table, cups in front of each of them. A man and a woman. They were the same blue-green color, which meant they'd been dead for some time. A pair of live peacekeepers stood guard over the bodies.

"The children?" I asked.

"Upstairs in their bed," DiCook said.

"What was his name?" Yanaba asked.

"Dante," DiCook said.

My body jerked at the name. "Dante?"

"You know him?" my protégé asked.

DiCook shot a look at me. "He was one of the peacekeepers I brought with me when the duke's staff found Sister Gretchen's body in one of his keep's wine barrels."

The idiot had been worshipping with the murdered priestess without his wife's knowledge or consent. Lucky for him, a truthspell cleared him almost immediately. I bit my tongue to keep from speculating that perhaps his wife had discovered his misbehavior after all.

"Chief Justice, if I may?" Yanaba brought me back to the present.

I smiled even though she couldn't see my expression. "Of course. The point of this exercise is to cultivate your experience, Justice."

She released her hold of the magistrate's arm and was quiet for a moment, no doubt gathering her thoughts before she started her questioning. "What are the positions of the adults?"

DiCook glanced at me, and I nodded for him to answer. "Dante's face and upper body are flat against the table top. His left arm lays beside his head, bent at the elbow. His right hangs at his side. His wife Barbora—" Malven's voice caught, and a wave of grief flowed from him before he could regain control. He must have been close to the couple.

"She's slumped against the back of her chair," the magistrate continued. "Her head is canted to her left over the top slat. Blood-flecked spittle is at the corner of her mouth. Both of her arms are straight down at her sides. She is dressed in her night clothes. He is wearing his uniform."

"Are there any items on the table?" Yanaba asked.

The magistrate cleared his throat. "A tea cup sits before each body. There's a pot next to Dante's head." He reached for the pale blue metal. "It's cold."

Yanaba folded her arms and slipped her hands into the opposing sleeves. The first week she was in my court, I'd deduced her gesture came when she was about to reach a conclusion in her reasoning. I prayed she didn't gamble at one of Thief's dens. Her body language was far too open and obvious.

"Have you had any problems with Dante's performance of his duties?" she asked.

"None." His single word matched the scowl on his face.

"If he was not one of the peacekeepers taking bribes, he had undiagnosed melancholia. No doubt it was a severe enough infliction that he felt the need to relieve his wife and their children of their lives as well."

I swallowed the urge to sigh. Gina had pointed out my own habit occurred whenever I felt as if another person's intellect was not equal to my own. And I was rather disappointed in Justice Yanaba at the moment.

"If I may point out something, Justice?" I said.

She stiffened. I didn't blame her. I still resented the Reverend Mother's constant dressing-downs in public.

"You read my reports on the incidents in Orrin over the last month, didn't you?"

She tilted her head to the side. "Yes, m'lady, but Dante's admitted indiscretion at the Temple of Love was minor. How does that relate to his death?"

"It may or it may not. However, you have not asked Wardens Noko or Daniel for their impressions of the scene," I said.

"You don't." A certain sullenness lay under her words.

Balance help me, had I been this arrogant when I was a freshly minted Justice?

Yes, Luc would have said silently if he were here.

"I can see to a certain extent," I said. "However, I still rely on our wardens for the things my sight cannot ascertain."

She seemed to shrink inside her robes at my rebuke.

"Also, both Magistrate DiCook and I provided you two important clues, which you instantly disregarded."

"Do both you and the magistrate believe it is murder and not suicide?" Despite the red glow of her face, her voice was thoughtful.

I looked at DiCook.

He sighed for me. "With all due respect, Justice, I wouldn't have gone to the temple to fetch you and the Chief Justice if I suspected otherwise." Maybe the magistrate had received the same lecture about decorum as I had from High Brother Luc.

"M'lady, I don't know if I can perform two reviews of the past in such a short period." Yanaba's choked whisper said volumes about what she truly feared.

"I'll take the children," I replied softly.

DiCook sent one of his peacekeepers to fetch someone from Light. We didn't have to wait long for the priest to arrive, but I was surprised Luc came himself, along with one of his own wardens.

When I said as much, Luc nudged me in the ribs. "I can't let Balance have all the fun."

"But Jeremy or Shi Hua—"

"I needed to get out of the temple for a bit. Istaqa is driving me mad." Silently, Luc added, *And I'm not putting the junior priests in the middle of this quagmire if I can help it.*

Unfortunately, the small shop and home quickly became too crowded with all these people. DiCook released all the peacekeepers back to their patrol routes, except the one he sent to collect Master Devin of the Healers Guild. Daniel accompanied me up the stairs to the three-room apartment over the shop. The odor left no question of which room was the children's bedchamber. My heart broke at the two tiny dark blue-green figures huddled on the straw mattress. Did they know what had been done to them, or had they slipped into Death's arms in their sleep?

"This is wrong," my warden murmured as he opened the shutters for a breath of fresher air, no matter the chill. "There was no reason to poison the children." He scuffed his boot against the wooden floor. "Are you sure you wouldn't rather wait for the high brother, m'lady?"

I shook my head. "First of all, it will be difficult for him to navigate those narrow stairs. I don't relish telling the Reverend Father of Light I got another member of his order killed should High Brother Luc tumble down the steps and break his neck."

"Secondly—" I softened my tone. "This is a prime example of why the high brother is training you and the rest of the Balance wardens in the non-magical aspects of his duties. We're losing Light priests faster than we're gaining justices. And these renegades have no care or thought as to who gets hurt."

Daniel bowed his head. "I meant no complaint or disrespect, m'lady."

I patted his shoulder. "I understand. This won't be easy on either of us." He stepped back to the corner of the room between the window and the door, the better to view everything.

Unfortunately, the room held no stone. The clay and brass brazier at the foot of the bed had cooled. Without anything else still alive in the room, it was the best I had to work my spell. I lifted the brazier from its stand, and placed it on the plank floor. At a minimum, I wouldn't have to worry about setting the building on fire.

The room chilled as cold air blew through the open window. I shivered as I sat cross-legged next to the brazier. Hopefully, Seamstress Barbora had prepared the container for the last few nights before putting the children to bed. Otherwise this whole exercise would be for naught. There wouldn't be enough of her residual energy on the brazier for a good reading.

Placing my hands on the metal and baked earthenware, I concentrated. Even though I had a semblance of vision, the figures and images were fleeting shadows when I rewound time. Therefore, I still had to rely on a partner to interpret them. Next to Little Bear, Daniel and Noko performed the task to my exacting specifications when a Light priest was otherwise engaged. And it made far more sense to have someone with Luc's experience assisting Justice Yanaba.

I still missed him acting as my eyes, though I'd never say so to Brother Jeremy or my wardens. After ten years of riding circuit together, he knew exactly what to look for without adding unnecessary description.

I yanked the threads of time back a little over a day. If the seamstress held typical motherly concern for her children's well-being, I could be more thorough. I let the threads slide forward. Shadows hovered over the bed before they darted to the pegs on the wall.

"The children awake," Daniel said, his voice gruff. "They change from their shifts into their day clothes. The boy runs from the room, but the girl walks more sedately."

I gritted my teeth against the strain of the time threads. While it would be easier to skip to the evening since I was fairly certain the children would not return to their room until bedtime, I couldn't take the chance of missing a pertinent clue.

"The girl has returned to the room." Daniel went silent, but confusion laced his tone when he continued. "She has something in her hand." He shifted to his left. "She's hiding it under this floorboard. Stop!"

My breath hissed between my teeth as he crouched next to the window. "Daniel . . ."

"It looks like a coin, but her hand covers it."

"Daniel, I can't hold the lines forever," I snapped.

"Continue," he murmured, but his attention was on the shadowy figure of the girl.

I let the threads slide forward once again.

"She's left the room." His attention was on the floorboard though.

"Warden! Witness me!" Despite my promise to improve my behavior, my fraying temper and the strain of the spell got the better of me.

"My apologies, Chief Justice." He rose to his full height and resumed watching the room.

The review of yesterday passed without anyone returning until Daniel said, "The seamstress enters the room and takes the brazier. Nothing, nothing. She returns. From her stance and the pads she uses, the brazier is full and hot. She sets it on the stand and leaves. Now, both children have entered the room. They are changing into their nightshifts and climbing into the bed."

His voice hitched. "Peacekeeper Dante comes in with cups in his hands. He gives them to the children. They drink whatever is in the cups and hand them back to their father. He sits the cups on the floor and tucks in the children. He kisses them on their foreheads. He gathers the empty cups and leaves."

"They fall asleep." My warden stepped closer to the bed, and his voice choked. "They have stopped breathing."

He continued to stare at the bed where the ghosts of the past have merged with the corpses of the present. Before I could reprimand him about his duty again, he shook himself and stepped back.

"Peacekeeper Jaime enters the room. Grief covers his face before he leaves." A bit of a pause passed before Daniel added, "Jaime returns with the magistrate. From the movement of his mouth, the magistrate is swearing. They both leave without touching anything."

Once the timelines slid into synchronicity, I blinked the sweat from my eyes, released the cold brazier, and shook the feeling back into my hands. "That wasn't very helpful."

"No, Chief Justice, it wasn't." Daniel shook his head. "May I check beneath the floorboard now?"

I nodded. As I climbed to my feet, Daniel knelt and pried up the wood. His gestures reminded me too much of High Sister Dragonfly's method of hiding evidence and valuables from my mother and her Assassins Guild cronies at the Temple of Love.

Using a piece of clean cloth from his pocket, my warden pulled a small round object from the space he'd uncovered. "Well, this certainly doesn't help clear the matter. It's not true silver."

I crossed to him and examined the coin he held up for me. He was correct. The metal appeared to be pewter. Unfortunately, my eyesight couldn't detect detail, and I didn't want to contaminate the metal by touching it. "What are its markings?"

"It has the symbol of the Temple of Thief on one side, though someone has scratched a cross through it. I don't recognize the symbol on the other side." He shook his head and carefully laid the cloth with the disk in my palm. "When has Thief ever minted coins?"

No sensation of magic from the metal pierced the weave. I frowned. "Never to the best of my knowledge. No nation would tag coins with a temple glyph, and all metalwork has been the province of Father on the nations' behalf until the Smiths Guild broke from them."

However, a trick Luc once pulled flashed through my mind. "Perhaps the high brother can cast a tracking spell."

I wrapped the coin carefully in the cloth and placed it in a pocket of my robes before I glanced at the dead children. Where had the girl gotten the coin? Why did she hide it? I didn't realize I'd spoken aloud until Daniel answered me.

"It could have something to do with their death," the warden said. "Perhaps Peacekeeper Dante needed the coin, and when he couldn't find it, he knew his family was doomed and that's when he poisoned—"

I held up my hand. "That's merely speculation at this point. We need more facts. The only thing we know for certain was Dante's daughter hid a strange coin, and the poison that killed her and her brother was most probably in whatever Dante brought his children to drink."

His face glowed a brilliant red. "Yes, m'lady."

Balance help me. I did it again. Treated a colleague as if he were a child. "Thank you for trying to look for solutions, Daniel."

He fidgeted. "But I understand your point, m'lady. We have very little evidence at this time. I won't presume to make any premature conclusions again."

"Good." I nodded. "Let's see what trouble Justice Yanaba and High Brother Luc have found."

I headed back down the stairs, perturbed. There was no reason for the children to be poisoned. None. Unless they weren't innocent bystanders.

After chiding Daniel, I had no right to speculate either. My own emotions were getting in my way. It had been less than a month since I'd learned my own mother had tried to abort me using poisonous mushrooms and herbs during her pregnancy. There had been no real reason for her actions as a sister of Love either other than her vanity.

We reached the first floor to find Yanaba looking puzzled. On the other hand, Luc's anger grated against my mind.

"What did you learn, Justice?" I asked my protégé.

She cocked her head in my direction. "I beg your forgiveness, Chief Justice, but I fear we have more questions than answers to the deaths in this house."

"How so?" My attention flicked from her to Luc and back again.

The younger woman hesitated before she began her recital. "Events during yesterday played out as I expected. Barbora plied her trade with the children assisting her. After the day ended, the evening meal was consumed prior to Dante's arrival. Barbora prepared two cups of milk and honey. Dante took them upstairs while Barbora set a kettle on and readied for bed. When he returned, they sat at the table and drank their tea."

Horror squeezed my heart. "Did Dante and Barbora use the same jar of honey for their tea as they did for the children's milk?"

Matching emotion flowed from Luc. "Yes."

I crossed to the table, removed the lid from the jar and sniffed. A hint of almond mixed with the honey but I couldn't be sure if it were poison or if the bees had harvested the nectar of a large number of almond blossoms last spring.

"Daniel, please go to the Wildling temple. Tell High Brother Jax I need the member of his order with the most accurate sense of smell."

With his quick glance at Noko and her answering nod, he strode to the front room. I couldn't miss the exchange. Noko would stay with me, regardless of Yanaba's safety. All of the Balance wardens had taken the attempts on my life far too personally. Daniel exchanged a word with the Light warden before the hinges squealed as the door opened and closed.

Oblivious to the silent exchange, my protégé focused on the matter at hand. "But, Chief Justice, several customers were here and put honey from that same pot in their tea with no ill effects."

"Did any of the patrons give something to the children?"

"Yes," Luc said. "A noblewoman from her dress and bearing. She gave a coin to the girl."

"Was she the last custom of the day?"

Magistrate DiCook spoke for the first time. "No, but she was here the longest, and she was the last to accept Barbora's offer of refreshment."

"What happened upstairs?" Luc asked.

My recitation to my audience was very short. At the end, everyone looked at the jar of honey sitting on the table.

"This makes no sense," Yanaba protested. "Why would a noblewoman want to poison a peacekeeper and his family?"

"You're jumping to conclusions again, Justice," DiCook said.

"I beg your pardon?" she said haughtily.

I grinned at him. "Do not take the magistrate's rebuke personally, Justice. He has had to learn logic in public, rather than in the classroom."

He inclined his head to me. "The Chief Justice and the High Brother of Light have been excellent teachers in investigative techniques. However, I do miss the days when Orrin's biggest problems were tavern brawls and petty theft."

"So, you don't believe she may have slipped the poison in the honey?" Yanaba asked.

I couldn't get a sense whether her confusion was over DiCook's statement regarding conclusions or his sentiment over misdemeanor crime.

"Oh, I believe the woman managed to slip a poison into the honey." He stroked his short beard as he considered the problem. "However, I do not believe the visitor was a local noblewoman." He shrugged. "In fact, she may not be a noble, or even a woman at all."

The young justice laughed. "In other words, your sight can be fooled, but—"

"Any sense can be fooled," I corrected. "Never presume one sense is better than another." I was harsh with her, but better here in a controlled environment than when we were in the middle of a battle for our lives.

"Comparing various sources of information will allow you to detect discrepancies, Justice Yanaba," Malven said, far more gently than I would have.

"You're becoming soft in your old age, Magistrate," I chided.

He chuckled and hooked his thumbs in his belt. "No, I simply would like one decent working relationship at the Temple of Balance."

I grinned. "I seem to remember your voice was one of the loudest calling for my head after the Samael DiRoy incident."

"And you spent nearly a year looking for a reason to take mine," he replied jovially.

Everyone else in the room laughed except Yanaba. When the humor died, she bowed her head. "I shall take the words from both of you under advisement, Magistrate, Chief Justice."

Maybe there was hope for the younger woman after all.

A loud series of knocks at the front door echoed through the small shop before I could answer her. Luc's warden exchanged words with a familiar voice.

Master Healer Devin strode into the back room. He took a good look at the scene before he nodded to me. "Another one, eh? Once again, I'm afraid you've called me too late."

I shrugged. "Unfortunately, I have need of your keen mind in helping us discover the culprit of these heinous crimes."

He shook his head. "It would be a change if you would summon us for something as simple as a hangnail."

"Admit it. You like the challenges I present you." I smiled.

Devin circled the table before he knelt next to Barbora's corpse. "I don't think you need a healer's expertise in this matter to know that they were poisoned, Chief Justice." He looked up at me. "But I assume you would like us to examine them more thoroughly at the Healers Guild's facilities."

"It will be the same terms as before."

Devin rose to his feet. "Understood. The guildmaster is considering permanently assigning a healer to assist the chief justice in these investigations."

"I'm sure there one or two that would volunteer for such duties," I answered.

"You know damn well that won't be acceptable," Devin muttered as he moved to examine Dante's corpse.

In other words, I could expect to hear more complaints from High Sister Bertrice about how I allowed the desecration of remains, but it was more due to politics and appearances within her own order. As a former healer herself, she was more than sympathetic to me and the investigative techniques of her old guild. But thanks to those same internal politics, I'd become the intermediary between the Healers Guild and the Temple of Death in Orrin.

When the guilds started breaking away from their respective temples after the last major demon invasion a century ago, the relationship between those who cared for the living and those that cared for dead had been especially contentious. Which meant either a member of her priesthood or I needed to observe the healers while they dealt with the dead.

Unfortunately, the healers preferred me.

I braced myself before telling Devin the rest. "Their children are upstairs, still in their bed."

The wave of disbelief, quickly followed by anger and sadness, flowed from the master healer. When the tide of emotion disbursed, he bowed. "We will show them all due respect, m'lady. Is there anything my apprentices should know before they start?"

"Yes. Don't eat the honey," Luc quipped.

Chapter 4

By the time the guild apprentices and our wardens loaded the bodies into Master Devin's wagon, Daniel returned with Sister Farrah from the Wildling temple. She shed her robes, leggings and tunic and placed them on the seat of the wagon before she shifted into her fox form. She examined the corpses before I led her through the building. She thoroughly sniffed everything in the seamstress shop and the apartment above, including the suspect jar of honey.

Once we were outside, she shifted back to human form. Master Devin averted his gaze just as he had when she first removed her clothes. However, he was the only one who did so. Social mores were different in the eastern nations of the Northern Long Continent, but I didn't know all the details, mainly because certain subtleties weren't documented by the Temple. They simply assumed their own common knowledge was known by everyone. I'd been meaning to ask the healer about his personal history over a social meal in an effort to know him, but with the recent troubles in Orrin, I had not had the opportunity.

Now, this investigation took precedence, and my invitation would have to be delayed again. I waited for Farrah to speak.

The normally light-hearted priestess's skin glowed a dark orange, and anger radiated from her. It took her several moments to calm herself to where she spoke a coherent human language.

"You were correct in your observations, Chief Justice. I could smell *kyaneos notos* in the used cups and in the honey." She reached for her clothes.

I frowned. "*Kyaneos notos?*"

"The poison used primarily by the Assassins Guild. Roughly translated, it means 'southern blue'. It can be produced by the manioc root or by bitter almonds." She tugged on her leggings. "That's the reason no one in the Healers

Guild noticed the substance when their stock was tainted last month. They use sweet almond oil which blended with and obscured the specific scent." Her coloring faded to a lighter shade as she shoved her arms into her tunic sleeves. "What I don't understand is how they managed to get a lethal dose into the honey."

"What do you mean?" I said.

Farrah mumbled something, but I couldn't understand with her tunic covering her head as she pulled it on. But Devin frowned. "She's right."

I looked at them both askance. "About?"

"The honey," the priestess and the healer said at the same time.

"Honey, fruit, sorghum grass," Devin continued. "Anything sweet can help offset the effects of *kyaneos* poisoning. It's not a remedy in and of itself, but a treatment of last resort or used in conjunction with a healing."

"So, the honey jar may have simply been the most expedient method of killing the peacekeeper," Yanaba said. "His wife and children may have been collateral targets." Before either I or the magistrate could say anything, she sighed. "But I'm jumping to conclusions again by assuming Dante was the primary target, aren't I, Chief Justice?"

"You're learning." I smiled even though she couldn't see it. "That's the important thing." However, the deep-seated feeling in my gut said my protégé was correct.

DiCook clapped his hands. "If we're finished here for the time being, Chief Justice, High Brother, I need to speak with you about additional patrol arrangements in Orrin."

From the way the magistrate rocked on his heels, that wasn't the subject he wanted to discuss, but it was good to know he was learning some discretion. Despite our efforts, the orders for Luc to visit Tandor weren't as secret as I'm sure both the Reverend Father of Light and the Reverend Mother of Balance would have wanted.

"I must accompany Master Devin first—" I started.

"Go take care of the magistrate." The healer made shooing motions with his hands. "I was leaving the Guild manse to check on Lady Katarina when Warden Daniel arrived. With her so close to her due date, the living need to take priority. Besides, Aaron won't do anything until you and I are both present. Or

I should say politics prevent him from examining our victims until I return and you're available. None of the other masters want to be directly involved."

I snorted at the melodrama between the Temples and the Guilds. "Your colleagues are certainly curious enough when I'm present."

Luc shuffled forward on the steel crutches Devin had designed for him with one of Orrin's master smiths. The devices were far more than the typical Y-shaped polished wood most injured amputees used. In fact, he'd been learning how to fight with them thanks to Shi Hua. "Do you mind if we have this meeting at my temple, Magistrate?" Luc grinned at Devin. "I know a healer who will be most irked if I miss my afternoon medication."

Devin shook a finger at Luc. "And I meant it when I told you if you miss a dosage, I'll haul you back to our manse."

"What? You mean Istaqa hasn't been making his daily report to you about everything that enters and leaves my body?" Luc mocked.

The healer crossed his arms and glared. "He tries, but you go out of your way to make his job difficult."

DiCook leaned toward Devin. "I totally blame Chief Justice Anthea. The high brother has picked up quite a few of her bad habits over their time riding circuit together."

"I know damn well who to blame, Magistrate." But the healer's sharp words were leavened by a certain amount of teasing.

The peacekeeper and our wardens tried to muffle their snickers, but a fair amount of dismay flowed from Yanaba. I would have laughed also, but somehow, I'd been accused as an accessory. Retaliation seemed more appropriate.

"Since I've been deemed guilty of corrupting a priest, maybe I should have you pay for our midday meal at an inn, Magistrate," I said.

"Oh, no." He waggled a forefinger in my direction. "I've seen you eat. You wouldn't leave enough scraps for a rat along the wharf, much less my children."

Even my protégé giggled at that rejoinder. It was good to see Malven relaxed around me, considering how bad our initial relationship had been.

It also meant I didn't have to be as careful about any remarks I made. "I'm surprised you wish to save your most cutting insults for a private meal." I tilted my head. "How can you possibly perform without an audience?"

"That's enough. All of you." Luc jabbed a finger in DiCook's direction. "Magistrate, I believe you've been equally corrupted. I seem to recall you quite peeved with the Chief Justice's jocularity when previous murder victims were found." He faced Devin. "And you threatened to tie down the Chief Justice in order to treat her wounds.

"I, on the other hand, am becoming quite cranky because it's past First Afternoon, I am hungry, and the one thing Anthea did right while we were on circuit was making sure we ate at regular mealtimes."

Laughing, I raised my hands in surrender. "Far be it for me to step between any priest and his meal."

Luc's warden brought his horse forward. Or rather his new mount, a placid creature unconcerned whether her rider mounted on the right side rather than the left.

My good humor fled at the sight. The use of the same poison meant we still had assassins operating in Orrin. Regardless of my rebuke to the magistrate months ago, and my protégé today, about making assumptions, I was sure of that fact. Balance help us, the alleged noblewoman could even be the skinwalker who was behind Luc's abduction and had eluded our fellow priests while we dealt with the demon.

While I was still hesitant about involving someone outside of the temples, there were few of my fellow clergy I truly trusted in this city. That meant I relied heavily on Magistrate DiCook over the last few months despite our personality clashes. And he may have some insight about the strange coin Daniel had uncovered.

We walked behind the healers' wagon until we reached the Temple of Light. Devin waved as he and his apprentices continued down the main thoroughfare. The clopping of the horse's hooves melded with the rest of the day's traffic.

I paused at the steps while Luc and his warden continued to the back gate of the Light complex. "Justice Yanaba, would you please review today's court reports? The clerks should have them ready for you."

Her lower jaw dropped, and her disappointment rolled across my psyche. She had hoped to be included in this meeting. "But, Chief Justice—"

I leaned close to her ear. "Your place is to obtain practical experience right now. And things are far too dangerous for both of us for you to continue arguing with me in public. I will inform you of our discussions when I return."

Her mouth closed, and she nodded firmly. "Yes, m'lady."

Good. Maybe she had some sense after all.

At my nod, Daniel took her arm from DiCook. She wrapped her hand around his bicep and let him lead her back to our temple across the thoroughfare. Noko, however, stayed at my side. Considering the Assassins Guild's first attempt on my life had been on these very steps, I knew any command I gave her to leave would fall on deaf ears.

At the top of the steps of the Temple of Light, the two wardens standing guard bowed as we approached. The man on my right opened the door behind him and guided me, Noko, DiCook, and DiCook's peacekeeper to the chief priest's private dining room. It wasn't like we didn't know the way, but with the infiltration of the temples by renegades, all protocols were being followed to the letter.

The murders of Love's entire contingent of wardens had left all Temple personnel even more paranoid than the imposter priest or the demons had.

Luc was already settled at the head of the table. I still expected Kam to take that chair though it had been nearly a year since he semi-retired in favor of Luc taking the temple seat. Now that he was dead . . .

I repressed a sigh. Balance knew I would have missed the old man even if he weren't my grandfather.

The Light warden gestured for DiCook's peacekeeper and my own warden to follow him, but Noko stood resolutely at my side. Almost as if she dared her opposite to physically remove her.

"This is a private meeting, Warden Noko," Luc said.

"With all due respect, High Brother, I will remain." She lifted her chin.

"Are you claiming either Magistrate DiCook or I would harm the chief justice?"

The color of Noko's skin didn't alter one whit at Luc's chiding. "Given the circumstances over the last year, the wardens of Balance are leaving nothing to chance. We will do our duty regardless of the pride of any official." Her gaze fell on me with that last statement.

I now had a very good idea what Little Bear and the rest of the wardens wanted to meet with me about over supper.

DiCook broke the tension by chuckling. "Let her stay, High Brother. Far be it for either of us interfere with the young lady's duties. I wouldn't want to lose my head should Justice Anthea choke on a fish bone."

Unease washed over me at the magistrate's jest. When had Luc and DiCook switched personalities?

I took a seat on Luc's left, but Noko didn't claim a place at the table. Instead, she stood behind me and slightly to my right, keeping her own sword arm free should the need arise.

Istaqa and two of his staff entered with platters of dried meat, cheese, dried fruit, and Cantan flat bread. Simple fare like we consumed on our circuit compared to Kam's extravagant gastronomic desires. Luc's personal attendant shooed the other men out, placed a pot of tea with Luc's medicine on the table before the chief priest, and poured DiCook and I each a cup of wine. Istaqa shot an irritated look at Noko before he too departed.

My stomach grumbled, but before I could pop a wedge of cheese in my mouth, Luc said, "Anthea, would you mind?"

I shook myself out of my maudlin thoughts of Kam. "Of course not." I circled the room, laying the wards that would keep anyone, including the nosy Istaqa, from overhearing our conversation. My stomach grumbled again when I finished. I snatched a slice of sharp cheese and shoved it into my mouth.

DiCook ignored the spread of delectables and folded his hands together. "You need to start including Justice Yanaba in these little war councils, Anthea."

"Why?" I said around my mouthful of cheese as I slid into my chair. "She needs to learn the basics first."

"She needs to be included," DiCook repeated.

"Did you actually watch her and listen to her conclusions at Dante's home? Balance, help me. Was I that arrogant when I was her age?" I muttered as I reached for more cheese.

"Actually, you were far worse," Luc answered.

"She needs to look deeper, or she will continue to miss the obvious," I countered.

"She needs to know what in the Twelve is going on in this city if she's going to be any use to me while you two are gallivanting around Tandor!" DiCook slapped the table for emphasis. The dishes and utensils rattled at the sharp blow.

Luc and I exchanged looks.

He's right.

I didn't answer the high brother's silent reprimand. I faced DiCook. "Was that all you wished to discuss?"

"No." He leaned forward. "What did you find at Dante's?"

"Four bodies," I said dryly.

He threw his hands up. "We're back to dissembling? I thought you and I had finally gotten beyond that."

I sighed. "I did plan on telling you, but I wanted to ask Luc about the evidence I found first so I'd have a solid lead to give you."

Luc leaned forward eagerly. "What did our assassin give Dante's daughter?"

I reached into my pocket and drew out the cloth. Both men watched breathlessly as I unwrapped it. Even Noko leaned over my shoulder to see it.

I carefully passed the unusual coin to Luc by the folds of Daniel's kerchief. "I was hoping you might be able to place a tracking spell on it."

His brows drew together as he held up the coin by a corner of the cloth and examined it under the overhead lamp. "I've never seen anything like this." He shook his head and passed the cloth and coin to DiCook. "I'm not going to be able to track the person who gave it to Dante's daughter."

"But you were able to track the gold piece your father gave you when that girl in Mountain Gate stole it from you years ago," I protested.

"Because it had more sentimental value to me than what the metal was worth, and I had carried it since I'd become a novice," he said.

DiCook cleared his throat. "This doesn't make sense. Minting coins has always been the province of the national governments though Father did the actual work, even at the height of the demon wars. It's not gold, silver or copper." His eyes met mine. "Why would an assassin give a child an essentially worthless coin?" He slid the disc nestled in cloth across the table to me.

"A very good question, Magistrate." I smiled. "High Brother Luc, if you don't mind me using your entrance to the tunnel system, I think it's time we ask the source. Anyone else interested in a visit to the Temple of Thief?"

Chapter 5

After our quick meal, the magistrate and Noko followed me into the tunnels from the hidden passage in Luc's bedchambers. I didn't need illumination to pick my way through the underground system between the temples. To me, the walls glowed a pale lavender. Some sort of tiny living creatures gave off a light I could see with my strange eyesight.

However, Noko and DiCook needed conventional flame. I led the way so their lamp didn't blind me with its heat. The balls of magical energy produced by the priests of Light would have been preferable for all of our needs, but once again, we were back to our problem of a shortage of able-bodied and trustworthy priests.

It also said how desperate the Reverend Mother of Balance and how unnerved the Reverend Father of Light were to send us both to Tandor with the recent upheaval in Orrin and the trade season about to start.

Thankfully, Luc didn't make some idiotic protest that he should accompany us to the Temple of Thief. I had equal gratitude our destination was next door to Light. I still had problems with anxiety in constrained places after the demon's attack down here. The shorter the walk in the tunnel system, the better for my fortitude.

As we approached Thief's underground door, magic vibrated against my skin. All of the temples had placed some kind of warning wards near their tunnel entrances after our latest demon encounter. No one wanted to face a possible invasion in their nightclothes.

I placed my hand on the granite door and whispered the words to unseal it. The door swung inward.

And I found a swordpoint at my throat.

The Thief warden holding the opposite end of the weapon quickly lowered it. "Apologies, Chief Justice. We were not informed of your visit."

I entered and gave her a slight bow. "My apologies to your high brother for the lack of notice, but times necessitate certain . . . avenues of action."

DiCook and Noko followed me into the high brother's private quarters. Some signal I missed must have passed between the two wardens because the skin of Thief's protector turned from medium yellow to bright orange.

She sheathed her sword. "One moment, if you please, Chief Justice." She marched across the bedchambers of her head priest, but she only opened the main door a crack. Whispered words were exchanged before she shut the door again and watched us.

In the meantime, I examined my counterpart's personal room. To my surprise, it was nearly as spartan as my own. I'd expected trophies of some kind. Maybe even the wood paneling or tapestries the other temples used to soften the harsh chill of the marble walls. Instead, the blue-green blocks were bare except for . . .

I peered closer. Magic sigils marked the walls. Not drawn, but carved and filled with various metals. The pale blue of gold. The warmer greens of silver and copper ores. It was odd to be able to see writing and not feel it as I normally would. My gloved fingers reached for the closest marking, the symbol for a veil.

"Find something of interest, Chief Justice?"

I dropped my hand and turned to find the seat of Thief standing in the doorway of his own private chambers. I smiled. "I always find things of interest in Orrin." I inclined my head. "I hope you'll forgive the intrusion, High Brother, but I found a bit of evidence at the scene of a crime today that necessitates a consultation with you."

High Brother Talbert wasn't a big man. In fact, he was shorter than me with a slight build. He kept his hair the length of a fingertip and appeared freshly shaven every time I'd encountered him. If it weren't for the leather leggings and silk tunic of the Temples, he'd pass through the city unremarked. I had the impression many people underestimated his skills in that regard.

He exchanged a look with his warden, and she left the room, closing the door behind her with the barest of sounds. He touched the sigil next to the doorframe. All of the symbols in the walls flared to life, and magic tingled across my skin.

"Impressive," I murmured.

"Given your entry route, I presumed you and the magistrate wish to keep this consultation private," Talbert said. "How may I be of service?"

During last month's convocation, I hadn't been sure where High Brother Talbert stood. He'd stayed carefully neutral until I proved Gerd had initiated false charges against me and she attempted to mind-control the magistrate.

But as Luc repeatedly reminded me, I needed to learn to trust people other than him. And I couldn't blame Talbert for holding back at the convocation until he learned the players and positions of Gerd's game.

And mine as well.

"I need any information you may have concerning a coin one of my wardens found." I pulled the kerchief from my pocket and handed it to the priest.

One of Talbert's eyebrows rose as he accepted the bundle from me. "I take it this is evidence from the site of this morning's murders?"

My eyes narrowed. "How do you know they were murdered?"

A corner of the priest's lips curved upward. "Peacekeeper Dante wasn't implicated in the bribery scandal, and the magistrate wouldn't have summoned you and High Brother Luc unless he had suspicions."

"So much for keeping this matter quiet," DiCook grumbled.

Talbert shrugged before he unwrapped the coin. "Our temple's role is to keep an eye on things."

"You did such a wonderful job the Assassins Guild nearly took over the city," DiCook snapped.

The chief priest of Thief neither flinched nor grew angry. "While our previous justice ignored my warnings concerning Love, our current justice handled the situation quite ably without my temple's assistance."

I groaned. "This mess started when Penelope was still chief justice of Orrin?"

Talbert nodded. "Yes, odd things have been happening long before your arrival. But Gerd accelerated her plans with her acquisition of the demon grimoire shortly after your appointment to the seat of Balance."

"You mean sentence," I said sourly, but the priest was no longer paying any attention to our conversation.

The subtle intake of his breath and the lightening of his skin were the only indications of his feelings.

"What is it?" I asked.

"Do you know the history of the Assassins Guild, Chief Justice?"

I shrugged. "They appeared before the demon wars. The first mention in the histories was three hundred years before the Battle of Toscana." The beginning of the demon invasions. A chill ran through me. My own Reverend Mother had confirmed her belief my recent encounters with demons were the prelude to another full-scale invasion.

Talbert's mien grew even more somber. "Just as the Healers Guild was originally part of the Temple of Death, and the Smiths Guild part of Father, the Assassins Guild was spawned from my temple. A fact we do not like to acknowledge."

I blinked. "Why?"

Talbert chuckled. "Why don't we like to recognize such a horrid past, or why such an organization was created?"

"The creation," I said. "I can understand not wanting to recognize it."

"Originally, the guild's purpose was to . . . ensure leaders stayed on task regarding preparations for the coming war with the demons. Our memories are so short compared to the gods though." Talbert sighed. "There were those within our own order who didn't believe Balance's warning of an invasion." He shook his head. "They preferred to sell their skills, and over time, well, they didn't think twice about extending their reach or their profits."

The idiocy of men never failed to amaze me. "But why are they here in Issura? And why now?"

Talbert sighed and rewrapped the coin. "I don't know the answer to either of those questions. We have been trying to discern their purpose and lost nearly a dozen of our own priesthood in the course of two years."

His admission jarred me, but not enough to speak when he was forthcoming with information.

Talbert stared at the cloth in his hand. "Our temple has worked too hard to keep them out of our queendom for the last two centuries." He hesitated for a moment before he said, "Why aren't you asking the most obvious question, Anthea?"

"Do you mean the reason for the coin?"

He nodded.

I smiled. "It's a warning to you they will continue to kill innocents if you assist me."

His own lips tilted. "And why don't you think it's a warning to you?"

Laughter spilled from me. "I'm at the top of their list of contracts to fulfill."

He cocked his head. "And how did you come by that information?"

I hesitated for a moment. "Would you mind terribly if I kept my source to myself for now? I would hate for the magistrate to request my presence at another murder."

A slight smile curved Talbert's mouth. "I understand your reasoning. If I may be so bold, Anthea—" He paused as if searching for the right words. "Maybe you shouldn't make your reports to Standora quite so thorough."

I watched him through slitted eyes. "Why?"

"Not even your temple is immune to infiltration," he said. "Don't ever make the assumption it is. Thief is the easiest for them because of our shared history, but we've also been on guard for exactly this possibility for centuries."

Talbert held out the cloth-wrapped coin. He'd given me quite a bit of information to mull over. It didn't quell my discomfort my own Reverend Mother had insinuated the same fear. What woman would deliberately blind herself to gain admittance to the order of Balance? Had the Assassins Guild recruited someone like me who resented being trapped in temple service? Or was our problem with the support staff the sisterhood depended on so much?

"Thank you for your analysis, High Brother." I took the small bundle from him, slipped it into my pocket, and turned to leave.

Talbert cleared his throat. "One more thing, Anthea—"

I faced him again.

"Bianca is far more dangerous than your mother ever was."

"Gerd is insane," I said.

"Even so." Talbert inclined his head. "However, Bianca is not. She found her association with Gerd quite . . . profitable. You ruined that."

"Profitable how?" I asked, though I had a sick feeling I already knew. Nathan, the squire I'd acquired last month, had mentioned Orrin's street children feared to approach Mother for aid, though caring for those in need was one of the Temples' primary responsibilities.

"I think you already know."

Anger burned through my blood. "And you didn't take action because . . . ?"

"Lack of proof and a senile justice."

Talbert's wry reply didn't help my mood. My anger turned into sheer rage. "Penelope knew?"

He shrugged. "I cannot tell you what she knew and didn't know during the last year of her life. All I can tell you is that your own Reverend Mother ignored the pleas of the staff at your temple for assistance. And that Penelope herself ignored much of what was happening in the city during her tenure despite my predecessor's counsel when she was still in control of her faculties. All I can say is be careful. While I will tender any aid you may require, don't make the mistake of trusting everyone."

I smiled. "And here the current holder of the seat of Light has recently lectured me on taking the chance of trusting someone other than him."

Talbert laughed. "Then my temple and I shall try to live up to High Brother Luc's opinion until the two of you return."

"Return?" I could feel my eyebrows climb my forehead.

"From Tandor. As I said, we try to learn everyone's secrets, Chief Justice." Another shrug from Talbert. "It's our purpose."

Of course, it was. "And how did you discover we were going to Tandor?"

"Reverend Father Farrell needs priests he trusts to ferret out problems in other Light facilities. Unfortunately, Justice Elizabeth's reports for the last several months sound too much like the ones Donella wrote for your predecessor. The only logical reason for Reverend Mother Alara to unofficially ask for your pardon would be for you to accompany Luc to Tandor."

I half-expected a smug expression from Talbert for his cleverness, but he gave off an air of worry. Another puzzle piece fell into place. "Your Reverend Father is getting similar reports from your counterpart, isn't he? Why aren't you accompanying Luc instead of me?"

Talbert relaxed a hair. "The Reverend Father is sending someone, but given the recent incidents in Orrin, he prefers that I stay here in case Justice Yanaba needs support. I apologize, but I do not have leave to reveal this person's identity."

What he didn't say added to my uneasiness. My own Reverend Mother was using me to flush out the problems in Tandor since I was near the top of their list of people to be eliminated. She'd said as much during her visit. This wasn't going to be a quiet investigative trip after all.

"Are there any other temple heads I need to warn Yanaba of while we're gone?" I asked.

He shook his head. "You already know the issues with Father Jerrod, but he's the only one Bianca can truly manipulate. Actually, the rest of us are breathing a little easier with you in Balance's seat."

Now, why did Talbert's reassurance send a giant surge of doubt through me?

Once we returned to Light and DiCook had departed to warn the rest of his peacekeepers about this new threat, Noko and I walked to the Healers Guild's manse.

Their facilities were more of an estate with two huge buildings in addition to the stables and storage sheds. One housed the healers and their staff. The other was for their patients. Once a person entered the patients' manse, they understood why the two were kept separate. No amount of lemon oil or other cleaning products totally masked the smell of sickness, festering wounds, or death.

We headed straight for the patient building. Journeywoman Bly opened the door before Noko had a chance to knock.

"Chief Justice, Warden." She bobbed her head. "Master Devin and Brother Xander are waiting for you." After we entered, she closed the door and set off at a brisk pace.

"Wait!" I hurried after her. "Brother Xander is here?"

"Yes." She glanced over her shoulder. "I'm afraid that's my fault. I asked to use the library at the Temple of Death."

"Why?" I asked as Noko and I followed the journeywoman into the examination room that had been set aside for Master Devin's use when dealing with the dead.

"Because we have a more thorough collection of signs and precautions literature when dealing with corpses, Chief Justice," Brother Xander answered. He smiled.

I was a little relieved at dealing with Bertrice's second. He didn't feel the need to put on condescending airs while the healers did the job I asked of them. But he still stood slightly apart from the other journeyman and master healer in the room with Devin.

I grinned at the priest in return. "When did you pull the stick out of your high sister's ass to get her to agree to the healers' use of your library?"

"When you and Master Devin nearly died thanks to the Assassins Guild," he said. "She let me convince our Reverend Mother the healers' efforts are absolutely necessary to help us stop the renegades."

I inclined my head. "Please relay my gratitude to your high sister for her cooperation in my investigation."

"Of course."

"If you two are finished playing political games, can we get started?" Devin said sourly. His feelings regarding diplomatic niceties matched mine, which was one of the reasons I liked the healer.

He lifted the sheet draped over the feet of the first corpse. His gusty inhalation said something wasn't quite right. He turned to Bly. "What are the signs of southern blue poisoning in a deceased person, Journeywoman?"

"The extremities shade from a red cherry to a red grape color," she dutifully recited. "Scholars deduce that tremors begin in the fingers and toes tearing blood vessels before the tremors involve the entire body. Oftentimes, the lips of the decedent are bluish in color from lack of air since southern blue stops the patient's breathing. If the poison is swallowed, there may be bleeding from the mouth."

Davin glanced at his male assistant. "Did you notice anything odd about the bodies when you were preparing them for examination, Journeyman?"

"The feet of the peacekeeper and his wife were dark purple, confirming Balance's report that they were found in a seated position," the young man replied. "The blood of the children's bodies had also pooled on the sides that touched the mattress. In all four cases, none of the fingers and toes showed the coloring from tremors."

Davin folded back the sheets from the feet of the other three bodies, verifying his assistants' observation. "Your report, Master Elena?"

"There was southern blue in the honey." The master healer hesitated.

"But . . ." I prodded.

She shook her head. "There wasn't enough in the honey to kill the adults. The fact that it was administered through honey makes me question whether the amount was sufficient to kill the children."

A series of Cantish curse words ran through my head. I'd hoped that the guild's evaluation would point me in the right direction to track down the Assassins Guild within Orrin.

"Is there a way to test for other poisons?" My gaze swept across the four healers.

"Some yes, some no," Devin finally answered.

"Any indication they were strangled?" I asked.

"None, m'lady," Journeywoman Bly answered.

"Could someone be trying to blame the Assassins Guild?" Xander ventured.

I threw up my hands in a helpless gesture. "Possibly, but why?"

"More likely they want us twisted in knots while they carry out some other plot," Noko murmured.

I stared at her.

"I'm not assuming anything, m'lady." She waved at the corpses. "No one would be foolish enough to point blame at the Assassins Guild. Such a maneuver would only invite the guild to exact revenge."

I turned back to Master Devin. "Is there anything to be gained from checking their innards?"

He scratched his chin through his short beard. "If Brother Xander doesn't mind, I'd like to check one of them to confirm the heart and lungs were damaged from a substance, even if we can't identify the actual poison used."

"Of course," Xander replied.

My discussion with High Brother Talbert sat like a weight in my gut as I watched the healers work. The Assassins Guild had been too honest in their desire to kill me so far. If Noko was right that no one in their right mind would pretend to be them, what made them change their tactics? And why now, right before Luc and I were to depart for Tandor?

In the end, Devin and Xander chose Dante as the least upsetting to the priest's colleagues. As the master healer suspected, the damage to the organs was caused by a substance, not external force. Master Elena would perform additional tests for poisons on the massive blood clots Xander agreed to let her extract from the lungs, but none of us held out much hope.

Unfortunately, I had other concerns besides the odd deaths. Upon returning to Balance, I summoned Yanaba to my office.

I smiled as Ming Wei carefully guided my junior justice to a chair at the little dining table in my workspace. The extra furniture crowded the already tight accommodations, but I had broken my fast while meeting with various officials lately. I could have those same engagements in one of the proper receiving rooms and had my own squire Nathan race back and forth, fetching various documents. However, I deplored wasting time.

Having another justice in residence also gave Ming Wei purpose as a squire since I didn't need two. Last month, Ambassador Quan of Jing had turned the child over to my care as a show of good faith. The girl had been terribly abused by her own parents and a Jing noble with a predilection for children. At first, the girl couldn't tolerate any adult touching her. Balance help her, she still couldn't with anyone else but Yanaba. But here at our temple, she started to come out of her shell, and we all had Nathan to thank for that.

And to the girl, a sightless woman wasn't a threat.

Yanaba pushed back her cowl. "Thank you for your assistance, Ming Wei."

The girl bowed even though the younger justice couldn't see her. "You're welcome, Lady Justice. Please summon me when you are finished." She shot me an impish grin and darted out of the room, closing the door a little too hard behind her. With Yanaba and I meeting, Ming Wei and Nathan would have some time to play.

The younger justice twitched in her chair. "I apologize for speaking out of turn—"

"Stop." I resisted the urge to hold up a hand as those with normal sight would do. I'd picked up too many bad habits once I'd given myself vision.

"This talk isn't a dressing down about your insubordination on the street earlier." I picked up one of the teapots Nathan had brought before Yanaba had arrived and poured her a cup. "With everything happening over the last month, we haven't had a chance for a frank conversation between the two of us. I did promise to inform you of the results of my meeting with the magistrate and High Brother Luc. And there are other things I need to share as well."

"A-all right," she said as I pressed the cup into her hands. She took a sip and grimaced.

I suppressed the urge to laugh at her expression. "To start, when were you planning to tell me you hate Jing black tea?"

Her jaw fell open. "H-how—you didn't probe my thoughts."

"I didn't have to." I sat and watched her reaction.

A wry expression ameliorated her disgust with my choice of teas. "I apologize, Chief Justice. I keep forgetting you can see."

"That doesn't necessarily mean I pay attention to everything I should." I took the cup from her hands before I poured contents from the second pot into a fresh cup. "I think you'll like this better."

She took a sip and smiled. "Rose hip. My favorite. Thank you."

"This brings me to the first issue we need to discuss. Honesty."

Shock marred her features. "You think because I didn't state my tea preference to you I am untrustworthy?"

I laughed. "No. That was simply manners. Something our staff reminds me I'm sorely lacking." I took a long swallow from the cup with the black tea to sooth my own discomfort. "I want us to truthspell each other while we have this conversation."

Yanaba's stillness reminded me of a rabbit, unsure if a predator had spotted her yet. Finally, she released the breath she held. "You fear I may have fooled the Reverend Mother and I may be a renegade priestess."

"Are you saying the same thought hasn't crossed your mind about me?"

She choked off her aborted laugh. "When the Reverend Mother first briefed me about my assignment to Orrin, yes. Now . . ." She stared at nothing before she added, "I think you're far too troublesome for the renegades to want to recruit. Are you sure you want to truthspell me?"

"Yes, but as long as you don't worry about offending me, it won't hurt you."

"You mean like killing the imposter who murdered Brother Mat and impersonated him?"

I sighed. "You heard about that."

"Except your staff—"

"Our," I corrected her.

"You didn't lose *our* staff's respect in that incident," she amended. "Which either means they conspired to commit treason with you, or you're forthright and committed enough to our purpose for them to follow you through the gates of the demons' realm if you asked."

I leaned back against my chair at her words. "I pray it never comes to that."

"As do I, Chief Justice." She shook her head. Worry sliced lines in her youthful features. "But I fear we may not have a choice."

Chapter 6

My truthspell session with Yanaba, as emotionally uncomfortable as it was, relieved both of our minds that neither of us were part of the conspiracy to destroy the Twelve Temples. I also revealed my meeting with High Brother Talbert and the oddness concerning Master Healer Devin's examination of the corpses.

Unfortunately, Yanaba's lack of experience meant she could provide no further insights, but at a minimum, she was forewarned the Assassins Guild was still active in Orrin. Part of me prayed the renegades and their allies would follow Luc and me to Tandor and leave the younger priest and priestesses at our Temples alone, but I feared the junior clergy would only provide more tempting targets.

When First Evening bells rang, I put aside the paperwork I had been reviewing. Talbert's warning continued to bother me. I was still wondering how to give the Reverend Mother adequate information without revealing too much to possible traitors within Balance. The entire process gave me a headache.

Stretching my cramped fingers, I headed for the courtroom. Since it was the largest room in our temple, it was also the most convenient place to have a nearly full staff meeting.

Or full staff meeting, I realized as I quickly counted heads.

Two tables had been shoved together. Wardens were placing benches around them while Sivan and Deborah directed the rest of the household staff in the placement of eating utensils, steaming bowls, and hot platters. Ming Wei watched over Justice Yanaba and kept her out of the way.

"Isn't anyone guarding our gates?" I asked to no one in particular.

Hogarth shuffled closer to me in order to be heard over the din. "Gina made deals with some of the wardens from Love and a couple of the Wilding priests.

People she trusts to watch our backs. They're protecting our walls for the next couple of candlemarks."

The Wildlings I understood. "Love?"

Hogarth shrugged. "You don't think Dragonfly and the rest of them girls didn't truthspell the demon out of their new wardens. Plus the priestesses owe you and Gina more than a few favors for getting them out of that mess they were in."

Such cooperation reassured me that we made some progress in repairing the relationships between the Temples in Orrin. Yet, I couldn't help but notice everyone, not just the wardens, were armed within our walls. Even our two squires and the kitchen girl had knife sheaths on their belts.

Their concerns plus the wardens' confrontation with me this morning made my next decision a little easier. "I'll ward the room as an extra precaution."

Hogarth nodded. "That would be best."

I reached for my shoulder and pulled my sword from its back sheath.

And every one in the courtroom immediately drew their weapons, too.

Everyone except Hogarth. Even Yanaba's blade was in her hands.

"Do I need to throw a bucket of cold water on all of you?" I snapped. Most of their faces gleamed scarlet.

Yanaba shrugged and sheathed her sword. "You cannot fault the wardens and staff for their uneasiness, Chief Justice."

"What was your excuse, Justice?" I asked as I headed for the basalt statue of our goddess.

"I heard you draw your sword," she said primly. "In my scant time assigned to Orrin, I've learned you never do so outside of a formal court session without a threat present."

My glare had no effect on her since she couldn't see it. However, the rest of the wardens and staff stowed their weapons amid stifled snickers. Nor did I want to destroy the good humor by pointing out we haven't had any capital cases since the chaos Gerd and the Assassins Guild had caused.

I turned to our cook. "Deborah, do you have everything you need from the kitchen before I ward the room?"

The residual snickers cut off abruptly. I hated ruining their moment of levity, even if it were at my expense, but I also wasn't taking any unnecessary chances with their lives. A single demon would make short work of those wardens and priests watching our walls right now. And even as fast as my people had armed themselves, one or two would die before any of us registered one of those bastards in the room.

"No, m'lady," Deborah said.

I knelt before the statue of Balance and sucked in a deep breath. The one helpful thing Penelope had done during her tenure was to place a padded kneeler at the base. The ancient invocation rolled off my tongue. Yanaba and the staff responded at the appropriate places of the prayer/spell.

I rose, and holding my sword perpendicular to the floor, I strode clockwise along the circuit of the room. Once again, I detected a presence at my shoulder, one I'd felt since the Reverend Mother sentenced me to the Orrin seat. While it would be comforting to believe Balance herself had taken a direct interest in the happenings of the city, I wasn't that much of a fool.

Maybe it was one of my predecessors. Not Penelope because she hadn't given much of a shit when she was alive. The more likely choice was Justice Thalia, who'd died protecting Orrin from pirates. But that was only wishful thinking on my part since I'd learned she was my maternal grandmother.

I brushed aside the wayward thoughts and concentrated on the spell. Residual power from centuries of my predecessors rose out of the stones and melded with mine as I circled the room. When I return to the statue, I slid my sword between her clasped hands. The wards settled into the walls, floor and ceiling of the huge chamber. No intruder would enter without my permission.

The energy pulsing in the stone made the courtroom feel far warmer than a hundred braziers ever could in winter. I removed my harness, gloves and outer cloak and placed them on the podium seat before I took my place at the head of the table.

I held up my goblet. "Thank Child for her bounty, and thank Mother for gifting Deborah the skills to make everything edible in the dead of winter. Let us eat."

That impromptu grace brought the humor back to the room. Once everyone had taken their fill, I raised my goblet to Little Bear. "You asked for this meeting, Chief Warden. Why don't you begin?"

His face turned a bright orange-red as he cleared his throat. "I'm speaking on behalf of the entire staff of Balance. Are you being permanently transferred to Tandor?"

Is that what they were worried about? I shook my head. "No, definitely not."

"Then why is Justice Yanaba here?" Leilani blurted. The junior clerk immediately slapped her hands over her mouth.

Thanks to the residual effects of our earlier truthspell, Yanaba's emotions rose above the others. She was more amused than angered by Leilani's indiscreet words.

I held up my own hand. "This is one time where temple decorum will be dropped. Everyone needs to know what's happening because all our lives depend on it. I want you to present your concerns." I turned to Yanaba. "Would you care to answer our junior clerk's question, Yanaba?"

She sipped her wine before she began. "The Reverend Mother sent me here for several reasons, chief among them was to see if my presence would ferret out further conspirators while Anthea is investigating the Balance Temple in Tandor."

"But why?" Tyra asked. "All our evidence points to their Temple of Light's involvement, not Balance."

"The Reverend Mother has noticed the similar discrepancies in Justice Elizabeth's reports that were in Penelope's prior to her death," I said.

"B-b-but—" Donella sounded like she was having an attack of nerves. Probably because she's the one who'd handled the bulk of Penelope's duties when the justice had become too senile to perform them.

"You're not in trouble, Donella," I said. "You informed the Reverend Mother of Penelope's condition." I couldn't help grinning. "Frankly, you, Sivan, and Little Bear were doing a better job of running the temple than your justice, which was why the Reverend Mother let the situation slide until she could find a way to force me to take the seat. So, to rest your minds, I'm not leaving Orrin anytime soon."

"That leads to the other main reason I'm here," Yanaba added. "If, Balance forbid, something has happened to Elizabeth, I'll be sent south to Tandor once Anthea is satisfied with my performance." She lifted her goblet again. "That's assuming our chief justice fails to get herself killed during the audit."

More snickers rounded the table. If the teasing kept the staff at ease given the dire circumstances we faced, the least I could do was graciously accept it.

Little Bear rapped his knuckles on the table. "Which brings us to our next concern, m'ladies. This trip to Tandor. We have no idea what's really happening down there. Anthea and Luc could be walking into a city already under the thumb of the Assassins Guild or demon dealers."

A murmur of agreement ran around the table.

"Or both. We are well aware of it," I said. "But someone needs to find out for sure before a demon army scales our walls on their march north. Given what happened at Love, our own Reverend Mother refuses to risk more lives than necessary in case Tandor has unknowingly fallen. Nor can the queen risk sending in conventional troops without raising the ire of the nobility."

I took a gulp of wine before I continued. "The reverend mothers and fathers in Standora made their decision, and I'm going to follow it. They need members of the clergy who they are sure haven't been compromised."

"Anthea, I don't mean to be contrary, and the Twelve know you're a pain in our collective backsides—" Sivan started.

"Aye," Deborah muttered.

"—but you need to be here," Sivan finished. "Whatever's going on, Orrin's at the heart of it."

"Once we know the condition and allegiance of Chief Justice Elizabeth and what the demon High Brother Dav is up to, we're coming back," I said, injecting as much reassurance into my voice as I could.

"Which brings us to our final concern," Little Bear said. "Who is accompanying the two of you?"

I sighed. "If I had my druthers, it would be just me and Luc—"

"That's unseemly," Hogarth snapped. "You're no longer a circuit justice. You're both temple seats."

"Thank you for stating the obvious, Reverend Mother," I said sourly. He returned my glare.

I turned back to Little Bear. "Right now, I can tell you who's not going. You and Gina are staying here. Yanaba needs the two most experience wardens if something does happen to me."

A smile twisted my lips. "Gina's already turned down Love's request for her transfer to their temple as their new chief warden, for which I thank you more than you realize, my dear." She bobbed her head in acknowledgment even as her face turned scarlet.

I leaned forward. "By the same token, Yanaba has requested you as her new chief warden if we discover the temple in Tandor has been thoroughly compromised."

Gina's attention flitted between me and Yanaba. "I-I don't know what to say."

The younger justice smiled. "You don't have to answer just yet. While I hope my planning becomes a moot point, I wanted to be ready in case. Anthea has already stated she won't give up Little Bear because she spent too much time training Sivan, and they are a package deal."

The assembly broke out in laughter, with Sivan muttering some nasty things about my hygiene even though she was smiling.

When the din died down, I said, "Have no doubt, this trip is extremely dangerous. We already lost Aglaia last month. Thief knows the odds of everyone involved in this alleged audit dying are damn high. That's why I'm asking for one, and only one, volunteer."

Tyra jumped to her feet. "I'm going."

The last thing I wanted was to hurt the grieving woman. She and Aglaia had been far closer than I knew before the battle at Love had cost Aglaia her life. "This isn't a revenge trip, Warden."

Tyra inclined her head. "I realize that, Justice, but you need someone who understands how both you and High Brother Luc work—"

Muffled banging on the main courtroom doors interrupted her justifications for her inclusion.

"Were we expecting guests tonight?" I muttered wryly.

Sivan chuckled. "Since you took the seat, nearly all guests are unexpected."

Whoever was at the door tried to enter. While my normal wards had a certain flexibility, the addition of centuries of power would have barred even our brothers and sisters from the Temple of Conflict along with the Issuran army from getting into the courtroom.

With a word and gesture, I dissolved the wards. Farrah, the Wildling second, nearly fell on her face when the door abruptly gave way and she stumbled through.

"Sorry to interrupt, Chief Justice." Her narrow countenance didn't look the least bit apologetic as she straightened. "But Ambassador Quan of Jing demands to see you over a matter of life and death."

Chapter 7

Sivan scrambled to her feet to intercept the ambassador and escort him to my office. While Hogarth and Deborah guided everyone else in the cleaning of our dining tables, Little Bear pulled me aside.

"Was there something else?" I asked innocently.

"You know damn well what I'm objecting to," he growled. At least, he didn't undermine my authority in front of the rest of the staff. He'd taken last month's lecture about discretion to heart. "You need more than just Tyra on this trip."

"I need you here more than I need you to watch my back," I murmured. "You saw Noko and Daniel's reports from earlier today."

"I also know about the coin Daniel found and what it means." Of course, Noko had informed her chief warden of my off-the-record meeting with High Brother Talbert. Little Bear raked his hands over his short hair, a gesture I seemed to provoke in many men these days.

"Which is exactly why I need you guarding Yanaba," I said. "I fear the Assassins Guild may target her next in order to make an additional point."

His eyebrow arched. "You're on the top of their list, not her."

I grinned. "They've lost too many of their people trying to kill me. They need easier prey."

"Like Dante's children?" His gaze felt like a knife slowly penetrating my ribs before it sliced into my heart. My smile faded.

"Yes," I whispered. "And Yanaba is just as vulnerable as they were. She needs you more than I do at the moment."

"You know Tandor is a trap." His hands clenched. He was probably imagining them wrapped around my throat in order to shake some sense into me.

"It's the not-so-obvious traps that worry me. And we have more than enough of them here in Orrin. I need you here, and that's the end of the discussion, Chief Warden." I pivoted on my boot heel and strode toward my office. Little Bear was following his duty, but he needed to learn personal feelings did not always mesh with those obligations. A bitter lesson I still had trouble swallowing.

This time, Quan's guards didn't question me entering my own office because I'd left my cloak in the courtroom. Therefore, my face, and especially my eyes, were visible to them.

I found the ambassador lounging in my chair with the missive from the queen in his hand. "Enjoying yourself, Quan Po?"

His answering smile sent the beads at the ends of his long moustache swaying. "I wasn't sure how long you would be, dearest Anthea, so I found some reading material to pass the time." He rose and bowed. "I've come to offer my services."

"Your services?"

There was one quick knock on my door before Sivan bustled in with a tray. Steam rose from the teapot, bringing with it the scent of my secret stash of expensive Jing black tea. The tray also held a selection of almond and cinnamon dessert pastries as well as teacups. The ambassador laid my pardon on my desk, but remained silent while my personal assistant set everything in place.

Sivan shot me a sharp look when she was done. My subtle negation didn't make her happy, but she left anyway. Two of my own wardens would be outside my door, challenging Quan's guards to a staring contest while the ambassador and I spoke.

While I understood my personal assistant's feelings on the matter, my relationship with Quan was a necessary one these days. I gestured for him to take a seat at the little table, which he did. He stayed quiet until I poured the tea and handed him the cup.

"The rumor among the fishwives is that you and High Brother Luc are riding south in a few days." He watched me over the rim of his cup, but I also knew when to remain silent.

His lips twitched in faint amusement. "It has been suggested to me that a sea route would be safer, quicker, and would catch our demon dealers by surprise."

I didn't need to ask who had made the suggestion. Shi Hua was a very clever young priestess. I snorted. "Hardly. They already know we're coming."

"But not when and not how." Quan sipped his tea. "The next high tide is at Second Night, and my ship is ready to launch."

His proposal had some merit. Sailing along the coast would get us to Tandor two days early. And if Luc and I could scout the city prior to officially approaching the temples, we would have a better idea of what was in store for us.

"And how long will your ship stay in Tandor's port?"

"Three days. The captain was supposed to go late tomorrow to pick up a shipment of pulque and azul wine. However, his first mate is a registered weather oracle—"

"Another storm?" I sighed and refilled both our cups.

"No ice this time." Quan saluted me with his cup before taking a deep drink.

"Thank Balance for that." However, this close to the spring equinox we should be having fewer storms, not more, regardless of the ice question.

I stared at the orange steam wafting from my own tea. Three days. Could we even begin to accomplish what we needed to in three days? "What about our horses?"

Quan shrugged. "It depends on how well they travel by ship. But are you sure you want to take temple-trained mounts with you, Anthea? If you hope to reconnoiter the city prior to your official arrival, such horses will be obvious to those enemies who are all too aware of temple practices."

"And you believe a red-eyed woman and a man with a missing foot won't prompt questions?"

"True," Quan admitted. "But human traits could be disguised. The horses will be far more difficult."

I didn't like depending on anyone else for transport, especially in a situation fraught with uncertainty, but Quan made a good point. "I still must speak with High Brother Luc first."

"As I surmised."

"If we're not at the docks when your captain is ready to cast off, he is not to wait," I said.

Quan laughed and set his cup on the fine ceramic saucer that accompanied the serving tray. "Trust me. He won't."

We both rose at the same time. "Thank you for your assistance, Ambassador Quan."

"My pleasure." We both bowed, and he departed.

While he was being more than helpful now, I had to wonder exactly what the Jing emperor's brother would want in return.

Chapter 8

After I gave instructions to Sivan about packing civilian clothing for both Tyra and me, I crossed through the underground tunnel over to Light. From his silhouette, Luc was already abed, reading Balance only knew what. His bedside lamp blinded me from any other details.

"Well, this is a pleasant surprise." He set his tome aside and extinguished the lamp for my comfort. When I could see, he wore his lascivious grin. The one I hadn't seen in over a month.

I groaned. "Oh, you have no idea how I wish it were that kind of visit."

All his lust and jocularity disappeared. "What's wrong?"

I crossed to his bed, my bootsteps softer on his wooden floor than the marble of my own chambers, and sat beside him. My conversation with Ambassador Quan spilled out, along with my semi-private conversation with High Brother Talbert. Luc was silent for a long time after I finished. I finally said, "Did Shi Hua say anything to you before she approached Quan about providing transport?"

"She suggested traveling to Tandor by sea would be a better tactical move, but she failed to mention that she'd already made arrangements." And by his tone, he was obviously not pleased by that exclusion.

"Then you don't think sailing to Tandor is a good idea?"

"I didn't say that." His sword arm crossed his chest. The elbow of the other rested on his forearm, and he rubbed his chin. That pose generally meant something that had been bothering him had coalesced into new knowledge inside his mind. "Have you noticed anything odd about our visiting priestess?"

I blinked and tilted my head. Usually, I could follow Luc's line of reasoning, but this time, I was at a loss. "Other than her penchant for climbing roofs and scaling walls?"

He regarded me. "That's part of it."

"And what is the rest?"

Instead of answering me, he reached over and rang the bell that sat on his night table. One of his wardens entered.

"Yes, High Brother?"

"Would you please summon Sister Shi Hua and Brother Jeremy to my quarters? And have Edberth prepare tea for Chief Justice Anthea." Barely contained anger tainted Luc's voice.

"Shall I send a warden to request her presence as well, High Brother?" Of course, the poor man sounded thoroughly confused. Between my uniform, hair color, and the lack of conventional light, he didn't realize I was in the room.

"That's quite all right," I said. "I think she can find her way here."

The warden jumped, his hand automatically reaching for his sword before he stopped himself. I could barely stifle my laughter at the expression on his face.

"That wasn't funny, Chief Justice," Luc chided.

"Of course, you are correct, High Brother. My apologies, Warden." My tone even managed to sound contrite.

"Would you like me to relight your lamp, sir?" Apparently, the aggrieved warden decided to ignore me.

"No, thank you," Luc said. Once the warden closed the bedchamber door, Luc flicked his thumb and forefinger. His bedside lamp flared to life.

I winced at the blinding white light. "Hey!"

"Serves you right. Now, fetch me a pair of leggings and a shirt."

I drew back. "Excuse me?"

"It'll take me too long to crawl over to the wardrobe, and you'll only harass Edberth if I summon him," Luc said sourly. "Not to mention, he's making your damn tea."

He was right. Even I needed help with certain aspects of hygiene and style since I couldn't see reflections with the bizarre version of eyesight I'd accidentally given myself. And Luc had spent ten years braiding my hair, so fetching his clothing hardly dented any recompense for his assistance.

I rose, crossed to his wardrobe and opened the doors. "You will need to tell me what to select."

"I don't need your pity." The skin on his face and torso had turned red.

"Good. Because you will receive none from me." I kept my voice low and even. "However, I pray you do not make the same mistakes I've made for the last thirty-one winters, and take your anger at the challenges the Twelve have thrown in you path out on everyone else around you."

Slowly, Luc's coloring faded to his normal cheerful gold. "I beg your forgiveness, m'lady."

"There's nothing to forgive," I said softly. "I seem to recall throwing my fair share of fits over the years." I ran my fingers over the silk hanging in the wardrobe. "Now, tell me which ones are proper Temple uniform shirts."

We managed to get him properly dressed and sitting at the medium-sized wooden table in his chambers prior to the junior clergies' arrival. From the number of chairs around it, I wasn't the only one who had been having morning meals while meeting with others.

Once Jeremy and Shi Hua arrived and Edberth left a tray with Jing tea on the side table, the warden withdrew and closed the door. Luc turned to me. "If you would please ward the room for me, Chief Justice."

His barely reined anger made me wonder if I'd made an error in judgment by not retrieving my sword and cloak, though neither of the Light clergy were armed with anything larger than a knife. And I also wondered how much of his anger was aimed in my direction. I tried to speak to him silently, but never had his thoughts been this closed to me.

I rose and quickly warded the room. And I remained standing, well out of reach of the other three.

"The chief justice was in the middle of a staff meeting tonight when she had an unexpected visitor," Luc began.

Jeremy's shocked visage shifted between Luc and me. "Light help us! It wasn't another attempt on her life by the Assassins Guild, was it?"

"No." Luc's gaze remained locked on Shi Hua. "Jeremy, you're here as my second. Recent events dictate that what I know, you need to know for the sake of our city.

"On the other hand, Shi Hua serves on the recommendation of the chief justice, and neither of us appreciate being manipulated."

The young priestess licked her lips nervously. "If I've done something inappropriate or that offends, please enlighten me, High Brother, so I don't re-peat my actions."

"The visitor was Ambassador Quan," I said quietly. Now, I knew what an-gered Luc. Maybe he was right, and their innocent suggestions might not be as helpful as they seemed on the surface. Granted, I didn't know Shi Hua as well as I wished, but I had trusted her.

Maybe too far according to the sick feeling in my gut.

"I'm going to ask you questions," Luc said. "And it will be under a truthspell. If you refuse the binding, I will have you arrested as a renegade, and let our na-tions' Reverend Fathers sort out the mess."

"High Brother—" Shi Hua began.

Luc held up his hand. "Before you agree to anything, the chief justice will perform the truthspell, not Jeremy or me. And I'm sure you know the results of someone trying to lie under her spell."

I sucked in a harsh breath at his pronouncement. He knew damn well why I didn't normally cast truthspells. I didn't have his finesse. The renegade who had killed and replaced Brother Mat had died when I interrogated him. Of course, he might still be alive if he'd answered my questions.

Then again, maybe not. He had gleefully admitted to killing a Light priest. I could have dismissed the truthspell instead of letting him die in agony, but usually, a person gave up their secrets long before the spell inflicted such a level of pain upon them.

Shi Hua bowed her head. "I will comply with the truthspell, High Brother."

Her agreement didn't make me feel any better about this. I glanced at Luc, but his eyes were hooded and his mind closed, almost as if he dared me to argue with him in front of his juniors.

"Have a seat, Sister," I muttered. "You might as well be semi-comfortable."

Once she did so, I took another deep breath, cleared my mind of my own wayward thoughts, and performed the two spells we needed. Last month, we'd discovered the Temple of Love had developed a blocking spell to keep their priestesses from being forced to reveal secrets they learned during pillow talk. Researching the matter, my grandfather Kam had discovered a spell to counter-act the blocker. Since we had reason to believe the renegades had learned of the blocker, we had to retrain ourselves to start with the counter before performing the actual truthspell.

I nodded to Luc once both spells had been completed and sidled toward the steaming pot. The hot tea was the one redeeming feature to this whole unpleasantness.

Luc leaned forward. "Why is it so important that Anthea and I be on the Jing ship when it leaves tonight?"

Shi Hua fought my truthspell for a moment, but must have decided her life was worth keeping.

"The Jing Temple of Thief discovered information that leads them to believe another cache of demon eggs is on its way to Cant." She rubbed her stomach. "The ambassador has been ordered to give Thief any aid to intercept and retrieve them if he can. I had made the suggestion of you sailing to Tandor to both you and the ambassador yesterday, prior to learning of the suspected demon eggs. The ambassador's ship was already scheduled to leave at tomorrow's high tide for Tandor to pick up a shipment of spirits. I meant no disrespect, sir. This is the first I heard the ambassador plans to send his ship sooner."

"What temples did you train at when you were a novice?" Luc asked.

"I—" Her face scrunched in pain. "At Light and Conflict."

Jeremy's eyebrows shot up, but Luc didn't seem surprised. It was highly unusual for any novice to split their time between two different temples. However, it would explain her better than average proficiency at fighting and wall climbing.

"Who did you train with outside of the formal temple structure?" Luc asked.

Shi Hua doubled over. "P-please, s-sir. D-don't a-ask—" She dropped to the floor, writhing.

Jeremy started to move toward her, but I stepped within reach and laid a hand on his shoulder to stop him. *Let this play out.*

He flinched when she let out a wail, but listened to my advice and stayed back.

I couldn't reveal this interrogation bothered me as well. This wasn't like Luc. I took a sip of my tea before I said, "You know if she dies under my truthspell, there will be a price to pay."

"This fiasco with the Assassins Guild has already cost my foot," he snapped.

It wasn't like him to focus on his personal grievances either. Two of my staff and Master Healer Devin had been poisoned. Kam and Sister Gretchen had been murdered, along with the entire squad of Love wardens as well as a warden from both mine and Luc's temples. The cost of that cursed demon grimoire had been too high for all of us.

I prayed Shi Hua wouldn't put my truthspell to the test and be added to that awful count.

She rolled around the wooden floor, screaming and crying, before she finally shouted, "Thief! The Reverend Father of Thief trained me. And my aunt who serves Love." She slumped to the floor and gasped for air.

"And that is why you shouldn't put yourself into a position where Anthea DiBalance truthspells you," I said to no one in particular.

Chapter 9

I continued to sip my tea while in halting motions, Shi Hua climbed back into her chair.

"Would you like some tea before we continue?" Luc's sudden graciousness didn't shock the young priestess.

She eyed me, then the extra cups on the tray before she said, "Yes, but given the circumstances, I'll pass for now, sir."

A short bark of laughter erupted from my throat. "He's not going to poison the tea or the cups when he's using me for his dirty work."

"All the same, Chief Justice, I'll wait and have a goblet of Pana red once the two of you are done questioning me." She clasped her hands on the tabletop. "High Brother, I respectfully ask you not to reveal what I've said here. All of you." Her attention shifted to include me and Jeremy.

Before Luc could respond, I snapped, "And I'll tell you the same thing I told Quan Po when he asked me to remain silent. If I have to choose between Issura, and especially Orrin, over Jing, I will choose my home."

"I understand," she said quietly.

Luc leaned back in his chair. "What is your aunt's status in Love?"

"She's a priestess at the main temple in Chengzhou." However, none of us missed her wince.

"What else does she do for Ambassador Quan or his brother?"

Another wince, but it was from pain. Shi Hua swallowed hard. "She assists the Reverend Father of Thief in intelligence gathering, and I believe she also worships with the emperor, but I dare not ask her that question."

I couldn't blame Shi Hua for not wanting to reveal that tidbit. It did make me wonder about her and Quan's real relationship, given the Jing Temple of Light required the same vows of chastity of its clergy.

"Why were you trained under four different temples?" Luc continued.

"The specific purpose was to become Prince Po's bodyguard. My aunt Yin Li was trained like me. She has been the emperor's bodyguard on several occasions when he was still the crown prince." Apparently, Shi Hua decided sharing information we hadn't requested would make things easier on her.

Foolish girl.

"Prince Po?" Jeremy's gaze swept the three of us.

I glared at Luc. "What was that load of manure about everything you knew, he needed know?"

The high brother shrugged. "I forgot a minor detail."

I turned to Jeremy. "Ambassador Quan is the Jing emperor's half-brother."

The younger priest frowned. "He is? Why is he really in Issura?"

Shi Hua glanced at me. "The emperor's father is waging an influence campaign against Prince Po and the prince's father. The emperor thought his brother would be more useful to him here in your queendom."

"And less likely to die," I muttered into my cup.

The young priestess nodded. "Yes, that, too. Other than our own seaport of Tianjin and Standora's, no other city on the Peaceful Seas receives as much traffic as Orrin. No one would question the prince's travel here like they would if he stayed at the embassy in Standora."

"Or in other words, he's here to spy on us." Luc's sour disposition was back.

"Not unless you are conspiring with the emperor's father to depose the emperor." Shi Hua's eyes narrowed, daring Luc to contradict her words.

"What is really happening in Jing?" I demanded. Shi Hua didn't answer because my question was too broad. I sucked in a cleansing breath, unsure if the irritation I was feeling was mine, Luc's, or a mixture of both, and rephrased my question to something I'd been wanting to know for months. "Why does the political situation in Jing necessitate that a priestess become the bodyguard of a member of the imperial family?"

She shrugged. "The schools of philosophy and magic vie, not just with each other, but with the Temples for influence in the imperial court. However, both the emperor and the prince implicitly trust Reverend Father Biming of Thief.

He recruited me for my ability to distance speak based on my aunt's recommendation. The prince can then send regular reports to the emperor."

I suspected I already knew the answer to my next question, but I asked it anyway. "Why does the emperor overlook the School of Sorcery's influence on his own father?"

"He doesn't," Shi Hua replied. "As you discovered last autumn, the emperor has had more than enough reason to suspect the School of Sorcery of treachery for some time. Both he and my own Reverend Father thought they had nipped our renegade problem with the raid and the discovery of the eggs. But now that my own order has been compromised, the imperial family's safety is of paramount concern, and my prince will do what he has to in order to protect his brother's family."

"Was it the main temple in Chengzhou that was compromised?" Worry replaced Luc's anger. "Or all of them?"

"Neither, sir." Shi Hua sighed. "It was one outlying Temple in the southwest. They launched an attack on Shakya to make it look like Jing aggression. Both Shakya's Reverend Father of Light and imperial diplomats have been working hard to smooth the king of Shakya's ruffled feathers."

"Surely, the king has been apprised of the recent demon incursions," Jeremy said.

"Yes." For the first time since I met her, Shi Hua looked far older than her twenty winters. "That doesn't mean he believes them."

I muttered several improper words under my breath before I added, "And if Shakya declares war, Maurya will follow suit since Shakya is their vassal state."

Shi Hua nodded. "That is the emperor's and our Temples' fears as well, Lady Justice."

"Well, now we know the renegades' interest in Tandor," Luc murmured. "It would be a perfect place to launch an attack on Cant."

I groaned. "And the Mecas would respond in Cant's defense."

Luc shook himself out of wherever his thoughts had taken him. "Who do you report to in Chengzhou?"

"Reverend Father Biming," she answered. "If he's unavailable, I deliver my report to Justice Mei Wen."

"Justice Mei Wen?" I cocked my head. "Why a junior member of Balance?"

"Because she's been one of my closest friends since we were novices, and I can form a rapport with her quickly and easily." A ghost of the Light priestess's old smile appeared on her face. "And she is training directly with our Reverend Mother of Balance."

"I see." I grinned in return and set down my empty cup.

Jeremy looked at me askance, not getting my joke.

Luc didn't wait for either Jeremy to figure out my bad pun or for me to explain it. He grabbed a piece of used parchment and sketched something with a stick of charcoal before he passed it to Shi Hua. "Have you seen a coin of this design before?"

The priestess's coloring faded to a sickly yellow-green. "Yes. It was on an assassin who tried to kill Prince Po while we were in the Fire Islands. Where—" Her tongue flicked across her lips and she glanced at me. "May I ask where you found one?"

I crossed my arms. "Tell us what happened in the Fire Islands first."

Shi Hua paused, as if considering whether to try to squirm around the truth since I hadn't asked a direct question. She sagged even further in her chair. "There were two of them. Our subterfuge with me playing the ambassador's concubine worked too well. They came for me, and I killed them. Reverend Father Biming suspects that incident was when I was moved to the top of the Guild's list of targets. A mere concubine couldn't have taken out two master assassins. He sent my aunt to our home village on the pretense of visiting her family. She learned someone had been asking questions about me."

Luc crossed his arms as well while he digested her information. His mental shields loosened.

Well? I asked.

I still think you put far too much trust in the girl.

She's the best chance for Jeremy and Yanaba to survive our little trip.

At his reluctant assent, I told Shi Hua about the deaths of Dante and his family.

"That doesn't make sense," she blurted. "From what Reverend Father Biming has told me, the Assassins Guild doesn't kill without purpose."

"Or without pay," I quipped.

"Unless Dante pissed off the wrong person here in Orrin," Jeremy offered for the first time. He'd remained quiet and absorbed the information flung about the room. No doubt he had hundreds of questions.

I know I did. High Brother Talbert's warning about High Mother Bianca rang through my head. If she and Gerd were as entwined in their business dealings as other evidence suggested, Bianca could have access to Guild resources. Perhaps even had dealings with the trader Ural DiSand my mother had mentioned during her interrogation. Dante could have been employed by someone seeking information, or maybe he had discovered something that was a danger to Orrin. I had more questions than answers at this point.

I met Luc's gaze, and he nodded. I said the word to dissolve the truthspell. "We're not going to solve anything sitting in your bedchambers. Shall we accompany our dear Jing ambassador to Tandor tonight?"

A wicked grin spread across his face. "By all means. I can truthspell him on the trip when his bodyguard isn't around."

Shi Hua didn't respond to his statement, though Jeremy did gasp at his senior's audacity.

"Can you relay silent speech from a third party when you distance speak?" I asked the younger woman.

She nodded.

"Good. When we return from Tandor, I want to have a little talk with your Reverend Father Biming."

Chapter 10

Little Bear insisted on accompanying Tyra and me to the docks. Like us, he wore nondescript clothing, nothing to betray our affiliation or rank. My chief warden made another impassioned argument on the ride across the city of why he should replace the junior warden on the trip to Tandor.

I finally cut him off with a violent gesture. "Are you saying Tyra's incompetent?"

He leaned away from me, and his mount whinnied softly. "That's not what I'm saying, and you know it."

I reined Nassa to a halt. "As I said earlier, I will not discuss this further, Chief Warden. Justice Yanaba requires your experience to keep the peace in Orrin as does Brother Jeremy and Magistrate DiCook. Not to mention, you need to instruct Warden Jonata on my preferences for court protocol. So, until you can perform your duties to my satisfaction, do not lecture me about who I select to join me on an investigation."

It wasn't fair to throw our newest warden's minor mistake in his face. She was fresh out of the academy and nervous as a pig going to the slaughter when she called a noble by the wrong title the other day in court. If Luc were here, he'd be silently chiding me for my harsh words to my chief warden.

Or maybe not, especially after his performance with Shi Hua tonight.

Little Bear stiffened in his saddle. The woolen edges of his own hood blazed orange from his body heat and anger. His horse whinnied again to protest the too tight grip on his reins.

"Yes, Chief Justice." He followed his tense acknowledgment by jerking his poor horse in the direction of our temple.

"I guess he's not taking our mounts back with him," Tyra remarked dryly.

I glared at her. When I was first condemned to the Balance seat, the quiet woman had barely spoken in my presence. Now, she unflinchingly gazed at me.

"Would you prefer to stay in Orrin as well?" I snapped.

"No," she replied calmly. "However, I'm not Little Bear, and I won't simply argue in the streets with you and gallop off in a huff. If I see you take unnecessary risks in Tandor, I will bind and gag you before I throw you on a ship for home."

My hands clenched around Nassa's reins. "I could have you flogged for insubordination," I bit out.

"You could, but I doubt you would be pardoned by the queen twice for stepping beyond your oath." She kneed her mount forward. "Are you coming, Chief Justice?"

I had Nassa follow. I fumed while the horses' hooves beat out a count of ten on the cobblestones before I asked, "What makes you think you can get away with your impertinence?"

"You wanted our honesty and discretion, m'lady," she said. "But there are times when honesty trumps discretion, and this is one of those times." She paused for a moment before she added, "Little Bear is justifiably concerned you will let your suicidal impulses control you on this investigation. However, the high brother needs you to be careful. His life depends on it. If you truly love him, you'll listen to me."

My blood froze. Luc and I had tried so hard to keep our illegal affair quiet. My grandfather Kam admitted he knew before he was killed. The Reverend Mother had deduced the truth and stated High Brother Jax of the Orrin Wildling Temple also knew. She'd added that High Brother Han of Conflict and High Sister Bertrice suspected the truth as well. The rest believed my mother had started the rumor simply to discredit me in her madness. And I clung to the last one in desperation.

"So now you're going to repeat rumors fostered by a priestess charged with conspiracy and treason in an attempt to control me?" I asked.

Tyra sighed. Yellow steam covered her face before the vapor turned green and dissipated. "I know because I saw the same fear on your face when he was abducted by the renegades I saw in my own reflection when Aglaia died. My observation will go no further than me, m'lady, but I stand by my counsel to you."

I'd underestimated this warden greatly. "Is that why you really volunteered? To keep me from killing myself?"

She chuckled. "As if I could stop you. I'm here to give the Light warden a hand in guarding the high brother."

"Thank you," I said sourly.

"You're welcome."

For once, the night was crisp, clear and fog-free along the coast, though I didn't doubt the forecast from Quan's weather oracle would fulfill itself in half a day. The night was clear enough I could make out the ships currently moored as well as the one headed out of the harbor. While I couldn't see the design of the flags flying on the mast, I recognized the voice of Captain Titus bellowing orders on board the duke's flagship, the *Mars Tranquilus*. Apparently, he hadn't become accustomed to his new position yet if he was personally supervising their departure.

The Sea Peoples' double-hulled ships bobbed at their moorings. Depending on the accuracy of weather oracles' forecast, the captains could start loading the stacks of Issuran goods sitting on the docks as early as tomorrow in order to leave once the storm passed. Past them sat the Jing junk that served as the ambassador's personal vessel.

But it was the strange ship anchored at the end of the longest pier that drew my attention. Three horses and one slim figure stood at the shore end of the quay where the unusually large vessel was berthed. Neither the saddles nor the person's cloak displayed the insignia of the Temple of Light, but I recognized Shi Hua's powerful essence. If that didn't give away her anger, the heat in her face beneath a merchant's cap did.

"What are you doing here, Sister?" I asked as I dismounted. Tyra followed suit.

Shi Hua bowed. "I am tasked with taking the high brother and his warden's horses back to the temple." She hesitated, watching my warden. "I can take yours back as well if you wish."

Tyra glanced at the junk, suspicion rolling off her in waves. "Why aren't we taking the Jing boat?" Her chin lifted in the direction of the strange ship. "This one flies the flags of the Iberian duchy of Valencia."

"Given the circumstances of both your task and my master's, he has accepted transportation that won't be associated with either of our nations," Shi Hua replied. "He and the captain of this ship trade favors."

I motioned for Tyra to board. From the set of her mouth, she didn't like leaving me alone on dock, but she grabbed her gear and handed her mount's reins to the priestess. Once my warden was out of earshot, I waited for the Jing sister to speak first.

"I have my loyalty to my emperor, just as you have yours to your queen," Shi Hua said softly. "But my first loyalty is to the Twelve. That's the only reason I have given you as much information as I have."

"And that makes manipulating me and the high brother acceptable in your eyes?" The problem wasn't my initial anger with her, nor hers with me. I was angry with myself for assuming we both had humanity's best interests at heart when it came to the demons threatening us.

"This joint voyage was not a manipulation, Lady Justice," she hissed. "If you believe so, flog me if you must, but please, *please*, do not hurt the ambassador."

Begging on Quan's behalf? Did she seriously believe I would harm him, or was this another game?

Balance, help me. I was so tired of all the political machinations. Kam had been right. I should have tried harder to convince Luc to run away with me to Cant. Or the Mecas. Or even seek sanctuary with Diné. If I had, Luc would still be whole, and Kam might be alive.

"You have my word I will not harm Quan Po unless he tries to deceive me, even by omission. Nor will I allow Luc or the wardens to do so. And I will relay the same statement to him when I board. I cannot give you more than that, Sister."

She bowed. "Nor can I ask more than that, Lady Justice."

I grabbed my bag before I handed Nassa's reins to Shi Hua. A tremor ran through me. Nassa had been my constant companion for the last eleven years. We hadn't been apart since the day I left Standora to begin my stint as a circuit justice in the foothills of eastern Orrin. Not having her within reach, available for a pursuit or an escape, was troublesome at best. I forced myself to turn away and marched down the pier to the gangplank.

When I reached the deck, the captain of the ship bowed to me. "Welcome aboard the *Unbridled*, m'lady." He deliberately spoke in Issuran, not the Peaceful Sea trade language or the Jing tongue. He also wore a fake beard, which probably meant he was Quan's man despite any claim of trading favors. He lowered his voice. "The high brother and Warden Yar have already boarded, m'lady, and the four of you have the use of my cabin."

Relief threaded through my nerves at the captain's mention of which warden Luc chose to accompany us. Yar was a mountain of a man, his ancestors from the northern steppes of the Old Continent. If we encountered trouble, he could literally sling Luc over his shoulder and run.

"Your generosity honors us, Captain," I said, returning his bow. I almost inquired about the ambassador when I noticed a nearby sailor staring at me.

Scraggly blue hair in a loose top knot. An equally scraggly beard. Well-worn clothes and skin chilled pale yellow from the winter air like his fellows. But he was paying more attention to me than the rope he handled.

Then he winked.

I tried not to react to the audacious man. Leave it to Quan to disguise himself as a common sailor. Either this was part of his plan to find the demon eggs. Or Shi Hua had warned him about Luc's threat to truthspell him.

Turning my back to the disguised sailor, I smiled at the captain. "Let me get out of your people's way before I trip over something and fall overboard."

The captain chuckled. "It would not do to cause a diplomatic incident by letting an esteemed passenger drown, even by accident, as we leave port."

As he escorted me across the deck, I took a good look. The ship was similar to the Iberian-style caravels the merchants along the western shores of the Long Continents preferred, but it was much larger with an extra mast. A new, faster design? I would have to ask the captain when he had a moment, but now was not the time.

He opened the door to his cabin and bowed again. Luc and the wardens sat at the single table. A blinding white oil lamp hung over the wooden surface and swayed with the waves beneath us.

Once the door closed and I took a seat, Luc said, "I was beginning to think you'd changed your mind."

I relayed my odd conversation with Shi Hua to him and the wardens. Tyra snorted in derision, but Yar's expression was impassive.

Luc frowned and rubbed his chin. "That doesn't make sense. We haven't seen the ambassador."

"I asked the captain if we were waiting on him when I boarded," Tyra volunteered around a wide yawn. "And he told me we weren't."

"He's already here." I held up a hand. "Don't ask me how I know, but I have half a mind to truthspell the bastard myself despite my promise to Shi Hua."

"Well, I didn't promise." Luc grinned. "I'll have to make sure I do it when you're not around to stop me."

Outside the cabin, the captain shouted orders. Timbers around us creaked and sails snapped. It was too late for us to change our minds about this trip unless we wanted to swim to shore.

I rose and stretched. "It's been a very long day for some of us. I'm going to sleep. If you're going to torture Quan, do it quietly."

Tyra yawned again.

Yar rolled his eyes. "I will keep the watch, m'lady." He stood and retrieved two sets of netting from a trunk tucked behind his seat.

"The captain left us hammocks," Tyra said as she stood. She covered her mouth again as her jaw cracked with a third yawn.

"No, you two take the bed." Luc tried to stand, but the ship tilted as the crew tacked into the wind, and he tumbled back into his chair.

Tyra glared at him. "With all due respect, High Brother, we do not need you falling out of a hammock and injuring yourself."

Luc opened his mouth to protest some more, but Tyra jammed her fists on her hips.

"I'll tell you the same thing I told the chief justice on our ride to the docks. If you continue to argue with me, I will bind and gag you."

Luc looked over at Yar. "She just threatened me."

"Yes, sir. She did." The warden didn't bother looking at Luc. Instead, he handed one end of a hammock to me and pointed to a hook on the wall where the end loop went.

"Anthea!"

I looked at Luc and shrugged.

He was still muttering imprecations under his breath when I fell asleep to the soft sway of the hammock.

Loud knocking woke me. I peered over the netting at Yar. The lamp had been extinguished. Yet, he sat, examining a map on the table.

"What time?" I whispered.

"Past Third Morning, m'lady," he murmured. He rose and peered out the window before he opened the door.

"Food for our passengers," Quan cheerily announced in an accent I didn't recognize. He carried a steaming pot and a stack of cups. The captain followed him into the cabin. In his hands was a tray full of baked goods from the scent.

"That sounds wonderful," Luc said as he sat upright and flung back his blanket.

Yar grabbed the map and rerolled it while the captain sat his tray on the table and stepped back to close the door. The captain crossed back to the middle of the cabin. He muttered under his breath, and his fingers made the gesture for warding.

In the moment between his spell and it settling into the wood around us, Tyra and I rolled out of our hammocks and drew our swords. Luc and Yar likewise produced weapons.

The alleged captain raised his hands in a conciliatory motion. "Sister Shi Hua said you wished to speak with me, Lady Justice."

Quan snickered. He dropped the odd accent. "Ignore her, my friend. Anthea can't think straight before two cups of her morning tea."

"I was more worried about her warden skewering me," the captain said mildly. "And I could say something about your incredible lack of manners. Why Chengwu thought it was a good idea to make you an ambassador is beyond me."

"And you're lucky we're not at home where I could have you beheaded for insulting a member of the imperial family." Quan cleared his throat. "Chief Justice Anthea DiBalance, High Brother Luc DiLight, may I present Reverend Father Biming of the Jing Temple of Thief."

Chapter 11

"What?" I glanced from Quan to his companion and back.

"You heard me the first time." The ambassador sniffed and began pouring tea.

Skewering Quan seemed like an excellent idea. I pointed my sword at him. "You couldn't have told me this last night?"

"It's unseemly for a common sailor to fraternize with a noble passenger," he responded, deliberately misunderstanding me.

While I searched for the words to spar with, Yar shoved his knife back into its sheath on his belt. "Do you need assistance, High Brother?"

Luc smirked. "I just need someone to keep me from pitching into the privy while I relieve myself. However, I don't trust the chief justice not to cause a diplomatic incident while our backs are turned."

"She won't, sir," Tyra said.

Only then did I realize I was the only one still holding a naked blade. Reluctantly, I sheathed it. "There wouldn't be a diplomatic incident if certain people didn't play games," I grumbled.

"It's an unfortunate necessity in these times," Biming said as we all studiously ignore Yar helping Luc. "However, Po, Shi Hua, and Talbert swore for your character and conduct. Else I would not have risked this meeting."

"Talbert?" I couldn't blame my sudden nausea on the pitch and roll of the ship beneath my bare feet.

"Justice, your temper is well-known, as is your temperance." Biming stroked the fake beard he wore. "I hope you'll listened to my news with the second quality before you make your decision about me."

I rubbed my forehead. This whole quagmire was rapidly getting out of hand.

Frankly, if the Jing priest was part of the renegades and wanted me out of the way, he could have had the crew throw me overboard long before now. I let out a deep breath. "How many of the crew are Thief?"

He chuckled. "Po truly does underestimate you. All of them. Four junior priests and the former high brother of Han Province. The rest are wardens, except for my personal cook."

I blinked and stared at the Reverend Father. "Could I please trouble you for some tea and headache powder before we continue this discussion?"

"The tea is easy." He smiled and motioned for me to sit at the table. "And I know a headache remedy better than most medicines."

While I took a seat, Yar helped Luc to the chair across from me. Biming stepped behind me and swept my hair over my shoulder. His fingers were hot as he probed my neck bones. A sudden stabbing flared down my spine and across my scalp, meeting at the spot in the center of my forehead that already ached. I gasped.

Luc started to rise. "What are you doing—"

Just as swiftly, all the pain disappeared. I blinked away my tears and held up a hand. "I'm all right." I looked up at the Reverend Father. "Thank you."

"I'm not finished yet." He sat cross-legged on the floor beside me and swung my knees around until my bare feet were in his lap.

When his fingers brushed my soles, I shrieked with laughter. Biming jerked his hands away. My reaction drew surprised looks from everyone except Luc.

"My apologies," I muttered.

"None are necessary." Biming smirked. "I can see why the Assassins Guild has failed so many times."

"What is that supposed to mean?" I resisted the urge to kick the man in the jaw.

His fingers dug into the bottom of my right foot. "They are using a dull broadax to slice a blade of grass." His thumbs pressed firmly on one particular spot. My neck and shoulder muscles were transformed into Deborah's bread pudding. I sagged in my chair.

"Better?" Biming asked.

I nodded. My tongue felt as liquid as the rest of my flesh.

"You need to show me how you do that," Luc said. "I would have paid you nine gold pieces to know your technique when Anthea and I were riding circuit together."

Biming's eyebrow rose. "Only nine?"

Luc grinned. "For the last nine years when she wouldn't shut up. Our first year, she refused to speak to me because she was angry about being assigned to a lowly rural region."

"Liar." I stuck my tongue out at him.

Quan set a cup of tea in front of me while Biming rose and served everyone cheese and day-old baked goods. Yar and Tyra sat on the bed while the Jing emissaries took the other two chairs.

Biming looked expectantly at me. "Where would you like to start, Anthea?"

I swallowed the bite of sweet corn bread. "Talbert couldn't, or wouldn't, tell me why I need to guard my words in my reports to my own Reverend Mother. Why should I do so?"

"My Issuran counterpart believes there is a spy within Balance. Your own Reverend Mother agrees, which is why she ordered Yanaba out of Standora and she's sending you to Tandor."

"Within Balance?" If I wasn't so damned relaxed from Biming's pressure techniques, my head would be pounding. "Have they eliminated the possibility of a corrupt courier?"

He nodded. "It's definitely someone within Balance itself. Alara is using the situation to feed false information to the renegades, which is how my own people discovered the existence of another cache of demon eggs."

The Jing Reverend Father used my own Reverend Mother's given name with impunity as if they were personal friends. However, he didn't sound much older than Luc or me. "You're terribly young to be guiding an entire nation's temple."

He scowled. "My predecessor had a heart seizure six years ago. Far sooner than one of his age and health should have."

"It wasn't from natural causes," I ventured as I picked off a piece of cornbread.

"Unfortunately, we had no proof against the perpetrators." He saluted me with his cup of tea. "Not until you revealed the existence of the demon at our Issuran embassy."

Biming cleared his throat. "In the interest of our cooperation and full disclosure, neither Shi Hua nor Quan intentionally misled either of you in regards to using a Jing ship to get to Tandor." His gaze shifted between Luc and me. "The prince didn't learn of my purpose and our mission until I arrived last night. He did plan on sending you with the merchant ship based on Shi Hua's suggestion. It was my idea to combine our tasks."

I shoved my cup to Quan to be refilled. "And you couldn't simply ask?"

"Not with so many people watching you." A wry smile tilted Biming's mouth.

"You couldn't point out the assassins to me?" I asked dryly as I accepted my hot, full cup from Quan. "Or are you afraid to become a target like your predecessor and protégé?"

Biming chuckled. "We, and by that, I mean all of Thief, not just my country's contingent or yours, aren't sure to whom all the watchers belong, and they are not all Assassins Guild."

"What he means is the spies are evenly split between those who want you alive and those we know wouldn't mourn your death," Quan offered.

"That's hardly reassuring," I muttered around another mouthful of bread.

"So who's your new concubine, Ambassador?" Luc grinned at the shocked looks on the Jing emissaries' faces. "Shi Hua's aunt?"

Biming frowned. "How did you learn of her?"

"The aunt or the concubine?" Luc's innocent face didn't fool me. I knew the game he was playing, and I was a little surprised both Quan and Biming bit on the bait. "I'm assuming she's guarding the ambassador while Shi Hua keeps an eye on Anthea for you."

Quan's eyes narrowed in suspicion. "That is none of your business."

However, Biming nodded. "Despite our careful planning, the Guild discovered Shi Hua was Temple long before she and Po arrived in Issura. Anthea's request for the sister's assistance in the Orrin temple seemed an opportunity too good to pass up and would make it harder for the Assassins Guild to reach any of you."

I leaned forward. "But Po's no longer the reason they're after Shi Hua, is it?"

Biming let loose a long, deep sigh. "No. You told your Reverend Mother she is a distance speaker."

Guilt at putting the young priestess in additional danger flared in my soul, but something in his manner disturbed me. "They're killing anyone with the distance speaking gift, aren't they?"

"Yes." He cocked his head and regarded Luc. "Shi Hua said you didn't ask about Po's new concubine when you truthspelled her." Biming glanced at the ambassador. "Apparently, you are not as careful as you think you are."

"Sometimes, it doesn't take a truthspell to learn a secret." Luc grinned.

Quan's look could have pierced solid steel. "How did you know Yin Li is Shi Hua's aunt?"

"Wait." I held up a hand. "Yin Li is already in Orrin?"

Quan looked at Biming. "I told you it takes two cups of tea before her mind can function."

If he weren't the Jing emperor's brother, I would have stabbed him.

"While I fully admit to truthspelling the sister, she volunteered the information her aunt serving Love was also one of her tutors when she was a novice." Luc shoved his untouched plate away. "While I like to think the temples work together, I've never heard of four different orders cooperating to that level, especially when training a novice. Therefore it stands to reason you would send someone with training similar to Shi Hua's, and it would have to be someone you trust implicitly, not to mention Yin Li has experience guarding the emperor himself."

Biming smiled. "High Brother, I think your own novice masters made a mistake in which temple you were assigned."

Luc inclined his head in acknowledgement of the compliment. Even I was surprised how much he'd put together, but then we hadn't had a chance to talk privately since the truthspell session with Shi Hua last night.

"Can we take a step backwards? Why did Quan give me a three-day deadline for staying in Tandor?" I asked.

"That was his plan before the *Unbridled* docked in Orrin yesterday." The Reverend Father grew somber. "If we intercept the eggs in Tandor, we had planned to return immediately to Orrin rather than take the chance of losing them again." He eyed Luc. "High Brother Dav's loyalties are suspect. I'd originally wanted to bring them to you in Orrin for destruction."

"And if they've slipped past you, you'll head down the coast to Tiwan," I said, guessing his next move. "From the capital of Cant, trade ships could carry demons or eggs down to the Grand Canal. The damn things would spread around the world faster than we could stop them."

"We don't have a choice," Biming said. "You know what one demon hatched here can do."

"I also know what will happen if they summon more of their brethren to this plane," I replied bitterly.

Quan took my cup to fill it again. "I'm sorry, Anthea, but our mission has to take precedence over yours."

"Do you realize it's all part and parcel of the same damn problem?" I retorted.

Neither the ambassador, the priests, or the wardens had a reply to that statement.

Late winter winds blew toward the coast, so the ship zig-zagged in a roughly parallel course. About the time land came into view, the pilot changed the *Unbridled's* heading to take us further out into the deeper and colder waters of the Peaceful Sea. However, the eerie sight of the sky and ocean blending into one solid blue-black had always unnerved me.

But in his restlessness, Luc cajoled me into accompanying him onto the deck. Tyra and Yar were off discussing warden matters with their Jing counterparts while both sides practiced each other's language instead of using the more common trade tongue. Luc was getting around better on the rolling deck with his modified crutches than I would have thought possible, though I was a bit thankful he didn't try climbing up to the forecastle.

Luc peered closely at me as we clutched the railing. "You're not getting seasick, are you?"

I sighed. "It's not the motion. It's the sight that bothers me."

He chuckled. "Close your eyes and give me your hand."

I did as he suggested. His warm palm covered mine. *It's an absolutely beautiful day. Too beautiful not to share. Look at it through my vision.*

His version of sight seeped into my mind. The water was dark, but not the awful blue-black I saw. White foam topped the waves, and flashes of silver marked a school of fish swimming beside us. A black and white form leapt above the surface before splashing into the sea.

A sea wolf!

There's a whole pack of them. He leaned over the railing so we could take in the others. Occasionally, a black dorsal fin sliced the blue water, but her companions remained in pursuit of their meal.

The sky was a clear medium blue with puffy white clouds that look as soft as wool. The sun was a blinding orb that Luc couldn't look at directly, not the bloody hue I knew. The familiar cries of gulls sounded from the stern of the ship, but these were bright white, not dark green, with their wings edged in black instead of blue.

Luc shifted so I could see the crew as they handled the rigging. To my surprise, only a third of the men and women were from the eastern region of the Old Continent. The rest were a mix from all over the world except the Lost Continent. And as far as anyone knew, the peoples of the Lost Continent had been butchered by the demons five centuries ago.

Or maybe they'd been eaten as a demon once threatened to do to me. Either way, the Sea Peoples stopped going to the Lost Continent after three generations. Some of the sailors claimed they heard the ghosts screaming in agony, and those with magic talents had gone mad after their visits.

With the mix of peoples, Biming's Thieves looked like any other trade ship's crew and would blend in at any port other than the fact they were sailing a new ship design. No, Thief would use the difference to draw in people in order to collect information. Perhaps they invested in the Iberian shipbuilders. Very clever of them.

The novelty of seeing the world through Luc's eyes couldn't stop the nagging worry inside me. I withdrew from our visual link and opened my eyes. *What do you think about Biming's story?*

He exhaled and his own concerns rippled across my consciousness. *He's telling the truth as he knows it, if that's what you're asking. Did you want me to truthspell him after all?*

No, I mean about a spy in Balance.

He raised an eyebrow. *You think your temple is above such corruption?*

No. I lowered my head, unable to look at him in my personal shame. *The renegades' mistake was not recruiting me before they harmed you.*

I could feel his utter stillness and waited for him to say something to my confession. Anything.

Instead of condemnation, he started laughing. Hard.

What's so funny?

Their real mistake was recruiting your mother instead of you.

Chapter 12

After much discussion that afternoon, we had decided on disguises. Despite Luc's not-so-joking suggestion that he and I pose as beggars, Biming's people scrounged adequate clothing for us to pass as down-on-their-luck minor nobles from the western side of the Old Continent with Yar and Tyra as our last two retainers.

A mourning veil would hide my eyes from close inspection. It also served to tamp down the obnoxiously bright oil lamp hanging in the cabin. Hadar, one of the Thief priests, convincingly sewed a boot to trousers to give the impression Luc's left foot was merely injured instead of missing.

When I complimented the young brother, he grinned. "Who do you think repairs storm damage to the sails?" He stood and circled us both.

"What are you looking for?" I asked.

Hadar shook his head. "With the high brother's merchant background and his coloring, he can pass as a noble from Valencia, but you, m'lady . . ."

"What?" I growled.

"That." He shook his index finger at me. "You're acting like a justice. Can you channel your duke's wife? Even a love priestess would work?"

Luc's head dropped into his hands. "Oh, gods help us."

My body shook. Part of me knew the young priest was trying to help, but all he managed was to dredge up my abominable past. Ironically, a past I unfortunately shared with the Lady Katarina of Orrin. We'd both been born to Love priestesses as a result of the Spring Rituals, and we'd both been abused by power-mad women who dealt in demon artifacts. My voice dropped even lower. "What is that supposed to mean?"

When I used that tone, most men wisely ran. Even Luc knew to back away from me.

The Thief priest did not. Instead, he crossed his arms and stared right back at me. "You're friends with Acting High Sister Dragonfly. How would she act in this situation?"

I matched his stance. "How do you know I'm friends with Dragonfly?"

"You didn't listen to a damn thing the captain told you at the midday meal, did you?"

A chill ran through me, and my eyes narrowed. "This cabin was warded."

He smiled. "Yes, it was."

My hands flexed.

Luc must have caught the rapid change of my mood. His head shot up and he nudged the younger man back with his right crutch. "If he was Guild, he wouldn't have bothered to tell you the truth."

I didn't take my gaze from the Thief priest. "Are you truly convinced of that, High Brother?"

Hadar gulped, finally realizing how much danger he was in. If Tyra had been in the cabin, he might already be dead. I muttered the two spells to solidify my questioning of him.

His breath caught as the magic settled into his flesh. "Why?"

"Because I'm tired of the games everyone around me wants to play with my life." I drew one of the knives I'd hidden in the dress when he was occupied with Luc's clothing, stepped closer to the younger priest, and rested the blade against his throat. I had to give him credit for not flinching. "Would you like your captain here while I question you?"

He sighed. The scent of mint wafted on his breath. Wooden hinges creaked to my left.

Reverend Father Biming cleared his throat. "I was under the impression you'd try to truthspell me or Ambassador Quan first, Lady Justice."

"Is that what Shi Hua told you?" I asked without taking my attention or my knife from his fellow priest.

"She mentioned you and the high brother weren't happy with how she handled things," Biming said dryly. "However, I would ask that you do not slice the throat of one of my crew. Finding a replacement in Tandor at this time would be problematic at best."

"You mean the Temple of Thief has been compromised there as well." Luc's words were more of a statement than a question.

"No, missing. Possibly dead given the Assassins Guild's activity in Issura." Biming stepped closer. "And that is your own Reverend Father of Thief's assessment, not mine. I offer myself for your questioning, Lady Justice."

"First, I want to know some things." I pressed the blade to make my point. This time, Hadar did flinch as blood beaded along the edge of my steel. "How did you learn the details of our private and warded conversation with your Reverend Father and the ambassador?"

"I didn't," he replied. "I guessed based on the Reverend Father's evaluation of your demeanor and the fact that you've been at the center of three separate demon attacks. And before you ask, everyone's aware you took the unusual step of supporting a *berda* as the new high sister of Love in Orrin. I reasoned that you two were on good terms."

I couldn't fault the youth's logic, except for one item. "And how do you know I wasn't responsible for unleashing the demon attacks to deflect suspicion away from me?"

The young priest blinked, and his mouth dropped open. Finally, he stammered, "Why would anyone do such a thing?"

"That would be an excellent subject for you to consider, Hadar." Biming couldn't keep humor from his voice. "If you're finished irritating our guest, the bilge pump needs tending to."

The younger man's face flared crimson before settling into yellow-orange. "Yes, sir."

I lowered my knife. As the priest turned to leave, I said, "Brother Hadar?"

"Yes, m'lady?" His back stiffened as he pivoted to face me.

"In the future, make sure you know your opponent before you engage her." I raised my left hand and dissolved my truthspell.

He bowed his head. "Yes, m'lady."

Once he left the cabin and closed the door behind him, I sheathed my knife and turned to Biming. The Reverend Father pinched the bridge of his nose as if his head ached.

"Do you have someone else on board who can also do the pressure techniques you used on Anthea this morning?" Luc asked. His unreleased laughter tickled my mental shields.

Biming looked up at Luc. "Yes, but I feel I deserve the headache." He turned to me and bowed. "My sincere apologies, Lady Justice. I encourage the crew to practice their intelligence gathering skills at every opportunity. However, I obviously need to work with Hadar on the subject of finesse. If you wish, I will submit to your truthspell."

If someone had told me a year ago that any Reverend Father would voluntarily submit to a lower ranked priestess's questioning, I would have laughed hysterically before dragging said person to the Temple of Child for treatment for their mental illness.

"And what if I simply pull out what I want?"

Luc's eyes widened at my blatant threat.

But Biming merely chuckled. "You may certainly try, Chief Justice. However, a truthspell would obtain better results."

I flung my own thoughts at him. My irritation at Shi Hua's manipulation. My anger at Hadar for suggesting I act like a priestess of Love. My fear that Tandor was already lost.

Nothing. It was like trying to capture a single raindrop under the surface of the ocean. And all the time he retained his bemused smile.

Luc shook his head. "You're a quicksilver."

Someone whose mind could not be broken, much less broken into, unless they allowed it. They were even rarer than distance speakers.

I cocked my head and regarded him with new respect. "How do you and Shi Hua manage to communicate?"

For an instant, I felt my own emotions mirrored, except Biming's frustration that the demons have eluded his grasp peeked over the others. Everything dissolved an instant later.

He smiled. "I can always hear her, but I have to concentrate very hard for her to hear me."

I took a deep breath, trying to will my neck and shoulders to relax. "Very well, Reverend Father, but is it acceptable if the high brother performs the truthspell? Mine have a tendency to be—"

"Deadly?" Biming offered with a chuckle.

I returned his smile. "I was going to say, 'extremely painful'. May I ask why you'd agree to our questioning of you?"

He blew out a deep breath and sat down at the table. "Because my own temple may be compromised without my knowledge. You two have a natural talent for flushing out problems. It's exactly the same reason I recruited Shi Hua five winters ago. We need as many clever priests and priestesses as we can find on our side. I would ask you to ward the cabin as well."

Luc and I exchanged a look, and he claimed the chair opposite from Biming. This was too good of an opportunity to collect information for our own protection, but even the Reverend Father worried about spies within his handpicked crew. While I warded the tiny cabin, Luc murmured the other spells under his breath. Both our magics tingled along my skin. However, the Reverend Father relaxed a bit. Almost as if he were glad to be forced to answer our questions. Maybe it was the only way he could unburden himself.

"Do you belong to any organization dedicated to bringing down the Twelve Temples?" I began.

"No." He smiled at what had become my standard opening question.

"Are you affiliated or partnered with anyone who has had dealings with demons?"

"Not to my knowledge."

"Do you personally wish the Twelve Temples to be eliminated or destroyed?"

"No."

"Have you ever used a demon spell or a demon grimoire?"

The Reverend Father's smile faded. "No."

Luc picked up the questioning. "Are any of the Jing Temples compromised other than the Light Temple on the Shakya border?"

Biming exhaled. "We don't think so, but I cannot guarantee it."

My itch to learn the ambassador's personal information was too great to resist. "How did you meet Quan Po?"

The Reverend Father chuckled. "When I was eleven winters and a novice and he was the same age and a civilian student at the Temple of Thief in Chengzhou."

I blinked and a rush of surprise from Luc mixed with my own emotions. Never had I detected any talent in the ambassador.

"Is he registered?" Luc asked at the same time I said, "What is his gift?"

"He can affect probabilities." Biming shook his head. "And no, he's not registered. His gift is latent. Passive. Totally subconscious. Po never figured out how to channel it consciously. Haven't you ever noticed his gift for attracting bed partners?"

"Everybody in Orrin knows," I said sourly.

Biming chuckled. "You're the only one who's been able to resist him. It annoys the demon out of him."

"He's not interested—"

"Yes, he is." A wave of jealousy rolled off Luc.

My face heated at the mix of embarrassment at Quan's previous innuendos and my lover's reaction. "It's not going to happen," I said severely. "Besides, he's been sleeping with Shi Hua." Who's younger and prettier, but I kept that thought to myself.

"No, he hasn't." Biming scratched at his fake beard for a moment before he forced himself to stop. "First of all, he's known her since she was fourteen, and he's not into children. Second, he wouldn't force himself onto anyone, much less a woman who has no interest in men. And last of all, she takes her vows quite seriously, and Po respects her for her dedication."

The Reverend Father grinned at me. "On the other hand, your regard for your vows has a certain moral flexibility. He's not above taking advantage of that fact."

"I believe I informed you thusly, Chief Justice." Luc's bad mood disappeared. I didn't like it being at my expense though.

"Our dear ambassador is not going anywhere near my bedchambers," I snapped, biting off the "again" since Luc didn't know Dragonfly had brought the ambassador through the tunnel system for our war council to rescue Luc from the renegades last month. It wasn't worth the argument because nothing had happened between the ambassador and me, nor was it going to.

I turned back to Biming. "Why was Quan sent to Thief for training when his father was a member of the School of the Dragon and the Phoenix?"

"Because the empress insisted on it." The Reverend Father shook his head. "It was the proverbial bone of contention between her and Master Quan that destroyed their relationship. He didn't believe Thief did enough to train his son." He eyed me. "You are aware the Jing imperial line carries Light talent, aren't you?"

I smiled wryly in return. "Just as I'm aware most of the royal lines around the world carry some talent." Spreading talent to as many people as possible is part of the reason for the Spring Rituals. But the empress's decision still didn't make sense to me. "Is Quan's talent lying along those of Thief the reason he wasn't named her heir as her eldest child?"

"That and the fact Master Quan, for all his inherent power, was a farm boy and not noble-born." Biming shrugged. "If Po had leaned towards Light as a passive, instead of Thief, the empress could have made a case for him to succeed her, but honestly, his heart would never have been in governing the empire."

Luc cleared his throat. "Can we get back to our pertinent questions, instead of gossip?"

"It's just as important to know your allies as well as your enemies, High Brother," Biming said.

"So there." I stuck out my tongue at Luc.

He ignored me. "Where did you pick up the trail of these demon eggs?"

Biming sighed. "Ironically, two of the renegades who attacked Shakya."

"Wait," Luc interjected. "How did you manage to capture even one? All the ones we've encounter have poisoned themselves."

"He and a fellow renegade were apprehended by our own Wildlings shortly after the attack on Shakya. They threw away their dosages after Shakya retook its outpost and ran. Lost their stomach for death after seeing what a demon egg hatching did to their prisoner." Biming stared at the swaying lamp for a moment before he shook himself.

"When my counterpart of Light questioned the renegades under truthspell, he asked about the renegades' relationship with the School of Sorcery. That led to the admission the school had more than one cache of demon eggs. Apparently, none of the groups of renegades are aware of more than one or two other groups."

A chill ran through me. Such an arrangement would protect the leaders of the nascent rebellion against the Temples, and keep us distracted trying to root them all out. "Did the group that attacked Shakya have any adult demons or just eggs?"

"They kept only the one egg." Worry and fear rolled off the Reverend Father. "Shakya was fortunate the prisoner used to hatch the damn thing wasn't strong enough. Both he and the infant demon died."

Luc muttered a Cantish oath. "That's why Quan's sorcerer gave the egg to Shi Hua."

Biming nodded. "They need a human lifeforce to hatch in this dimension."

"That's the only reason we're not hip-deep in the damned things yet," I muttered.

"How many eggs were there at the border Temple?" Luc asked.

"We're not sure of the actual count." Biming subconsciously scratched at his fake beard again. "The rest of their cache was split in two. One headed east, which I'm chasing, and one headed west, which another priest of rank is tracking."

The damn things needed people in order to hatch. A terrible thought occurred to me. Was that the real reason my mother had been selling children in Orrin? No. It couldn't be. The demons would need a full-grown adult. Someone healthy and strong like Shi Hua.

"What are you thinking, Anthea?" Luc drew me out of my reverie.

I shook my head. "Dante's family. If they could use children to hatch the demons, the Assassins Guild would have kidnapped his little ones instead of poisoning them." I clenched my fists in an effort to keep my tears of anger at bay and drew a deep breath. "Where did the Jing renegades send the egg cache you're chasing initially?"

"Pagonia."

"Multnomah?" Luc asked.

Biming cocked his head. "How did you know?"

"The Pagonian Reverend Father of Light discovered renegades there," Luc replied.

"How do you know the eggs are going to Cant?" I asked.

"We don't." The Reverend Father stared at me. "The two survivors we interrogated said the eggs would be used in Cant."

Luc muttered something in Cantish I'd never heard before.

"Excuse me?" I stared at him.

His wave of worry was tinged with fear. "They *are* going to use Tandor to launch an attack on Cant."

Biming nodded. "That was your Reverend Father Farrell's evaluation as well. He apologized for not sending any more of his people to Tandor to assist us, but he doesn't trust anyone beyond you and Brother Jeremy at this point."

Luc frowned at the mention of his superior. "Surely, the Reverend Father wouldn't dump the problem with one of his parishes on you."

I couldn't comprehend any of the Issuran Temple heads doing so. Given the circumstances, I'd still put any regard or orders of the Jing Reverend Father of Thief behind my own Reverend Mother on that issue, but I didn't give voice to that thought, or even silently relay it to Luc, so I continued pacing in the small confines of the cabin.

"Normally, you would be correct, High Brother." The Jing priest wiped his hands down his face. "From Multnomah, the eggs were taken south by someone disguised as a priest of Light. In Standora, we lost the tracking spell. The same day, one of Reverend Father Farrell's personal staff disappeared."

I paused in my pacing. My borrowed skirts swished far too much for my liking. "Did you find a skinned corpse anywhere?"

Biming's eyebrows rose. "Yes." His surprised expression turned to a frown. "How did you know?"

"Because contrary to Thief's evaluation of me, I don't put everything in my reports." I'd told my own Reverend Mother about the skinned body of Brother Jon in person when she arrived in Orrin nearly four weeks ago. "Do you know what a skinwalker is?"

Biming shook his head.

"It's evil magic." Luc's voice was somber. Jon had been one of his order, a novice master. No one knew how or why his skinless corpse had ended up in an empty manse outside of Orrin proper, other than a skinwalker had been wearing the dead priest like a cloak when he abducted and tortured Luc.

To lose another Light priest in this manner, Reverend Father Farrell would be furious. Luc definitely was. "I wouldn't be surprised if the spell was from a demon grimoire. It allows the caster to become the person whose skin he wears."

I leaned closer to Biming. "Are you a skinwalker?"

"No, but then, you already know I'm not a demon," he said.

"Why didn't you mention any of this when we broke our fast?" I asked.

"Because Po was in here and because what you said to both him and Shi Hua needed to be addressed privately between us."

I straightened at his answer. "What exact words of mine are you referring to?"

"Choosing between one country and another."

Irritation itched under my skin, the same irritation I felt when my own

Reverend Mother chided me. "Are you saying you wouldn't put Jung's interests above any other nation?"

"I'm saying our priestly vows are to honor the gods by protecting their creation, which means all of humanity, not the portions we choose."

I slapped my hand on the table. "And my vows included upholding the laws of Issura."

Biming exhaled a long, drawn-out breath. "There was a time when all nations had one law—do anything to survive and defeat the demons. The problem is we are weak compared to the gods, and we often put our petty concerns above the welfare of the whole."

"Like your own Reverend Father of Conflict?" I said sharply.

"Chen is more of a danger to himself than to anyone else." The Jing senior priest scrubbed at his face for a moment. "And that has more to do with his pride over a young Light novice defeating him in a hand-to-hand combat contest during the Spring Rituals years ago."

Luc's laughter jerked me out of my bad mood. "I've warned the personnel at Orrin about that."

I cocked my head and regarded Biming. "You also believe our missions are related?"

"Of course." He smiled. "What I don't need in this task is the distraction of you and Po performing your diplomatic dance. This *is* a Temple matter."

His emphasis took me by surprise. "And the ambassador, even though he is someone you regard highly, is not Temple."

He shrugged. "Even so."

"So why is he here? Shi Hua said he was ordered to assist you in the egg situation. She didn't say anything about him accompanying us."

Biming chuckled again. "The emperor told him to render any assistance to me. He took it upon himself to come on this trip. The reason I refused to allow Shi Hua to come is because she is too desperately needed in Orrin." Another chuckle. "I stand by my assessment he would not have the patience for ruling Jing. Not enough adventure for him."

An ugly suspicion occurred to me. "Are you expecting us to watch over him while you and your people search for the cache?"

"No. Actually, he will be your excuse for visiting the Temple of Light. Quan told you the truth in a certain regard. His captain *was* supposed to pick up a shipment of spirits. Your story will be that you contracted with him to transport the goods due to unexpected repairs to his own ship. Of course, you are demonstrating your new ship design since it is the last asset you and your brother own after the terrible accident at the Valencia shipyards that claimed the lives of your father and husband. It is, after all, the beginning of the trade season." Biming smiled when he finished spinning our false tale.

"That won't hold up under a truthspell," I muttered.

"It will if we use the blocker," Luc said. "If the imposter Micah didn't get word out to his fellow conspirators, and I don't think he did since you didn't leave him alone long enough to do so, we can use it to spin our narrative. When they interrogated me, they were only concerned about the whereabouts of the grimoire, and they definitely didn't use the counter to the blocking spell."

I stared at him. We hadn't spoken about what the renegades had done to him beyond the obvious loss of his foot. They'd tortured him. Maybe not in the same way they had Sister Gretchen of Love, but they had tortured him. And like Gretchen, he'd resisted the torture and used the blocker to sow confusion.

I wanted to throw my arms around him and beg his forgiveness for not finding and rescuing him sooner. I also wanted to gut the bastards who'd harmed him, even though all of them but the skinwalker were dead.

But I had to push aside the stew of my emotions and focus on the problem at hand. "That doesn't mean the renegades didn't obtain the counter through the Multnomah temple before the Pagonian Reverend Father discovered the infiltration."

"If you have a better idea, I'll listen to it," Luc replied quietly.

That was the problem. I didn't have any better ideas for getting into either Light or Balance in Tandor without being identified by the renegades. Once their spies realized we weren't in Orrin anymore, they'd send word south. Gods help us if they had a distance speaker among them.

And if half of Orrin already knew we were leaving, then there were already people in Tandor watching for us.

No, I didn't have any better idea. I wish I did. I shook my head.

"May the Twelve watch over our endeavors," Biming murmured.

Luc dissolved the truthspell with the other priest's benediction.

I, on the other hand, bit my tongue to keep my own bitter words from spilling out. The gods hadn't helped us so far. Why on earth would they start now?

Chapter 13

After a second full day of sailing, we arrived at the port for the city of Tandor roughly a candlemark after Second Night. Biming chose to anchor in the harbor rather risk docking in the dark. The lanterns that normally marked the wharves' boundaries and any hazards weren't lit, which wasn't unusual for a smaller city at this time of year, but that wasn't the real reason for his decision. The crew and passengers needed their last chance at sleep before we began our respective missions.

Except Death's temporary touch eluded me. I rolled out of my hammock and eased through the cabin door. Only the lookout and another warden from the way he prowled the ship were awake. They merely nodded in acknowledgement as I crossed the main deck and leaned on the railing.

The city's centuries-old fortress loomed on a cliff high above the shops and warehouses. It had been the first Toscan stronghold built on the Northern Long Continent after the devastation the demons had wrought along the western shores, and its squat, blocky shape reinforced its foreignness. Only the domes, towers, and spinnerets of the temples drew more attention to themselves on the skyline.

Being on the edge of the Valley of the Lost, the desert that separated Issura from the Cliffdwellers and Diné, Tandor's vegetation was dominated by scrub. The late winter rains had flushed the plants with life. Soon they would bake under the spring sun until the entire region was a tinder box by summer. I watched the city and hoped for a hint of what we were up against, but quiet reigned.

"What do you see?"

I jerked at the voice behind me and whirled. Ambassador Quan stood there. He no longer had the unkempt appearance of a freelance sailor, but neither did he wear the attire of a royal-born emissary. He wore loose pants and a leather vest so he could have been anyone from anywhere. The only things that hinted of Jing were his moustache and beard. Even then, he'd replaced the gold and precious gem beads that decorated his facial hair with ones made of ceramic and bone.

Not even I could detect which bead held Luc's counterspell. It was the only assistance we could offer the ambassador, Biming, and the crew, as little as it was. I found myself sending a silent prayer to Thief that he'd watch out for his priests and wardens.

"What do you mean?" Compared to the lap of the waves and the knocking of only a handful of ships against the wharf in the distance, my voice sounded terribly loud.

He stepped up to the railing and gestured at the city. "You're staring at Tandor as if you are interrogating it. So, what is it you see?"

I chuckled and quickly covered my mouth to stifle the sound. "I see a sleeping city, Your Excellency. It's what I hear that bothers me."

"What do you hear?" He frowned at me.

"Listen," I commanded.

He tilted his head, his frown turning into an expression of concentration. After a while, he murmured, "I don't hear anything."

"That's just it." I waved toward the buildings. "The equinox is two weeks away. We only passed one outgoing ship in the harbor. Barely a handful of ships are docked, and all of them fly the flag of the Duchy of Tandor. Also, where are the loading and unloading crews? Where are the merchants' warehouse supervisors? At a minimum, people and goods from the mountains should be making their way to the city in preparation for the arrival of trade ships.

"In addition, the initial visitors for the Spring Rituals should be arriving." I pointed toward the Temple of Love. "On such a clear, calm night, we should hear laughter from the sisters and their patrons even at this hour."

He stroked his moustache. "The Sea Peoples fleet already passed through Tandor last month."

"Exactly. So where are any Meca ships? The Wari? The Tiwanaku? No ships from the western side of the Old Continent or the Cradle I can understand, especially if the Panthalassa Sea is also having more storms than normal like we are. However, even merchants from Diné should be delivering their wools and the Cliffdwellers their ceramics."

Quan's lips twitched, and the motion sent his beads swaying. "Could the renegades have already conquered Tandor and launched their invasion of Cant?"

"Normally, I would say no." I waved at the harbor. "No sign of sentries. No black spots to mark the passage of demons. They can't touch anything in our plane without contaminating it."

"So the eggs may have hatched on the other side of the city, out of your sight, and they're already marching east."

Once again, I stared at the city. A chill ran through me that had nothing to do with the late winter air. "That's what I fear. We may be too late." I looked at Quan. "Do you have alternate plans with Shi Hua in case she does not hear from you?"

"Yes," he said, but he did not elucidate.

Nor did I ask. The less I knew, the less I could reveal if I was truthspelled, and my captor knew the counter to the blocking spell. Or if we were tortured.

Luc and I had made similar arrangements with the caveat that neither of us knew what other arrangements our seconds had made. We only knew Yanaba and Jeremy assured us backup plans had been arranged.

We simply couldn't plead for the Reverend Father to turn the *Unbridled* around and head for home. Not on the chance he and his people could intercept those damned eggs. And Luc and I had to ferret out what was going on in the Tandor Temples. After the news from Pagonia and Jing, we couldn't let the renegades successfully brew a false war between humans.

"Where is our captain?" I said.

"Asleep before his head hit the pallet. Biming—" Quan shook his head. "I swear the man could sleep through the blasting of the Grand Canal. And that's while laying on rocks next to flash-bangs with very short wicks."

I laughed. "Luc has the same talent. He can even sleep on horseback." My humor died. "I envy that gift."

Quan sighed. His breath steamed a brilliant yellow before it dissipated. "I never had the luxury to develop that skill."

His admission surprised me. "I would have thought your parents and their servants would have doted on your every wish."

His gaze met mine. "My mother sent me to Thief for training as a child. I wasn't much older than you were when Balance claimed you."

"I'm sorry," I whispered. Quan wasn't the confessional type, and I hated to disturb this . . . thing between us. "In your case, I'm sure she was trying to protect you."

"No." The bitterness in his tone sounded more like me than him. "She was trying to find a place for me away from the throne and the schools." His gaze shifted back to Tandor. "If anyone understands what it's like to be a pawn in someone else's game, it would be you. Good eventide, m'lady."

He pivoted and stalked toward the smaller cabin he shared with Biming.

Uncertainty filled me. Should I have said something to sooth him? I'd always worn my resentment at my lot with the same openness I wore my Temple robes. However, there was no doubt my talents belonged to Balance.

I couldn't imagine being in Quan's position. So many possibilities, and yet, not able to take advantage of any of them. My fingers clung to the railing, and I stared at the dark, silent city. It had never occurred to me that my position could be far worse than blindness and an insane mother who wanted me dead while I was still in her womb.

The air held a hint of dampness when the *Unbridled* docked shortly before Second Morning. In the distance, another storm roiled. Not the one we managed to miss leaving Orrin, but the third one following on its heels. Fortunately for us, all of them had stayed north of us.

We disembarked, and my eyes itched thanks to the scant sleep I achieved. It had been fitful and full of strange dreams.

There was movement along the wharves as the five of us strode toward the Temple district, along with the expected interest in the *Unbridled*'s design and Luc's crutches. But the activity was still far less than Orrin's wharves during a major winter storm. It almost made me wish I had sided with Reverend Father Biming when he objected to the ambassador accompanying us. Quan insisted he was perfectly safe between me, Luc, and our wardens on our scouting expedition.

Does this seem too quiet to you? Luc whispered in my mind.

Quan and I noticed the same thing from the deck when we anchored last night.

Shock and a flare of jealousy rippled across our mental link. *Any other insights the ambassador managed to share?*

I didn't dare look at Luc behind me. More citizens were out and about the farther we traveled from the docks. *Where the demon is this attitude coming from?*

Maybe it's because he's seen more of your bedchambers than I have lately? Nor has he made any secret of his attraction to you.

I didn't bother to hide my irritation. It wasn't my fault all the Orrin tunnel connections terminating at a Temple did so at the seat's private rooms. *We're in the middle of what could possibly be enemy territory and you want to throw a jealous snit now? Reverend Father Biming already pointed out any so-called attraction is Quan's ego at play. If we weren't in such a dangerous predicament, I'd drag you to the Child's temple seat for treatment.*

Sullenness wasn't something I'd ever felt from Luc before, and the experience bothered me more than I cared to admit. For all his respect for my independence, had he viewed himself as more capable than me, even with my twisted version of sight? Or did he truly blame me for the loss of his foot?

His tantrum did remind me to keep a closer eye out for the telltale signs of demons. I took more interest in my surroundings as surely a foreign noblewoman would do. And this truly was the first time I *saw* Tandor.

During my last visit, I had been twelve winters and still blind, on a lesson trip with Justice Rose, my novice master, and three other Balance trainees. I'd accidentally stumbled upon the healing spell in the library of Tandor's Temple of Death designed for those without the actual healing gift. It took me three more years of study to bastardize the spell to the point I was confident it would give me normal sight.

But I couldn't give myself something of which I had no comprehension at that point of my life. And my own Reverend Mother had the staff and wardens watch me closely and carefully once I was allowed to leave the isolated room I was kept in for another year.

I shook aside the maudlin memories and paid more attention to the people and the architecture. This city was so much drier than Orrin was. Adobe and stucco dominated the exteriors of the buildings. The scrub trees in the area simply didn't provide straight enough wood with which to build, and they provided even less shade in the occasional garden we passed.

Their Government House along with the temples used sandstone. Any sturdier building material went to Tandor's fortress on the cliff. Unlike Duke Marco's family residence, it intimidated the other buildings instead of blending in with them. The Toscans who built it said it was a monument to the Apache and Chumash who'd sacrificed their lives to keep the demon invasion from spilling through the pass and flooding the Plains Nations with death and destruction. However, the surviving Chumash had a different opinion.

No one knew what the Apache would have thought.

From clothing and accessories, Tandor was as culturally mixed as Orrin though there was definitely more Cantan influence than Issuran. Like the vegetation, the people seemed stunted and twisted. Or maybe it was the fortress weighing them down. No one would meet Quan's gaze, much less return his friendly greetings. Everyone kept to themselves and hurried by, intent on their own business.

Where are the children? Luc asked.

That's an excellent question. And one I didn't have an answer for. Even when I'd been here nearly twenty years ago, I'd heard the high-pitched laughter of children, especially on the side avenues.

The roadways remained dirt until we reached Temple Street. Despite the brick thoroughfare, a low cloud of dust swirled around the feet of people and camels. With water more precious than gold here, horses and oxen were simply too expensive to keep.

I glanced at the Temple of Balance. Something was off about the warden who stood guard at the closed main doors. Something more than the lack of magical essence if court were in session. Something I couldn't quite place. It wasn't his bored expression either. That I could totally understand given the lack of activity at any of the Temples.

Instead, we approached the Temple of Light as we had planned. I found myself wishing I'd borrowed Dragonfly's scimitar before we'd left Orrin since I couldn't carry my own Temple-forged sword. My knives and magic may not be enough if we had to fight our way back to the *Unbridled*.

The main doors were closed, which was highly unusual for Light at this time of day, much less the season and the warmth of approaching spring. The warden at the doors of the Temple appeared as bored as the one at Balance. Or he was until we approached.

"What do you want?" he snapped.

Luc's tension at the rude greeting by a retainer of his order poked at my psyche, but he forced his hackles down and his tongue to remain silent.

"I am Ambassador Quan of Jing." Quan bowed to the warden far more deeply than he normally would to one of such minor rank. "My own ship was to pick up contracted goods at your lovely port this week. However, the hull took damage in a storm." He gestured at Luc. "Lord Stefan's ship was available on short notice, and he agreed to ferry my spirits. Unfortunately, to meet the original contract, we had to leave before we could make the arrangement formal. Therefore, I require the services of a brother of Light."

The warden glared at Quan, but said nothing.

"I'd be more than happy to compensate any other merchants for their loss of time, and I would make a generous donation to the Lord of Light."

More silence. Now, even Yar and Tyra's anger grated at my nerves.

I reached into my purse and produced a silver. I handed it to the unknown warden, keeping my head bowed. "For your assistance, kind sir."

He pocketed the coin. "This way, Ambassador." The warden opened the door and gestured for us to enter.

The audacity—

I pinched Luc's arm to still his diatribe before he said anything incriminating. Balance only knew who had the gift of silent speech in this place, much less whether they were strong enough to eavesdrop on our link.

A priest approached us, his smile reminding me of the two wardens outside. Something was off, the hint at the edge of my mind and I couldn't quite reach it. "How may I help you, children?"

Quan repeated the same speech as he did outside with the warden. This time, he picked up on the hint to bribe the priest at his first blatant silence.

The brother slid the gold piece into his robes. "I'll be happy to assist you, Ambassador."

Quan sniffed. "Surely, there is someone higher ranked than the junior-most priest available. I want to make sure this is contract is sealed correctly."

The priest's coloring didn't change one iota at the insult. It remained a steady, solid yellow. A frisson of unease shuddered down my spine. Even the easy-going Jeremy or the always cheerful Shi Hua would have bristled at such a derogatory statement, though they wouldn't have changed their facial expression one bit.

"Such assistance would require a larger donation." The priest's gaze flicked down and back up Tyra's body, his manner leaving no question of his price.

I stepped between them. "Touch my retainer, and you'll find something far more pointy to play with and maybe a few more holes to play in."

Scarlet shot through his face and hands, and he edged away. He ignored me and cleared his throat. "Y-you and Lord Stefan will have to be truthspelled during the drafting and sealing of your agreement, Ambassador."

"Of course," Quan said amiably. "Wouldn't have it any other way." He turned to me. "Do behave yourself while we're gone, Lady Miriam."

"Absolutely, Ambassador," I murmured. And like a child, I crossed my fingers we would leave this cursed place without resorting to holes in anyone. Most especially Luc.

The two wardens and I took turns pacing the main sanctuary of the Temple of Light. Any comfort I normally took from Light's benevolent expression was swallowed by my nervousness. Or maybe the statue reminded me too much of the Tandorian brother's simpering smile. No other warden and no staff checked on us while we waited near the private conference chamber where Quan, Luc, and the unknown priest had gone. This time of year should have been busy for the Temple of Light here, too, but no other merchants arrived for contract drafting and sealing either.

If anyone from this Temple watched us, it was from hidden spyholes. And the thought of such in an actual building of the Twelve turned my stomach.

Finally, the magic in the alabaster globe, showing the conference room in use, faded and the door opened.

"Well?" I asked the two men as they exited.

Quan held up a sealed contract, but Luc shook his head and said, "We need to leave. Now."

His urgency scared me, and I didn't argue. We headed for the main doors of the Temple when they burst open.

Men dressed as wardens poured into the sanctuary. Far too many for a Temple the size of Tandor's. All armed to the teeth. The hard mien of their faces reminded me of the assassins and mercenaries who had secretly replaced the wardens of Love in Orrin. Of the imposters who'd abducted Luc. They quickly surrounded us.

My fingers flexed at the desire for my sword, but it sat in the main cabin on the *Unbridled*. Twenty against five. It would be difficult to escape in a straight fight if we were more heavily armed.

Now . . .

A final man, dressed as a priest but with absolutely no insignia on his robes, strode in from the hallway to the priests' private quarters. His color was far too green to be human, but neither was it the empty black of a demon. Luc's recognition and alarm trilled in my mind, and my heart lodged in my throat.

The skinwalker.

I hadn't had a good look at him while we rescued Luc from his abductors. I'd been a bit too busy dealing with the demon. But Luc had given a detailed description of their leader to Leilani. Her drawing had been sent to the capital, and their answer had chilled us. The Reverend Father of Light had also sent a hair sample so we could confirm his missing priest was the skinned body we'd discovered in Samael DiRoy's manse.

"Did you really think you were going to walk in here without me knowing, High Brother?"

Luc said nothing.

The skinwalker turned to me. "And any woman accompanying you would have to be the Red Justice."

"And we know you're not the Light novice master Brother Jon," I snapped.

"I never said I was," he mocked. "Do you even know who or what I am?"

When I didn't answer, he smiled. "Well, your two wardens will be useful later. Let us start by questioning the non-powered Prince Po of Jing."

Tyra and I drew our knives, and Yar, the sword he borrowed from the crew.

"No." Quan had to be insane. He stepped between me and the skinwalker. "It's not worth your life." His hand cupped my cheek, and I probed his surface thoughts. *I am a distraction to make you despair. You know what you came to learn. Find a way to alert your Temples and queen.*

I took his hand and squeezed it. "Survive." I shifted and glared at the skinwalker. "Drop your weapons, Wardens." My knives clattered against the tiles.

For an instant, I didn't think Tyra and Yar would obey. But their steel clanged on the floor as well. A strange sense of relief filled me that none of us had given up our blessed Temple weapons.

"Take the wardens down to the gaol. The cripples deserve slightly better accommodations," the skinwalker sneered.

Luc bristled at the insult, but he didn't resist the renegades while they searched us and collected the rest of our weapons. They also made a point of touching mine and Tyra's bodies inappropriately. Another attempt at intimidation. I was thankful everyone kept their heads as the renegades dragged all of us in three different directions.

Luc and I were taken down the hall to the Temple's private quarters. They tossed us through the door of the high brother's chambers. For once, I was thankful for the wood those of Light chose for their interiors. The paneling had to be extremely expensive to import, which was why it was only used in the private quarters.

But it was far gentler to our bodies than the sandstone and ceramic used elsewhere in the Temple. We both rolled with the momentum. The result in my case was a couple of bruises. Luc's crutches clattered against the floor when one of the renegades threw them in after us. The door slammed shut, and a bolt thudded into place.

Luc pushed himself to a sitting position. "Well, that was enjoyable."

"At least, one of us is partially armed. Are you all right?"

"Do you mean am I bleeding?" He carefully felt inside the sewn-on boot. "No."

His assessment was a bit of a relief. The master healers had warned him about additional damage to his leg since it would take another two or three weeks for the flesh over the stump to fully recover.

I flipped the widow's veil off my face. No sense bothering if they knew who I was. Surprisingly, neither the skinwalker nor his men had taken the pins for my veil or hair when they took my additional knives. Maybe I could put them to use.

I climbed to my feet and examined the room. All normal furnishings for a high brother were missing. Instead, the smell of urine, excrement, and unwashed bodies filled the room. There was nothing here but a bundle of rags in the corner of the high brother's chambers next to the bathing room entryway.

No, not a bundle of rags from the faint yellowish glow. A person. I tentatively approached the huddled figure.

Luc's familiar magic tingled along my back. "Who is it?"

I glanced at him. From the energy centered in his palm, he'd produced a light ball in order to see. I crouched next to the figure. The facial hair indicated he was male.

"Hello." No response.

"My name is Anthea."

He stirred, and his eyes blinked. "Don't hurt me." He turned away and shielded his face from the light.

I looked over my shoulder. "Can you tone down the glow?" I had to assume he did as I asked because the stranger peered through spread fingers at me and didn't squint quite as hard.

"We aren't going to hurt you." I held out my empty hands. "We're prisoners, too. Can you tell me your name?"

"I-I don't remember."

The horrid stench of his breath nearly made me gag. I tried to smile past the odor. "What do they call you here?"

"D-dav." Tears cleared away the grime on his face. "By the Twelve, please kill me."

Tandor's high brother of Light. Gerd's former lover. *Balance, please don't let this man be my birth father.*

Like any offspring of the Spring Rituals from Love, I held fantasies that my birth father would come and take me to his much better home. The broken man before me didn't match my childish dreams.

I hadn't asked my birth mother, the former high sister of Love, about my unknown father when I interrogated her about the demon grimoire. In the aftermath of Kam's confession and death, I had known I could not bear her answer. Not without slitting her throat. I slammed down on the emotions that threatened to transform me into the same gibbering mess as the priest. "Dav, do you know how long you've been here?"

"I don't know!" he wailed. He sobbed in earnest.

I laid a hand on his shoulder.

"No! Not inside me! Not again!" He jerked from my touch and scrambled to the opposite corner. His terrible shrieks became more incoherent until his voice hoarsened, and he collapsed on the floor, weeping.

I stood. Dav needed the ministrations from someone of Child. He wouldn't be any help in our escape.

I eyed Luc. *Do you think Tandor has the same tunnel system as Orrin?*

I would assume so. The renegades certainly knew about ours before you and I did.

I faced the wall where the secret passage had been in Luc's quarters. My fingers trailed over the wood panel until I felt the warm tingle of Light magic. I whispered the words for opening the way.

"Anthea! Get back!"

A wash of virulent energy spiked in my brain. I couldn't counter the magic. Couldn't even think straight. The physical force threw me across the room. My landing knocked the air from my lungs.

"Anthea?" Luc whispered. He brushed loose locks from my eyes. In the corner, Dav's weeping had devolved into a strange keening sound.

Pain radiated across my pelvis, and I groaned. "Why do I always land on my right hip when I'm thrown around?"

"Must be your special talent," Luc joked. "Can you sit up?" I must have lost consciousness if he'd crawled clear across the room without me realizing it.

"Yes." I carefully pushed myself upright, my body protesting every motion, and leaned against the wall. "What the demon was that? I've never felt anything like it."

"The best I could describe is an odd mix of demon and human magic," Luc murmured.

"Well, I'd say it confirms Tandor has a similar tunnel system, and the skin-walker didn't want Dav escaping through it." I rubbed the back of my neck. All of Biming's pressure work on my muscles over the last two days had died in that odd blast of energy.

"What about the bathing room?"

"The pipes!"

I pushed myself upright and stalked over to the other door and yanked it open. My one heartbeat examination said we weren't going to crawl through either intake or outflow pipes. I quickly closed the door and returned to my seat on the floor next to Luc. "The spouts have been removed and the wall stoned over. You don't want to know what the bathing pool is filled with."

"From the smell, I can guess," Luc said dryly. It was nice to hear his old humor. "At least, Dav retains enough of his faculties to not defecate out here."

"For the amount in the bathing pool, I'd say he's been here close to a year." I wasn't sure whether to rage or to despair. When I discovered Samael DiRoy's treason, I had assumed, had hoped really, it was only the work of a jealous relative. This went so much deeper . . .

Something clicked as my brain started working again. "That spell on the tunnel entrance reminds me of the demon grimoire Gretchen stole from Gerd."

"What?" Luc cocked his head, his expression aghast. "You used the grimoire?"

"Well, it's good to know there's a possibility more shocking than the idea I'd ever join Quan in bed."

He sighed. "All right. I apologize for even entertaining the idea you would accept the ambassador's offer for bedplay. So, why does the spell guarding the passage remind you of the grimoire?"

"It was more how the grimoire felt when I touched it whether with gloves or my bare hands. Like it was alive." I hesitated. "I ripped out a few pages of the grimoire to contaminate *High Brother Euclid's Theories on the Geometric Progression of Spells*, and—"

"You-you ruined, then burned, our only copy of Euclid?"

"Kam said I could borrow it before you officially became high brother," I spat. "Leilani translated it into Balance code so we'd have a copy in our library, and she's creating a new copy for yours."

"You burned a book, priceless not only for its knowledge but its actual history, and your excuse is 'I made you a copy'?" Luc hadn't been this enraged with Istaqa the other morning.

"Its history?" I squeaked.

"It was one of the original copies in Euclid's own handwriting. A gift from the Temple of Light in Athenos to the Issuran clergy. And you burned it? Why? Because you couldn't read it?"

"I burned it because I damn well wasn't going to give the original grimoire to some shapeshifting, people-skinning sorcerer!"

We glared at each other.

Then we started to laugh at the ridiculousness of our argument. We laughed so hard we both howled, and tears ran down our faces.

When I could catch my breath, I wiped my face. "Balance help me, I can't believe I burned a Euclidean original."

"I can't believe the demon fell for it." A thread of his excitement burrowed past his outrage and humor. "You didn't have weeks to contaminate the book like the casket that brought the demon egg to Orrin last autumn. How'd you hurry the process?"

"I manipulated the strings of time by pulling a future version of the book back to my point," I lied. I couldn't tell him I'd sacrificed seven days of my life. We couldn't afford another ridiculous fight over something that was done.

"But if you burned the book—"

"Can we save the lesson on calculating probabilities for another time?" I rubbed my still-aching forehead. "Maybe one where we're not about to be interrogated, tortured, and killed?"

"I was thinking if you could demon-contaminate a book, could you reverse the process and—"

"—remove the spell and escape the city," I finished. I rested my chin on my knees and stared at the offending spot on the wall. "Possibly. What about Tyra, Yar and Quan?"

He shuddered. "You're right. We can't leave them with that monster." He eyed me. "Can you get a message to Shi Hua? Get her attention some how?"

I frowned and looked at him. "Why can't you? You're her superior."

His cheeks blazed red. "You're not the one who let their anger get the better of them."

"So, you no longer believe she was actively trying to deceive you?"

"I admit I was being an idiot because she's Quan's woman." He expelled another loud breath. "You still didn't answer my question."

"Because the closer her relationship with someone, the easier time she has maintaining contact?" I smirked. So he had listen to some of what Shi Hua had said when he interrogated her. "If I can reach her, are you going to have another jealous fit?"

"No, Lady Justice." His endearing grin, the one he'd used to originally seduce me, appeared on his face.

I waggled a forefinger at him. "That's 'Chief Justice' to you."

He inclined his head to me. "My apologies, Chief Justice."

"All right. Let's try contacting Shi Hua first." I rolled my head in an effort to relieve the muscle knots in my neck.

"What about Quan? Light only knows what they're doing to him at this moment."

I glared at Luc. "It will take me less effort to contact *your* junior priestess than it will for me to break the spell on the secret door. Besides, a little torture may improve the ambassador's disposition. Now, hush, and let me concentrate."

"Yes, Chief Justice."

I ignored him and closed my eyes. Silent speech with someone nearby was one thing. Attracting the attention of a distance speaker was another.

My mind reached for Orrin—

I gasped as magic was pulled, no, yanked from me. My very bones vibrated at the deep alarm bell. And just as abruptly, the sensation disappeared.

"Anthea!" Luc grabbed my shoulders.

Even the damaged Dav stopped his keening. His head rose and he stared in the direction of Tandor's Temple of Balance.

I realized what I'd felt was the defensive wards of my home Temple. By the Twelve! What was happening in Orrin that Yanaba activated them?

Another realization hit. I was hearing the dying peels of Balance bells here in Tandor. The same pattern had echoed in every spot dedicated to Balance in Issura thanks to my junior priestess. No one activated the alarm spell lightly. And it hadn't been heard in a century. My heart rose in my throat. If Yanaba hadn't set off the alarm bell, there was only one other thing that could.

Orrin was under attack by demons.

Chapter 14

Closing her eyes, Shi Hua leaned her head back against the ledge of the pool and luxuriated in the hot waters of the bath. When she'd dismissed Istaqa, the head of Light's household had acted relieved. She smiled to herself. He was a man devoted to propriety, and from the gossip shared by the wardens, the high brother had threatened to send Istaqa back to Standora if he said anything else regarding her presence or her gender.

But his over-obsequiousness for the last three days set her teeth on edge.

"What's so funny?"

She opened her eyes to find Jeremy lowering himself into the opposite end of the bath and laughed. "Aren't you afraid Istaqa will find you in here with me?"

Jeremy chuckled. "You've only been here a month. He can be a lot worse." He shrugged. "It's not like we men don't share the facilities. A good soak used to be High Brother Kam's way of having morning status meetings."

She'd only met High Brother Luc's predecessor twice, both times when she had accompanied Ambassador Quan to contentious trade negotiations because he wanted her input. Despite Kam's jovial persona and outlandish love of luxury, she had the impression he was exactly like Brother Lin, her novice master back in Chengzhou. Very little missed either priest's eyes.

Her laughter died at the thought of the murdered Kam. "Istaqa has had the luxury of being born during a time of peace. We all have. It colors our perceptions. The Issuran order of Light may have to change its ways if we're facing another round with the demons. We can't afford not to have more people with Light talent within our ranks if that's the only way to kill the demons hatched here on our plane."

Jeremy frowned as he considered her words. "You mean enroll women in our ranks?"

She nodded. "And eliminate the vow of chastity. According to a friend, the Temple leaders in Jing are considering a hold on such for this year's Spring Rituals. At least for the older novices."

Jeremy ducked his head under the water. How much of this action was due to discomfort at her words?

Frankly, she wasn't sure how she felt about the news Mei Win and Jian had relayed last night. Jian had sounded almost jealous of the novices, but then he also found women as enticing as she did.

Except two women could not produce a baby, and that's what the human race needed right now. More children with Light talent to fight the demon invasion the older clergy feared was coming. She wasn't quite sure how'd she feel if she were commanded to lay with a man in order to produce a child with the same talents she had.

Jeremy's head broke the surface, and he wiped the water from his eyes. "Istaqa would have a fit if our Reverend Father issued such a decree."

"But he's not a priest," Shi Hua murmured. She handed the dish of soap to Jeremy, but held her tongue on asking him his personal feelings on the matter.

"No. He wishes he were though." He scooped out a dollop of the herbal-scented mixture and started scrubbing his scalp. "From what I can tell, he's not interested in relations with any gender."

"I see." In fact, that one simple statement explained much about the head of the household staff. He had no talent, but he wanted the prestige of belonging to one of the Temples. Service as support staff or warden would bring a measure of status to someone who might have none otherwise. Istaqa wouldn't be the first person to cling to whatever good fortune he found.

Maybe even cling a bit too hard and end up losing everything.

Jeremy ducked his head to rinse the soap from his dark strands. When he rose, he swiped locks back from his face. "I wonder if that was the original purpose of the Spring Rituals. Spread as much seed as we could in order to produce more individuals with talent."

She considered his idea and nodded. "That would make sense. It's probably one of those tenets so commonly held that none of our forebears thought it was necessary to document." She smiled. "Like why trees and foliage must be cleared for a league from any fortress or palace."

He nodded. "When I was researching for the high brother, I found obscure items along those thoughts scribbled in the margins of some of our older tomes and scrolls."

She stared at him. "When have you had time to do any research?"

He grimaced. "This was before the chaos with the Assassins Guild started."

"Anything interesting?"

"More confusing than enlightening." He cocked his head. "I want to invite Justice Yanaba to dine with us tonight. I'd like your opinion and hers on some things I found."

"That sounds acceptable." As if to punctuate her sentence, the bells tolled out Second Morning. "And I will be late for court if I don't leave now. Shall I relay your invitation?" She stood and climbed up the steps of the bath.

"Yes, please." Jeremy chuckled. "While time may be different in Jing, you're late now."

She shook her head as she dried off with a towel. "No. Yanaba canceled court yesterday and delayed court until Third Morning today. She wanted to give the chief justice as much time as she could before the spies watching Balance send word to Tandor."

He wiped his hands down his face. "This mayhem is beyond our rank."

"There's no one else the Reverend Father of Issura can rely on at the moment." She yanked on her dressing robe.

Jeremy sighed. "Believe me, I'm very much aware of that fact. When this audit is over, I want to sleep for a week."

She hesitated at the door. "Let us pray we don't take the final sleep in this mayhem."

The gallery was already half-full when Shi Hua arrived at Balance, but the tension she detected didn't come only from the spectators. No, it also came from across the room where Magistrate DiCook whispered furiously and gesticulated wildly at Chief Warden Little Bear.

Warden Gina stood next to the truthspeller's bench. She nodded as Shi Hua approached. "You arrived just in time for the pre-court entertainment," the warden said in a low voice.

The corner of Shi Hua's mouth quirked. "Let me guess. A personage is not happy the chief justice failed to inform him of certain events. And worse, we haven't made any headway on his peacekeeper's murder."

"Even so." But the warden's deep brown eyes weren't focused on the arguing men. Instead, they flicked over the gallery.

Shi Hua followed her gaze. There was an abnormal amount of Sea People seated. Scowls marred their visages. "What happened? Things have been quiet since their fleet arrived."

In fact, Jeremy had worked day and night to wrap up a specific trade contract so they could depart two days ago. Their shallowed-bottomed vessels didn't rely as heavily on the tides as the Long Continents' caravels did, but they suffered the same risk of smashing into the cliffs surrounding Orrin's harbor in rough seas. The bad weather for the third day straight could have pricked moods.

"Mmm-hmmm." Gina's expression darkened when an Issuran sailor argued with the two Balance wardens at the door. "If you'll excuse me, Sister." She strode toward the escalating disagreement.

Shi Hua looked over at the clerk's bench. Donella's worried look mirrored her own gut feeling. And the atmosphere in the court mirrored the fierce storm about to break open the skies outside.

She edged closer to the senior clerk. "What the demon is going on?" she whispered.

Donella's not-so-amused snort didn't help. "That is the question, isn't it?" she replied in a low voice. "A fight broke out in one of the seafront taverns between a local dockworker and a Sea Peoples captain. The dockworker was stabbed. The prince was involved, and he claims to have been the one who actually stabbed the victim."

"When was this?"

The clerk shrugged. "According to the peacekeeper report shortly after Second Night the day before last."

A chill ran through Shi Hua. Second Night two days ago had been high tide. When Reverend Father Biming left with the chief justice and the high brother. Was the incident designed to keep them in Orrin and simply didn't proceed on schedule? Or had it been timed for immediately after their departure to keep the chief justice's staff and allies off balance?

Or it could simple be coincidence?

Except nothing had been a coincidence since she had been recruited as the prince's bodyguard.

And she was right back to the wallowing that had kept her awake for the last two nights. Disappointment she'd been excluded from the mission to Tandor ran thick inside of her, despite Quan's reassurances he needed someone to keep an eye on things here in Orrin.

More spectators settled in the gallery. Issurans and Sea People gave each other wary looks, but for the most part ignored each other. The number of people inside the courtroom kept it toasty without the benefit of braziers so she removed her outer cloak.

A little hum ran through the crowd when Shi Hua brushed back her hood. Part of her wondered how many people came to watch the day-to-day drama at Balance because they had nothing else better to do this late in winter. Having a foreign priestess of Light act as the court's truthspeller was probably too normal for them.

No. She smiled to herself. They would never expect a *priestess* of Light. For them, that was the novelty.

The argument between the magistrate and the chief warden broke off, and the magistrate stomped over to sit right behind her in the section reserved for peacekeepers and witnesses. He hesitated when he caught sight of her.

"They left you out, too?"

She shrugged. Biming had drummed discretion into her head. Now was not the time to sympathize with the magistrate.

He shook his head as he took his seat. "Then things are worse than Little Bear wants to admit. Have you discovered anything new regarding Dante?"

"I'm sorry, Magistrate." She bobbed her head. "The healers did not find anything on the victim's bodies we could use for tracking spells." She turned to Leilani. "Did you finish the sketch of our suspect?"

The junior clerk nodded. "I'll fetch it for you after court, Sister." Leilani focused on something across the room.

Shi Hua followed her gaze.

The door to the gaol opened, and another Balance warden escorted a prisoner to the small railed area directly in front of the justice's podium. Prince Alika, the youngest son of the Sea Peoples king, wore the gray shift of a prisoner and not his usual brightly colored woven loincloth and feathered cloak. He stood proudly in the accused's box.

A chill ran through Shi Hua. He'd been a person of interest when the chief justice had been investigating the brutal murder of Sister Gretchen of Love due to his worship with the priestess, but Anthea hadn't bothered to question him about the priestess's death when he arrived in Orrin last month since she'd discovered the actual murderer.

If it hadn't been so long since Shi Hua had broken her fast, she was sure her vomit would be decorating Balance's marble floors. Things had gone beyond simple coincidence. Why else would an incident with the prince have occurred right after Anthea and Luc had left?

Shi Hua scanned the spectators. No one stood out, but then the Assassins Guild took great pains to blend in with their surroundings. She rose to alert Gina. Unfortunately, Little Bear chose that moment to slam his ceremonial staff against the floor three times.

"All rise! The honorable Justice Yanaba presiding!"

Another murmur ran through the crowd as they stood. Why get this excited? Yanaba had been sitting at the podium for nearly two weeks now.

The justice entered, her young squire guiding the priestess's steps to her seat in front of the giant statue of Balance herself. Yanaba drew her sword and banged the pommel against the podium.

"Be seated." Her voice didn't have the same husky quality as the chief justice's, but it was clear and sure. She sat on her high stool behind the podium.

Shi Hua's nerves jumped, and her gaze skipped over everyone present. Where was the threat coming from? Who was the target?

"Sister!" Donella hissed.

Shi Hua jumped and realized she was the only one still standing. She dropped to her bench, ignoring the magistrate's muffled snicker.

The clerk cleared her throat. "Justice, the first case involves Alika of the Sea Peoples. He is accused of assault with intent of death against Piotr of Orrin." Any titles of an accused or a victim were eliminated during the course of a trial.

Yanaba turned to face the prince. Developing the same body language as people who were sighted was a talent few justices could master, but she excelled at the stunt. She would be a formidable chief justice someday, if not the Reverend Mother of Issura.

"How do you plead, Alika?"

His arrest hadn't bowed the prince one whit, but neither did he display the arrogance so common in many royals. "Self-defense, Lady Justice."

Yanaba shifted in the direction of her staff. "Sister Shi Hua, if you would please truthspell the defendant?"

As she stood, some logic in her subconscious linked disparate events. The attempt on her own life last autumn. The problems in Tandor. The attack on Shakya. All designed to pit nation against nation.

The incident with Prince Alika wasn't a random event. He was the next target, and if he were assassinated in the Orrin courtroom . . .

Her gaze darted across the gallery again, but nothing and no one stood out.

"Sister, we are waiting." If anything, Yanaba had learned Anthea's tone of voice that brooked no disobedience.

"I beg your pardon, Lady Justice." What to say? What excuse to use to get both Yanaba and the prince out of here? Because if the Assassins Guild had the opportunity to kill everyone in Balance, they'd take it.

Thief, be with me. Shi Hua stumbled toward the accused's box. "I believe I'm going to be ill."

Little Bear frowned and took a step toward her. She mouthed, "The justice." His eyes widened.

"Get down, Your Highness!" Using the warden's bench to launch herself, she vaulted up and pivoted with arms outstretched, focusing her wards on the corners of the accused's box like she would a room. Surprisingly, Prince Alika listened and he ducked below the railing. She landed on top of him, and they both tumbled to the hard floor.

Darts pinged. Her invisible barrier held her and the prince safe. Shouts and screams echoed off the domed ceiling. Above the cacophony, the chief warden's voice bellowed orders.

Power thrummed through the marble. Power her own energy responded to, leaving her gasping. Together, the two currents sought out those who would harm someone in their mistress's home.

The release at finding its targets rocked the temple and set the bells in its tower tolling. No, not just any bells. The alarm bell rang its deep note.

Demons. And they were inside the temple itself.

When her own head stopped ringing from the power surge, Shi Hua rolled off the prince. "Are you injured Your Highness?"

"Other than bruises from you falling on me, no." A frown twisted his brow. "What the Child is going on?"

Yanaba's clear voice called out. "It's all right, Sister. Our wardens have them."

Shi Hua peered through the slats of the accused's box. The Balance wardens had hauled three bodies in front of the podium. Two wore Issuran clothing. The other dressed in the woven leggings and cloak of an islander.

Only the temple's guardians were armed. A few wardens, who must have been on the night watch, wore cottons shifts. Or in one case, nothing at all. A couple of swords, including the magistrate's, and a multitude of knives lay scattered around the floor.

What she wouldn't give for Anthea's peculiar sight right now, but nothing suspicious stood out. She dissolved her personal wards and climbed to her feet. She held out her hand and pulled Prince Alika upright as well.

"Warden Jonata, please take the prince to our receiving room, and return his personal effects," Yanaba commanded. "Chief Warden, secure the prisoners in the gaol for questioning."

After each warden's affirmation, the justice pushed back her hood. Her milky white orbs swept over the crowd as if she could see their very souls. "The rest of you, take your seats. No one is leaving until I question you. And I wouldn't suggest touching any weapons until I give you clearance to leave the temple." An ugly smile filled her face. "Unless you desire another demonstration of Balance's true power."

In the distance, the other Temples echoed the deep alarm bell of Balance. A sound no one had heard in four generations.

A shudder ran through the crowd as they recognized the pattern. A few made warding gestures, but they all took their places on the gallery's benches. The justice flicked her fingers in a peculiar pattern, and the ringing abruptly ceased.

Jonata led the prince and a companion from the courtroom. Little Bear, Gina, and another male warden were checking the unconscious men for weapons.

Since the wiser course of action was to stay out of the wardens' way, Shi Hua forced herself to relax as she resumed her seat. She couldn't help but notice the slight smiles on the clerks' faces. No doubt there would be some teasing in her future. Maybe she was fitting in as a priestess in Issura after all.

DiCook leaned forward and murmured, "Do you always jump on princes to protect them before alerting any guards?"

She kept her expression neutral and said, "According to our emperor, yes."

Her answer set Donella and Leilani into another fit of silent giggles. But she could feel the magistrate's questions brewing for later because she had the same ones. The attempt on Prince Alika's life made sense in the context of trying to start a war. But what had set off the demon alarm, and how in Light's many names did it connect to the murders of Peacekeeper Dante and his family?

Because the damn ball of ice in her gut said it did.

"Sir, the one who threw the darts at Prince Alika and Sister Shi Hua is dead." Gina's voice was steady but held a thread of anger as she searched the body. She looked at Little Bear. "It appears to be poison."

"Nathan?" the justice called out.

"Yes, m'lady." Anthea's squire came out from behind the statue of Balance. Mei Wen poked her head out, too. The two children must have used the basalt figure as cover when the madness cut loose.

"Go to the Healers Guild and request Master Devin's attendance at our Temple," Yanaba said.

"Yes, m'lady." The boy raced out of the courtroom.

"Justice?" Little Bear held up what looked like a sapphire the size of a hen's egg. "The other two are alive, but we have a problem."

"Found another one, sir," the male warden, who had been checking the Sea Peoples man, held up a second jewel-like object.

The people in the gallery muttered in confusion, but the staff of Balance wore horrified expressions. Thank the Twelve, the wardens wore gloves. The skin of Shi Hua's throat burned at the memory of one of those things trying to suck her very life force from her body.

Demon eggs.

Now they knew what had set off the alarm bell.

Chapter 15

"Orrin's under attack," I whispered, not quite believing the words.

"Light, help us." Shock and rage warred within Luc and battered against my mind. "Those damn eggs must have never left the city."

"We need to go. Now." I struggled to my feet and took two steps toward Luc's crutches.

The door to Dav's chambers burst open and slammed into the wall. I yanked the pins for my widow's veil. Fake wardens rushed into the room. I stabbed at the bastards, but I might as well have been empty-handed. They seized me before I harmed them, much less before any spell could form in my rattled brain. Luc shouted behind me as they dragged me from the room. A fist hitting flesh was the last sound before the door slammed shut again.

Stop wasting time with those idiots and contact Biming!

The pain trickling through the link from Luc wasn't as bad as I feared. *And how, pray tell, m'lady, do you propose I touch a quicksilver mind?*

He'll hear you, I reminded him.

So will everyone else in the city!

Does it matter at this point?

His silence reassured me he'd do what was necessary. I severed our link. Luc didn't need to be distracted by the skinwalker's plans for me.

The renegades dragged me into the main sanctuary. My attention was taken by the corpse on the floor. The priest Luc had questioned under the pretense of Quan's request for contract sealing. Cooling blood spatter covered the front of the statue of Light as well as the altar. Enough blood had been spilled the eternal flame had been extinguished as well.

Which was a good thing when the renegades tossed me against Light's altar.

My skirts didn't catch fire. Unfortunately, the builders didn't use wood for the altar. The dark blue marble was threaded with pale blue veins of gold. It barely made a sound when my shoulder rammed it. I, however, made a slight whistling sound at the pain as I collapsed.

Fingers dug into my jaw and dragged me to my knees. "How'd you do it?" Spittle sprayed my face.

I blinked, and the greenish mien of the skinwalker stared into my eyes. "You need to be more specific," I mumbled.

He released me, and his backhand cracked across my cheek before I could duck. The force of the blow brought tears to my eyes.

"Balance! How did you activate the bells?"

"I didn't."

"Truthspell the bitch," another voice said. This one was more female. I peered around the skinwalker. A tall woman dressed as a Balance court clerk stood over a kneeling figure, a knife to her prisoner's throat.

It was the second person who grabbed my attention. Justice Elizabeth was the only one who'd shown me any kindness after I'd given myself my odd sight. I hadn't seen her in nearly sixteen years, and I had often wondered if she'd been assigned to Tandor as punishment for showing me any consideration.

Her hair had been shorn the length of two knuckles, and her temple robes were little more than rags. Her eyes stared into nothingness. But there was a straightness to her spine that had nothing to do with the blade on her neck. A straightness that had definitely been missing from High Brother Dav. Magic tingled against my skin, a harsh buzz, yet still familiar. She was under a truthspell.

"It's good to see you again after all these years, Elizabeth," I said.

A strained laugh erupted from the other justice. Had I misjudged her mental state?

"Ah, Anthea. I take it our dear Reverend Mother never figured out how to reverse what you'd done to yourself, little deathwish."

My ignominious nickname from my novice days at Standora. Her way of saying she was intact.

I snorted. "The harpy couldn't find her ass if you placed both hands on her posterior for her."

Under the cover of Elizabeth's laughter, I activated the truthspell blocker.

"Have you met my new clerk Minerva?"

"Shut up!" The other woman yanked Elizabeth's chin higher. "One more word and I slit your throat, old woman."

"Old? She only has ten winters on me—" My words dissolved into choking when the skinwalker's hands wrapped around my throat. The same alien magic I'd felt sealing the door to the underground tunnels tried to penetrate my soul, but his truthspell lay on top of the blocker like a layer of oil on water.

"There we go." The skinwalker smiled at me. "Did you activate the bells in Balance?"

"No."

The skinwalker eyed me as if he didn't quite believe me. "Who activated the spell for the demon alarm?"

I braced myself against the possible pain if the blocker didn't work. "I don't know."

The searing sensation in my gut didn't come. Practicing with Luc, Jeremy, and Shi Hua at home had been one thing. I feared the blocker wouldn't work against the skinwalker's magic. But then, Kam had said he discovered the information about the blocker and counter in a treatise on demon grimoires.

The thought of the old man brought fresh anger to the surface. This was the bastard who orchestrated my colleague, my friend, my *grandfather's* death.

Despite his assumption the truthspell worked, the skinwalker's frustration spilled into another slap across my cheek. "Can only a justice activate the bells in that manner?"

Despite the taste of blood in my mouth, I said, "Yes." Another lie slipped by his truthspell.

He leaned away and watched me. "Now, Elizabeth says no, but you say yes. One of you is lying."

My eyes narrowed, and I flashed a vicious smile. "Or maybe a fool is asking the questions. Your boy Samael DiRoy was equally sloppy during his interrogation last summer when his demons captured me."

The skinwalker shrugged. "You did me a favor by executing him. He wasn't the most reliable ally."

I tilted my head. "And Duke Benedetto and Lady Cora DiMara were?"

"Discovering all my secrets won't be that easy, my dear justice." He turned to one of the imposter wardens. "Let's see if we can convince her of my sincerity."

My heart lodged in my throat and refused to beat. This bastard had used

Luc against me before. What would be worse? Allowing my imagination to run wild? Or watching the skinwalker slice my lover apart piece by piece?

"Bring in all three men," the skinwalker said.

"What about the wardens in the gaol?" one of them asked.

An ugly smile filled the skinwalker's face. "Take them over to Love. Our people haven't had much respite since all the priestesses decided to die rather than join us."

A sick game. That's all he wanted. Helpless people for his entertainment.

Please, Balance, let Luc get his warning out to Biming. I wasn't sure why I bothered with the prayer. My Goddess hadn't answered in all the time I'd served in Her Temples. But if the Reverend Father and his crew escaped, they'd be able to warn the queen that Tandor was lost.

The renegade asking questions strode across the floor to the same conference room Luc and Quan had used earlier and knocked. Two of his compatriots dragged out the ambassador. A deep red bruise circled one eye. Hot pink blood dribbled from the corner of his mouth. But he was alive.

The man who followed them drew my attention. He wore the mail shirt of Conflict. The badge on his shoulder indicated his rank was high brother. And he was huge, equally the height and mass of Yar. I couldn't hope to fight him physically.

I mentally reached for Elizabeth. *Did your Conflict seat defect?*

Yes. A wagonful of fury lay behind her single word.

A third blow across my face knocked me to the floor. I caught myself before my head hit the stone inlaid around the statue of Light. The bastards still had not deigned to bind my wrists. Maybe some of Shi Hua's hand-to-hand techniques would be useful. I merely had to wait for the opportunity.

"If you two are going to talk, say it so we all can hear it," the skinwalker drawled. "What did you tell her?"

I glared up at him and slowly sat up. A little truth sprinkled between the lies could do wonders. "I asked the chief justice if the Tandor high brother of Conflict had defected to your cause."

He turned to Elizabeth. "Is that what she truly asked you in silent speech?"

"Yes," she spat.

A puzzled look crossed his face. Or rather Brother Jon's face. He'd stolen the Light novice master's skin over a month ago from what we had determined. In

Dav's quarters, Luc and I had been too busy sniping and planning an escape for me to ask if it was the features or the essence of the skinwalker Luc had recognized. With the peculiar version of eyesight I'd given myself, nearly everyone looked the same to me.

Except demons and this skinwalker.

I deliberately ignored him and turned back to Elizabeth. "Chief Justice, who else has joined these . . . people?" I didn't want to let on how much I knew about them.

She remained silent, both audibly and mentally for a moment, despite the truthspell. "The high brother of Light has been used by this one somehow." She grimaced at the reference to the skinwalker. "However, Dav's many indiscretions are the cause, not a genuine desire to join them."

Elizabeth's voice caught. "High Brother Aduba and our captor told me everyone else is dead." *Except the junior Wildlings.* Her raw emotions shielded her silent words to me.

Do they know the Wildlings are alive? I asked.

They do, but they've lied to me about it. I overheard the ones guarding me one morning. The juniors have employed strike-and-run tactics to slow down whatever their plan is. Dark humor tickled my mind. *Thank you for carefully wording your question, Anthea.*

"Really, Chief Justice?" Quan's voice was strong despite his injuries. "You're not even going to ask as to my well-being?"

I laughed. "I was fairly certain whoever interrogated you, my dear Ambassador, would surely have killed you out of sheer annoyance before now."

"Quit playacting." A sneer lifted one corner of the skinwalker's mouth. "We already know how close you two are."

"Everyone knows that," a familiar voice quipped from the hallway to Light's private quarters. Surprise sparked in me when Luc entered the main sanctuary under his own power with his crutches. He must have played up his missing foot. Or else the renegades didn't think he was much of a danger to them.

Or both.

Out of sight of the skinwalker, the fingers of Luc's right hand flicked. He repeated the motion. Thank Balance, he'd managed to contact Biming or one of his people. The contingent of Thief had been warned. The fate of our world was now in their hands.

It didn't mean I wouldn't do my damnedest to get Quan, Luc and our wardens out of this mess alive.

Shrieking echoed down the same hallway Luc had come from. The imposter wardens appeared, and they had their hands full with the slavering, struggling Dav. He fought with the desperation of the truly mad despite the manacles on his wrists. His incoherent wails sent a dull ache through my already ringing head.

"Someone gag him!" the skinwalker roared.

One of the imposter warden shoved a wad of cloth into Dav's open mouth, but it only muffled the awful sounds he made. From the sorrowful expression on Elizabeth's face, this was not a new occurrence.

The skinwalker turned to the traitor priest. "Get them."

Aduba crossed to the altar and retrieved a woven basket behind the marble. After he placed the container in the skinwalker's hands, he removed the cover. The skinwalker lowered the basket so I could see what was inside.

Horror ran through me. Objects blacker than anything on this plane lay inside. Demon eggs.

"Beautiful, aren't they?" the skinwalker murmured.

"No," I whispered.

He jerked and shoved the basket back into the traitor's grasp before he bent and peered into my face. "What did you say?"

"You asked me if I thought they were beautiful. I said no." I straightened until our noses nearly touched. No heat radiated from him.

Of course not, my internal voice chided. *He's wearing a dead man's skin and he consorts with demons.*

"You should take care in how you speak to me, woman." His spittle flecked my skin.

"And you're an idiot," I added. "Don't ask rhetorical questions around someone you've truthspelled."

He straightened and started laughing. His hand dipped into the basket. He held up a single egg. A black darker than anything known in our plane of existence spread over his fingertips.

What the demon was happening in Orrin? If Yanaba was dealing with a demon there, but the eggs were here—

When the logic melded inside my head, I realized our fatal mistake. The renegades had been distributing the eggs to all the major cities along the Issuran coast. Had the Balance alarm cut off because my junior and staff were dead? Or because Yanaba, Jeremy, and Shi Hua had defeated the demons? Did any of the justices in the other cities understand the reason for the alarm?

"You have been a pain in my backside, bitch," the skinwalker said. "I'm going to enjoy watching the baby devour your body and soul."

"No!" Quan struggled with his bonds, but the imposter wardens had a firm grip on him.

Luc, on the other hand, limped over to the closest bench and dropped to it with a heavy sigh.

Both the skinwalker and the traitor's gazes flicked between the two men. Those certainly weren't the reactions they were expecting.

Aduba chuckled. "I think your bitch in Orrin named the wrong person as Justice Anthea's lover."

Luc laughed as well. "And if your comrade had any sense, Aduba, he would have recruited Anthea to your cause instead of Gerd."

The skinwalker cocked his head. "But you traveled the western Orrin circuit with her. We confirmed that piece of information."

Luc made a disgusted face. "Are you referring to the ten years of torture because I pissed off the Reverend Father of Light? *You* didn't give me a chance to join you either. You didn't even ask. No, you decided to lop off my foot because Gerd is just as much of a greedy, lying bitch as her daughter." He waved at me. "Look at what she did to herself to escape Balance."

"Bastard!" I screamed. Love, help me. I wanted to run across the room and kiss him senseless. "You ungrateful—" I launched into every insult in every language I could manage.

Luc rocked on the bench, roaring with laughter. I finally ran out of breath. Thankfully, Quan merely scowled at us both, instead of breaking the illusion.

The skinwalker stalked over to hover over Luc. "And how do I know you're telling me the truth?"

Luc shrugged. "Go ahead and truthspell me if you wish. It's not like you haven't done it before."

The skinwalker turned to me. "What is your compatriot hiding?"

I glared at Luc. "He's hoping you'll be foolish enough not to truthspell him."

"Why?"

I shook my head. "You are truly a fantastic idiot."

His hand rose again. "Answer me."

"Then ask me the right question, you fool!" I shouted. "You can't ask a generic question. For the love of the Twelve, don't you even understand how a truthspell works?"

The skinwalker lowered his arm. "Do you know what he is planning to do to me?"

"No," I ground out.

"Do you know what he's planning to do to the demon eggs?"

I smiled. "If you try to hatch the eggs in here, even if you kill both him and Dav, the wards will automatically activate and incinerate us all."

Chapter 16

A thread of frustration ran hand-in-hand with exhaustion through Shi Hua by the time they were ready to question the prisoners. The demon eggs hidden on the two living renegades had triggered the alarm spell when Yanaba activated Balance's defensive spells. So, nearly everyone from the other Temples had raced to Balance in response.

The better question was why weren't the alarm bells triggered the moment the renegades stepped through the doors of the Temple.

However, Yanaba took advantage of the other Temples response to gather more clergy who could help truthspell the spectators to make sure no other renegades escaped. She ignored Father Jerrod's disparaging remarks and sent the rest of the wardens back to their respective Temples.

Still, it had taken several candlemarks to truthspell everyone in the gallery, even with the Balance wardens helping with the questioning. The pandemonium and demon eggs had frightened the spectators enough they didn't argue about being trapped in the Temple for a good chunk of their day.

But in the end, only their original two prisoners and the dead assassin were suspects in the attempt on Prince Alika's life. And the prince wanted to be involved in the renegades' interrogations. So much so, he'd broken a few pieces of furniture in expressing his desire to be a participant.

Yanaba pointed out if he could remain calm and stay within the Temple of Balance, she would share any information she recovered from the renegades. Otherwise, she'd bind him, both literally and magically, and ban the Sea Peoples fleet from Orrin for the rest of the current trade season. His chief captain Iakepa pointed out the loss of revenue, because no doubt their own justices would uphold Yanaba's ruling given the demon situation. However, it was the captain's mention of how the Sea Peoples king would be highly displeased at the loss of trade that convinced the prince to cease breaking furniture and semi-graciously accept her offer.

In contrast, Master Healer Devin and High Sister Bertrice had worked together to ensure nothing else dangerous was on the body of the dead assassin, especially when the wardens discovered the darts the assassin threw at Prince Alika and Shi Hua were poisoned, too. Once Devin confirmed the cause of death was due to poisoning from southern blue, likely self-administered, they transported the body to the Temple of Death.

By that point, the rest of the clergy had left, except for High Brother Han of Conflict and High Brother Jax of Wildling.

"Sister Shi Hua, if you would stay with Prince Alika and Captain Iakepa while I—" Jeremy started.

"No," she and Yanaba said at the same time.

The priest crossed his arms. "I'm the current senior at Light. Neither of you have any say in the matter."

"Which is exactly why it should be me." Shi Hua matched his stance.

"She's right," Yanaba added. "Or have you forgotten everything you were taught?"

An undercurrent lay in the justice's words. Too much training with Reverend Father Biming gave Shi Hua the answer. The senior clergy still didn't trust her even after they had truthspelled her. Even worse, Biming had pointed out how sloppy she had been when she complained about their treatment of her.

The biggest blow was the two people she'd started to consider as friends here in Issura had been ordered to not trust her either. Their seniors didn't want both of them alone with her. So why did Jeremy propose the joint dinner tonight?

"I know none of you give a rat's hairy ass about my opinion, but the ladies have a point." Magistrate DiCook hooked his thumbs in his belt and rocked on his heels. "Given the circumstances, Brother, you should stay up here. We don't know what other surprises those two might have on 'em."

"You're right. It's not your business," Jeremy spat.

"Yer lettin' yer pride get in the way of your duty, son." Han's rumbling bass was the first time either of the temple seats had spoken. "Right now, you and Sister Shi Hua are the only ones we've got who can destroy those blasted eggs."

"In fact, it might be a better idea for me to accompany Justice Yanaba in questioning the renegades." Everyone except Jax jumped at the quiet voice behind them. High Brother Talbert stepped out of the shadows of the foyer.

High Brother Han shoved his partially drawn sword back into its scabbard. "How the demon did you get in here?" He glanced at the temple's main doors, which Yanaba had ordered locked.

High Brother Talbert's wry smile was aimed at Yanaba. "Lady Justice, while the Chief Justice is indisposed, I would suggest you station a warden in her bedchambers."

The younger woman sighed. "You are, of course, correct in the matter of guarding all egresses, High Brother. However, may I ask why you should be my choice as a truthspeller?"

He smiled at her. "As Han said, we have every incentive to keep Brother Jeremy and Sister Shi Hua alive at this point. This questioning is merely an opportunity to kill another one of our Light clergy, something they failed to do a few candlemarks ago in your own courtroom." He paused for a moment. "If you wish another to act as your truthspeller, my pride will not get in the way, but as both High Brother Han and High Brother Jax can attest, my skills would be better suited to your needs."

"And that means what?" Yanaba asked.

Shi Hua couldn't help laughing. Maybe she'd simply spent too much time with Reverend Father Biming. "He means where the chief justice is a sledgehammer when it comes to truthspelling, he is the trickle of water that can carve stone."

High Brother Talbert inclined his head to her. "Even so, Sister." He turned back to Yanaba. "However, the decision is always yours, Lady Justice."

"I accept your offer, High Brother." Yanaba cocked her head as if she could see. "However, I still want Sister Shi Hua downstairs with us. Just in case, they have any other demon-related surprises."

She must have heard Jeremy's slight inhalation of breath when he opened his mouth, and she held up her right hand. "This discussion is done, Brother. You're in charge of destroying those damn eggs before they glom onto an innocent person and hatch. Use whatever resources you need. I would suggest you start with High Mother Bianca and High Father Jerrod."

Shi Hua suppressed her smile at Jeremy's shock, but the move made sense given Orrin's internal political situation. And from the appraising looks the three high brothers were giving the justice, they weren't going to underestimate her again.

Yanaba rested her hand on DiCook's arm. "Magistrate, I know the chief justice often includes you in interrogations, but if these renegades have other tricks, I will feel much better if Brother Jeremy has your wise counsel and experience to depend on."

"Woman, could you lay the compliments on any thicker?" DiCook grumbled.

"I could, but then the high brothers would know I value your counsel above theirs, and I'm not sure their egos could bear it."

The magistrate's cheeks and ears pinked at Yanaba's flattery. For once, he didn't have a rejoinder.

Shi Hua blinked. She never would have thought a justice could flirt better than a priestess of Love.

Yanaba turned her head toward the receiving room. "Ming Wei, please attend me."

The squire trotted around the doorway and immediately to the justice's side, though the little girl eyed the men suspiciously and her hand curled around her knife handle. "Yes, m'lady?"

Yanaba gazed at the girl fondly, or appeared to do so to anyone watching them. "I must go to the gaol to interrogate our prisoners. Once you've escorted me down the steps, I want you to go to the kitchen and assist Deborah until I summon you. Understood?"

"Yes, m'lady," the little girl replied.

"Thank you." Yanaba turned to Shi Hua. "If you're ready, Sister? High Brother Talbert?"

At their assents, the justice headed down the hallway to the gaol door. Even with his higher rank, Talbert had no problem bringing up the rear of their little group. And the fewer adult men around, the more at ease Yanaba's squire appeared.

At the entrance to the gaol, Warden Jonata, stood guard. Obviously, Little Bear wasn't taking any chances.

Shi Hua followed the justice as Ming Wei led Yanaba down the steep, winding staircase. Thank Light, the builders had carved a railing into the bedrock that served as the foundation of the temple. The flickering flames of the oil lamps produced shadows that could cause even a sighted person to misstep.

At the bottom of the stairwell, Warden Gina also kept watch. Donella waited with her, arms full of parchment, quills, and an inkpot. Ming Wei escorted Yanaba to the furthest cell door.

"Thank you, Squire." The justice smiled at the small girl. "Please carry out my instructions."

"Yes, m'lady." Ming Wei executed a perfect curtsey, even though her justice couldn't see it, before she dashed past the other clergy and up the stairs.

Yanaba waited until the door above them slammed before she said, "Warden, if you please?"

Gina unlocked the cell door. Inside a naked Sea Peoples man was shackled to the wall, his arms and legs spread. The position was barbaric and cruel, but after a renegade managed to commit suicide in the same cell last month, the Balance wardens obviously weren't taking any chances. In fact, Chief Warden Nicolas at Light would have done the same thing. Little Bear stood inside the cell, watching the prisoner.

The renegade didn't look afraid or concerned. A chill ran through Shi Hua that had nothing to do with the coolness of the underground cells. His expression reminded her of the assassin inside the Jing Embassy, the one High Brother Luc's tracking spell had inadvertently revealed during the chief justice's investigation into Sister Gretchen of Love's murder.

Gina handed a stool to Little Bear. Donella flicked a nervous glance at Yanaba.

"Let me know when you are ready to document our proceedings," the justice said.

"Yes, m'lady." The clerk scurried inside the cell and prepared to record the interrogation. Talbert guided Yanaba through the doorway as well.

The entire time the prisoner stared at Shi Hua. He was a huge man with a broad, powerful chest and equally powerful thighs. His dark hair had been unbound when the wardens searched him. It flowed over his shoulders. He towered over even Little Bear, and would be considered attractive if it weren't for the dead look in his eyes. But he ignored everyone in the cell, his gaze fixed on her through the little window after Gina shut and locked the cell door.

There's no way he can escape. The manacles holding him were spelled to cancel any talents he may have. Maybe the others were right. Maybe the attempt on Prince Alika's life was a ruse to attack the defenders of Orrin, especially anyone from Light.

"Ready, Lady Justice." Donella's voice trembled faintly.

Shi Hua couldn't blame the poor woman. Ambassador Quan told her what had happened when the chief justice interrogated the imposter priest from Light. He had chosen to die rather than reveal his leader.

"What is your birthname?" Yanaba began.

"No one."

"What did your birth mother call you?"

"The dead can't speak," he sneered.

"What did your birth father call you?"

"You'd have to ask him. I never knew."

"What did those who raised you call you?"

"Scum, most days. Offal or shit, on special occasions."

Shi Hua frowned. What the demon was going on? High Brother Talbert had laid the counter to the blocker and the truthspell itself. She could detect both spells active and working.

Gina nudged Shi Hua's arm and inclined her head toward the prisoner, then the high brother.

She nodded to the warden's unspoken question of whether the Talbert had done his job properly. Something else was going on here.

"What do you call yourself?" Yanaba patiently continued.

"Your enemy." His grin was pure evil. And it was wasted on the justice. Therefore, it was meant for Shi Hua. But why? Was she still at the top of the Assassins Guild's list of targets?

"Where were you born?"

"On a ship."

"Which ship?"

"I don't know."

"Where was this ship?"

"On the sea."

"Which sea?"

For the first time, the prisoner faltered. A grimace clouded his face.

"Which sea?" Yanaba repeated.

A low moan rumbled out of him.

"Answer my question. On which sea was this ship when you were born?"

He looked like he was about to vomit, but he said nothing.

High Brother Talbert's face appeared in the window. "Warden Gina, if you would be kind enough to let me out for a moment?"

"Justice?" the warden called.

"Do it," Yanaba responded.

Gina unlocked the door. The Balance wardens really were taking every precaution if Little Bear did not take a key inside the cell with him.

High Brother Talbert step out, and Gina relocked the door.

He beckoned Shi Hua to follow him. They stopped in front of the cell door for the other prisoner, and Talbert slid back the metal plate on the top half of the entrance. "Look," he ordered.

She peered through the window set in the door. Warden Dezba stood inside, watching the prisoner. The man, who had been dressed as an Issuran sailor in the courtroom, had been stripped and bound like his compatriot. However, he sagged from his chains, and he panted as if he were the one resisting a truthspell. She extended her senses. Talbert's signature was definitely on this man, which shouldn't be possible since he hadn't truthspelled this prisoner yet.

But there was something else. Something she would have sworn wasn't there when the men had been captured.

Talbert slid the plate back in place. "Your opinion, Sister?" he asked softly.

She felt as if she were fourteen winters again, spending her days between Light and Conflict and her evenings between Love and Thief. And even more exhausted than she had six years ago while training nearly every hour of the day.

Shi Hua kept her voice at a murmur as well. "Some kind of deep empathic link to share the pain load of an interrogation under truthspell." She laid her index finger over her lips for a moment as she considered the problem. "It would probably take someone from Child to break it, assuming it could be done without damaging our prisoners. But why go to these extremes to keep them alive? Every other time, the renegades killed themselves rather than answer the chief justice's questions."

Talbert nodded in approval. "Exactly my question, Sister."

"Do we truthspell them both at the same time?" she asked.

"You will not."

"But I'm—"

"More of target than Prince Alika if a mutual friend of ours is correct." He smiled to take the sting from his words. Of course, Reverend Father Biming had visited with Talbert during the few hours he was in Orrin.

Shi Hua frowned. "If not me, then who else?"

"The very person you suggested, my dear Sister." He strode down the hallway and looked inside the cell. "Justice, would you mind a short recess? Sister Shi Hua has made an excellent suggestion to resolve our current dilemma."

"Of course, High Brother."

The priest jogged up the hall and climbed the steps. A moment later, the slam of the door to the gaol echoed down the stairwell. Little Bear insisted the justice and her clerk not wait inside the cell. Shi Hua expected Yanaba to throw a fit. Anthea certainly would have. But the younger justice readily agreed. No one asked what Talbert was up to, though the chief warden's scowl indicated he wasn't pleased about being excluded.

Shi Hua didn't dare say a word. The less the prisoners knew of Talbert's plan, the better. She had finished counting the rivets on the cell door in front of her when footsteps came from the stairwell.

The high brother of Thief appeared, but it was the woman behind him who garnered the most surprise from Shi Hua's companions. Like those of her order, High Sister Mya of Child rarely left her temple. The press of a large population's emotions overwhelmed their sensitive talents.

The empath was tall, and her pale green formal robes did nothing to hide her almost painfully thin physique. She had pushed her hood back. Her brown hair was trimmed above her ears, and her equally brown eyes were almost too big for her face.

She inclined her head to Yanaba first, then Shi Hua. Most temple seats rarely showed such courtesy to their own juniors, much less another temple's. "High Brother Talbert said you have need of my talents, Justice."

Yanaba smiled. "Sister, if you would explain your theory to High Sister Mya?" Of course, she couldn't explain. She didn't know.

Shi Hua bowed to the head of Child. "Are you comfortable using silent speech, High Sister?"

"Comfortable?" Mya's high laughter resembled a wind chime. "No, but I can tolerate it for short periods."

Shi Hua quickly relayed Yanaba's earlier questioning, Talbert's suspicions, and her own theory of how the renegade was resisting the truthspell. The high sister then examined each prisoner.

"I believe you're right." She shook her head. "But it's more than these two. I can feel at least ten others in the link."

A chill ran through Shi Hua. High Brother Luc had suggested there were more assassins in Orrin than even he and the chief justice realized. The only reason to share the pain load of a truthspell was if the assassins were expected to act in concert and all of them needed to be alive to do so. Otherwise they would already poisoned themselves . . .

Oh, sweet Light!

She reached for Yanaba's arm. *They have more than just the two eggs here in Orrin.*

Shock from both priestesses ran along their mental link.

The whole cache your Reverend Father Biming is after? the justice asked.

Shi Hua's heart hammered, and pain echoed from High Sister Mya. She took a deep breath to calm herself. They needed Mya's help. Overwhelming the high sister would be counterproductive. *If the one he's tracking is the size of the one my temple found in the School of Sorcery in Chengzhou, then no, not the entire cache. But I'd say they are definitely part of it, and were left here when the couriers passed through Orrin.*

So Anthea and Luc are chasing after this cache of demon eggs, and the audit in Tandor was merely a ploy? The priestess from Child tilted her head as she regarded Shi Hua.

Not at first, but the information from another Temple of Thief indicated the cache was passing through Issura, and they hoped to intercept it.

Mya smiled. *You're not telling me the whole story.*

We cannot tell you at the moment, Yanaba interjected. *Please do not ask us.*

The high sister's humor floated along the link. *Talbert said much the same thing to me this morning. Very well then. Do you want me to trace the link or break it so you can question these two?*

While Shi Hua knew her own choice, she'd learned enough to know it was wiser to defer to Balance. *This is your interrogation, Lady Justice.*

Yanaba didn't hesitate. *Trace them. If Shi Hua is correct, finding those eggs is our priority, but please, give me a moment.* Yanaba broke the mental connection and called, "Chief Warden."

Little Bear stepped to her side. "Yes, m'lady?"

Yanaba reached out, and he automatically wrapped her hand around his elbow. "Walk with me," she said. They strode down the short hallway. Little Bear's shoulders tensed at the justice's silent instructions. She turned and strolled back toward Shi Hua without aid while the chief warden raced up the stairwell.

"How do you move without running into the walls?" Shi Hua murmured.

Yanaba chuckled and tapped her forehead. "Good memory. Jeremy will let you know when they're ready upstairs."

Of course. Little Bear was getting Temple eyes on the spies who had been watching Balance and Light since midwinter. It had become a game among the wardens and peacekeepers to identify them all. Now, they needed to see if any of their suspects reacted to Mya's trace.

A horrible thought occurred to Shi Hua. Had Dante spotted someone? An assassin who realized he or she had been identified? Was that why the peacekeeper and his family had been killed? Or had he spotted the eggs and not realized what they were? She had a sinking feeling there was more to Dante and his family's deaths than a simple warning to the chief justice or High Brother Talbert.

"Aren't you going to finish your questioning, Justice," the Sea Peoples prisoner called out. No one answered him.

The silence and stillness had become unbearable when Shi Hua felt a tickle at the back of her mind.

Tell the justice the magistrate and I are ready. Anger and confidence rushed into her mind from Jeremy.

"Your orders have been enacted, Lady Justice."

Yanaba inclined her head. "If you would care to proceed, High Sister."

"I need all of you out of my way." Mya gestured for the rest of the little group to go further up the hallway. "Talbert, would you cloak them please? Don't forget the other warden in the second prisoner's cell."

Once the wardens, the clerk, and all the clergy but herself crowded together at the end of the corridor by the stairwell, the high sister set to work.

Or she went through the motions anyway. Shi Hua couldn't See any of the colored streamers indicating active magic like she normally could.

She glanced at High Brother Talbert. He returned her look with a wry tilt of his lips. Of course. He was a quicksilver like Reverend Father Biming. And he'd extended his talent so none of their emotions interfered with Mya's delicate magic.

The high sister finished murmuring under her breath. Her arms extended towards each cell. Nothing seemed to happen for a long time.

Mya screamed, a high, piercing cry that could have shattered ear drums. Talbert raced for her and caught the high sister before she hit the stone floor.

Strange grunting came from each of the cells. Then the sound of ripping flesh.

Talbert glanced inside the closest cell, and his eyes widened. He slung the unconscious high sister over his shoulder and rushed toward the exit.

Yanaba drew her sword. "Gina! Dezba! Get Mya and Talbert upstairs! Now!"

Shi Hua automatically drew her own sword. Now, she wished she'd told Istaqa to put a rush on the new bow she'd commissioned. Beneath her feet, stone vibrated as Balance's alarm bell rang for the second time the same day.

Talbert raced between her and Yanaba, hauling the unconscious priestess. Dezba followed them up the stairs.

Gina hesitated. "Justice—"

"Go!" Yanaba roared. The sound she made was reminiscent of the chief justice.

The warden obeyed and raced up the steps.

Shi Hua charged forward and tried not to see what was inside the second cell as she slammed the plate back in place over the window. She placed her palm over the metal and whispered the words of her spell. The entire door glowed a dull red from the heat she produced. The thing inside screamed in frustration

She whirled for the other cell, but she was too late.

A black form oozed through the open window and dribbled down to the floor. The disconcerting thing about the puddle were the red eyes glaring at her.

Her breath caught, and old terror gibbered in her mind.

The prisoners weren't human.

Chapter 17

The skinwalker turned to the traitor priest. "Is she telling the truth?"

Aduba shrugged. "Possibly. Each Temple has its own secrets."

The skinwalker regarded him through narrowed eyes. "Yet, your Temple has no such defense?"

The former Conflict priest's teeth gleamed red against his yellow orange skin. "We have no need for tricks. We're warriors. I also wasn't trying to destroy you or keep you out."

Aduba's answer obviously didn't satisfy the skinwalker. He loomed over me again. "Who set off the alarm bells at Balance?"

"I don't know," I repeated. "Justice Elizabeth has been your prisoner, and I didn't have a chance to visit the Temple of Balance here yet." I leaned to the side to glare at the traitor before I looked up at the skinwalker again. "Are you sure you killed or captured everyone from the Temples not already committed to your cause?" I leaned forward again. "Or are you relying on someone else's word?" I pointedly looked at Aduba again.

So did the skinwalker.

The traitor chuckled. "Nicely played. The Red Justice hopes to sow discord among us."

"Maybe it's more than that." The skinwalker's attention returned to me. "Perhaps she knows how to subvert a truthspell like my precious little Gretchen."

"Holy Light." Luc made a disgusted sound in the back of his throat. "The bitch is right. You two are dumber than a box of rocks. Has it occurred to either of you that Gerd played you the entire time? She sold the damn grimoire to Quan."

"I truthspelled Gerd myself," the skinwalker hissed.

Luc shrugged. "You only thought you did. Just like you think you've got her—" He lifted his chin toward me. "—truthspelled. Near as I can figure it's a quirk of the family line. It's how the red-eyed freak is jerking you around. And she was right. Part of me was hoping you'd incinerate yourself." He lifted his stump before flashing the skinwalker a vicious smile. "The revenge would have been so sweet."

The skinwalker crossed to Quan. "Did you truthspell our darling prince?" he spat.

"Of course," the traitor replied, his voice mild.

The greenish form raised a hand and muttered the words for a truthspell. Normally, successive truthspells didn't have an additive affect on the subject or interrogation, but we had no idea of what the effect would be on top of a blocker.

Fear and desperation flowed from the ambassador as he stared at me.

"Did you purchase, trade, or barter with High Sister Gerd for the demon grimoire?" the skinwalker said.

"No," Quan choked out.

"Did she give it to you?"

Quan squirmed and groaned. My heart sank. The double truthspell bypassed the blocker we'd given him.

"Y-y-yes." The ambassador collapsed to the floor.

I thought my heart would stop. Damn Quan! I never knew he was that good of an actor.

The skinwalker yanked the ambassador up by his hair. "Why would she give it to you?"

"To keep it out of your hands, of course."

Aduba grunted. "I guess that confirms your spy's story."

The traitor's comment along with Quan's sent the skinwalker into a frenzy. He kicked the ambassador repeatedly until Aduba stepped between them.

"Don't be a fool!" the traitor snapped. "We can't use the prince if you kill him!"

For an instant, I wondered if the skinwalker would take his fury out on one of his own again. I had no doubt that was the reason for the death of the Light priest Luc and Quan had questioned.

The skinwalker stalked over to Elizabeth and yanked on her ear. Other than a sharp inhalation, she didn't react to the pain. "Since I know my truthspells work on you, where's the safest place in Tandor for me to hatch my eggs?"

She deliberately fought the truthspell to add to the deception. In the end, we both knew how she'd answer because the idiot had asked the wrong damn question.

"Balance," Elizabeth gasped.

The renegades finally shackled my wrists before they herded all of us across the thoroughfare.

The metal binding my arms wasn't spelled. Their second mistake. And they were escorting me to a home temple. Their third. Obviously, the skinwalker hadn't broken Elizabeth the way he had Dav, or he would be taking more precautions with the two of us.

On the way, more of the skinwalker's men grabbed civilians off the street and forced them into the Temple of Balance. The two who tried to resist had swords shoved through their hearts, and their bodies were left to rot on the bricks.

And I couldn't help them. Not without revealing the skinwalker's mistakes, and I didn't dare. There was too much at stake with demon eggs involved.

Bile rose in my throat. More deaths to lay at my feet. Had Yanaba and Di-Cook discovered the truth regarding the murders of Peacekeeper Dante and his family before the chaos cut loose in Orrin? Or had their deaths only been the beginning of whatever madness was happening at home?

The two renegades wrestled me into the Temple of Balance. Tandor's version of a courtroom was smaller than Orrin's. The sandstone walls were painted, which gave it a rich green color instead of the marble blues of home. But the basalt image of our hooded goddess was the same, and power thrummed beneath my light sand boots. It was all I could take in before the renegades forced Elizabeth and me up the two steps of the dais and to our knees before the statue.

The skinwalker kicked over the podium and stool, no doubt so the civilians, who cowered in the benches of the gallery, could have a better view of their coming deaths.

Luc hobbled over to the bench reserved for the court's truthspeller and sat. I first thought it was from habit, but the renegades placed Quan and Dav on the floor next to him. Quan was the only one besides me who noticed when Luc picked the pocket of the renegade escorting the ambassador.

A moment later, more renegades dragged in Tyra and Yar. Our wardens looked to be in the same shape as the ambassador. Cuts and bruises, but still relatively intact. They were both bound with ropes. Relief spilled from Tyra's mind when she and Yar were slammed to the floor across from me.

"Are you all right, Justice?" she whispered.

I winked at her.

"Lock the doors!" the skinwalker bellowed.

Elizabeth tried to hide her smile, but Tyra grinned openly. Yar's gaze bounced between the three of us as he tried to decipher what we planned.

Tyra subtly leaned closer to his ear, his bulk hiding her movement. "Follow my lead when the justice breaks our bindings." Her words were breathed more than said, but Yar's taut muscles relaxed a fraction at the news we had a plan.

The traitor carried the woven reed basket of demon eggs to the dais and stood between me and Tyra while the skinwalker extolled his cause to the poor civilians. He grinned at me. "I'm going to enjoy watching you die."

"What are you getting out of this, Aduba?"

"Revenge," he spat.

I lifted one eyebrow. "Revenge for what?"

"My parents sold me to the Temple," he snapped. "And not just any Temple, but one on the opposite side of the world. They said they couldn't control me. That I was too violent to be around my brothers and sisters."

"Were you?"

His silence spoke volumes.

"You hate them for trying to help you find discipline for your rages?" I asked.

"Shut up." His fingers curled and released as if he imagined he were choking the life out of me. Strangling women, as the renegade Marsden had done to poor Sister Gretchen, seemed to be a theme running through these idiots. "You have no idea what my life was like."

I waited for a moment before I looked up at the hidden face of my goddess. "Oh, Balance. Is this how ridiculous I sound?"

"Yes," Tyra answered.

My attention whipped to her. "I am going to transfer you when we get home," I muttered.

"You can't." She grinned at me. "You already promised Gina she could be chief warden down here, and sending me back to Standora would make you short-handed."

"Excuse me," Elizabeth exclaimed. "I'm still alive. I have a say in my staff."

"Take it up with the Reverend Mother," I shot back. "She's the one who assumed you were dead."

"I shall certainly have words with her the next time we meet." She paused. "Is it just me or is it terribly quiet in here?"

I leaned forward to see the rest of the courtroom. Everyone stared at us. Horrified amazement rolled off the civilians and renegades. Luc and Quan were trying to hide their humor. And the skinwalker's visage had changed from a sickly greenish color to an even worse dark yellow.

Power surged beneath my shins an instant before the Balance alarm bell started tolling again. The deep booming clangs shifted the civilians' fear to outright terror.

I closed my eyes and listened to the code. Orrin. Demon invasion.

Despite our lies to the skinwalker, Yanaba or another clergy member didn't have to be alive to set it off. Not if demons were within the walls of the Temple itself. This time, I didn't experience the yank on my magic. What in all the names of the Twelve was happening at home?

Chapter 18

Nausea threatened to splatter Shi Hua's breakfast over the stones of the gaol floor as the demon forced itself through the cell window. She flexed her free hand and summoned a fire ball.

Power flared around her, a deep throb that hummed in tune with her own.

"How'd you kill the ones before?" Yanaba said.

"The chief justice froze them in time, and then a lot of light balls."

"Is that all?" Sarcasm dripped from Yanaba's voice. "Get behind me, and start make those blasted balls."

The justice's left hand waved in a complex pattern while Shi Hua created more light balls. She floated them above her head to keep them out of the way. Her sword pommel was starting to feel uncomfortably warm in her hand as it absorbed the heat her magic generated.

"Yanaba?" Her voice shook. The last drops of demon fell to the floor.

"I'm trying," the justice said through gritted teeth. She repeated her spell.

The demon wasn't stopping though. It oozed along the floor toward them, as if it couldn't keep a solid shape. It moved with the consistency of the thick mulberry syrup Shi Hua loved through a bowl of snow.

"How many fireballs do you have?" Yanaba trembled with the strain of slowing the demon, and that was all she could manage.

"A dozen," Shi Hua answered. She dimly remembered High Brother Luc and Jeremy needing more than that when the imperial sorcerer had unleashed one at the Jing embassy. And Jeremy had used fewer in the tunnels beneath Orrin's Temples only because they'd injured the demon while rescuing the high brother before they'd brought tons of rocks in the Death Gate section down on the damn demon's head.

Maybe it was a good thing they didn't have flash powder. If she and Yanaba tried that stunt here, they'd bring most of the Temple of Balance down and bury themselves alive.

"Launch your light balls," Yanaba ordered.

"And if it survives?" Shi Hua eyed the black mass flowing toward them.

"We get it to chase us to the courtroom." There was an awful certainty in the justice's voice.

"I hope to the Twelve you know what you're doing," Shi Hua muttered. She gestured and her light balls flew down the hallway.

Another high-pitched scream rent the air of the gaol. The release of magic blinded her, but she managed to catch hold of Yanaba's robe and tugged her away from the wailing demon.

The sounds the demon made changed. They almost sounded like cursing. An odd feeling crawled over Shi Hua's skin.

She launched another light ball for good measure before she sheathed her sword, grabbed Yanaba's free hand, and dragged her toward the stairs.

Behind them, the demon screamed again. Its compatriot, trapped in the other cell, answered its call. The second demon said something in what sounded almost like a language, but its cadence and the crawling sensation on Shi Hua's skin said the second demon was casting a spell that would free it.

She pulled Yanaba up the steps, but the door was locked as the justice had ordered. A clang of metal on stone echoed up the stairwell.

"Let me," Yanaba said.

They carefully switched places. A shadow appeared at the bend of the stone. Shi Hua drew on the energy of the oil lamps and directed it at the inky spot. Another shriek rewarded her.

The back of her neck tingled, and she heard the door open behind her. She pivoted in time to jerk Yanaba back from the sword thrust at her chest.

Chief Warden Little Bear wore a sheepish look for only an instant. His expression immediately transformed to one of horror. He yanked the justice past the doorframe.

Shi Hua whirled and shot a light ball in the direction of the bend. Another shriek rattled her eardrums. She pivoted, leapt across the threshold, and slammed the door shut. The bolts automatically dropped into place. Metal vibrated beneath her hands as if an ox rammed the door, but the locks held.

For now.

The rest of the Balance wardens and High Brother Jax crowded around them.

"Evacuate the entire Balance complex," Yanaba ordered. "Everyone out, including wardens."

"B-but—" Little Bear stammered.

"My command is not open to debate, Chief Warden." For being blind, Yanaba did an excellent approximation of the chief justice's bloody glare, but she'd left something out.

"Wait!" Shi Hua tried not to wince as the two demons beat on the gaol door. The heat she fed into the metal no longer deterred them. "What about the spies High Sister Mya traced?"

Jax nodded. "The wardens and peacekeepers caught five of them. My people are tracking the rest from those captured."

"Bring the captured to the courtroom," Yanaba said. "And hurry. If they're like the two in our gaol, they're hiding demons inside of them as well as the eggs."

That statement drove the Wilding seat and the wardens into a flurry of activity.

The justice rested a hand on Shi Hua's shoulder. "I need you to hold the door until I'm ready. When I call, run straight for the statue of Balance."

"Yes, Lady Justice," she hissed. Despite the tight fit of the door to its frame, the demons tried to slip through the miniscule gaps between them. She shifted so one hand rested on the metal doorframe, and with the other tried to ward the gaps around the door itself. The Balance gaol might be unusable once she and the demons were done with it, but the demons would have to eat her before she'd let them harm her friends.

Maybe Quan was right. Maybe she had started thinking of Orrin as home. She gritted her teeth as the demons poked and prodded her wards, looking for any fissure, any crack to slip through.

High Brother Han appeared beside Shi Hua, and he braced himself with both hands against the door. His magic felt rough, a cat's tongue cleaning and reinforcing the tortured steel door itself from the virulent demon magic.

He smiled at her through his bushy red beard. "Just a few moments more, Sister."

Compared to the priests of Conflict she knew in Jing, Han didn't have the elegance of her instructor Brother Shang or the arrogance of Reverend Father Chen. Instead, he had a steady reassurance that he'd die before he allowed the demons through this door.

The alarm bell continued to ring. The other Temples had taken up the claxon, and the cacophony throbbed through her body.

Another sound underlay the bells. Soft, subtle not-quite music.

It was a prayer. Or a summoning.

She heard the incantation in her head, but the words grew louder. No. Han muttered them under his breath. The first invocation any novice learned. The oldest litany of the Twelve.

Shi Hua joined in, and she felt the power swirling around and through the surrounding marble. Now, she understood why Yanaba said to run for the statue of Balance. It was the center of the maelstrom of magic gathering around them. The proverbial eye of the typhoon.

Even the demons must have felt it. They redoubled their efforts to break down the door.

Now.

Shi Hua wasn't sure she'd actually heard Yanaba until Han grabbed her by the waist and tossed her over his shoulder. He ran for the statue, his giant strides making up for his lack of grace.

Behind them, without their talents blocking the spaces between door and frame, the demons slithered around and over the metal. Scarlet eyes filled with malicious glee at their escape, and Shi Hua's stomach turned in a way that had nothing to do with the high brother's shoulder ramming into her abdomen with each footfall.

Han set her down and pressed his body against hers. "Hang on!" She clung to the carved folds of Balance's robes and peered beneath his arm.

Yanaba stood in front of the representation of her goddess, facing the statue, her arms upraised. Her chanting changed to something else, a language so old Shi Hua didn't recognize it.

Behind the justice, two men and three woman had been lashed to the steel railing that formed the accused's box. They screamed as blood spurted from their splitting flesh. As black tendrils crawled out of their red wounds.

The two demons from the gaol charged into the courtroom. They now had some semblance of limbs and claws as the old records described. Their venom-ous red gaze focused on the unprotected justice's back. The black forms leapt.

Something from the dawn of time, from when Balance herself first became self-aware, flooded the courtroom. It was nothing and everything at once.

Shi Hua couldn't see, couldn't hear, couldn't feel the basalt beneath her fin-gertips. Twelve, help her, she couldn't even feel her own heartbeat.

Then, she could see . . . *her*. A justice stood over the disintegrating demons and the renegades who'd brought them to Orrin. Not Yanaba though. She looked up at Shi Hua. The woman's cowl covered the top part of her face, but the prominent nose and the full lips . . .

If Shi Hua didn't know Anthea had left nearly three days ago, she would have sworn the chief justice watched her. A slight smile curved the figure's mouth, and she laid a forefinger over her lips. Dark mist swirled, and everything was lost in the maelstrom of nothingness once again.

And it felt like the nothingness would remain. Would be the only thing she would know.

Ever again.

Until the end of time.

A groan came from nearby. Shi Hua blinked. Once again, sunlight poured through the high windows of the courtroom. Yanaba lay on the floor.

"What on earth—" Han whispered in her ear.

Dust. Everything was dust. Not just the demons. The human remains. The wooden benches. The tapestries. Anything that wasn't metal or stone had been turned to dust.

Everything except the three clergy who stood or lay on the dais.

"You all right, Sister?" The high brother couldn't raise his voice above a whisper. Or he was afraid to.

She nodded. "Yanaba?" She forced her fingers to straighten and release their hold on the statue. Many of the clergy at home had spoken of feeling the touch of their home Temple patron. But nothing like this ever happened to her.

Muscles and joints seemed to forget how to work. Step by step, she made her way to the fallen justice and knelt beside her. Shi Hua brushed back Yanaba's hood and the strands of dark hair the wild magic had pulled loose from her braids. Two fingers found the justice's pulse on her throat.

"What in Conflict—" Han's voice grated against Shi Hua's ears.

She followed his gaze. Everywhere sunlight touched the dust, the latter dissolved, as if the beams scrubbed away the contamination.

She realized what else was wrong. The alarm bells had stopped ringing.

Shi turned back to the justice. "Yanaba? Can you hear me?"

When there was no response, she reached into the other woman's mind.

There was nothing. The body lying on the floor was an empty shell.

Chapter 19

The tolling of bells pounded through my head. Not just Balance's, but every Temple in Tandor had joined in the cacophony of sound.

"Stop that racket!" The skinwalker surged across the podium and seized my chin. "Stop it now!"

"We're not doing it, you idiot!" I shouted back. "It's your people spreading eggs up and down the coast of Issura!" I smiled as viciously as I could, given his painful grip on my lower jaw. "The Temples are reacting, and the gods are coming for you, traitors!"

He opened his mouth to respond, and an arrow with bright green fletching sprouted from it. The skinwalker's hold on me relaxed, and he stumbled before he started falling forward.

I threw myself to the right and rolled to avoid his body. An arrow probably wouldn't kill the bastard, but our chance had come.

Tyra and Yar were already on their feet. Luc sawed at his warden's bonds. Balance only knew how he'd gotten hold of a knife.

Beyond them, a half-dozen new people in civilian clothing and four animals engaged the fake wardens. They'd come from behind me, from the door to the private sections of the Temple. The tingle of magic flared, and one of the renegades clutched his chest. My own heart leapt.

The surviving clergy.

The innocents, dragged into the Temple by the renegades, seized the weapons of the fallen and joined the fray against their oppressors.

Luc gave the blade he'd appropriated to Yar, who freed Tyra in turn, while I stood in order for him to unlock my shackles.

A woman snatched something from a fallen renegade and leapt onto the dais. Luc raised a crutch to strike the woman rushing toward Elizabeth when the woman dropped to her knees in front of my fellow justice.

"After all the trouble of saving my behind nearly eleven years ago, you're going to kill me now, Brother Luc?" She held up another key.

"Reby?" Out of anyone I expected, she was not it, but I couldn't dispute the familiar glass-sharp energy of the girl from my very first case as a circuit justice. Except she was no longer the dirty young woman angry with her father and the world. However, I couldn't be sure she'd given up the light-fingered part from the way she knew where to find the key to the shackles.

Luc lowered his crutch, bewilderment flowing from him.

She smiled, lifted the manacles on Elizabeth's wrists, and unlocked them. "It's been a while, Justice."

"Yes, it has," Elizabeth snapped, but a slight smile curved her lips. "Now, help me up instead of flirting with the high brother."

"High brother?" Reby grinned. "Moving up in the world, Luc?"

"Yes, Luc. Why don't you make yourself useful?" I held out my arms.

He unlocked my shackles while muttering something insulting in Cantish. Reby answered him in kind.

Ignoring their byplay, I surveyed the fighting, which was quick and dirty and already over. From the fury and grief bouncing off my mind, the people of Tandor had been as ill-used by the renegades as the sisters of Love back home, and they showed their opponents their extreme displeasure. Only Aduba still stood, his back to a corner and his sword slashing at the wolf and two pumas who prowled well out of his reach. The third cat lay on his side, a nasty cut across the ribs bleeding hot pink.

Underneath the clanging of the alarm bells came pounding on the main doors of the Temple.

"Anthea, we're going to have more company in a moment if you don't do something," Luc said.

He was right. The assassins and mercenaries inside hadn't expected the civilians to rise up. We wouldn't be as lucky holding off the multitude of fully armed men and women attempting to break down the Temple doors.

I crossed the dais to the image of Balance. My fingers itched, and I desperately wished for my sword. It wasn't just any weapon. It was my focus in directing a greater working.

"If we don't have our swords, then we use the Goddess's other symbol," Elizabeth said softly. She stood next to me in front of the statue and held out her hand.

I grasped her palm in mine and extended my senses. Our free hands clasped Balance's stone ones. Like my own courtroom in Orrin, the leftover essence of Elizabeth's predecessors permeated the very walls of the Temple despite the skinwalker's attempts to mold it to his own ends. We chanted the words of warding together.

Power snapped into place. At the very least, our wards muffled the pounding on the Temple doors and headache-inducing clamor of the alarm bells.

I turned to examine the ones who rescued us and recognized another familiar face. "Hadar?"

He bowed. "At your service, m'lady." From beneath his cloak, he pulled two familiar scabbards.

Relief washed through me as I accepted my sword. "Thank you. Where's your captain?"

"On board the *Unbridled*, leaving Tandor, and sailing for Tiwan." Hadar nodded toward Reby as he handed Luc's sword over to him. "Tandor's Wildling second confirmed the rest of the eggs are headed south."

I eyed Reby who was removing Quan's shackles. "Second, hmm? What were you insinuating about aspirations earlier, Sister?"

She shot me an impish grin.

I turned back to Hadar. "And why are you here and not with him?"

The young priest shrugged. "I am to be the nursemaid for a certain misbehaving sailor while you and High Brother Luc attempt to set things right in the city."

I shook my head. "Best of luck with that job."

Abruptly, the alarm bells stopped. Everyone in the room looked around before their gazes settled on Elizabeth and me.

"Whatever is happening in Orrin is over," she said.

"Yes, but what was the outcome?" I replied.

She was no longer listening to me. Instead she appeared to stare in the direction of our remaining opponent. In Aduba's corner, a man standing on the other side of the pacing animals muttered a spell under his breath. The traitor stopped swinging his sword as abruptly as the bells had ceased tolling.

"Are you back with us, my friend?" the man asked. He had to be a priest as well since neither the Wildlings or Elizabeth tried to stop him.

"Gah! Where is that son of a bitch?" Aduba roared. "I'll rend that damn skinwalker limb from limb."

We all looked as one at the body of the skinwalker. A greenish-black mist rose from the corpse. The skin it had been wearing emptied faster than Kam could empty a wineskin. The mist hovered for a moment before it fled down the corridor leading to the staff offices.

One of the pumas shifted back to his human form. "Sorry, old man. You don't get to beat anyone today."

Aduba launched into a tirade in an unfamiliar language while he sheathed his sword. From his emphasis, a great many of the words shouldn't be used during a state dinner at the capital.

Elizabeth, what just happened? I asked.

It would appear Aduba, Nantan, and the junior Wildlings came up with their own plan, she said dryly.

"What do we do now?" one of the civilian women asked once Aduba lost steam. She sounded on the verge of tears. Everyone looked at Elizabeth, who turned to me.

Glancing around, I could understand the civilian woman's dismay. Bodies were strewn around the courtroom. What I suspected was the deceased Brother Jon's skin lay on the dais. It was rapidly starting to stink now that the skinwalker's magic was no longer keeping it intact. Renegades surrounded the temple, and from the muffled noise were still trying to force their way into Balance despite the addition of our wards.

And to top everything off, we needed to deal with a basket full of demon eggs that could possibly hatch any moment.

I turned back to Elizabeth. "Lady Justice, does your cook have a baking oven?"

She gave me a perplexed look. "Yes, but I doubt if it's lit."

"Luc, Yar—"

"Brother Jon's skin and salt. We're on it." Luc took off toward the kitchen on his crutches. Yar grimaced, but he whipped off his cloak and used it to gather the remains of the former Light novice master.

"Reby, can you find us hammers? We need to smash the demon eggs, then burned them as soon as the oven is hot enough."

She nodded, and the Wildlings dashed down the main hallway toward the rear of the temple.

The one who must be Nantan stepped forward. "Aduba and I can handle the deceased with some assistance, assuming there's enough salt and oil left in the kitchen." He eyed some of the civilian men and women who had helped with our rescue. They all nodded.

I inclined my head. "Thank you. However, we need to talk when you are done."

His gaze swept the remains of the mayhem before he looked at me. Sadness rolled off him. "For every life, there is a death, Lady Justice. Sometimes, all the survivors can do is continue."

The Temple of Death. He'd answered my first question. And he'd make sure neither the skinwalker or the demons could possibly use the deceased.

I turned to Tyra as they other started on their tasks.

She chuckled. "A couple of civilians and I can watch High Brother Dav and the chief justice."

"I do not need to be watched in my own temple," Elizabeth snapped.

"Actually, you're mine, Justice." I glanced at Hadar, but he was already tending to Quan's wounds. The ambassador flicked his fingers impudently in my direction, indicating he didn't need additional assistance. Good to know the skinwalker's torture hadn't broken him.

Dav sat in a corner, keening softly. He didn't appear to be aware of anyone around him.

"Please be gentle with the high brother, Warden. The skinwalker destroyed his mind."

"Yes, m'lady," she answered softly.

I wrapped Elizabeth's arm around mine and led her toward her quarters. Once we were out of hearing range of the rest, I asked, "Where did the skinwalker keep you captive?"

She snorted. "In my own gaol. He didn't take any chances. He used our own spell-threaded chains to keep me from contacting anyone, much less warn them." She sighed. "I don't suppose we have time for a bath, do we?"

"I think we can manage a quick one and some clean clothes." I patted the hand encircling my elbow.

"She poisoned all the wardens and staff," Elizabeth whispered.

I forced myself to relax despite her words and continued down the hallway. "Your clerk?" Her body had been among the dead in the courtroom.

"Minerva." The grief Elizabeth must have held in check for so long filled her voice. "She was shocked when she walked into my bedchambers and found me alive. Unfortunately, she'd brought her new master with her."

"You didn't eat that night?"

"I nibbled on some bread while I read. I didn't touch the stew." She sighed. "I never thought my distaste for goat stew would save my life."

"Why on earth would your cook make a dish you detested?"

Elizabeth's chuckle carried a sad note. "I never told her because everyone else here loved that stew. I usually managed to dump it down the privy before anyone came to collect my tray. The couple of times I couldn't, I'd claim I wasn't feeling well, and I'd ask for more bread to settle my stomach."

We reached her bedchambers, and I pushed the door open. In so many ways, the room looked exactly like mine. But the air was stale from weeks of disuse.

"Elizabeth, is there a tunnel system beneath Tandor?"

"Of course. Nearly every city with all Twelve Temples has one. Didn't your predecessor tell you?"

One more piece of knowledge that was passed from seat to seat, and lost because no one recorded it anywhere. Over the last several weeks, I'd wondered if Penelope had even known about the tunnels. She hadn't been assigned to Orrin until after Justice Thalia's death.

And I still had trouble conceiving the legendary justice of Orrin as my maternal grandmother.

Elizabeth took control and led me further into her private area. Her lips moved as she counted paces. When she stopped, she gestured with her free hand. "On your right should be my armoire. Two stones to the left of it is the Balance entrance to the system." She released my arm.

I crossed to the wall and knelt before the block she'd indicated, a mirror of the same one in my own bedchambers, and held out my hand. The familiar tingle of magic, untainted by the skinwalker's power. However, we couldn't use it with the entire Temple warded.

Even more likely, the renegades had people stationed on the other side of the block, waiting for us to drop those wards. And we had an incorporeal skinwalker trapped inside the Temple with us.

"Where are the contingency exits outside of the city walls?"

She grimaced. "Unfortunately, Tandor only has two that are still usable. One connects with the duke's exit to a very small cove on the other side of the northern cliff. The other ends several leagues away in an outcropping of the eastern desert. The rest have collapsed due to the loose soil of the region. The Reverend Mother—"

Her pursed lips and the bitterness of the last three words said everything I needed to know, but I voiced the thought anyway. "Didn't feel the tunnel upkeep was a good use of Temple funds."

A mirthless laugh rippled from Elizabeth. "My apologies, Anthea. I forgot who I was speaking with."

"My admiration for her has only grown," I muttered, sarcasm thick in my voice. Except now the old biddy had plenty of knowledge concerning my personal relationship with Luc. The question was when would she use it against me. Or was that the real reason I was ordered to accompany Luc to Tandor? We both survived despite her efforts?

No, I couldn't think that way. I'd become as paranoid as Gerd if I continued.

I pushed myself to my feet. "Any ideas on how to trap a bodiless skinwalker?"

"No." Elizabeth sighed. "If I've counted my days correctly, a contingent from the Diné should have arrived by now. Some of their own clergy accompany the merchants for spring trading. They might know . . ."

I could hear her underlying fear. The renegades might have been killing trade delegations as they arrived in Tandor. It would explain the lack of ships in the harbor as well. Kill the crew, then sink the captured caravels in the Peaceful Sea's drop-off a few leagues from shore where no one would be the wiser.

Or possibly take the ships to a sympathetic port where they would be manned and used against us.

First, we needed to focus on things we could control. "Let's take care of that bath before we worry about our next step." I took her hand once again. "I often find my brain gets cleaned along with my body during a good soak."

Surprisingly, the Temple of Balance still had hot water despite the kitchen fires having been extinguished. Elizabeth explained all the buildings had water tanks on the roof, filled from the aqueduct that diverted some water from the Tandor River, a thin trickle making its way from the mountains to the sea. Some tanks were designed to keep water cool. Others designed to use the abundant sunshine to heat the water.

Her continual patter was intended to keep me from asking about the bruising on her body. Bruising that was terribly familiar. It was the same pattern that had covered the body of Sister Gretchen according to Luc and Master Healer Devin. Thank Balance, the bastards hadn't cut Elizabeth. A very small grace though in the scheme of things.

I also had a strong suspicion my colleague explained the workings of Tandor plumbing to keep from breaking down as I helped her wash. My suspicions were confirmed when I left her to soak in order to search her armoire for clean clothing. I waited until the sobbing died before I re-entered her bathing room. I wished I could have given her more than those few moments to grieve for herself and her people.

Once Elizabeth was dressed, we needed a war counsel with the other clergy. *Luc?*

We're on the back porch.

I led Elizabeth down the cross hallway to the temple's kitchen. From outside came a lot of cursing and the sound of metal on stone. Inside, the Balance-awful smell of the baking oven encouraged us through the door to the fresher, drier air outside.

While the huge porch of my own temple was designed to protect from the rain, this one protected its occupants from the blazing sun. It was also arranged to capture any hint of a sea breeze that wended its way through the city.

Luc sat with Nantan, Hadar, and Quan. The four of them watched Aduba take his rage out on the eggs. The Conflict priest set a scarf or napkin on the beheading stone. Using a pair of cooking tongs, he placed a demon egg in the center of the cloth. With a series of colorful words that neither invoked his deity or any spell, he swung a huge hammer down on the awful black egg.

Reby darted forward and gathered the damp cloth by its corners. She dashed past us and flung the egg-soaked napkin inside the white-hot baking oven.

Now, I knew the source of the atrocious smell.

Behind Aduba, another fire burned in the sparring area. It wasn't the carefully constructed funeral pyre the members of Death would normally build for the deceased. I recognized bits and pieces as benches from the courtroom and stall doors from the stable. But the blaze did the job of burning the remains to charred bits the demons couldn't use against us.

I led Elizabeth to a chair and settled her. She seemed so much more fragile now, as if the dirt and blood of her captivity had held her together. What she really needed was a proper healer and the mental care of someone from Child, neither of which I could get for her any time soon. We were essentially trapped in Balance until we came up with a plan.

I crouched and peered up through the slats covering the porch at the roofs of the Temples on each side of Balance, but I couldn't tell if any people were up there from the heat shimmering off the stucco. "Anyone from Mother or Knowledge take potshots at us?"

"Two from each," Nantan answered as I straightened. "Your wards are holding. The quarrels bounced off them. We've only let them see Aduba and Reby destroying the eggs, plus Sisquoc patrolling in his puma form."

"They're probably assuming we'll stay put during the hottest hours of the day," Hadar offered. He looked up at me. "Some of these people wouldn't last long in the midday heat of the desert if we left now."

He was careful not to name either civilians or clergy. Maybe he'd learned something from my truthspelling him. Or Biming had lectured him about rank and propriety after our encounter aboard the *Unbridled.*

Technically, it was still winter, but this far south, the heat and lack of water would be a problem. Even if we stuck to the National Road, it swung away from the coastal canyons for several leagues into the northern edge of the desert. Balance knew taking the Road would mean capture and death no matter which direction we ran. And we risked drowning from flash floods or suffocating in a mudslide if a late winter storm caught us unaware as we climbed in and out of canyons. Our injured couldn't possibly handle the physical trials of that terrain anyway, and we'd condemn them to something far worse than death by leaving them here.

"Any horses or camels in the stables?" It was a rhetorical question, and I knew it.

"No," Nantan answered. "The renegades also took most of the root vegetables and fruits from the cold room, all the dried meats, and the more exotic and expensive spices."

"On the other hand, we have plenty of corn meal, wheat, barley, and oats." Luc shrugged and grinned. "Plus onions, beans, oil, and Cantish sauce. I remember my mother's recipes."

"And we have water in the roof tanks," Elizabeth added.

"But they've shut off the aqueduct to Balance," Nantan amended.

"Better shutting it off than poisoning it," Luc murmured. "It gives us time to come up with a plan."

"So we've got food and water for a few weeks," I murmured. Out in the sun, Aduba removed his mail and silk shirt. His skin glowed a deep red from his exertions. "Maybe the high brother should take a rest before he collapses from heat exhaustion."

"I'll rest when the Twelve-forsaken—" The rest of his words devolved into a stream of obscenities even I was loath to use, all of which concerned the destruction of the demon eggs and the humans who sided with our enemies. He brought the hammer down with such force I was surprised he didn't crack the headstone.

"Nantan, are you going to tell the rest of us what insane plot you and Aduba came up with?" Elizabeth tilted her head. "And before you answer, should I have Luc truthspell you?"

I couldn't blame Elizabeth for the edge in her voice. However, I hadn't questioned her thoroughly either. I didn't have the heart to do so after what she'd been through. But if the skinwalker had driven Dav insane, Balance only knew what the skinwalker had done to her.

After throwing another egg-soaked rag into the baking oven's fire, Reby leaned against a pillar. "We all need to truthspell each other. It's the only way to be sure."

"You're actually going to sit still for that?" Luc asked.

"None of us have a choice," she said, rather calmly. "And it's been nearly eleven years ago. Is it really healthy to hold a grudge that long, High Brother?" She drawled out his title.

Aduba stomped past her with the last rag full of demon egg remains.

Elizabeth chuckled. "Oh, there's a story I want to hear."

The conflict priest reappeared and leaned against the doorframe. "As do I,"

"Once we can trust each other and we have a plan to retake Tandor," I started. "I'll tell you all the tale about the night Luc was attacked in the forest by a giant polecat while he was taking a piss."

Everyone laughed except Reby and Luc.

After gathering the younger priests and priestesses, we met in Balance's receiving room. Yar and Tyra were included as the only two trustworthy wardens left in Tandor. Luc and I explained the truthspell blocker and its counterspell before we did a round-robin question-and-answer session with no one from the same Temple sitting next to each other. Luc and I told of the recent events in Orrin. Hadar explained the cooperation between the Reverend Fathers and Mothers of Thief from the Cradle and the Old Continent after the attempt to start a war between Jing and Shakya.

The others' stories sent a wave of horror and sorrow through me. Death had been the only Tandor Temple that had survived the renegades' take-over intact. It was almost exactly what those bastards had tried in Orrin, and it showed just how close we came to losing everything.

Tandor's high brother of Thief had been the first to notice the change in Dav's behavior and the addition of a new brother of Light named Jon. Then came a complete re-staffing of the Light wardens. Suspicion fell on Aduba as well since he'd only been assigned to Tandor a year ago. After a truthspelling session with Thief and Child, Aduba volunteered to investigate the newcomers. The other two seats created a subpersonality of Aduba's using his childhood resentment, one that would survive a truthspell and fit in with the Temple additions.

Unfortunately, two things happened about the same time: Aduba discovered his second Tighan was truly a renegade and I was named to Orrin's Balance seat

The skinwalker accelerated his plan to poison the clergy and their staffs in order to secure Tandor first. Tighan decided he didn't want to wait for the poison, but Aduba saved most of his people

Nantan had discovered the plot by his own cook. Everyone at Death took another drug that lowered the heartbeat and breathing to simulate the poison had taken effect.

All the clergy at the Temple of the Wildling God were suspicious of their new washer woman. Why she thought they wouldn't smell the poison in their evening meal was beyond even me. Their high sister died from a thrown knife laced with poison when they confronted the cook.

The Assassins Guild wanted to make a point with Thief. The bastards snuck in through the tunnels. The people in Thief gave a spirited defense and managed to kill a few of the bastards before they were overwhelmed.

Everyone else had the same awful ending as the staff of Balance. Everyone except Dav and Elizabeth.

Aduba and Nantan managed to use a sleight of hand with a few dead assassins and civilian corpses in Death's cold storage to make it look like everyone from the Temples had been accounted for. In the meantime, a priest or priestess from each of the surviving three temples accompanied their staffs in fleeing east in the hopes of warning the Cliffdwellers and the Diné.

Then the remaining survivors except Elizabeth and Aduba launched their hit-and-run campaign against the renegades, believing they were buying time until help arrived. Thankfully, the high brother of Child had trusted Nantan with the counterspell to reassert Aduba's real personality. He continued as a spy for the surviving clergy as they waited for assistance from the east.

I leaned forward. "Why not send word to Orrin or even head south to Cant?"

"Because the National Road would be the first place they'd look for us," Nantan said. "And since this Jon allegedly came from Standora, we weren't sure we could trust the home temples."

"One of mine, Sister Rabbit Runs, is part Diné," Aduba added. "She's the one who told us what this Jon really was. According to the Diné legends, a skinwalker cannot attack you in your home unless you invite him in."

Luc swore under his breath. "And Dav would automatically invite a fellow brother of Light into his Temple."

"Rabbit Runs' background and knowledge is why I sent her with the group headed east," Aduba said.

"We also weren't sure of the reception we'd receive in Cant," Reby interjected.

Luc glared at her. "Why?"

"Get your hackles down, High Brother." She smirked at him, but quickly sobered. "According to a fellow Wilding from Tiwan I met at the border, the villages along their eastern and southern edges are being raided."

I frowned. "Why would the Mecas—"

"They didn't," Reby said. "But someone's been trying hard to make it look like it was. The priest I met was responding to the first report of a raid on a northern village."

The other, unspoken, problem was if our group fled to Tiwan while Biming was trying to recover the demon eggs, we'd tip off the renegades already stationed in Cant. Biming would never find the eggs until it was too late.

Or we could start the very war we'd been sent here to prevent.

I turned to Luc.

He looked at me. "Just like the incident between Jing and Shakya. We can't let them turn us into scapegoats either, saying we're an invasion force from Issura. Not if the king's already on edge about border raids."

"Speaking of Jing—" Hadar fished a package out of his shoulder bag. "—I have something for you, Anthea, courtesy of our captain."

I accepted the twined-wrapped canvas. Familiar round objects met my fingers, and I couldn't help my grin. A dozen flash-bangs.

Hadar grinned in return. "A certain mutual friend said you were quite handy in using them against demons."

"I think Aduba has adequately taken care of the demons here," I said. But my black humor quickly died at the thought of what could be happening in Orrin.

Sensing my mood shift, Luc said yet again, "Our juniors have contingency plans in place."

"That doesn't answer why the alarm bells went off twice," I snapped.

"I hate to say this," Elizabeth said softly. "But we may have face the fact that Orrin is lost, too."

I jumped to my feet. "You've given up on Tandor already?"

"We are under siege in my own Temple. We've lost a majority of our priesthood. There's a disembodied skinwalker floating around Balance knows where in here." Elizabeth threw up her hands. Their color matched the bright red of her face. "If you know how we can escape this mess, I want to hear it!"

I paced, trying to come up with a reasonable plan of action. My first choice would be to take the northern tunnel and head home. But we had no mounts. On foot, we would be so much demon fodder. I had no doubt that the skinwalker had other demon allies nearby. And as much as I hated to admit it, too, Orrin may already be lost. Even now, the queen's army and Temple troops should be marching south due to the triggering of the alarms.

I rubbed a hand over my mouth as an idea sparked. "How smooth are the tunnel floors between here and the eastern exit?"

Reby smirked. "If you mean for those of you on two feet, then fairly smooth."

"She means for those of us on one foot," Luc said dryly.

"Actually, I was thinking of the injured," I said, matching his tone. "A trek across the desert will be bad enough for anyone healthy and intact. If someone becomes incapacitated in the tunnels, we aren't going to be able to carry them."

Elizabeth sighed heavily. "We can't take Dav with us either. The skinwalker broke his mind."

"We can't leave him here alone and defenseless," I protested.

"Anthea, the skinwalker can see through Dav's eyes." Elizabeth faced my general direction since I paced the area behind the chair I'd been using. "Possess and control him. It wasn't Aduba who left these bruises on me. And the skinwalker's been using him to spy in Orrin. If we take him with us, the renegades will be on us within a couple of candlemarks."

"What are you suggesting?" My voice didn't sound natural because deep inside, I knew exactly what she was insinuating. And I knew it would be a mercy for the insane priest.

"Don't act the fool, sister. It doesn't become you." It should have been an insult, but from her expression, her heart was breaking. "You know exactly what I'm suggesting."

"I'll do it," Nantan murmured.

"No." Elizabeth held up a hand. "He's my counterpart. I'll do it." Her voice faltered. "If I could borrow a blade."

Reby silently placed her knife in Elizabeth's hand and wrapped the justice's fingers around the handle.

I stepped forward, but Tyra pushed away from where she leaned against the wall and grabbed my arm. "You know it needs to be done, Anthea. He's already gone. Let her do this for him." It was the first time either she or Yar had spoken the entire meeting.

None of my wardens addressed me by name unless they were trying to point out I was being an idiot. And down in my soul I knew Tyra was right. But this was one more loss, one more life I didn't save, on my ledger. I couldn't point fingers at Dav for breaking his vows of chastity. Balance knew I certainly had.

But that didn't mean either of us deserved to die.

"Is that what we're going to do on our trek east?" I bit out the ugly words. "Slit the throats of anyone who can't keep up?"

"If we have to, then yes." Nantan watched me, his skin color remaining yellow. "Or would you prefer to be eaten by a demon. Or worse, used to hatch one of those damn eggs."

"This is just so easy for you, isn't it?" I spat.

"Our goddesses are the beginning and the end of the universe, Justice," he said. "You know what happens if we activate the defenses of our own Temples. I'd rather be stabbed in the heart than to be forced to use those measures. Or have you forgotten what happened to the isles of Britannia?"

A shudder ran through me. The spells within Balance and Death wouldn't only destroy demons. The cluster of islands off the western coast to the Old Continent were inhabitable centuries after the clergy of Death had launched their only recourse when they were overrun. Despite their efforts to evacuate, the cost had been horrendous.

Please, Twelve! Don't let Yanaba have resorted to them. I trusted Bertrice, Orrin's high sister of Death, to think twice before taking that path. But my junior justice was young and headstrong and . . .

Everyone in the room was silent.

"We can't go north," Luc finally said. "We don't know what's waiting for us there, and neither of us have been able to contact Shi Hua. Even if we could take one of the ships still in the harbor, none of us, but Hadar, have the skill to sail it."

Everyone looked at the Biming's protégé. He shrugged. "Trying to teach all of you while we're in the midst of a running fight would only be signing our death warrants.

"If we stay here, these renegades will simply allow us to die of thirst long before help arrives," Aduba added. "Assuming help does come. Both the Temples and the Issuran army may have their hands full even if we set off the alarms here. And our people fled east months ago. No help has come from that quarter."

"I guess we don't have a choice." I sat heavily in the chair I'd abandoned. "We head east. Even if the Cliffdwellers and the Diné have chosen not to become involved, we can try to negotiate passage through their territory to Kulshra'jek Pass. The snow will be melted soon and the pass open."

"What about the civilians trapped in here with us?" Sisquoc's gaze was as unblinking in his human form as it was in puma form. His attention shifted from person to person around our circle of chairs. "Many of them have spouses and children here in the city. Even if we talk them into leaving with us, the renegades will use their families against us. Somehow."

"How do you propose we get their families out?" Elizabeth asked.

"I'm not," the Wildling said softly. "I'm proposing some of us stay. The only people the renegades can confirm inside these walls are Aduba and Reby. If Balance sets off the alarms here, it could provide enough of a distraction to enable us all to slip out.

I chuckled. "You're forgetting the skinwalker is in here with us. He could be in this very room, listening as we speak."

Elizabeth's breath whistled. "No, that will be perfect."

The morbid excitement rolling off my sister justice chilled me, but it gave a clue to the logical conclusion she'd reached. "You can't do this."

The fingers of her right hand twitched and flicked as she worked out the spells she needed in her mind. "I'm almost as much of a hindrance to you as Dav is. But with your help, I can force the skinwalker into Dav's body. I'll set off the alarm bells to cover your escape to the eastern tunnel while Sisquoc and whoever stays with him takes the civilians out through Love. And then . . ." Her voice faltered.

Realizing the implications, the rest fell silent at her pronouncement.

I stumbled over to her, landing on my knees, and grasped her hands. She still held Reby's knife. "You can't do this, Elizabeth."

"The Reverend Mother has already picked my replacement." She pulled her empty hand free and cupped my cheek. "If you taught her, she will have survived whatever has happened in Orrin. And this way—" A tear ran down her cheek. "—none of you will have to fret over whatever awful thing the skinwalker may have planted in me because, my dear, I have the same damn fear."

Aduba crouched next to me. His huge calloused hand covered both of ours. "Lady Justice, you cannot sacrifice yourself this way."

"He should have killed me the moment he learned I was still alive," she whispered. "At a minimum, I was the bait to trap Anthea because she can see these cursed demons."

Minerva. She was the leak within Balance the Reverend Mother feared.

I scrambled to my feet. "Wait! We're missing something." I whirled to face Luc. "The skinwalker had that demon with him at Samael DiRoy's mansion."

"If you mean the demon my second burned in our tunnel system, then yes," he said dryly. "But what does that have to do with—"

"The thing that's in this temple with us now is not the same skinwalker!" I slapped my palms together. Irritation raged through me. I'd long since healed from the poisoning and other assorted injuries the Assassins Guild had inflicted on me over a month ago. My mind should have picked up on the difference in the skinwalker's skin. "The skinwalker is corrupted from wearing the skin of a dead priest, but his body didn't show any demon contamination until he picked up the egg."

"That doesn't make sense," Luc protested. "Let's say you're right. The skinwalker who abducted me did touch his demon. The contamination you see would have been all over Jon's skin. And trust me, the skinwalker who captured us here—" He jabbed his forefinger toward the floor. "—was definitely wearing Jon's skin."

"But the demons that touched me last year, the ones summoned by Samael DiRoy—" I patted my collarbones with both hands. "My cloaks, my boots, my sword. None of my belongings had any contamination."

Luc frowned. "We know there's a difference between those that are summoned and those that hatched on our plane."

"We were fairly certain the one with the skinwalker was hatched in this plane." I waved my hands as if that would bat away my confusion. I was on the tip of some revelation. I knew it. "It was too slow to be otherwise."

"What if it wasn't?" Nantan entered the conversation. In my obsession with the demons, I had forgotten Luc and I weren't alone. "We have no idea what a demon's lifespan is. What if it was left behind during one of the earlier invasions?"

"But the last invasion was a century ago!" one of the Wildlings protested. He was the wolf, but I couldn't remember his name for the life of me.

Also, I couldn't deal with a lecture from Luc for slipping back into my old habits. "Nantan's correct though. We've learned the demons left Balance knows how many eggs behind. It stands to reason they could have left some of their people behind to watch out for their young." Damn, I wish I had seen the skinwalker last month, but I'd been so focused on rescuing Luc and killing the demon, any other concerns had fled my head at the time.

"Slow down a moment." Luc waved his hands. "The Jing imperial sorcerer who wore his demon as a sash? You said the sorcerer's clothing didn't show the contamination either."

I tried to wrap my mind around all the clues, but nothing quite fit. "Are you saying the one we killed in the Jing embassy was an old one left behind?"

"I'm not saying that either," Luc said. "The only thing we know for sure is the eggs and the grimoires contaminate what they touch. And if you're right that the grimoire bindings are made from demon skin—" He frowned as he tried to work out the discrepancy. "But Shi Hua touched the egg in the embassy—"

"Except Jeremy ripped off a good chunk of her skin getting the damn thing off her," I said sourly. I examined my hands. "She healed without a sign. Like my own fingers did after touching the grimoire."

"So prior to life, and after death?" Aduba stood as well and wiped his brow. "That's what causes this contamination you see?"

I paused in my pacing and shrugged helplessly. "Apparently."

"So, all of this was what?" Reby scowled at all of us. "A Temple exercise in logic?"

"No," I answered. "Spies had already informed the renegades Luc and I were headed to Tandor for a Temple audit. Actually, everyone in Orrin knew we were coming south. Various factions have been watching us since we were appointed to our respective seats." I yanked on my braids. Whatever my subconscious mind had noticed about the skinwalker had faded in my frustration and our discussion of demon contamination.

"Maybe you're correct about it not being the same skinwalker who wore Jon's skin back in Orrin. Otherwise, why didn't the skinwalker use what he learned about us during the attacks last month while he had us prisoner at Light today?" Luc said. "The renegades have been trying to use us against each other from the beginning."

"Maybe because he figured out Gerd lied to him because she was furious I stretched out her birth canal," I muttered. The rest of the clergy except Hadar and Elizabeth stared at me. I'd forgotten not everyone knew the sordid details of my past.

"No." Luc matched my gaze. "You're right. This isn't the same skinwalker. They traded Jon's skin, hoping to confuse and intimidate us."

"You think the other one went south with the eggs while disguised as someone else?" Aduba asked.

"Possibly." Luc rubbed his chin. "Or it could still be here and organizing the renegades trying to find a way in here. What do you know about a local merchant named Ural DiSand?"

The Tandor clergy exchanged looks before Nantan said, "I know of him. He's one of the wealthier traders in the city. He mostly acts as an export broker, sending Issuran goods south and east. Why?"

"Dav often travelled to Orrin with him." Luc shrugged. "He may have simply thought he was doing the high brother a favor. Have any of the rest of you spoken to him or even been in his presence?"

I watched the other priests and priestesses carefully as they all said no. The truthspells were still in effect, and there was no change in their color. No change whatsoever in color or demeanor. No one knew anything relevant about this mysterious trader.

Or maybe Aduba wasn't the only one who had another personality imposed on them.

"None of our speculation matters," I answered. "Going back to what Aduba said, we're ineffective while we stay here, and we have no way to send a message about the possibility of multiple skinwalkers involved in this mess in addition to the demons and their damned eggs. The only way to save your city is to find help."

And I tried not to think about the possibility that by losing Dav and Elizabeth, we may have lost the battle before we'd begun.

Chapter 20

Shi Hua watched as Master Healer Aaron and one of his journeywomen looked over Yanaba. Han had carried the unconscious woman to her private quarters. The room was smaller than the chief justice's, but just as sparse. When Shi Hua had pointed out a couple of weeks ago Yanaba didn't need to emulate her senior, the justice had joked there was no point in decorations when she couldn't see them.

Warden Gina slipped into the room. "Sister, Brother Jeremy and the magistrate need to see you."

"It can—" Shi Hua snapped.

Gina lowered her voice further. "No, it can't wait, Sister." Her gaze flicked to the healers. "I'll watch over her. That's my responsibility. Yours is to this city and its people."

Master Aaron looked up at Shi Hua. "We'll take good care of her, Sister."

Reluctantly, she left Yanaba's bedchambers. Light Warden Mateqai stood at attention in the hallway.

"Where are they?" she asked.

"The Temple of Death, Sister." He fell in step beside her. "To warn you, the rest of the seats are being called in as well."

"I can find my own way." She knew she sounded angry, but beneath the veneer of irritability was a wagonload of fear for Yanaba. Is that why Chief Justice Anthea was always annoyed? To hide her fear and worry? And she could already hear what Mei Wen would say—that acknowledgement and control of your emotions were necessary so they would not control you.

Nor did she want to treat Mateqai poorly. He was one of the few people at the Temple of Light who treated her with the accord of her station.

"With all due respect, Sister, you will not leave our Temple without a warden escort," he said.

Her anger flared. "Because I'm from Jing?"

"Because we have demons and demon eggs within the city walls as well as an active Assassins Guild," he replied evenly. "This is a dangerous time. All of the priesthood is subject to the same restrictions from their wardens."

Mei Wen would be right Shi Hua was acting the fool. "I apologize," she said softly. "I'm not upset with you."

"I gathered as much." He put a hand on her arm, and they both paused in the corridor. "Losing over half our own priests and now all the justices has put everyone on edge. But whether you realize it or not, Brother Jeremy needs you. He may be a couple of winters older, but he has not had your—" Mateqai's tongue swept his lips, a nervous gesture as he tried to find an adequate word. "—autonomy. With the high brother on his mission to Tandor, Jeremy requires your support. You've been in Orrin longer than he has. He very much needs your political acumen right now. My only question is where does your loyalty lie."

"What is that supposed to mean?" She tried to keep her voice level, but it vibrated with irritation anyway.

"Is your allegiance with your Temple or your nation?"

"Well, that's interesting." She scowled at him. "Especially, since both Chief Justice Anthea and High Brother Luc have been adamant their first concern is Issura."

"And for all of her brilliance, the chief justice can be too stubborn to see a situation truly at times." He looked away for a moment before his steady gaze returned to hers. "And regardless of Istaqa's own type of idiocy, the rest of us at Light need to know we can rely on you. The high brother had justifiable concerns over your loyalty—"

"I didn't lie to him." It took all of her control to not shout at Mateqai.

"No, but you did allow yourself to be put in a position where your word would be questioned." The warden cocked his head. "Given that our former high sister of Love's lies lost the high brother his foot and too many lives in this city, did you really expect him to behave otherwise?"

Shi Hua stared at the marble in front of her boots. Mateqai was right. Oh, Light help her, Reverend Father Biming had tried to point out her mistake, but it took a warden to truly kick the lesson home.

She met Mateqai's gaze once more. "My allegiance is to Light. It can't be any other way. Not with demons on the loose."

He nodded as if her answer satisfied him. "In addition to the five spies on the street and the . . . leftovers in the gaol, another five bodies have been reported." He continued down the corridor toward the main doors of the Temple.

And had already been taken to Death, which was why Jeremy and the magistrate waited for her there.

Shi Hua hastened her pace to keep up with him. "That would bring the total to the twelve people High Sister Mya sensed in the link. All of them had demon eggs on them, didn't they?"

"And demons inside them," Mateqai said. He nodded to the Balance warden, who unlocked the doors and allowed them through.

Outside, Warden Daniel stood guard in front of the black lacquered doors. Bright sunshine glowed in a counterpoint to the dour mood on the street. Her attention swept the avenue. Traffic wasn't as prominent as it normally would be this time of day. Clusters of pedestrians huddled on the corners. The most discomfiting part was the closed entrance to Light with one of their own wardens acting as a sentinel. On a warm day like this, the huge polished oak doors should be wide open.

The small hairs on the back of her neck rose as she and Mateqai jogged down the temple steps. Spectators on the avenue watched the two of them stride down the cobblestones before they returned to trading conjectures with their companions.

"Is the entire city on edge?" she asked as they headed south down the street.

Mateqai gave her a surprised look. "Have the main alarm bells sounded in Jing during your lifetime?"

"No," she sheepishly admitted.

"Couriers have been dispatched for the capital, but the odds are the queen's army and Temple troops will be marching south before any messages reach the palace or home temples." The warden shook his head. "Maybe that's a good thing."

They both remained silent the rest of the way to Death. Again, a warden was stationed in front of the main doors of this Temple, just like the other eleven. The warden turned, and she knocked a specific rhythm. From the immediate unlocking of the doors, they were waiting on Shi Hua and Mateqai's arrival.

The second Death warden eyed them before allowing them through. For some reason, the black lacquered wood doors seemed to pronounce doom when they slammed shut and the warden on this side of the entryway shoved the bolts into place.

Mateqai escorted Shi Hua down a side corridor and to another painted door. This one was royal blue, which meant a university certified library. She expected Jeremy, Magistrate DiCook, and High Sister Bertrice, since this was her Temple after all. What she hadn't been expecting were the other nine seats already in attendance. The presence of Chief Warden Little Bear wasn't as much of a surprise. Someone from Balance had to attend this impromptu war council. The door closed quietly behind Mateqai, leaving Shi Hua feeling slightly bereft.

Bertrice crossed the room and pulled her into a huge hug. "Are you all right?" She leaned back to examine Shi Hua.

"Yes, High Sister. I'm fine." She couldn't bow without knocking her head into the other priestess's. "The justice was the only one—" Injured? Damaged? She wasn't sure how to describe what happened to her friend.

"Give the child some breathing space, Bertrice," Dragonfly admonished. The acting high sister of Love rolled her eyes. "You know Master Devin went over both her and Han with all those nasty little instruments of his."

"How's Yanaba?" Han asked. The high brother of Conflict's face held the same worry Shi Hua felt.

She shook her head. "The healers don't know yet." She turned to Mya. "If you could go back to Balance, High Sister—"

Unlike the other senior clergy, the seat of the Temple of Child was barely upright. She curled up on a large chair with arms, surrounded by lots of pillows. Her smile was sad and regretful. "I'm in no shape to aid the justice at this time. I've already appointed one of my best priests. He's preparing now."

Shi Hua approached Mya and knelt before her, but she didn't dare touch the priestess. "But it's as if her mind isn't in her body!"

Talbert stood behind Mya. His hand rested on her shoulder. "Balance always demands a price for her help, Sister," he said softly. "You're not a novice who needs to be taught that lesson. Yanaba knew there would be a sacrifice to invoke the Temple's protections."

Shi Hua focused on his hand. That's how the high sister managed to attend this meeting. He extended his quicksilver ability over her so everyone else's emotions wouldn't expose her mind to further damage. The tracing of the renegades' link she'd performed must have inflicted much more severe injuries to her psyche than Shi Hua had realized.

"I beg forgiveness, High Sister. The demons—"

Mya's lips twisted into a wry smile. "They tried to kill. They did not succeed. And our colleagues found all of the eggs. I'll be all right, but it will take some time to recover." She sighed. "Unfortunately, time is a luxury we do not have."

"Balance and Light should have told us about these blasted eggs." Bianca, who held the seat of the Temple of Mother, did not hold kindly feelings toward Anthea after Gerd, Dragonfly's predecessor at Love, had manipulated her. Shi Hua's order was simply guilty by association.

"They did if you bothered to read the chief justice's report concerning the incident onboard the duke's flagship and the Jing Embassy," Jax said dryly. The Wildling seat loved poking his counterparts just to see what would happen. "Those Twelve-forsaken renegades tried to assassinate Sister Shi Hua last fall with one of those blasted eggs."

"If you all are finished with your pissing contest, I need to borrow the Lights for a moment," Magistrate DiCook interjected.

"And what could you possibly need them for," Bianca sneered.

"Some of us are still trying to do our jobs," the magistrate drawled. "Three days ago, one of my peacekeepers and his entire family were murdered. Prior to them leaving for Tandor, the chief justice and High Brother Luc believed the Assassins Guild was behind the murders. I concur, and it might all be related to today's attacks." He inclined his head toward Shi Hua and Jeremy. "I need them because I'm down a justice, which means I need to work fast to make sure the bastards didn't have a backup plan to kill all of you."

High Father Jerrod spoke for the first time. "We have our wardens to protect us, Magistrate."

DiCook's eyes narrowed. "Nothing against the wardens, but there were twelve demons and twelve eggs within the city walls. Some of them inside your temples. If you don't want my help, that's all right with me, but I am the duly-elected magistrate of this city, and I aim to keep the rest of Orrin safe whether you like it or not."

"Are you insinuating we don't care about the people of this city?" Bianca's voice rose when she was insulted, a bit of knowledge Shi Hua filed away.

Apparently, Jing wasn't the only nation dealing with petty rivalries among the clergy.

DiCook flashed Bianca a nasty smile. "I'm not saying my house is squeaky clean, but bribes are one thing. It wasn't one of my peacekeepers dealing in demon grimoires." He waited a heartbeat before he added, "High Mother."

"Enough," Bertrice snapped. She gestured for Shi Hua to follow her. "The magistrate wanted yours and Brother Jeremy's opinions on one of the reported deaths before you destroy the rest of the eggs and demons."

"And why do you get to be a part of their conversation?" Jerrod protested.

"It's my morgue," Bertrice said sweetly.

Shi Hua tried to keep a neutral expression on her face as she followed the high sister of Death. Jeremy, DiCook, and Little Bear trailed after them. Considering the tension in the library, she wasn't sure how High Sister Mya managed. She felt like she was being smothered by the senior clergy's collective egos.

Bertrice led them to a doorway approximately in the same place as the gaol doors in Balance and Light. Shi Hua couldn't suppress her shudder after what had happened within Balance this morning.

"Are you sure you're all right?" Bertrice examined her once again.

"We're dealing with things no one in our world has for a century." Shi Hua offered her a slight smile. "If anyone else told me they were all right after demons ripped their way out of human bodies, I'd send them to Child for an examination of their mental health."

The high sister chuckled. "That's the smartest thing I've heard anyone say today. I don't suppose you could light the way."

Shi Hua produced a light ball with just enough energy to produce adequate illumination. It bobbed above their heads as they took the winding staircase down to Death's cold storage room. Bertrice unlocked a second door, and they entered.

The room was incredibly frigid after the warm sunshine of earlier. Special alabaster lamps charged with magic provided the light by which the clergy of Death worked. Ice blocks packed with sawdust formed the walls. Any extra heat, such as that of oil lamps, would make the ice melt faster.

Wooden shelving stood in front of the ice walls. The shelves themselves were wide and long enough to hold an average-sized man, and every single shelf contained a corpse. Several of the bodies were oddly contorted. Thankfully, they were all covered.

A black basalt block formed a table in the middle of the room, and a white-covered figure lay on top. Like some of the other corpses, it was an unusual size and shape. As if two bodies were merged into one.

Or one body tried to separate into two.

Shi Hua jerked at movement near her, and she belatedly realized there were two of the living among the dead. Bertrice's second Xander conferred quietly with the other man who dressed as a warden of Death. It took her a moment to realize he wasn't a warden, but Master Healer Devin.

Given that the Healers Guild broke away from the Temple of Death decades ago, High Sister Bertrice had to resort to subterfuge for a healer to consult on a suspicious death when the chief justice wasn't around to bully any recalcitrant clergy into agreement.

The healer grinned at Shi Hua. "Still intact I see, Sister."

"For now." She returned his smile. "It's not for the lack of effort on the part of the Assassins Guild."

Magistrate DiCook stepped forward and flipped off the sheet. "I want your opinions on this."

Blond hair stood out against the bluish-white skin of the deformed corpse. Such colors were unusual for this part of the world, but not unheard of, especially with the influx of settlers and skilled tradespeople from the northwestern quarter of the Old Continent after the Chumash had been decimated in this region a few centuries ago. However, it was the thing tearing its way out of the body's abdomen that bothered her the most.

Shi Hua looked at Magistrate DiCook. "Who is she?"

"According to Justice Yanaba's review of the timeline, she looks just like the woman who poisoned Peacekeeper Dante and his family." The magistrate hooked his thumbs in his belt and rocked on his heels.

She remembered when the request for assistance came three days ago. High Brother Luc had insisted on going himself and left the negotiations over a series of grain shipments in her hands. His reasoning had been she needed to review some of the basic responsibilities as a member of the Temple of Light. She'd resented his implication at the time. Now, she wished desperately he and the chief justice hadn't left Orrin.

"Take a closer look at the deformations," Little Bear said quietly.

Jeremy bent over the corpse's head and frowned. "She's not showing the skin damage I would expect for a crushed skull."

Shi Hua turned to Little Bear. "You only found skins in the gaol cells, didn't you?"

He nodded.

Shi Hua tried to sort out the information, but her soul wanted to curl up in a ball on her bed with her covers over her head. "So are the skinwalkers actually demons?"

"Not according to Gina's grandmother who's Diné." The corner of Little Bear's mouth quirked. "Skinwalkers are people so corrupted by demon magic they are no longer truly human."

Jeremy nodded to himself as he circled the corpse, examining it. "This is a perfect disguise for infiltrating the enemy. The demons could have taught the skinwalkers the trick. It's not like humans siding with those bastards is unheard of."

He crouched at eye level with the body before he glanced at the healer. "When did you realize there were no bones in the head and chest?"

"When I realized it looked like my undershirt without me in it," Master Devin said dryly. "You deliver enough babies and you learn to see a second being's structure through the woman's womb." He pointed at the obscenely distended lump in the corpse's chest. "That's the demon's head."

"Their magic must preserve the human skin somehow," Shi Hua mused. "Enough so that the Temple alarm didn't register the actual demons underneath until they ripped their way out of their flesh suits."

"But the eggs—" Bertrice started.

"Were spell-shielded somehow," Shi Hua said. "Given Prince Alika's rank, they expected Brother Jeremy to attend the trial." An unamused chuckle forced its way out of her. "For once, I wasn't the primary target. The assassination of the prince was merely a distraction in order to plant the eggs on Yanaba and Jeremy. When she activated the main Temple wards, they must have cut through any glamor or shield protecting the eggs."

"I doubt if they cared which Light priest they killed," Little Bear growled. "They would have been ecstatic if they managed to kill all three of you."

But the chief warden's grumbling faded as Shi Hua noticed her fellow Light priest staring at the corpse. "What is it? What are you seeing?"

Jeremy muttered an oath under his breath. "The demons are still alive."

Both Xander and Devin exhaled, and their breath steamed. Xander nodded. "That was our conclusion as well."

Shi Hua mulled the implications. "When High Sister Mya turned their killing spell back on them, it incapacitated them?"

Bertrice tilted her head as she regarded the thing on the slab. "We think it was a combination. Mya did incapacitate them momentarily, but it was Yanaba's initiation of Balance's defensive spells that froze them."

Shi Hua looked over at Jeremy. "You're being terribly quiet."

"They're not just frozen." He shook his head. "They're terribly old."

"Of course." Bertrice nodded. "Balance can manipulate time to a certain extent. The protection spells would accelerate time to kill the invaders through old age."

"But it only went forward far enough for bones and wood to decompose," Shi Hua said. "The metal and stone in the courtroom were still intact."

"Not totally intact," Jeremy murmured. When she looked at him, he said, "Those showed signs of unusual wear. However, they would last much longer than animal or plant material. And the effects were more intense the closer they were to Yanaba. The only exception was the statue of Balance and the base on which you and Han stood."

"This makes sense though," Devin interjected. When everyone looked at him, he waved his hands. "According to the old lore, it took all Twelve Temples working in unison to stop the invasions. No one power is superior to the others. It takes all of them working together."

DiCook nodded. "It also explains why the renegades are working so damn hard to sow dissension between the Temples themselves—"

"Not to mention between us, the nobility, and the populace," Xander said.

"And we're down one Temple," Shi Hua said softly.

"Not really." Bertrice's smile had a rueful quality when she gazed at Little Bear. "The Balance staff ran their own damn Temple after Penelope lost her mind. They may not have the magic, but they have the knowledge."

He inclined his head at Bertrice's compliment.

Shi Hua fidgeted. She'd been so used to keeping secrets. Like the priesthood of Thief, staying silent had become second nature to her. But after what she saw during the destruction of the demons and their minions in the courtroom, maybe they did have more help than they realized.

She turned to Jeremy. "I don't believe we're as alone as we think when it comes to Balance."

His brows drew together. "What do you mean?"

The chief justice trusted the living people in the morgue. Shi Hua's recounting of Yanaba's spell spilled out of her, including the strange figure she saw. When she finished, she waited, expecting them to tell her she was mad.

Little Bear frowned. "Are you sure you saw Anthea?"

Shi Ha shrugged helplessly. "I couldn't see her eyes. Her cowl covered them. But the lower face, especially the jawline, resembled the chief justice. The nose wasn't as prominent though, so—" She lifted her hands in a helpless gesture. "I'm not sure of anything at this point, Chief Warden. I believe in the Twelve, but I've never had an experience like this. If it were the Goddess Herself answering Yanaba's prayers, why would she look like one of Her priestesses?"

Bertrice and DiCook stared at each other.

"I don't believe in ghosts," the high sister said.

The magistrate shook his head. "I was a new groom of twenty winters when that last pirate attack occurred. I don't know if I'd recognize her now. Did High Brother Han mention seeing someone else in Balance robes during the justice's spell?"

"No, he didn't." Bertrice ran her hand through her short silver hair. "But then, he was assigned to Orrin twelve years ago. He might have thought he was hallucinating. Or that he saw the Goddess. Assuming he did see the woman Shi Hua describes."

"It couldn't be her." DiCook stared at the demon in its human skin for a moment before he added, "But then, they never did find her body, and it never washed up on shore."

Shi Hua hugged herself and tried to blame her goosebumps on the ice. "What are you two implying?"

"Would you allow me to see your memory?" Bertrice inclined her head toward DiCook. "And then share it with the magistrate?"

Shi Hua glanced at Jeremy, who nodded. Good, he was as curious as she was. "Only if you tell me why first."

Bertrice shared another nervous look with the magistrate. "We think the person you saw was Justice Thalia, Anthea's grandmother."

Chapter 21

I went to visit Quan while Luc and one of the civilian women argued the finer points of cornmeal porridge recipes in the kitchen. Hadar had put the Jing ambassador in the former chief warden's quarters to rest.

When I entered, Quan definitely was not resting. He looked up from a scroll he read at the previous occupant's desk and smiled. Or tried to. The swelling on the right side of his jaw transformed the expression into a grotesque parody. "To what do I owe this pleasant distraction, Chief Justice?"

"I came to see how you were feeling."

He chuckled. "Come now, Lady Justice. I thought you and I were beyond such subterfuge."

I clasped my hands behind my back. "Very well then, I need you intact. Have you had any contact with Shi Hua?"

His smile fell. "Given our projected arrival in Tandor, I knew I wouldn't have any news for Orrin or Chengzhou until First Night today. I can only hope to hear from her at our designated time." He leaned back in his chair. "I take neither you nor High Brother Luc have been able to gain her attention."

"It hasn't been for lack of trying."

"That's the problem with distance speaking. They have to find you." He set the scroll aside. "Shi Hua, Yanaba, and Jeremy are intelligent, capable young clergy. They would give their lives before they would let anything happen to your precious city."

"That's exactly what I fear given the alarm bells in Orrin were activated twice today," I murmured.

"You must have faith your city has not fallen." He picked up another scroll.

"However, I did find some interesting reading from Justice Elizabeth's chief warden. Would you like to hear?"

I'd learned over the course of our acquaintance over the last five months that when the ambassador found something "interesting", it was very significant.

"Very much." I crossed the room and perched on the edge of the bed.

Quan must truly be in pain since he didn't make any remarks regarding the bed or us being alone. Either that, or leaving the door open was one of my better decisions in the last three days.

"Most of this is his duty log, but there are some pertinent personal observations. Here we go." He held the scroll at an angle for the best illumination from his single oil lamp. "This is an entry from the twentieth day of summer."

A chill ran through me. I had been tried and sentenced seven days prior to the warden writing this note.

"'Our clerk Minerva acted in a most unusual manner after returning from the Temple of Light this afternoon. When I mentioned having a reception to welcome the two new wardens recently assigned to Light, she told me not to bother. She normally assists me with such planning. When I said not doing so was rude, she told me that groveling to other temples was beneath Balance.'"

I rested my elbows on my knees. "So he's very courteous, and we have the benefit of hindsight—"

Quan shot me an annoyed look. "There's more, and you need to hear it all. The next entry is dated twenty-one days later." He resumed reading. "'Minerva has been avoiding me since we parted ways. When I caught her after court yesterday, I asked her why. She would not tell me. However, when I entered my quarters today after training with the Conflict wardens, I found her rifling through my reports and journals. When I asked her what she was doing, she claimed she was searching for her personal belongings. I told her I had returned everything. She accused me of lying and stormed out of my quarters.'"

I dropped my face into my hands. "Balance help us. I can see where this is going."

"Do you think everything at your temple would still be efficient if Little Bear and Sivan parted ways?" Quan asked.

I lifted my head and glared at him. "None of your business and continue reading."

He chuckled some more. "'Fiftieth day of summer. Spoke with my counterpart at Thief. Conflict's second Tighan is highly irritated he was passed over for the seat. Allegedly, the wardens at Conflict are taking sides in the matter. I passed my concerns to the justice.'"

Elizabeth hadn't said anything to me, and when we did the mutual truthspelling session, I hadn't known to ask about her staff's observations.

Quan continued reading. "'Sixty-first day of summer. I was headed to my quarters when I heard noises in the courtroom. I investigated and discovered Minerva in the middle of intimate relations with Ural DiSand, a prominent merchant and a close friend of the duke's. I don't think I would have minded as much if they weren't on the dais and in front of Balance herself.'"

I straightened. "That isn't amusing, even to me."

"Nor me, m'lady." He returned to the chief warden's account. "'Sixty-fifth day of summer. Duke Enzo passed today, the fourth death this week. Something is odd about Duchess Nadine's reaction to the loss of both her son and her husband in such a short period. While I want to investigate, the magistrate insists they are all from natural causes, and it's simply our bad luck, or in the case of the duke, heartbreak. The justice said she would consider my petition.'"

Quan looked up at me. "The other three deaths before Duke Enzo were his infant son of course, the city's chief healer, and Ural DiSand's main rival, a merchant named Amarantha DiRoma. In all fairness, three of the four were over forty winters. A heart seizure or a brain storm isn't unheard of at that age. Nor is an infant's death from a fever."

"Did Elizabeth grant his petition?"

Quan shrugged. "You would have to ask her. That was his last entry."

Balance help us. He would have been poisoned at dinner that very night.

The ambassador set the scroll aside. "I heard all of the priests and priestesses trapped here participated in a mutual truthspell this afternoon. Are you sure you trust Justice Elizabeth?"

Balance, I wished I was on my old circuit again. It had been tedious at times, but the problems had been the normal problems between humans. Not this political intrigue where innocents were pawns and no one was safe.

When the silence stretched too long, he added, "Even I realize you have to know the right questions to ask."

I glared at him. "She's willing to give up her life to cover our escape."

He made a disgusted sound low in his throat. "You are not that stupid, Anthea."

"No." I rose. "I'm not. I also don't trust anyone these days."

Quan cocked his head. "Not even Luc?"

I snorted at the ambassador's teasing. "Him least of all."

New questions fluttered through my mind as I stalked out of the room. Quan wasn't stupid either. Maybe he was couching his terms carefully, knowing the skinwalker's non-corporeal form haunted the hallways of the temple. Or he could be steering me toward the target he desired to eliminate.

Or maybe I let old sentimentality for one of the few people to show me any kindness in my life cloud my judgment.

After our meal, my lack of rest the night before caught up with me, and I took a nap in the wardens' barracks. I couldn't have been asleep more than a candlemark or two when Reby shook me awake.

"The renegades are trying something new, Lady Justice."

I rolled off the bed, pulled on my borrowed boots, and followed her to the back porch. The sickly sweet stench of death filled the air. Aduba, Luc, and one of the younger Death priests watched through the roof slats. I crouched next to Luc's chair and peered at what had gained their attention.

Crude gallows were set atop the garden walls of the neighboring Temples. Cold blue bodies swung from the gibbets. Hanging had been outlawed for centuries after the Temples had learned the demons could siphon the energy of the slow deaths.

We may have destroyed the demon eggs, but the sight of something so taboo had its effect on all of us. "Does anybody recognize them?" I asked softly.

"I thought you could see," Aduba remarked.

I smirked up at him. "In a manner of speaking. Surely, Elizabeth has mentioned how I tried to remove myself from Balance's service?"

He laughed, a deep baritone note. "Everyone in the Long Continents and quite a bit of the Cradle has heard that story, but what does that have to do with your sight?"

"If I gave you a tail like the Southern Long Continent monkeys, would you know how to swing from a tree limb with it?" I asked.

"Ah, so since you were born blind . . ." He tapped his nose. "Point taken, m'lady." He looked back up at the corpses, swaying in the slight breeze. "The two on Mother are our city's cobbler and his eldest son. They were killed earlier on the street when the skinwalker dragged you into Balance. The two on Knowledge are their wives. Their deaths were not as merciful."

I didn't need an explanation for the two additional poles on each roof. Their presence was warning enough of what would happen to more civilians if we didn't surrender. I rested my hand on Luc's arm. "We go tonight?"

"We go tonight," he growled.

Chapter 22

Shi Hua blinked as the shock of High Sister Bertrice's words settled into her. She had attended the funerals last month of those members of the Temples the renegades had murdered. Ambassador Quan had insisted the Jing embassy staff be present at the state funerals, even though she'd planned to go anyway since one of those killed had been High Brother Kam of Light, Luc's predecessor. Along with everyone else attending, she had heard Chief Justice Anthea's story of Kam's deathbed confession, that he was her maternal grandfather due to his blasphemous and illegal affair with Thalia, the former chief justice of Orrin.

But Bertrice's idea of the ghost of Thalia haunting the Temple of Balance . . .

"That's impossible," Shi Hua said. "Wouldn't she be seventy winters now?"

"Seventy-one," Bertrice said absently.

"The woman I saw definitely wasn't that old," Shi Hua protested. "Besides, I was only reassigned to Orrin's Temple of Light last month. Surely if this were Justice Thalia, she'd reveal herself to High Brother Han, too, as a long-standing seat even if they didn't personally know each other! She died long before I was born!"

Bertrice's focus returned to the here and now, and she smiled. "Child, you have the unusual talent for walking more Temple paths than the rest of us. I wouldn't be a bit surprised if Balance staked her claim on you as well. That's part of why I'd like to take a look at your memory."

Shi Hua turned to Jeremy, more than willing to defer to him in this insane idea.

He rose to his full height and shrugged. "I'm curious myself, but I'm not going to force you into a link, Sister."

A little sliver of relief wound through her. Jeremy trusted her. He wasn't going to be cruel as Luc had been over a misunderstanding because of her sloppy handling of information. It was her decision to enter the link. And she found she wanted someone to tell her she wasn't insane, considering what she saw in the Balance courtroom.

She locked eyes with Bertrice. "High Sister, would you mind if we not perform the link down here?"

"Oh, I wholly agree with you on that count." Bertrice chuckled before she turned to Jeremy. "When would you like to start with the demons, Brother?"

"I hate to even suggest this, but—" He looked at the ancient demon again. "This may be an excellent opportunity for the other Temples to practice their skills. As both Master Devin and Sister Shi Hua have pointed out, we've forgotten how to fight the demons in just four generations. We need to relearn and quickly."

Bertrice looked at the demon, too. "Let's have this discussion upstairs. I have a bad feeling that these things are listening to everything we say."

Once upstairs, Jeremy suggested they perform the memory viewing later that evening after dinner at his Temple. Given that the other nine seats were waiting in Bertrice's library, the high sister reluctantly agreed. No one asked why. Jerrod and Bianca would protest Little Bear representing Balance no matter the current circumstances. And they would accuse Bertrice of betraying her Temple if she allowed any healer, much less Devin, to attend a convocation, even if it was an informal one.

Shi Hua suppressed a sigh. Part of her was relieved, but Jeremy's plan only delayed the inevitable.

While Little Bear and Devin left to attend their other duties, Jeremy and Shi Hua followed Bertrice back to her library. Their entrance immediately drew the attention of the other nine seats, each with varying expectancy and annoyance in eight of their faces. Jax wore his perpetual expression of amusement.

"Well?" Father Jerrod asked impatiently.

"The five below were all demons wearing human skins," Jeremy said, a defiant lift to his chin. "And they're still alive."

Shocked silence met his pronouncement.

High Sister Mariana of Knowledge finally asked, "Did you destroy them?"

She's close to Thalia's age, Shi Hua silently said to Jeremy. *Would she recognize the justice?*

"No," Jeremy answered both aloud and silently. *Mariana was named to Orrin's Knowledge seat after Thalia's death*, he added to Shi Hua.

"By the Twelve, why not?" Han exclaimed.

"Because Justice Yanaba is trapped in the same spell she used to freeze them." The realization of what had happened to her friend hit Shi Hua as she said the words. "If we burn them, we'll kill her."

Surprise emanated from Jeremy, but his expression didn't change.

Jerrod frowned. "Of course. The girl must have slipped up casting the spell."

Shi Hua glared at him. "More likely she sacrificed herself because they were outside her reach, and she knew Jeremy would destroy them for her." The words came out far more harshly than she intended.

Jerrod's face turned poppy red. "How dare you."

"Foreign bitch," Bianca muttered.

Bertrice stepped between Shi Hua and the two seats. "After the conduct from both of you last month, you're lucky you still have your precious positions—"

"Enough!" Han's voice cut through the words and tension in the room. He turned to Jeremy and Shi Hua. "You two have an idea of how to extricate Yanaba without setting those blasted things loose again?"

Shi Hua exchanged looks with Jeremy before she said, "Maybe. But we'll need a little time to put it together."

"'Maybe' isn't good enough, Sister," High Brother Ben of Vintner said, but his words had no bite. "We cannot let those things loose." He shot a glance at Talbert, and a half-smile appeared on Ben's face. "Thief was watching over us today. I doubt we will be as lucky a second time if we don't destroy those things now."

Jeremy folded his arms over his chest, a mirror of their own high brother's stubborn stance. "All we're asking for is a few candlemarks to go through the Balance records and a meal before we try to free Justice Yanaba. If it can't be done, we'll quickly find out, and we'll destroy the demons downstairs. But I'd prefer to try to salvage a priestess if we can. We've lost too many clergy to these damn renegades and their demon masters already."

Mya smiled. "Well said, Brother. Not even Balance Herself could come up with a more logical plan."

Han nodded. "My people and I will help you guard the demons until Light is ready, Bertrice."

She sighed. "Thank you. I'll have to . . ." Her voice faltered, and she shook her head. "In all my years, I never thought I'd have to prepare to activate Death's defenses."

"Until Second Evening then, sirs and ladies." Jeremy inclined his head to the seats, pivoted on his booted toe, and marched from the library.

Shi Hua hurried after him. Wardens Nicholas and Mateqai fell in step behind them as they exited the Temple of Death.

They were halfway back to Light when Jeremy spoke. "I hope you weren't blowing smoke up their collective asses back there."

She sighed. "You and me both. Remember the spell-in-the-box stunt the chief justice pulled in the Jing embassy last autumn?"

"Are you joking?" He shook his head. "I still have nightmares about that afternoon."

"That makes two of us." Her wry smile faded as she looked up at him. "I think Yanaba tried a variation of that, but without defined solid surfaces, she used something else."

He frowned. "Like what? The city walls?"

She shrugged. "Maybe."

"Or she used her soul," Mateqai said.

Jeremy and Shi Hua both stopped short, whirled around, and stared at the warden. Even Nicholas looked at him askance.

Mateqai shrugged. "I'm a passive. Spent a few years studying at Knowledge before I transferred to the Warden Academy."

Her facial muscles tightened as she gave him a wicked grin. "You and I are going over to Balance before our dinner meeting. We're going to put your Knowledge experience to the test."

Maybe, just maybe, they might have a chance at saving Yanaba after all.

Chapter 23

I shared Quan's discovery with Luc as we searched the Balance storeroom for kits to carry supplies for our flight into the desert. I'd already borrowed a set of robes from Elizabeth to protect me from the cold, but I'd feel a lot better if I could wear a proper uniform.

Especially since desert nights would be as chill as days were hot.

Luc shook his head. *All these oddities make sense in hindsight, but taken one at a time, I can see why Elizabeth didn't notice them. Especially given they came on the heels of a relationship dissolution.*

It's the rapid occurrence of the deaths that bothers me. That and the fact that Elizabeth's staff didn't have Sivan and Deborah's organizational skills. I shoved the box of yarn I'd just searched back on its shelf. *Could the renegades have recruited Duchess Nadine?*

It's possible. But given what they've done to Dav, it's just as likely the skinwalkers may have possessed her. Luc shuffled to the next set of shelves.

A shiver ran through me. *This is too similar to the events in Orrin with Duke Marco's parents last summer.*

All part of the same plot. The renegades panicked and got sloppy once they learned you can see demons. If the Assassins Guild hadn't rushed trying to kill you, if they had continued playing their long game and made your death look like an accident or illness, they would have taken Orrin, too. "I found the water skins," he said aloud.

"Good. Those are more important than equipment bags." I yanked another box from the shelves and touched the contents. "Blessed Balance, I found uniform tunics."

Why are you assuming Orrin defeated the demons? I silently added as I searched for one that would fit me and another for Tyra.

Because I trust Jeremy. He killed the demon in our tunnels and saved our asses.

I think we need to truthspell Elizabeth again, I said as I tossed two tunics over my shoulder and continued my examination of box contents on the next set of shelves.

"Quit shopping for new clothes. We still need the packs to carry supplies," Luc said. He slung waterskin straps over his head. *What knowledge do you think she possesses that you absolutely must retrieve before she sacrifices herself?*

I found leggings in the next box and held each pair to my lower half. *I don't know. And that's the other problem.* Only one pair long enough to fit me, but there were a couple that should fit Tyra. No luck finding footwear my size in the third box, though I did find a pair for my warden. I was stuck with the soft sand boots.

What do you mean?

Finally, my fingers found equipment bags. I divided the packs and stuffed the majority into three. *What if she hasn't been compromised by the skinwalker? We've lost too many clergy to these fools. Remember the stasis spell I stashed in the transport casket to trap the demon at the Jing embassy?*

Yes. Even with silent speech, he drawled the word.

I grinned at him. *I have an idea to trap and kill the skinwalker as well as save Elizabeth.*

He hobbled over to me with his load of waterskins. *What if Elizabeth doesn't want to be saved?*

"I'm going to give her the same choice she gave me in Standora sixteen years ago," I replied.

Thankfully, the renegades hadn't bothered to clean out the Balance armory either when they took the Temples. At least, we weren't leaving the junior priests and priestesses remaining behind totally defenseless. After I set secondary wards on the kitchen entrance to the Temple, we assembled in the courtroom to divide the equipment and food.

I didn't have to ask Elizabeth if she had completed her task. Her secondary wards in the courtroom grated like sand along my senses.

Without the temple bells and with my disturbed sleep pattern, I couldn't tell what hour it was. According to Hadar's reading of the stars he could view from the back porch, it was near Second Evening when I wrapped my fellow justice's arm around my elbow and guided her to the top of the dais.

I felt a little more myself wearing a Balance uniform again when I turned to face the small crowd around us. "The instant Elizabeth and I bring down the major wards, our opponents will flood into this temple. If Thief is with us tonight, they'll assume it's a trick and delay their entry. Hopefully, that will give us enough time to evacuate."

"And if it doesn't?" the civilian woman who had been arguing recipes with Luc called out.

"Then you retreat back here to the courtroom," Elizabeth said firmly. "We'll re-engage the wards."

"To face dying of thirst while those bastards wait us out." The woman snorted. "I'll take my chances in your tunnels."

"This situation is exactly what the original builders of the temples planned for," I said dryly. "A way to get to safety when a city was under siege."

"If any of you have changed your minds about heading east with Chief Justice Anthea to seek allies, now's the time to say so," Elizabeth said. "Once she and Sisquoc tell me each group is clear of Balance, Dav and I will bring the temple down on as many of these bastards as we can."

As one, every person in the room turned to look at the Light priest. He sat in the corner where the clerk's benches and tables normally rested, rocking and muttering the same two phrases over and over, "It's in here. Please kill me."

"With all due respect, Justice, you cannot be serious!" The civilian man standing next to the first speaker gestured in Dav's direction. "The high brother's mind is gone. How is he going to help you?"

"I'll be here until the last moment," I said firmly. "In case those of you with Brother Sisquoc's group run into trouble. Dav's condition is why Elizabeth volunteered to stay behind. We need help. All of you heard the alarm bell today. There may be more demons in Tandor—"

"And you're racing into the desert because you're afraid," another civilian male spat.

Luc hobbled to the front of the group. "If you have a better idea how to save Tandor, we want to hear it. In case you forgot everything the brothers and sisters of Knowledge taught all of you as children, the alarm bell wasn't triggered here in Tandor. It was an echo of the alarm bell at the Temple of Balance in Orrin. We don't dare take you north because we haven't heard from the distance speaker at my own Temple."

The man couldn't meet Luc's gaze.

Aduba stepped up beside Luc. "The skinwalker disabled our own alarms, and Justice Elizabeth spent a good chunk of the day re-establishing the spells here. Part of what she will do is set off her own alarm bell to let the rest of Issura know what's happened to Tandor. But we're caught between Orrin, which may be lost, and Cant, where these damn traitors have riled our neighbors into thinking the Mecas and Issura are about to invade them. What exactly would you have us do, Master Weaver?"

Their argument sounded like it was a repeat of one that had probably happened earlier between the high brother of Conflict and the craftsman.

Reby stepped forward as well. "Enough debate. We're losing precious night cover. We need to leave now."

Her sharp words stirred the civilians into action. In the end, the same three civilians were heading east with us, a peacekeeper and two young men from the Butchers Guild. Two of the Death priests and the wolf Wildling remained in the city with Sisquoc and the civilians.

Luc paused and looked at me. *Don't stay too long.*

I won't. I winked at him before he followed the two groups filing out of the courtroom.

Aduba would wait in the tunnel for me as long as he dared while Luc and Nantan led the rest out. I sure as Balance couldn't carry Elizabeth all the way to the Valley of the Lost, much less across that cursed wasteland. But I could get her to her own chambers.

The thump of Luc's crutches disappeared down the hall.

Heart hammering, I turned to Elizabeth. "Are you ready, sister?"

Before she could answer, another voice did. "What are you two petty worms up to?"

"Dav?" Elizabeth's voice was barely a whisper.

"Not exactly." From the cadence of his voice, his body movements, and the greenish-yellow cast of his skin, it wasn't the high brother who addressed us. He rose to his feet. The blanket covering him dropped to the floor. He gripped a sword with which he mockingly saluted us.

I drew my own blade. "How did you manage to get a weapon?"

The skinwalker laughed as he stalked toward me. "Your precious peasants cannot count."

"Do it, Elizabeth." I inserted myself between the skinwalker and my fellow justice.

The buzz in the back of my mind disappeared as we dropped the Temple's main wards, and the deep sound of the Balance alarm thrummed through my body. The skinwalker raised his sword, and I parried his first strike.

Chapter 24

"Light bless you, Sivan," Shi Hua murmured when Balance's head of the household produced both Anthea's notes on the bastardized spell that had saved Quan and the Jing embassy staff last autumn and the Balance grimoire with the primary spell. That relief pushed away the discomfort of being in the chief justice's private quarters without her present.

Sivan blushed. "I'm sorry I only managed to enter the written notes into her personal papers. I was supposed to give them to Donella for dissemination to the home temple and Knowledge. I just . . ."

"You knew where to find what I needed." Shi Hua skimmed the written notes before she looked at Sivan. "Do you know if Yanaba knew about this time-line freeze?"

Balance's head of household held up her hands in a helpless gesture. "I couldn't presume to know for sure."

Chief Warden Little Bear frowned over his partner's shoulder. "You suspect Yanaba tried one of Anthea's damn fool stunts."

Shi Hua nodded. "However, I can't take credit for the idea." She waved toward Mateqai. "It was my warden's notion. We think she may have tried to piggyback High Sister Mya's empathic trace and freeze the demons in order to destroy them. The problem was that five of the demons were outside of Balance's walls."

"When she tried to reach them, she may have extended her mind too far and became trapped in the spell herself," Mateqai added.

"Balance help us!" Sivan started pacing the chamber.

"But you don't know for sure." Little Bear raised a questioning eyebrow.

"No." Shi Hua shook her head.

"Could the other person you mentioned be keeping her body alive?" he asked hopefully.

Damn. She'd forgotten he was in the morgue when she confessed her vision to High Sister Bertrice. However, he must not have mentioned her story to Sivan. She looked as equally confused as Mateqai.

Shi Hua shrugged. "I don't know. We're guessing about everything at this point." She wanted to hit something to relieve her frustration.

"Here." Sivan waggled her fingers for the page from the chief justice's official record. "Let me stamp out a quick copy of Anthea's notes so we have them, and you can take it and the Balance grimoire with you to study before your dinner this evening.

"I don't want to take your only copy of the Temple grimoire," Shi Hua protested.

"We have . . ." Sivan's voice faltered for a moment before she collected herself. "Yanaba has her personal copy as well as the two we have in the Balance library." It only took her a moment to make a copy of the altered spell with the raised code the stamps created.

"Thank you, Sivan." Shi Hua tucked the parchment back into the grimoire and placed them in her satchel. The same bag with her necessaries for court she'd collected this morning. Except entering the courtroom seemed like it had happened days ago, not hours.

"I'd like to check on Yanaba before we leave." She bobbed her head. "If you don't mind."

"Of course." But Sivan's smile was too sad to be reassuring.

Nor was Mateqai about to let her out of her sight. He followed Shi Hua and Sivan to Yanaba's room. Outside the door to her bedchambers, Warden Gina stood with Master Healer Aaron, one of his journeywomen, and a warden from Child. The familiar tingle of wards danced along Shi Hua's skin.

"What's going on?" Sivan asked. Her gaze darted between the two men and a furrow creased her brow.

"Brother Turtle needed some space and quiet to work," Gina said.

At Shi Hua's side, her fingers made the youthful gesture for good luck. If the priest from Child could help Yanaba, Jeremy and she wouldn't have to worry about harming the justice when they destroyed the demons stored in Death.

The tingle faded from her skin a moment or two before the door to the bedchambers opened. Brother Turtle stepped out, a short round-faced man Shi Hua didn't remember meeting before. His shape resembled his public name. His somber expression told the story before he said a word.

"The justice simply isn't there." Brother Turtle shook his head. "I don't understand how she is breathing or how her heart is even beating. There's no connection. No thread. She—" He scrubbed his face as if he could scrub away the dark circles under his eyes and the lines etched in his skin. "The only time I feel this . . . emptiness is when the soul leaves the body." He held his hands up in a helpless gesture.

Shi Hua exchanged a glance with Mateqai before she addressed the other priest. "We think we know where she is, but has there been any instances in your records of retrieved souls being put back?"

Brother Turtle's round brown eyes slowly blinked. "There's quite a bit of lore about those whose hearts or lungs have stopped and they claim to see Death and Light before medical aid is rendered, but the other way around?" He shook his head. "No. There has always been a bit of soul still attached to the body to bring them back."

"Would you be willing to help Sister Shi Hua later?" Mateqai asked. "She and Brother Jeremy believe the justice has become trapped in her own spell."

Everyone turned to stare at him. Rarely did a warden speak out of turn to those in their assigned Temple, but to do so with another priest was unheard of.

Brother Turtle tilted his head as he regarded the request. Finally, he nodded. "Yes, but I need the high sister's approval. And—" His wry smile gave him some life. "I need to leave you for rest, or I'll be unable to assist you tonight."

"We're meeting at Light. You're welcome to join us for dinner," Shi Hua offered.

Turtle held up a hand. "I thank you for the invitation, but I won't be much use to you if I socialize before we try this retrieval. I will research the matter and join you, say, a candlemark past First Evening."

"You have my gratitude, Brother." She bowed. *Please Lord Light don't let me be wrong about this.*

By the time the Temple bells rang First Evening, Shi Hua wondered if she'd be blind and crippled before this madness was over. She stretched and bent her fingers, trying to ease the shaking and cramping. Mateqai had been a Lightsend with his perfect memory as she worked out the possibilities of how to extract Yanaba from her own spell. She could see why he'd been shunted to Knowledge at first.

When she rose and stretched her back, she realized what was really bothering her. The Temple library was quiet. Too quiet. She'd gotten used to Jeremy making jokes, or Chief Warden Nicholas's grunting every time he shifted in his chair while he read one of the histories. Or even Istaqa fussing at her for bringing tea into the library.

"How did you end up at Light?" she asked as she donned her harness. Wearing weapons to dinner would have earned a stern reprimand back in Chengzhou, but here in Orrin, it had become standard procedure. Given everything that happened since last summer, no one from any of the Temples went anywhere unarmed.

Mateqai chuckled. "When it became obvious I would never develop an active talent, they tested my suitability for other occupations. I had excellent scores in weapons and strategy so I chose the Wardens Academy, and I couldn't activate a spell from any other Temple but Light."

She gathered her notes, and they headed down the hallway to the high brother's dining room. This morning in the temple bath, Jeremy had suggested they invite Yanaba to Light for this very meal. Now, it had turned into a desperate attempt to save the justice's life.

Jeremy, High Sister Bertrice, and Magistrate DiCook were seated when she and Mateqai arrived. Chief Warden Nicholas, a warden from Death, and a peacekeeper stood against three of the dining room's wall, flicking suspicious glances at each other.

Mateqai leaned close to Shi Hua's ear. "Am I supposed to stand and act intimidating, too?"

"No." Magistrate DiCook pointed at the empty chair next to Jeremy. "This insanity is as much your responsibility as theirs." He waved his hand to indicate the two Light clergy.

"I beg your pardon," the acting high brother had an affronted expression, but she knew it was a sham. "You are not the host."

"Really?" DiCook glared at Jeremy. "You're going to adapt Istaqa's etiquette routine now?" He jabbed a thumb at his own man. "Your wardens already have my peacekeepers and the duke's guards in a paranoid uproar."

Just as Shi Hua and Mateqai took their seats, the dining room door burst open. Chairs crashed to the floor, and everyone reached for their weapons before the realization it was Little Bear sank in.

"Forgive my tardiness—" His eyes widened a bit as he took in the tableau. "And the next time, I will knock before one of you accidentally slices my throat."

Jeremy eyed DiCook. "I see what you mean about the paranoia."

The magistrate grunted and slid his half-drawn sword back into its scabbard.

The food itself was light. Cold venison, boiled potatoes, and dried blackberries. She and Mateqai took turns relaying what they'd learned between bites.

"It's not much different than when a justice replays a timeline outdoors," Shi Hua said. "She uses natural barriers, a tree line, a garden hedge, a row of flowers, as one of their anchor points. Inside, it's the same thing as any other clergy warding a space. We need length, width and depth. Only Balance deals with the fourth factor, time itself."

She pulled out her sketch. "Since Yanaba had to reach outside of the Temple of Balance to find all the demons, she used the walls of Orrin. However, we are not landlocked, and our other border is the sea shore. But the shoreline is constantly changing. Waves and tides are affected by the motion of the moon. Yanaba had to let go of her body in order to anchor the time effect of the moon on the shore."

Bertrice's eyes narrowed. "If Yanaba let go of her body, how is she alive?"

"That was Brother Turtle's question when he examined her this afternoon," Shi Hua answered. "Like I said before, we're getting help. Someone, something is keeping her body going until we can put her back."

"A woman cutting off her soul isn't like spilling dried beans on the floor!" DiCook slapped his hand on the table.

"No, it isn't," Jeremy said quietly.

"Then why do you think she can be put back?" DiCook spat.

"That's why I still want to see Shi Hua's memory," Bertrice said. "Her vision may be the key to recovering Yanaba."

"You want proof of who I saw in Balance earlier today." Shi Hua shook her head. "I don't know if I can offer that."

Bertrice leaned her elbows on the table and smiled. "If you saw a woman who was dead before you were born, that will satisfy me as proof the Twelve are helping us." She turned to DiCook. "Would it satisfy you though?"

"I—" DiCook's mouth opened and closed twice before he slumped in his chair. "You're the one dealing in faith, Sister. If you say it's her, then . . . yeah, it'll satisfy me."

Bertrice faced Shi Hua again. "Are you ready, Sister?"

"Yes, m'lady." She rose and took the seat Little Bear vacated next to the high sister.

Bertrice clasped Shi Hua's hand in her right one. "Let me do the work. You need your strength to save Yanaba." With her left, she took the magistrate's hand.

"How come you aren't asking if I'm ready?" DiCook grumbled.

Bertrice laughed. "Because you will never be ready."

There wasn't any easing into the link. One moment, Shi Hua was sitting at the high brother's table. The next, she leaned against the door to Balance's gaol again, High Brother Han next to her as they desperately fought to keep the demons from oozing around the seam between frame and door.

Yanaba's mental shout.

Han picked up Shi Hua and ran.

The sharp edges of the statue beneath her fingertips.

Fear eating through her Temple discipline.

The wild storm of nothingness devouring the demons.

And the figure in Balance robes standing in the middle of the disintegration of everything. Her cowl still covered her upper face. Shi Hua forced herself to peer closer. No. The lips were slightly off. The nose a hair crooked. It wasn't Anthea.

Except this time, the figure didn't raise her finger to her lips. Her smile was still there though. "I will see you soon, my friend."

She wasn't talking to Shi Hua. Another person in black robes stood next to Yanaba's fallen body. The figure pushed back her hood. Short, silver hair. The second person turned toward Shi Hua.

High Sister Bertrice.

In shock, Shi Hua let go of the statue, and she was swept into the maelstrom.

Chapter 25

"Twelve help me, I miss being a lowly peacekeeper dragging Kam's drunk ass out of taverns."

The magistrate's gruff voice drew Shi Hua back to the here and now. She blinked.

Little Bear pressed a goblet to her lips. "Drink."

Mateqai stood over the Balance warden, concern etched in his features.

Bertrice abruptly released Shi Hua's hand and raced from the room. Her warden jogged after her.

Shi Hua latched onto the goblet and greedily gulped the contents.

"Slow down, Sister." Little Bear tugged the rim from her mouth. "We can't have you drunk tonight."

"I don't know about that," DiCook muttered. "Sounds like an excellent idea to me."

Shi Hua looked at the magistrate, but she still didn't feel quite connected to her body. Was this a sample of what Yanaba experienced?

"That wasn't how it happened the first time, was it?" DiCook appeared . . . frightened.

She blinked a few times before she said, "No." She turned back to Little Bear. "May I have a little more wine, please?"

It wasn't until Mateqai refilled her goblet that she realized she had drained it. She'd been so busy discussing how to save Yanaba during dinner she hadn't touched her wine.

This time when Little Bear handed her the goblet, Shi Hua carefully sipped the Pana red.

"You two want to tell the rest of us what in the name of the Twelve just happened?" Jeremy asked. "Why'd Bertrice run out of the room?" He had the same expression of concern as everyone else in the room.

Everyone except the magistrate. Shi Hua reached over and touched his hand. He jerked away.

"Did you see what happened?" she asked. "Was it . . . ?"

"It sure as Balance looked like her." DiCook reached for the decanter and poured himself a healthy portion of wine. He took a huge gulp and swiped the back of his hand across his mouth. "What scares me more was what she said to Bertrice."

"What are you talking about?" Jeremy demanded.

Shi Hua met his gaze. "Everything started as I remembered. Yanaba ordering the evacuation of Balance. High Brother Han and I fighting to keep the two demons from breaking out of the gaol. Then him hoisting me over his shoulder and running for Yanaba and the statue."

She took another sip to sooth her suddenly dry mouth. "Yanaba performed her spell and collapsed. The figure appeared amongst the crumbling demons, but she addressed Bertrice who was standing next to Yanaba's body. She told the high sister she would see her soon."

Jeremy's frown deepened. "You didn't mention Bertrice in your vision."

"Because that's not how it happened this afternoon." Shi Hua reached for her goblet again, but her hands were shaking so bad Little Bear had to lift it to her lips so she could take another sip.

A knock sounded on the door. Chief Warden Nicholas checked before he allowed Brother Turtle to enter along with the warden who had accompanied him earlier to Balance.

"Are we ready?" The priest from Child's cheerful smile fell. "What went wrong?"

"High Sister Bertrice's examination of Sister Shi Hua's memory of the incident that fell Justice Yanaba." Jeremy turned to the magistrate. "You're sure it was Justice Thalia?"

"This is way beyond my position." DiCook downed the rest of his wine. A couple of drops escaped and dribbled down his short beard to land on his doublet. "But yeah, it sure looked and sounded like her."

"Ah, so someone *is* keeping our young justice alive." Brother Turtle actually sounded relieved.

"You're taking the idea of a dead justice running around Balance in stride." Jeremy's dry tone sounded exactly like High Brother Luc's.

Turtle folded his arms, inserting his hands beneath the folds of his cloak. "I believe the gods will not forsake us when demons come." His wasn't some arch appraisal or superior attitude. It was sincere assurance.

Shi Hua pushed herself to her feet. Turtle was right. They weren't alone in this fight, even though she had problems with the idea of a ghost in the Temple of Balance. But that was her personal issue to work through. And if they could get Yanaba back, all the better. "Chief Warden Little Bear, if you would take Brother Turtle and his escort to Justice Yanaba, Brother Jeremy and I will see what we can do about freeing her soul so he can make sure it goes back where it belongs."

Upon leaving the dining room, they found High Sister Bertrice sitting on a bench in Light's main sanctuary, her head bowed as if in prayer. Both her warden and another from Light watched her, but didn't interfere with the priestess.

Little Bear glanced at Jeremy, but said nothing as he led the men from Child out of the temple.

"I'll see about adding extra patrols," DiCook murmured. "My bad feeling about all this is getting worse."

"Would you object to some help?" Jeremy asked quietly.

"Not tonight." The magistrate looked as if he would lose his supper any moment.

"Nicholas?"

"Yes, sir?" The chief warden stood so straight Shi Hua feared he would crack.

Jeremy suddenly looked far older than his twenty-one winters. "Send a messenger to the duke. Tell him we need all the fighters he can gather to assist the magistrate. Then go to every temple, but Balance and Death. Get as many wardens as they can muster, and we need a priest or priestess at every city gate and the five tunnel entrances."

Nicholas's confused expression would have been comical if the circumstances weren't so dire.

"But, sir, the Wildling and Death tunnels have collapsed."

Jeremy's hard look melted the chief warden's resistance. "I've seen demons ooze around rock, and earlier today, they flowed underneath Balance's gaol door. And if any of my esteemed colleagues don't like my precautions, they can haul their Twelve-damned asses down to Death's morgue and deal with the remaining demons themselves."

Despite the bite of the words themselves, Jeremy's tone remained even and calm through his entire delivery. And it had a much larger effect on the magistrate and the Light wardens listening than Shi Hua would have believed during their bath this morning. A thread of confidence spun from all of them, an assurance now that someone seemed to know what he was doing.

"Yes, sir." Nicholas pivoted smartly, and soon wardens and clerks were running in all direction with a sense of committed urgency.

Shi Hua rose on her toes and whispered to Jeremy, "Let me talk to the high sister."

He gave a curt nod. "Don't take too long." Underneath his reply was his unspoken worry Yanaba may be running out of time.

A worry she shared.

"Yes, sir." She crossed to the bench and sat beside Bertrice.

"High Sister, forgive me for imposing—"

"No." Bertrice took Shi Hua's left hand in a tight grip. "It's I who must beg your pardon. I'm the one who pushed for the review. I apologize for the pain I caused you."

"You didn't." Shi Hua bit her bottom lip. The last thing she wanted was to cause the older priestess more discomfort. Seeing someone the high sister had known and obviously respected had to be disconcerting for the stoutest of hearts.

"She's the one who recommended High Brother Kai sponsor my late admission to Death after I lost my healing ability." Bertrice's gulp was audible. "She invited me to the noon meal once a week. Asked about my welfare. Offered to help with my studies. It wasn't until after her death I realized she blamed herself for asking me to save Gerd's baby."

Shi Hua wasn't sure what to do about such a personal confession, especially about events that had happened eleven winters before she was born. It was one thing to gossip with Ambassador Quan about the personal drama of Orrin's clergy. It was another to see how it affected their lives.

"High Sister, there's a justice we can save," she said softly. "However, Brother Jeremy and I need your help. We don't dare move those demons to our Temple."

Bertrice straightened and took a deep breath. She patted Shi Hua's hand and rose. "You're right, of course, but thank you for listening to an old woman's maudlin stories."

Shi Hua stood and smiled. "Any time you wish to share a meal and tell me your stories, I will be available. But tonight—"

"Tonight, we have our duties." The high sister's brisk tone almost sounded like herself. "Brother Jeremy, what are you dawdling over there for! We have a justice and a city to save!"

Shi Hua foolishly crossed her fingers again as she followed the high sister and her warden toward the Temple's main doors. *Please, Light, don't let Justice Thalia's words be a prophesy.*

Warden Gina from Balance met them at the bottom of the steps of Light. The only traffic on the street were Temple personnel and peacekeepers heading to their assigned posts.

Jeremy frowned when she fell in step beside him. Shi Hua noticed Mateqai was the only one of their own wardens with them.

"What do you think you're doing?" Jeremy said.

"You're going to need someone from Balance with you," she said firmly.

"I told Nicholas not to—"

"If what the sister—" Gina inclined her head in Shi Hua's direction. "—saw is the truth, you need one of us there. We'd offer a justice but we're fresh out so you're stuck with me."

"Little Bear told you of tonight's vision." Displeasure set Jeremy's mouth in a grim line.

Gina stepped closer and lowered her voice. "We are in this mess because of secrets. Let us not compound our problems by forming more."

Shi Hua laughed. She couldn't help it. "Let it go, Brother. She's practicing to be Justice Yanaba's chief warden."

Gina frowned. "How do you know about that?"

Shi Hua plastered an innocent expression on her face and remained silent.

Jeremy shook his head. "These kinds of quips are exactly what got you into trouble with High Brother Luc. At the rate you're going over the last three days, you will find yourself on the wrong end of a lash for insubordination."

She lowered her eyes. "Yes, sir." He was right. She'd been letting her personal feelings for the people in Orrin loosen her tongue.

"If you children are finished with adolescent attempts at one-upmanship, we have duties to perform," High Sister Bertrice barked.

Shi Hua dared to look at the temple seat. Despite Bertrice's tone, sparks of humor lit her eyes. She pivoted and marched toward Death, her own warden at her side. The rest of them scrambled to follow.

"So do you two actually have a plan on how to burn the demons after we extract Justice Yanaba?" Bertrice asked when they caught up with her. "Because if we do it in the morgue, we'll suffocate if we don't drown in the ice melt. The room wasn't designed for a fire."

"I don't think we have a choice," Jeremy said. "We can't risk moving them to the first floor. Once we break Yanaba's time spell, there's too much of a chance of one getting out of the Temple of Death despite our best efforts. You haven't seen how fast these things can move."

Bertrice shot a glance at Shi Hua. "Yes, I have, Brother."

Good. The high sister had paid attention to the entire memory. She wasn't underestimating the danger. That bit of relief didn't quell Shi Hua's nerves, but she and Jeremy would have Death's cooperation.

"There's a secondary air vent into your morgue, correct?" she asked. "That's how they're designed in Jing."

"Yes," Bertrice said. "I see. Force air down through the stairwell and smoke out the vent, but we'll need someone with wind talent."

"Prince Alika," Gina volunteered. "It'll be faster than searching the Orrin registry, and he owes Sister Shi Hua."

"Where's he staying?" Bertrice asked.

"The Green Lady," the Balance warden answered.

The high sister made a disgusted sound low in her throat. "Of course he is." She turned to her warden. "Axton, tell him what we need and that we need it now."

"But High Sister—"

She cut the poor man off with a wave. "I'm with people who have defeated demons in this generation. I doubt the Assassins Guild will succeed in killing me tonight if they're mad enough to try. Oh, and if the prince denies you aid, tell him the request is from the little Jing priestess who saved his worthless hide this morning. Go."

Instead of running up the street, he arrowed for the Temple of Love.

Jeremy frowned. "Isn't that the wrong direction?"

The remaining two wardens and the high sister started laughing. Shi Hua yanked Jeremy's cloak in the direction of Death. "I'll explain the ways of men and woman to you later. Right now, we have priorities."

Her stomach roiled so much by the time they reached the Temple of Death she wondered if she would vomit caterpillars. Little Bear had been right. She shouldn't have drank so much wine. But she didn't have the fuzzy-headedness of spirits. If anything, everything was sharp. Too clear.

She could die tonight. Even worse, if they had miscalculated what Yana-ba had done, they could be condemning the entire world to cold and rot and darkness.

Most of all, she was thankful for her cloak when they reached the bottom of the stairwell. The morgue seemed far colder than it should have been. Beatrice joined them a few moments later after she issued orders to her staff on how to secure the morgue should such an event become necessary.

"We're going to have to leave both the upstairs and downstairs morgue doors open to get the air flow we need," the high sister said.

"Mateqai and Gina, upstairs," Jeremy ordered.

"No," they answered in unison.

"We can't have too many people down here," he said more gently. "Shi Hua and I need one person to ward the room and one person to shift the smoke while we deal with the demons. Anyone else in this tight of space will be a lia-bility, and you both know it."

"You've both seen these things," Shi Hua added. "Been involved in battling them. Both in rescuing Luc and today's events. The priests and priestesses up-stairs will know if the wards fall."

"And when they melt the door to the frame and poor concrete down the ventilation shaft, you'll be trapped down here," Gina said. Her anger lashed against Shi Hua's mind.

"If my wards fall," Bertrice said. "We're already dead."

"Then we'll see you when you're done." Mateqai clapped Shi Hua and Jeremy each on the shoulder and headed up the stairs. After one more anguished-filled look, Gina followed him.

"The alarm spell will automatically be triggered once we break Yanaba's hold on the demons," Jeremy said.

"Good," Bertrice said. "The rest of Issura needs to know how bad things are here. Nobody at Standora seems to be taking mine or Anthea's reports seriously. If I have to activate the main temple defenses…" She shrugged. "Let's just say I'd rather not have a repeat of what happened to the isles of Britannia."

Shi Hua shivered beneath her cloak. Every child knew that story. The evacuation of the islands was as legendary as Empress Bao De's army holding back the last demon horde. But it was the Death priests' desperation that destroyed both the demons and all life on the islands. The magic they left behind was so destructive even centuries later, nothing grew, and anyone who tried to land on the islands' shores perished instantly.

The body they had inspected earlier still lay on the slab in the middle of the room. Jeremy gestured for Shi Hua to assist him, and they carefully stacked the other four demon bodies on the stone along with the first.

Without a word, through silent speech or otherwise, she and Jeremy began creating light balls. The magic globes hovered overhead. They wouldn't last long without something solid to contain them, but Shi Hua had learned through bitter experience no lesser Light magic would actually destroy a demon.

Bertrice paced to keep warm while they worked, even though it couldn't have been more than a quarter of a candlemark since they'd entered the morgue. Shi Hua jumped at footsteps on the stairs.

But it wasn't Prince Alika. Captain Iakepa appeared around the bend of the stairwell and entered the morgue. He raised his hand to shield his eyes. "I hear you need a wind talent." A grim smile followed his words.

"Are you sure about helping us with this?" Jeremy asked. "I cannot guarantee any of us will survive."

The Sea Peoples fleet captain glanced at Shi Hua. "Your sister in Light did her duty this morning. I'll do mine this evening."

Bertrice nodded curtly. "Then let us begin." She murmured under her breath as she circled the room. Already the sawdust darkened with ice melt with the amount of heat produced by active magic in the morgue along with four living bodies.

A secondary throb echoed beneath Bertrice's wards. Brother Xander and the other four Death priests and priestesses laid a secondary layer of warding over the Temple itself. It wasn't as powerful as Death's last ditch defenses, but it would give the other clergy a fighting chance to keep the demons contained if this crazy idea failed.

We cannot fail, Shi Hua told herself firmly. As her novice master said years ago, failure was simply not an option to be considered in the equation.

Once Bertrice finished with her warding, she planted herself in front of the stairwell, her sword drawn. Iakepa waved his hands in an easy, graceful motion. A breeze ruffled Bertrice's short, silver hair and stirred the ends of his longer locks.

Shi Hua closed her eyes, feeling her way along the complex magic entwining the demons and their human skins. A spell like this should have been far simpler. Most people with talent shed their magic like they would a strand of hair or a chip of a fingernail.

This was . . . Yanaba herself. Whether she deliberately let go of her body or her soul was dragged away by the demons was a question to be asked after they untangled her.

This was far worse than the mess created when Shi Hua had let one of her kittens play with a skein of her grandmother's silk thread. Aunt Yin Li's punishment of untying every single knot and re-wrapping the thread around its spool had been most effective. But this was far more complicated, nor would it merely result in cramped fingers and a wasted afternoon.

A bead of perspiration trickled down her temple. She could feel Jeremy working his way toward her, his own impatience beginning to fray his nerves.

Settle, she whispered through their link. *We can't afford a mistake. Not now.*

You're right. He took a deep breath and released it before he continued unsnarling Yanaba's spell.

The magic they released melded into the justice's familiar presence, but she didn't feel quite right. Shi Hua gritted her teeth. She simply had to trust Brother Turtle would be able to reconnect Yanaba's soul with her body.

Shi Hua wasn't sure how long it took her and Jeremy to get to the last knot and loosen but not release it. Sweat soaked her small clothes and dampened her silks and leathers. With the breeze flowing through the morgue, her body was more chilled than when they started.

"Ready?" Jeremy rasped as if he hadn't used his voice in years.

She nodded. In her peripheral vision. Bertrice and Iakepa tensed.

They tugged the knot. Magic parted with a rush and snapped back together, whole and hale. Shi Hua would have sworn she saw Yanaba for a brief instant, but she was already leaping back from the stone slab. With a gesture, her mass of light balls joined Jeremy's and surged forward. The top most demon ripped off its human face.

Fire flared, so white-hot she had to shield her eyes. The demons screeched in their piercing, high-pitched way. Heat prickled her skin and evaporated a great deal of the moisture in her clothing. She wanted to bury her head and protect her brain from the light and sound. Her eyes watered and her nose ran, but not from the smoke. The odor of the demons burning was worse than anything she'd experienced before. Not even the sulfurous reek of rotten eggs was this bad.

When she could see again, four of the demons had crumbled to ash. The one on the bottom had been partially protected. It fell more than leapt off the slab in her direction. She raised an aching arm and concentrated. Her light ball hit the demon at the same moment as Jeremy's.

Ash exploded. Iakepa's wind swept most of the finer particles out the ventilation shaft, but enough were left to set everyone to coughing.

"Stop, Captain," Bertrice called out through the cloud. The breeze ceased, and the demon remains settled on their heads and shoulders, the preparation slab and the other corpses, and the floor.

The low throb of the alarm bell vibrated through the stone under Shi Hua's feet. How odd. Balance's bell had ceased when Yanaba killed the demons within the temple's walls.

"Well?" Captain Iakepa asked.

Jeremy pulled a dagger from his belt and poked at the ash on the stone slab in the middle of the room. "That went better than I thought it would." He sheathed his dagger.

"Brother Xander must have forgotten how to stop the alarm spell," Bertrice grumbled. With a wave of her hand, she dismissed her wards and yelled up the stairwell, "Dammit Axton! Tell Xander to stop that blasted bell!"

"It's not just ours," Jeremy said. "Listen to the tempo."

Bertrice's brows drew together as she listened, then came her shocked expression. "That's the Temple of Balance in Tandor!"

"But why is Orrin's alarm still sounding?" Captain Iakepa asked.

Shi Hua turned to Jeremy and shock froze her for an instant. The hand on the corpse behind him moved. "Bertrice! Wards! Now!"

Rushing forward, Shi Hua drew her sword and swung as the dead girl crawled off the shelf and latched herself around the priest's neck.

Chapter 26

I kept the skinwalker's attention on me. He wasn't expecting real resistance, much less any fighting skills. And I fought with every dirty trick Luc and Shi Hua had taught me.

Unfortunately, he knew just as many nasty stunts, his upper body strength was greater than mine, and I couldn't just kill the bastard and end this farce. Luc and Nantan needed as much time as I could stall for, and if I did strike the skinwalker down, only Dav would die. The skinwalker would simply possess me or Elizabeth and use one of us to kill the other.

I just prayed to my goddess the skinwalker had as much of a headache as I did from the tolling of Balance's alarm bell.

The pounding on the Temple's main doors had resumed with the dropping of the main wards and the beginning of the alarm. I barely parried another jab to my chest. My responses were slowing, and my lungs fought for every breath.

"Finished!" Elizabeth shouted.

The skinwalker skittered away from me, and his sword crashed to the floor as he stared at his hands. "What have you whores done to me!"

"Sorry." I shot him an evil smile. "Wrong temple." I threw a small bottle at his feet. When it smashed against the flagstones, he froze in place.

"I wish we had time for you to teach me that trick," Elizabeth said wistfully.

"So do I." I sheathed my sword, reached into my other pocket, and produced a second bottle. The last thing I wanted was to assault someone who had shown me kindness. I hoped someday she would understand, even if she never forgave me. "Is the main defensive spell primed? I don't want him getting loose before I clear the Temple."

"Yes." She reached out her hand in my direction. "It was good hear your voice one last time, Anthea."

I seized her head and poured the few drops of soma tears into her mouth when she opened it to scream or curse me. "I'm sorry for this, Elizabeth."

Guilt consumed me. It was too easy. She was too weak from her captivity. I only hoped I hadn't given her too much and accidentally killed her in the process. I threw up a haphazard ward over the main doors as her concentration failed. The ward wouldn't last long, nor was it meant to.

"Traitor." Her voice slurred. "How could you join themmmm—" She passed out before she could finish her accusation concerning my loyalty. I lowered Elizabeth gently to the dais and tossed the bottle aside. It shattered just like the one I'd thrown at the skinwalker. The chaos we left in the courtroom should puzzle the renegades as they tried to understand what happened during our escape.

Assuming we succeeded.

I examined the skinwalker, but he was still frozen in my time spell. Unfortunately, my experiments had shown that without a physical frame such as walls, my spell dissipated in moments. And I couldn't waste what little energy I had left on freezing the entire room, then trying to extract myself and my fellow justice from the spell.

Reaching out with my senses, I also checked Elizabeth's work. She had properly primed the defensive spell. No one had ever tried setting it off remotely before, as far as the chronicles said. I hoped this was another common trick they simply forgot to record.

Hefting Elizabeth over my shoulder, I strode to her bedchambers as fast as my exhaustion and sore muscles allowed. Her primed defensive spell prickled along my skin. I dropped my wards on all the doors when I reached the passage to the tunnels. Shouts and the rattle of steel echoed through the corridors of Balance.

A bright orange face poked through the opening. "The younger priests have cleared our way, but it won't remain safe for long." Aduba reached for the unconscious Elizabeth as I lowered her, and he carefully pulled her through. "Justice?" he asked when I didn't follow her.

I crouched to look at him. "Go. I need to seal this block before I release the defensive spell."

"You're not planning on doing something stupid, are you?"

"Everything we're doing is idiotic by any definition." I grinned at him. "I don't plan on dying today. But we need the renegades deep inside the Temple before I launch the defenses, or our efforts are worthless. Now, go." I waved him toward the eastern exit. "I'll catch up because I'm not carrying dead weight."

Aduba chuckled. "Yes, our justice will be most vexed with all of us." He lifted Elizabeth, and my last view was his thick calves and huge feet as he jogged for the desert exit.

Time was a luxury we could no longer afford. The echo of voices and the tromp of booted feet came closer to Elizabeth's quarters. I could feel the tight threads of my time spell binding the skinwalker loosen.

I ducked through the open passage, turned, and laid my hand on the invisible sigil that would fold the sandstone block back in place. "Looking for us?"

My shout had the desired effect—the renegades panicked.

I reached out and triggered the flame spell Luc had laid on the shortened wicks of the two flashbangs planted above the doors of the kitchen. From the rolling booms of falling sandstone and screams of pain, the explosions had collapsed the kitchen ceiling and outer wall as planned. I sealed the tunnel passageway.

Sucking in a deep breath, I stood and placed both hands on the sandstone foundation of the Temple of Balance. All justices were taught the last stand defenses of our Temple, but I'd never actually triggered such a spell. None of my sisters had in a century. Part of me wondered if Yanaba had been forced by circumstances to enact those very defenses when the Orrin alarm bell had sounded this morning. Had she been smart enough to stand within the statue of Balance's protective circle when she did so? None of us knew what would happen if a justice launched the Temple's defenses outside of that circle on the dais.

The alarm bell's rhythm changed as if in answer to my question. Alternating between Tandor and Orrin. But it was Death's signature this time.

My heart seized in my chest. Two different Temples in one day. For all my hatred of Orrin from my awful childhood, it had become home again. Bertrice, Xander, nor any of the other clergy at Death would trigger the alarm for a petty reason.

I may not be able to save Orrin, but I could damn well even the odds here in Tandor. I reached out with my mind and set off the defense spell. Power throbbed, and I was thrown against the opposing tunnel wall. My only satisfaction as I lost consciousness was feeling the skinwalker's horror as he realized Elizabeth and I had outsmarted him.

Chapter 27

Shi Hua aborted her sword stroke. She couldn't get at the dead girl without hitting Jeremy.

Three more corpses were moving. One fell off its shelf and started clawing at its own face. Pale flesh parted showing black underneath. That's why the alarm bells in Orrin still rang.

More demons.

Jeremy thrashed and jerked as he desperately tried to pry off the arm choking the life out of him. His motions only stirred up a cloud of ash.

"Jeremy! Stop!" she shouted aloud and through silent speech.

He froze in place, but panic showed on his nearly purple face.

Summoning what little strength she had left, Shi Hua shot a light ball at the demon in a dead girl's flesh. It screamed its outrage and the smell of fried eggs filled the morgue. But it released her fellow priest.

And launched itself at the Sea Peoples sailor. Captain Iapeka was ready for the demon.

Or thought he was.

His obsidian battleax passed through the demon, and it leapt for his head. A pulse of power from Bertrice slammed it into the ice wall before it touched the captain.

Jeremy dropped to one knee as he tried to catch a breath. Shi Hua inserted herself between him and the other three demons. Thank Light, the last two corpses on the shelves showed no indication of moving. Instead of wasting her strength on light balls, she charged her sword.

"Bertrice, we need those wards!" She launched a series of strikes against the closest demon, which still wore a man's face. A very familiar face.

"Working on it!"

But the first demon, realizing the older priestess was a greater threat, charged Bertrice. Iakepa had learned from his first encounter. He used his ax to direct a blast of air at the demon. The creature slammed into an empty set of shelves. The wood collapsed under the weight of the demon.

Shi Hua's blade drew blood from the second demon she engaged. The droplets spattered across the basalt slab. They sizzled against the stone, and the slab cracked in a series of sharp reports. The demon spat something in its language. What she wouldn't give for a flashbang to shove down its horrid mouth full of sharp, sharp teeth.

Regardless of her lack of explosives, she needed to figure out a way to end this, and quick. Bertrice battled the original demon, and Jeremy struggled keeping the other two at bay. Iakepa used his blasts of wind to keep any of the demons away when they made a dash for the stairwell.

She slashed at the demon's neck. It ducked and swiped at her arm. Fire ran across her skin, and her fingers went numb. A part of her knew she was damn lucky to still have her limb. She'd seen one of these things gut a man with one stroke of its claws.

Shi Hua switched her sword to her left hand. The demon barked, the odd staccato sound that was their laughter, almost as if it tasted victory.

Behind the demon, Iakepa gestured at her sword and his ax. She prayed she understood what the sea captain meant. She whacked at the demon in a half-hearted manner. When it laughed again, she thrust her sword straight out and slightly raised.

The demon leapt back, only to be caught in a blast of wind. Before either she or the demon could react, its head was impaled on her sword. Its flesh ignited. The flame flared. Its weight disappeared the moment her arm was dragged downward. Ash exploded into the air.

Trying not to breathe in more demon dust, Shi Hua whirled to help Jeremy.

The demon still wearing a woman's skin didn't see her coming. She stabbed the damn thing through the base of its skull, forcing her power through her blade. The demon exploded into ash.

Its partner in the shape of a boy made its fatal mistake when it whirled to face her. The third demon's angry screech abruptly cut off when Jeremy parted its head from its shoulders. Its body collapsed in a gray cloud.

The one wearing the corpse of the little girl made a desperate dash for the stairwell. Bertrice's strike sliced it in half at its waist.

Shi Hua's stomach somersaulted as the upper body seized the ankle of its lower body and tried to crawl toward Iakepa. A light ball from Jeremy ignited its flesh, and one last burst blasted ash through the morgue.

When they could breathe again, Jeremy remarked dryly, "Well, that wasn't so bad."

"You're calling that easy?" Iakepa stared at the priest in disbelief.

"We were lucky they were babies." Bertrice picked up a discarded shroud and wiped demon blood from her blade. The cloth hissed as it dissolved. "They were too inexperienced to shift their density as fast as an adult demon can. And they were too hungry to notice the air vent. Otherwise, we'd have a lot of dead people in the streets right now."

Shi Hua kicked at the ash on the floor. "These were the poisoned peacekeeper and his family, weren't they?"

"Yes." Bertrice sheathed her sword. "The demons had a backup plan in case the first twelve failed to kill the Temple seats. It had to be the real reason for their murders."

"Eggs planted inside their corpses somehow?" Shi Hua asked.

"You've seen the way they can alter their shape and density. The adults may have implanted the eggs without damaging the humans' skin and without their knowledge." Jeremy tried to brush ash off his clothes and only succeeded in stirring up more. He frowned. "But the high brother didn't mention seeing anything like that during the chief justice or Yanaba's rewinding of time."

"The bastards could have done it before the time Luc viewed." Beatrice scratched the top of her head, and ash cascaded down her shoulders. "In fact, they would have had to in order for the eggs to suck in enough life force to hatch."

"Makes sense." Jeremy nodded. "A suspension spell on the egg and something else designed to detect when the host is dying so the infant can glom onto the life force."

"Or the adults you and the sister killed fed the last of their life force into the eggs for them to hatch now," Iakepa offered.

"That's possible as well," Bertrice admitted.

"But the chief justice had Master Devin check Peacekeeper Dante's body for internal damage," Shi Hua protested. "Surely he would have found one of the eggs."

"Not if the older demons used their powers to adjust the mass and laid a glamor over them. It's the only way Anthea wouldn't have been able to see them I can think of." Bertrice sighed and brushed at her cloak. "All I know is I desperately need a bath after we check on Yanaba. I swear I have demon ash in every crevice of my body."

Something else was wrong. Amid her older colleagues' analysis and jocularity, Shi Hua couldn't put a finger on it at first. It was silent in the morgue. Too silent. "Did the alarm bell cease when we killed the babies?"

"It should have, but the Balance alarm bell for Tandor has gone silent, too," Bertrice murmured.

Shi Hua glanced at Jeremy. His expression held the same worry as she felt. Had Chief Justice Anthea won her battle?

Or had she sacrificed herself to save Tandor as Yanaba had for Orrin?

Chapter 28

I regained consciousness and immediately started coughing from the dust in the air. The sandstone blocks in front of me glowed a faint green from the residual heat of the unleashed magic, but the tiny creatures that produced the pale lavender light I depended on when I was underground had been obliterated by the dust or by the Temple's defensive spell. I was back to only having four of my physical senses.

My dizziness didn't help. It took me a couple of tries to regain my feet. I stumbled forward. My hands touched warm rock. The spell to open the way back to Balance was gone as was the residual signature of centuries of justices blessing this Temple. I reached inside with my senses but felt nothing. Had the defensive spell worked?

Or had the renegades managed to escape despite our plans?

Death, I pray you took Brother Dav into your embrace, and he's no longer suffering. After everything the skinwalker had done to the former brother of Light, he deserved that small mercy despite his shortcomings.

I didn't dare reach out for Sisquoc or the clergy accompanying him. No sense revealing they were still within the city. If the spell had worked as the ancient texts described, only dust would be left inside the Temple. Any surviving renegades on the street should assume we killed ourselves in a desperate attempt to destroy them.

Another coughing fit took me to my knees. When it was done, I felt along my skull for injuries and found none. Hopefully, the power backlash had been the cause of my blackout.

I climbed to my feet again. The wall of Balance was rapidly cooling, and I needed to get moving before I totally lost all sense of direction down here.

Keeping the fingers of my right hand on the tunnel wall, I headed for Knowl-edge. A familiar tingle of magic met my touch.

The tunnel entrance to the neighboring Temple was still active. Good to know. Without the skinwalker or the demon eggs, the renegades might not have anyone who could seal the entrances to the other temples.

That was assuming I was wrong, and there was only one skinwalker in Tandor.

A few paces beyond Knowledge, the lavender glow returned, and I could see where I was going. A gray sigil ahead resolved into the symbol for Conflict. Bless Luc's heart. Remembering my description of the incredible creatures that emitted the light my peculiar vision could detect, he had marked the way for me.

I picked up my pace. Nothing but my own harsh breathing met my ears. A new fear struck me.

At least one skinwalker had possessed Dav. The renegades could know more about the Tandor tunnels than anyone at the Temples. Could they have set up a trap down here? Is that why no help came from the east after all these months?

One problem at a time, Anthea. But even my inner voice didn't sound so sure.

Long after I'd passed the gray symbols for Death and Vintner, an indigo spot grew up ahead. A fat tail sprouting green fur brushed the edge of the tunnel exit. None of the others were supposed to wait for me, so the creature could be an untamed animal searching for food or shelter.

I slowed my approach. The tail disappeared and a blue nose eased around the corner. It sniffed a couple of times and withdrew. A nude human woman stepped in front of the exit.

"Justice, it's me. Reby."

I relaxed my grip on the hilt of my sword and strode to her. "You're lucky I didn't have a crossbow. And why did you disobey instructions?"

"Because my silent speech range isn't very far," she said.

"And because we weren't leaving you to those bastards," Tyra said, stepping from behind another boulder.

Reby quickly pulled on loose pants, a tunic and boots. "Sisquoc said you lost consciousness when you set off Balance's defensive spell."

"Magic backlash." I shrugged. We set off in the direction of the gold ovals on the cooling sand and rocks. "I'd already gotten a dose when I tried to circumvent the skinwalker's seal on the Light passage to the tunnel system."

"You sure you didn't hit your head?" Tyra asked.

When I didn't answer, she muttered, "That's what I thought."

Reby grunted. "Either way, we need to find you a healer."

"And how do you propose to do that in the middle of the Valley of the Lost?" I snapped.

She sighed. "I don't know. I just—" She remained silent for a good thirty paces before she said, "I'm worried about my father."

"You want to run back to Mountain Gate."

"Yes."

I understood her feelings more than I cared to admit. Yet, I aimed for reassurance. "He's probably in the safest place in Issura right now."

"There's no safe place when it comes to demons." Her bitterness was warranted. We'd both come by that lesson the hard way.

"It's safer than being caught between skinwalkers and the queen's army."

She looked at me. Over the years, she had grown to my height. "Do you really think the queen will respond?"

"The demon alarm bells haven't rang in a century," I answered. "But they did ring. She has no choice. And even if she disregarded her duty, the Reverend Mothers and Fathers in Standora wouldn't disregard theirs." I hoped.

She grunted again, but Tyra picked up the argument. "We should have—"

"What? Fought and gotten yourselves killed to prove your loyalty?"

"No, I . . ."

When Tyra didn't continue, I decided it was time for some other answers and turned to Reby. "Why didn't the renegades capture the Sea Peoples fleet?"

"Too many with talent for the renegades to handle." She shrugged. "They made excuses to Prince Alika that storms had washed out roads from the interior so we didn't have many goods to trade yet."

"How'd you find this out?"

She snickered. "Because they were dumb enough to have this discussion in a tavern. Also, the prince mentioned he had dispensation from his father to marry an Issuran woman he'd gotten pregnant, and he was anxious to sail up the coast."

A shiver ran down my back. I feared I already knew the answer, but I asked anyway. "Do you know the name of the woman?"

"Gretchen. He was quite in a hurry to go to Orrin to request her hand, so the Sea Peoples fleet was only here for a day since there was not much for them to trade."

Of course. The murdered priestess would have used any means to escape my mother. I wondered if she plotted her escape with the prince before or after she learned about the demon grimoire in Gerd's possession. And was the child Gretchen carried when she died actually Alika's?

But that was a question for the prince some other time. However, it did explain his demeanor at the funerals last month. "What about the lack of ships from the Mecas?"

"We don't know." Worry laced Reby's voice. "A few merchant vessels came in and left that we are aware of, but they didn't unload any goods for trade, nor did they pick up any. Neither have any caravans come up from Cant, but that could be due to the border problems." She shook her head. "We're only a fortnight from the Spring Rituals, but not even craftspeople from the outlying areas of Tandor Province have arrived."

"So practically no contact from the outside world for nearly a year?"

She shook her head again. "Not exactly. Even after the duke's death, the renegades kept normal business going in Tandor until the winter storms set in about a month before the Solstice. The renegades didn't crack down on the civilians until the Smiths Guild was caught sneaking weapons to us a couple of weeks before mid-winter."

Which was right about the time Sister Gretchen was murdered. Once again, a coincidence that was too close for comfort.

"Reby, what's your opinion of the other Tandor clergy?" I asked.

She stopped in her tracks, and Tyra and I halted as well. I held up my hand when Tyra automatically reached for her sword.

Reby merely shook her head. "After the truthspells and counterspells and blockers, you don't believe them? Do you even trust me?" She propped her fists on her hips in the same defiant manner she had in her youth.

"I don't know if I asked the right questions, and frankly, I wouldn't trust my purse with you, but I do trust you to give me an honest evaluation."

"You and Brother Luc are never going to let that incident in Mountain Gate go, are you?" she bit out. "I'll bet you still even have the locks you cut from mine and my father's hair."

"For your first question, no, I won't, but I cannot vouch for the high brother. For your second, yes, I do."

She threw her hands up in an exasperated gesture and began trudging in the direction of the fading tracks. I strode after her. Tyra followed after a moment.

When I didn't think Reby would answer my question, she said, "Don't you think if I'd joined the renegades, I would've stolen my hair from you?"

"Yes, I do." A slight smile curved my mouth. Tyra snickered beside me

"I trust Nantan and the others with my life." Reby turned to look at me. "And I have for the last seven months."

We walked further before she added, "You're right. You didn't ask me about Orrin directly. Without the others' knowledge, I sent two of my Wildlings north for help. One four weeks after the Autumn Equinox. The second five weeks after the Winter Solstice. They never came back, and they would have gone straight to High Brother Jax."

"Assuming they made it past the DiRoy mansion."

"DiRoy?" She looked at me askance.

"You could barely call him a renegade," I muttered. "A distant cousin of the queen with delusions of grandeur and a demon grimoire."

But her revelation disturbed me. Jax had been playing his own game from the beginning. He made no secret of that. But surely he would have said something if he'd received a message from Reby about the situation in Tandor.

"How did you explain the disappearance of two of your own priests to Aduba and Nantan?"

"I said Talia had been killed during one of our raids against the renegades. For Brick—" Her face flamed bright orange. "I-I claimed I'd learned he was a renegade, and that I'd killed him."

"Both stories passed a truthspell?"

"Not every priest is as adept at questioning as a justice." Shame replaced the slight humor in her voice with her next words. "By the time Nantan thought to question me about them a second time, it had been long enough that I knew they were dead and I told him the truth."

"So deep down, you don't trust High Brother Nantan?"

"I-I wasn't sure at first." Sorrow tainted her words. "Wildlings . . . I've never had to play the political games I see in the other Temples. When my own high sister confronted the new cook and was killed, I didn't know who to trust besides my own people."

"I'm sorry, Sister," I murmured. "Talia and Brick's deaths aren't your fault. You did the right thing sending them for help."

"I just pray every night their deaths were more merciful than those who were poisoned," she said softly.

We saved our breath for the journey. We'd walked at least a league before distant howling broke the uneasy quiet between the three of us. Reby's head lifted, and she paused to listen. "Coyotes. About fifteen leagues away."

"That far?" But she was right. I saw no telltale green fur in the distance as I scanned the horizon around us. "They sound much closer."

"Any noise carries out here in the desert," she said.

Another series of high-pitched howls came from another direction.

"Opposing packs signifying their territories." She nodded curtly and continued walking.

"Too bad it's not that easy with humans," I remarked.

"Or demons," Tyra added.

We caught up to the rest of the group shortly before dawn. A light blue mist hugged the ground, and the Tandor people deemed it safe enough for a small fire under a rocky overhang to cook the handful of hares the two other Wildlings had caught despite the priests' injuries.

"Everything went as planned?" Luc asked when I collapsed next to him. Tyra made a point of spreading her cloak on my other side as Yar had done with Luc, but they gave us a little space to converse without overtly eavesdropping.

"I wish I knew for sure," I replied to Luc. A small drink from my waterskin didn't quench my thirst, but the contents had to last. And the liquid would be needed far more desperately when the sun baked our surroundings. "I would have checked more thoroughly, but not getting caught by the survivors seemed to be the smarter option."

I silently relayed my conversation with Reby to him.

That news is something to mull over, he said.

Could Jax be part of the conspiracy?

I want to say no, but I have nothing to confirm or deny her story at the moment.

I sighed. *I could say the same thing about Reby. Eleven years is a long time. People change.*

You don't.

I resisted the urge to smack his chest. "How's the ambassador holding up?" I said instead.

"As well as can be expected after torture and a trek through the desert," Quan answered loudly.

Most of the group chuckled before they returned to finding spots, without too many rocks, to sleep.

I rose and crossed to where Hadar was changing Quan bandages. "Did you hear from Shi Hua last night?"

"No." That single syllable carried a huge weight.

"She can take care of herself," I said. "She's taken out how many members of the Assassins Guild?"

"It's the demons that worry me, Lady Justice," the ambassador said far more quietly. "Fighting one at a time is not the same as battling a dozen."

"No, it's not," I admitted. "But she's not alone."

His snort displayed his lack of faith in my fellow clergy.

"Well, if you don't trust Issurans, then have some faith in her." I patted his uninjured arm before I returned to my seat by Luc.

You'd better hope that's the case, he said. *Quan regards her as a daughter.*

As I settled down for the day, I found myself praying to Balance everyone in Orrin had survived whatever was happening there.

Once more, the goddess didn't deign to answer.

I was roused from my fitful sleep by what sounded like a woman shrieking obscenities. My eyes teared from the blinding whiteness of the sunbaked sand, and I drew my hood more tightly around my face despite the heat. Luc breathed evenly beside me. Otherwise, it was quiet.

Just another nightmare of my mother's interrogation then.

I closed my eyes in an attempt to go back to sleep, but the silence was merely Elizabeth drawing a breath to continue her tirade.

"You were supposed to let me die!" Her scream shattered the stillness of the midday desert, and the wave of her rage burned across my psyche. "Traitors!

Renegades!" She switched to a Cantish word that indicated someone's mother was a donkey with questionable taste in breeding partners.

"I thought you were the justice with the death wish," Luc muttered beside me.

"Apparently not." I rose on my elbows and tried to look around.

The huge, shadowy outline of Aduba sat beside Elizabeth. He tried vainly to calm her down, but she was having none of it. As a precaution, he and Nantan agreed it would be best to keep all weapons out of her reach until we could explain things.

I rose, stumbled over to the spot the shrieking came from, and knelt beside the smaller shadow. "Elizabeth, stop it. You'll give away our position."

"Blasphemous whore!" She struck at me, but she had no strength behind the blow she landed on my left bicep.

I grabbed her fist as she drew back for another punch. "The Reverend Mother delivers better insults and cuffs me harder than you, so settle down, or I'll drug you again."

"Demon dealers," she hissed. She wrenched herself from my grasp, but she didn't try to hit me again.

"No, we aren't," I said sternly. "I know the skinwalker made Dav do terrible things to you, but I am not losing another priest or priestess to these renegades. Tandor's people needs your help to free them."

"That bitch Alara already gave me up for dead." Elizabeth's voice rose in pitch again. Now, everyone was awake from the stirring around me. "You're traitors!"

"Elizabeth, we need you," Aduba said. He tried to stroke her back, but she jerked away from him.

I wanted to cringe and hide myself. Touch was our sisterhood's greatest tool outside of magic, and it had been turned against poor Elizabeth. And her manner reminded me too much of little Ming Wei.

"You should have let me die." Her last word devolved into sobbing. Her time alone in her bath had given her the resolve for a short time. Enough for the respite she sought. But now, the mask had fallen, and we had no one from Child who could ease her emotional pain.

"Try to get some sleep, Brother," I said to Aduba. "I'll stay with her."

"All right." He reached over and brushed my own tears from my cheeks.

I wished I could tell him they were from the white-hot glow of the sand around us, but such a declaration would make me sound even more callous than what so many thought of me. Nor was I quite sure it was the whole truth either. Not when her agony beat against my mental shields.

"Why?" The single word came through her sobs.

"The same reason you tried to talk me into letting a healer see me all those years ago," I said softly.

"I can't do this anymore." More tears followed her words.

"Do what?" I closed my eyes against the glare of the sand and simply listened.

"Survive."

"So, you'll condemn others to what you suffered through over the last several months?"

"That's not fair," she spat.

"No, it isn't. Neither is the fact that my squire suffered heart damage from a poison the Assassins Guild meant for me. Or that Yanaba's squire was sold to a noble who used her as cruelly as the skinwalker used you. Except in Ming Wei's case, the noble tried to burn her alive when his misdeeds were discovered."

According to the rhythm of their breathing, our entire group of escapees from Tandor were now wide awake and listening to my words. And it wasn't like I hadn't admitted my next words to all of Orrin during last month's funerals.

"And it wasn't fair I ended up in Balance's service—"

"You're rehashing old grievances, Anthea." Anger tinged Elizabeth's words. Good. That was better than despair and self-pity. Anger I knew how to work with.

"I'm blind because my birth mother tried to abort me with poison, even though I was a product of the Spring Rituals. She was discovered, but the healer burned out her power trying to fully restore me."

The sound of Elizabeth's weeping abruptly stopped, and she sniffed. "I never dreamed Thalia would be that foolish."

"Thalia?"

My fellow justice sniffed and coughed a few times in conjunction with the rustle of cloth against skin. "There was a rumor when you first came to Standora . . ." Her voice trailed off into embarrassment.

"That I was Thalia's daughter?"

Elizabeth remained silent for the space of five heartbeats before she said, "Yes."

I laughed. Hard. I couldn't help it.

When I finally got my mirth under control, I gently nudged her with my elbow and said, "Want to hear a secret?"

"You're really Alara's daughter?"

We both laughed at that one, and I heard more than a few snickers from the people around us.

"You're almost right about Thalia. Just add a generation." For the first time, I found I wasn't as worried about the repercussions of my scandalous heritage.

"Granddaughter, hmmm?" Elizabeth felt for my hand and clasped it. "It explains the Reverend Mother's fury with her over the decades."

"No, she's more pissed that Thalia got herself killed in the pirate attack on Orrin."

"Didn't she know about Thalia's indiscretion?" True curiosity lay behind her words. She was no longer wallowing in her own misery, but I wasn't sure how I would keep her distracted the whole time we crossed the desert.

"She claims she did, but why she failed to discipline Thalia is something only she knows."

"Is your birth mother's deed why you cast that spell on your eyes?" Elizabeth asked softly.

I sighed. "No. The Reverend Mother was correct in her assessment of my contrariness when I tried to restore my sight. But I was born blind because they couldn't get another healer in time after—" I swallowed hard. "After Bertrice burned out her healing gift in saving my life."

"High Sister Bertrice of Death?" Real curiosity lay behind Elizabeth's voice, as if she were putting together the last pieces of a puzzle, instead of the morbid need to know another's secrets.

"Yes. I only learned the truth last month." The faint scratch of something crawling on the ground interrupted the breathless silence of my audience. "My grandfather confessed on his deathbed."

"I'm sorry for your loss." She squeezed my hand and was quiet again.

Unfortunately, Reby decided to fill the emptiness. "You can't end that story without telling us who caught Justice Thalia's attention."

A chorus of affirmations followed.

"I'd like to hear the end of your story as well."

At the strange voice above us, everyone scrambled to seize weapons. I forced my eyes open.

Yellow-orange shadows rose from the sand. The same voice said, "I would suggest you put down your weapons." A ripple of magic tingled along my skin, the harsh rasp of it reminding me of High Brother Han's talent.

"Who are you?" I demanded.

He, and I was fairly certain the person on the rock above us was a man, chuckled. "Someone smart enough not to give his name to a lady with talent, Justice Thalia's granddaughter."

I rose to my feet, and the creak of arrows being drawn followed me. I pushed back my hood, and tears immediately coursed down my face.

"She has red eyes, sir," a woman shouted from ahead of me.

I expected a chest full of arrows following her words. Instead, a couple of dislodged stones clattered as the man above us climbed down.

When he stepped into view, his clothes were bright yellow to me after being in the sun so long. He pushed back his own hood to display orange skin and blueish-green hair. "Chief Justice Anthea of the Orrin Temple of Balance in Issura?"

I lifted my chin. "You need to make sure you're killing the right person? I would have thought my eye color was a dead giveaway."

"No, my lady. Simply surprised you made it south so quickly after Tandor's alarm bell sounded."

"Not quite, but you have me at a disadvantage. You are?"

He grinned. "I am Nizhé'é', Reverend Father of Conflict, Diné Nation. We're here to rescue you."

Chapter 29

Despite the aches in every muscle and joint, Shi Hua kept pace with Jeremy and Mateqai's long strides as they ran for Balance. Apparently, Warden Gina had left Death as soon as Brother Xander had relayed the all-clear from High Sister Bertrice.

Please, Light, let her be all right.

Chief Warden Little Bear waited for them at the Temple's main doors. "Are the demons dead?" he asked as he escorted the three of them past the courtroom and down the main hallway.

"Yes," Jeremy answered between gasps for air. "Yanaba was entangled by her own spell as we suspected. We freed her, but . . ."

Little Bear shook his head as he led the way to Balance's receiving room. "We're still waiting for their word on her condition. Neither Master Healer Aaron or Brother Turtle have come out of her bedchambers yet."

Inside the receiving room, Magistrate DiCook paced. He looked up expectantly at Little Bear who shook his head.

DiCook turned to Jeremy. "The demons?"

"Magistrate, you might want to sit down—" Jeremy began.

"Your superior doesn't bother to sugarcoat the truth," the magistrate snapped. "Neither does the chief justice, so spit it out."

Unlike DiCook, Shi Hua sat gingerly. Envy of Jeremy's position didn't remotely cross her mind.

"Sister Farrah of Wildling was right. It wasn't the poison that killed your peacekeeper and his family. They had demon eggs planted inside them."

Little Bear cursed under his breath. The magistrate blindly reached for the chair beside him and dropped into the seat.

Finally, DiCook looked up at Jeremy. "Why?"

He released a deep breath. "As near as we can surmise, they were the backup plan in case something went wrong with their first scenario of killing Sister Shi Hua and Justice Yanaba. As to why Dante and his wife and children—" He shrugged. "They may have been chosen because of your trust in him, or because he was the first peacekeeper they could grab, or they could have been picked randomly. I doubt we'll ever know the true reason."

Sivan poked her head around the door of the receiving room and withdrew again. "They're in here, Chief Healer!"

A moment later, Master Aaron strode in, looking as exhausted as Shi Hua felt. "The justice is alive and awake." He held up his hand when Shi Hua rose and Jeremy took a step toward the door. "She's not exactly coherent at the moment. Brother Turtle said he'd never seen a soul stretched so far and then snap back without some damage to the person."

"So, it was stretched, not broken?" Shi Hua asked. Her initial joy had plummeted with the healer's evaluation.

"I'm not well-versed in the aspects of mental health as those serving Child." Master Aaron gripped the back of another chair. "Brother Turtle has sent young Nathan to fetch another member of his order. The brother strained his own abilities helping Yanaba reel herself back to her body."

"But she's alive?" Shi Hua pressed, needing the reassurance to make sure she hadn't misheard him the first time.

"For now," the healer replied gently. "The pressure in her blood vessels is too high. I gave her a drug to lower it, but she's in danger of brainstorm if her condition doesn't stabilize on its own."

"She's too young," DiCook protested.

"I've never had a patient entangled in a spell to kill demons before, Magistrate." Master Aaron held up his hands in a helpless gesture. "I hate to say this, but I'm guessing here. All of my guild is. One of my journeywomen spent the day at Knowledge's library in the hopes of finding some mention of this. I sent a courier to the Guild Hall in Standora just before you and the Temples decided to seal the city gates. If you have a suggestion, I'm more than willing to hear it."

"I wish to the Twelve I did," DiCook said fervently. "Having a senile justice when we were at peace was one thing." He tugged at his beard. "During wartime, we're in very deep trouble."

No one said anything. There was nothing to say. Not when everyone in Orrin had heard the alarm bells tolling. Not when demons were in Tandor, too.

Temple bells started ringing, and everyone jumped. Sheepish glances were exchanged as they recognized the higher-pitched bells sounding the hour.

Second Night.

Shi Hua almost felt like crying in relief. No wonder she was so damn tired. It was only the second night she hadn't contacted home since she arrived in Issura. The first had also been due to a demon.

"Brother Jeremy, with your leave, I was supposed to contact Ambassador Quan last hour."

He muttered an oath under his breath. "Here we are fretting, and I'm ignoring the obvious solution. Of course. Warden Mateqai would you please—"

She held up a hand and smiled. "I can do it here if everyone can remain quiet for a few moments."

Everyone murmured their assent and she resumed her seat at the table. Closing her eyes, she concentrated and threw her mind south. Nothing. She couldn't hear Ambassador Quan at all.

She switched tactics. Perhaps he'd left Tandor and headed to Cant with the *Unbridled.*

No Quan.

Reverend Father Biming?

Again, no answer. Not even a hint of the ship along the coastline. She focused on Tandor once again.

High Brother Luc?

Nothing. She couldn't feel any priest in Light either.

Anthea!

There was a blank spot where the power of Balance should have been. Each of the other eleven Temples tingled, though Light felt off somehow. But she sensed no clergy or other talents, and she received absolutely no impression from Balance at all.

As if the Temple itself had been destroyed.

Icy fear ran deeper than it had earlier tonight fighting the demons in Death's morgue. Her eyelids fluttered and opened.

Everyone looked at her expectantly.

"I can't find them," she whispered. "I can't find any of them. And Tandor's Temple of Balance is gone."

Chapter 30

The Diné's Reverend Father of Conflict and his scouts joined us under the outcropping. Introductions were made. And they had a healer with them.

"Thank you," I said. "Ambassador Quan has been trying to hide his pain."

The Reverend Father shook his head. "He would not have made it across the Valley of the Lost in his condition. But I understand why you brought him with you." The corner of his mouth lifted. "I'm more impressed by your Light priest. He does not allow the loss of his foot to stop him, does he?"

I turned to watch Luc in the farthest recess of our small shelter. He hovered over Quan, watching everything the healer did. And Yar loomed over Luc's shoulder, ready to yank the priest out of the way if the healer so much as twitched in his direction.

My own mouth curved at the sight. "No, he doesn't."

On the other hand, Tyra practically crawled on top of me. The only reason she didn't push the Reverend Father away from me was she knew I'd stab her. I'd be the first to admit no sleep and no tea made me an exceptionally surly justice.

"Our distance speakers relayed the news that two of Issura's cities have been compromised." The Reverend Father's statement wasn't a question, but he waited with an air of expectancy. This close to the border, Tandor's alarms would have triggered their counterparts in Cant, Diné, and the Cliffdwellers' territories.

"I don't know what happened in Orrin after we left." Four days ago, I realized with a start. It had only been four days ago that DiCook's man had found the bodies of Dante and his family. A little over three days since we'd boarded the *Unbridled* to come south. "We were sent to Tandor by our own Reverend Father and Mother to investigate problems in conjunction with discovering a renegade within our city's Temple of Light."

"The audits, eh?" The Reverend Father frowned. "We need to compare stories while we wait for our clergy and warriors to catch up with us."

"You're a scouting party?"

"You sound surprised." And he seemed highly amused by my disbelief.

"To risk a Temple leader—"

He leaned close to my ear. "Unlike your Issuran leaders, we have no problem getting our hands dirty. Especially when it comes to demons."

Aduba joined us. "M'lord, we sent survivors from Tandor's temples to you months ago, our staffs and younger clergy. I . . ." His voice died at whatever he saw in the Reverend Father's expression.

"Do you know what happened?" I asked softly.

"According to our own justices, they were picked off one by one." The Reverend Father reached into his pocket and pulled out a piece of folded parchment. "This was discovered on the first body our outriders found. It was addressed to you, High Brother. Forgive me for reading it, but it was necessary."

Aduba gingerly accepted the parchment and opened it. Hot, raw grief flowed from him. "Rabbit Runs," he whispered. His face turned a brilliant scarlet, and he crumpled the parchment. "Your justices? They verified it was a skinwalker?"

The Reverend Father nodded. In the subsequent silence, I realized everyone was listening to our conversation.

"What exactly are they?" I asked. "To my sight, they don't appear human."

"They aren't. Not anymore." The Reverend Father shook his head. "We don't speak of them."

I poked him in the chest. "Then we've got two problems. First, secrets, no matter whose they are, are getting people killed." My voice resembled High Brother Jax's when he was halfway between his human and wolf forms. "Second is forgetting the important things that everyone thought were such common knowledge a century ago no one bothered to record them. We're blind in a deadly situation."

However, it wasn't the Reverend Father who reprimanded me.

"Get off your high horse, Anthea," Elizabeth said. "Some of us are always blind in deadly situations."

I glared at my fellow justice, but my action was wasted on her. On the other hand, both our group and the Reverend Father's found Elizabeth's comment hysterically funny.

Ignoring the others, I turned back to the Reverend Father. "Did you salt and burn the bodies?"

He hesitated, which sent an awful feeling through my stomach. "We did the ones we could find on our journey west."

Luc swung closer to us on his crutches. "How many bodies?"

"Forty-two bodies," the Reverend Father answered. "The problem is we only found thirty-nine skins."

"Balance, take them," I muttered. "How many of these skinwalkers are after us?"

"Enough that no one goes anywhere alone, even to take a piss." Luc's scowl swept the entire assemblage, but no one argued with his order. He turned back to the Reverend Father. "If you would please answer the chief justice's question, what are these skinwalkers?"

The Reverend Father sucked in a deep breath and released it. "They were, are, sorcerers seeking power by whatever means possible. According to legend, they were the ones who first invited the demons into our world, exchanging their souls for the demons' grimoires."

"So it isn't just the eggs and the disaffected clergy," I muttered, more to myself than anyone else. "The demons who remained here since the last incursion have been actively teaching their ways to those with any magical talent willing to learn from them."

"It would explain Samael DiRoy," Luc answered.

"Hold on." The Reverend Father raised his hand. "What's this about leftover demons and eggs?"

"You're right, Reverend Father." I grinned, but the expression felt tight because there was nothing funny about this whole mess. "There's much we need to discuss while we wait for your army."

Chapter 31

The next morning when Shi Hua arrived at the Temple of Balance, Master Healer Aaron gave her permission to see Yanaba.

"A very *brief* visit, young lady." He waggled a forefinger at her.

"Yes, sir." But the fact that he allowed the visit at all gave her some hope for Yanaba's recovery.

She tiptoed into the justice's bedchambers. Yanaba lay in her bed, her skin grayish against her white linen nightshift and her black hair. Warden Noko smiled and rose from her chair beside the bed.

"You don't have to leave," Shi Hua whispered.

"Noko said you were here." Yanaba didn't quite sound right.

"And I need to get our justice some more water," Noko added, grabbing the pitcher on the stand next to the bed.

Shi Hua eased closer. Yanaba's milky orbs stared at the marble ceiling. Not that Shi Hua expected the justice to see anything, but she generally would face the direction of someone's voice out of politeness.

"I came to see how you were feeling. You gave us all quite a scare." Shi Hua gingerly sat on the chair beside the bed as the warden left the room and closed the door behind her.

"Please tell me you killed all the demons." Yanaba's fists curled in her blanket as if she feared the answer.

"Yes."

"The wardens and the healers have been lying to me," Yanaba said, her tone fierce.

Shi Hua shifted on the wooden slats. Was this what the master healer meant when he said the justice wasn't in her right mind last night? "Lying to you? About what?"

"Count them for me," Yanaba demanded. "All of them."

"There were twelve demons wearing human skins as disguises, the two in your gaol, five more out on Temple Street, and five more scattered through the city. Each one of them carried an egg. We presume the eggs would be used to kill the seats of each Temple." She hesitated a moment. Yanaba had been to the seamstress's shop. Had helped with the chief justice's investigation into the family's death. She deserved to know the whole story.

"Or me if the opportunity presented itself, which it did in court yesterday morning. There were also four eggs implanted inside the persons of Peacekeeper Dante and his family. We're fairly certain those eggs are what really killed them, not the poison. However, there seemed to be some kind of spell that delayed the demons from fully hatching. The working theory is that they were a backup plan if the demons couldn't get to their original targets. We think the last surviving disguised demon in the morgue used the deaths of her four compatriots to finish the hatching."

Yanaba sighed. It almost sounded like relief. "Twenty-eight total. That's what I counted, too."

Shi Hua reached for Yanaba's fist and covered it with her palm. "So, we did find them all?"

The justice nodded. Her eyes closed, and tears leaked from beneath her lids. "All that were within Orrin's walls. I wanted to tell you, but if I tried in the middle of my spells, I would have lost all the demons."

"You shouldn't have tried casting the time freezing spell at the same time as the Balance defenses." Shi Hua immediately regretted her rebuke. It wasn't fair when Yanaba was recovering.

"I don't think I did," Yanaba whispered. "At least, not by myself."

"Of course, it was—" Shi Hua's hands trembled. It took her a moment to realize the justice was trembling as well.

"You sensed her, didn't you?" Yanaba's words weren't an accusation. More like a plea for reassurance.

The same reassurance Shi Hua needed from High Sister Bertrice that she wasn't insane when she allowed the seat of Death to review her memories.

Especially after High Brother Han said he saw no one else in the courtroom when the Temple's defenses destroyed the demons.

"If you mean the other justice, I saw her, yes."

"Other justice?" For the first time, Yanaba turned to face Shi Hua.

She squeezed Yanaba's hand. "Maybe we're talking about two different things. Who did you sense?"

Yanaba swallowed hard. "Balance Herself. It wasn't my power. It was Hers. She held me together when I lost touch with my body, wh-when I tried to bind all the demons. I thought Death had come for me. But She held me together…"

A soft chuckle erupted from Shi Hua. "That makes far more sense than what I thought I saw."

"I wouldn't laugh about the gods." Yanaba actually sounded frightened, but her fist relaxed a bit.

"At first, I thought Chief Justice Anthea had come back, but there's no way a mere human could stand in the middle of Balance's defensive spell." Shi Hua sighed and lifted Yanaba's hand. She gently massaged the knots until her friend's fingers relaxed. "The nose was the same, but I couldn't see her eyes, and her lower face wasn't quite right. When I tried to describe the person I saw, High Sister Bertrice wanted to see my memory."

"What did she think we saw?" Yanaba asked.

"She and the magistrate swore it was Justice Thalia."

"They think a spirit of a dead justice is haunting this Temple?"

Shi Hua released Yanaba and played with the hem of her cloak. "Is that idea any more ridiculous than Balance herself taking a hand in earthly matters?"

"No," Yanaba said softly. "Not when Justice Thalia's body was never recovered." She quivered beneath her blankets. "Actually, neither idea is ridiculous. According to the Temple texts, Balance was the one who originally warned us the demons were coming. Why not act against this latest incursion through a justice who died in the line of duty?"

Shi Hua jumped to her feet and started pacing. "This type of contemplation is far beyond my training."

"A difference in our nation's cultures, or a difference in our training?"

The question stopped Shi Hua in her tracks. Maybe Yanaba would understand. "It's more a personal issue. I admired my favorite aunt, wanted to be just like her, wanted to be of service. When I entered the Temple and was assigned to Light, I thought I would be helping people to find common ground in their disputes."

"Joining the Temples was never about your personal beliefs?" Yanaba said softly.

"No." Shi Hua resumed her pacing. "It's not that I don't believe in the Twelve. It's been nearly two thousand years since Balance appeared to warn the human race of the demons. It's been a thousand years since the records say the Twelve appeared to fight the demons. So why now?"

"You sound like the chief justice," Yanaba said.

Her comment brought Shi Hua to a halt again. "How so?"

"She doesn't believe in anything she can't perceive with her senses either."

"And?"

Yanaba shrugged. "We in the Temples ask the people to have faith the gods will help us in our battle against the demons. So, why don't we have the same faith?"

Shi Hua sat down again. "You don't believe in them?"

"I had my own doubts, but after what happened to me, I can't help but to believe now."

Shi Hua's conversation with Yanaba about faith rolled through her mind for the rest of the day while she performed her duties. Brother Fang's philosophy lectures were tame compared to experiencing . . . well, whatever she had experienced inside Balance's protective circle.

Part of her hoped Yanaba was right that the gods were taking a personal interest in the recent demon incursions. But having a previous justice watching out for her city was quite . . . overwhelming. Either way, they had some extra assistance in the war, for that is what it truly was though only High Brother Han had the courage to say the words aloud, which gave her some peace of mind.

However, twenty-eight demons within the walls of Orrin disturbed Prince Alika enough he ordered half of the Sea Peoples fleet to sail straight for home during with the afternoon's high tide. Warning the rest of their islands took precedence since no one in Thief knew exactly where eggs were deposited. The prince ordered all of his captains and sailors to be truthspelled before they departed. She hoped his precautions were enough to prevent any demon eggs from being smuggled to their territory from Issura.

When Shi Hua could finally retreat to her own chambers, she was torn between taking a bath or crawling into her bed. However, if she headed to the bathing room, one of the wardens would have to accompany her due to the paranoia of all the chief wardens thanks to the demon threat.

And Istaqa would launch into a tirade about propriety.

She was too damn tired to deal with Light's chief of household at this hour. Instead, she changed into the loose silk pants and shirt she wore for sleep. By the time she finished her nightly routine and sat on her bed, the Temple bells tolled First Night.

Jeremy had extracted a promise that she would attempt to contact Ambassador Quan again, though she didn't hold out much hope. Not when it had felt as if Tandor's Temple of Balance was simply . . . gone.

And if Reverend Father Biming didn't answer her either tonight, she needed to warn Mei Wen of the events here in Issura.

Sitting cross-legged. Shi Hua closed her eyes and threw her mind south once again. The spot where Balance should be was as blank as it had been last night. The other eleven were uninhabited. Carefully sweeping the minds of the inhabitants only showed some with talent, but no one felt familiar. She didn't dare make contact. Not when she didn't know who was still loyal to the human race and who had sided with the renegades.

She tried a different tactic for the Reverend Father and searched for a blurred spot amongst several with talent. The *Unbridled* definitely was no longer docked at Tandor. Nor were there any groups within the city that matched what she was looking for if, for whatever reason, the clergy of Thief had abandoned the ship.

Stretching a little further, she searched for any ship on the Peaceful Sea between Tandor and Cant's capital Tiwan. Again, nothing.

That was odd. This close to the Spring Rituals, there should be some traffic, no matter how light. The absence of anyone scared her back into her own head. Time to inform her Temple superiors in both Jing and Issura of the unusual happenings.

She blinked her eyes and stretched before she settled back into her cross-legged position, her hands resting loosely on her knees with her palms upright and her thumbs touching her middle fingers.

Mei Wen?

A comforting, familiar touch filled her, but a third person entered the link. *I am here. Reverend Father Jin is with me.*

Has something happened? With the recent events in Issura over the last two days, one more disaster seemed apropos.

Yes, a great many things. The Reverend Father's mental voice sounded terribly grim. *Have you spoken with Biming in the last two days?*

No, sir. I could not contact him or the ambassador last night. Shi Hua swallowed hard. *I missed last night's contact with Justice Mei Wen because we had a demon invasion in Orrin.*

How many? he asked.

Twenty-eight in total. She relayed the new methods the demons used to get inside the Temples. Mei Wen's alarm at the new tactics buzzed through the link, and the Reverend Father grew even more somber.

I spoke with my counterparts across the world, he said. *We've made a decision many will find unorthodox, but is very necessary for our survival as a species.*

As Shi Hua listened while he laid out the plan of the Reverend Fathers of Light, unorthodox didn't begin to describe it. And if the civilian populace didn't understand the why of the plan and rebelled, the Reverend Fathers may have sentenced the world to death.

Chapter 32

One of the Diné Wildlings took the form of an eagle and flew east to inform the forces marching toward Tandor of our presence. While the rest of our combined camps dozed, the surviving Temple leaders of the city, Luc and I shared recent events with Reverend Father Nizhé'é.

The strange impression I'd felt of someone looking over my shoulder since I was sentenced to the Orrin Balance seat seemed even stronger here than it did at home. And it approved of the Reverend Father, even though I couldn't give a logical reason why this feeling permeated me.

However, Reby insisted on the same round-robin truthspelling session we'd performed in the Temple of Balance back in Tandor. I couldn't blame her, especially since I couldn't come up with a rational thought of why we shouldn't take a reasonable precaution.

When it came to renegades, the interior of the continent hadn't any known encounters of imposters within the Temples. The Reverend Father shrugged. "We've received the messages from our Light counterparts from the western seaside nations and Jing. Either these renegades of yours are more careful in hiding themselves among our nations, or they haven't been able to infiltrate our communities to the same degree. We're insulated from foreign ships."

"We can't blame everything on other nations," I protested. "Samael DiRoy was our queen's own cousin."

"I wasn't blaming anyone, Lady Justice." His lips twitched again as if he found me very amusing. "I am merely pointing out that a stranger is more likely to be noticed in our cities and villages than in a trade center such as your Orrin."

"The border between Jing and Shakya doesn't touch the sea," Luc pointed.

"Even so," the Reverend Father admitted.

Attempts to place blame were getting us nowhere. Time to steer the conversation to our immediate problem. "I first heard of skinwalkers last month from one of my wardens whose grandmother was Diné."

The Reverend Father shook his head, and his bemusement tickled my psyche. "Surely, your grandparents would have told you such stories before you were taken to the Temple of Balance."

"Why would you think that?"

"Pardon my assumption, Lady Justice." The Reverend Father inclined his head. "I thought surely your grandmother Justice Thalia would relate more of her heritage."

My mouth fell open. I'd forgotten that tidbit from the historical chronicles. Thalia's parents were Diné weavers who were in Issura for trade when her mother had become ill midway through her pregnancy. She delivered Thalia too early.

Those of us born blind weren't tested for talents. It was simply assumed we were chosen to serve Balance, and we were claimed by the closest Temple. And the percentage of those supposedly chosen who survived infancy and didn't have talent was so small as to be negligible.

Thanks to my confession of my scandalous parentage in Tandor, Reby's giggles at my slip turned to outright guffaws, earning her glares from those nearest us who were trying to sleep.

The Reverend Father leaned toward Luc. "What did I step into?"

"Anthea actually forgot for a moment that Thalia is her maternal grandmother." Luc's tone said he was barely able to control his own humor at my faux pas.

I cleared my throat. "No, she didn't. There were . . . issues between her and my birth mother Gerd. I take it you knew Thalia, Reverend Father?"

"Not personally." He shrugged. "I saw her once when I was a novice. A training exercise with our counterparts in Orrin." He chuckled. "During Spring Rituals as a matter of fact. For not using her eyes, she was one demon of a swordswoman."

"If I ever met her, I don't remember," I said. "I was sent to Standora for training at three winters. The sisters there don't encourage tall tales."

"I see." Humor and something else lay in the Reverend Father's voice.

An odd sensation filled me at his tone but I was too scared to examine it further. "Back to the skinwalkers. I can see them, but how does a person with normal sight detect a skinwalker?"

The Reverend Father cocked his head. "First, would you please tell me how they look to you?"

I lifted my hands helplessly. "All creatures of our plane are bright and colorful. Demons are the blackness of non-existence. But skinwalkers are—" I struggled to find the words. "They're an awful gray-green to me. As if they're caught between life and nothing."

He nodded. "That's the best way I can explain them, too. Each bit of magic they perform with the intent to harm corrupts them. As for how they look to us, they simply no longer fit in this world. Maybe the skin is too loose or too tight. Maybe they do not react as we expect. Sometimes they forget to blink. It's like they've forgotten how to be human."

"But we harm by our Temple's very nature," Aduba protested. "Are you saying these skinwalkers are what we will turn into?"

"No." The Reverend Father's sharp negation roused a few of the sleepers. "We fight to protect the universe. We do not battle because we enjoy hurting others or for personal gain."

"That sort of explains why they would join with the Assassins Guild," Reby murmured. She stared at her toes until she realized we were waiting on her to expound her thought. She looked around our little circle. "C'mon. None of you have met someone in desperate need of Child's help? Someone who likes inflicting pain on others?"

"If someone like that has talent," Nantan said. "Then, yes, they would be very attractive to the Guild."

I rubbed my aching forehead. "The whole situation is turning uglier by the moment."

"Nothing we can do except retake Tandor, then march for Orrin," Luc said.

I shook my head. "You make it sound so simple."

"The best plans are." He grinned at me.

We woke early, around a candlemark after Third Afternoon. By the time we ate a bit and packed our gear, an argument had broken out. It was led by

Ambassador Quan who insisted he head back to Tandor with us, instead of going to the closest Diné village for appropriate medical care.

He folded his arms over his chest. Despite the healing, his color was still a pale yellow. "Sister Shi Hua will be looking for me in Tandor or onboard the *Unbridled.* That's probably why she didn't contact me last night. I wasn't where she could find me."

"And we're fighting for our city, Lady Justice," one of the barely-healed Wildlings insisted.

I looked at Reby who merely shrugged. So, I turned to the Reverend Father.

He grinned. "I'm not the senior Issuran clergy here, and we are in your queendom without an invitation."

Technically, Nantan outranked Aduba, Luc, and I through sheer seniority. I glared at the Death seat.

"We need their help, Lady Justice," he said mildly. "At this point, we're too far from Diné. We can't spare anyone to accompany the injured, and we already know more skinwalkers are prowling the desert. Ambassador Quan and the other injured would merely be bait for them."

I fumed before I finally bit out, "Fine."

The Tandor Temple contingent was smart enough not to gloat, unlike the ambassador. I could have pulled rank on him over a foreign emissary's safety, but I needed to know what was happening in Orrin. He was my best chance at contacting Jeremy and Yanaba through Shi Hua. And the last thing I wanted was to lead our allies into a trap.

We retraced our steps back to Tandor. The Diné forces caught up with us a candlemark after First Evening. And it wasn't just our immediate neighbors. Various factions of the Plains Nations had joined them. Their Wildling and Thief scouts surged ahead of the main van while Reverend Father Nizhé'é' updated the other leaders.

He also had to translate between us and the three foreign high brothers of Conflict. Their mastery of the trade tongue of the Peaceful Sea was limited, and our knowledge of the various Plains languages wasn't much better. The Plains Nations priests and priestesses of Light questioned Luc thoroughly about our demon encounters through a fellow Diné brother.

On the plus side, a contingent from the Cliffdwellers and Commanche Temples were making their way through Kulshra'jek Pass according to the newcomers. They were disguised as traders heading for Standora for the Spring Rituals, and they had a distance speaker with them. If our own capital was compromised, we would know in the next few days. Even better were the extra camels our injured could ride.

Most surprising though were the horses. Brother Hadar had laughed in delight at the sight of them. Apparently, the Commanche Nation had bartered for and were breeding animals from the priest's homeland of Hejaz. Steeds bred for arid and desert terrains.

We headed west again in much better spirits than when we fled Tandor.

I walked alongside the camel Luc rode while Warden Yar paced on the other side of the beast. Thief in his guise as Luck had been gracious. Luc's stump hadn't bled due to our recent misadventures, and the healers riding with the combined Diné and Plains Nations forces had the medicine he needed to keep the appropriate blood flow through his still healing leg.

This time, the trek through the desert gave me too much time to think. "After speaking with the Reverend Father, it sounds like a much longer game is being played than the incidents that have taken place in the last year."

"How so?"

"You can't simply slide a non-believer into a Temple—"

"They certainly did with Mat," he grumbled.

The reminder of that bastard didn't improve my mood. Nor did I regret that he died under my truthspell. Part of me hoped Light Himself shoved that evil man into whatever hole He and Balance had originally banished Love and Conflict. "What if they recruited the current renegades from within the Temple when they were novices?"

"That would mean—" Luc's breath whistled as he released it. "It would mean the imposters would have infiltrated the Temples a generation ago."

"I'm thinking three or four." I shrugged. "Why else would the demons leave their people and their unhatched eggs behind? They lost the war and were driven out of our plane. They wanted revenge for the loss."

Luc bobbed on his camel as he tried to poke holes at my theory. "They haven't lost if they're still fighting. It wasn't just your assignment to a Temple seat. It was mine and Aduba's as well that triggered the acceleration of their plans."

"I hear my name being taken in vain." The Tandor Conflict seat's jovial mood was at odds with our discussion when he dropped back to converse with us. But then, those from Conflict relished a good fight, and one was definitely coming within the next day.

Either I was about ruin our working relationship, or I was about to stumble on something critical to figuring out how to find the renegades. "I don't mean to be rude, High Brother, but this is important. Why did our Reverend Father of Conflict assign you to Tandor?"

"You mean because I'm from the Cradle and not the Long Continents?" he teased.

"No, I mean you, when Tighan was passed over for the seat."

Aduba sobered. "I asked my Reverend Father that very question after he pulled me from the eastern border. He merely said Tighan needed more experience."

I looked up at Luc. "Sound familiar?"

He shook his head. "No. My assignment was Kam's machinations."

"But Mat claimed Kam passed him over because of the experience issue," I continued.

"And how many lies did Mat tell over the course of the last seven months of his life?" Luc snapped.

"The best lies are leavened with the truth," Aduba offered.

The disturbing thought finally clicked inside my brain. "What if Justice Penelope wasn't senile? What if Kam suspected something of both her and Mat, but he couldn't prove anything? Just like he did the DiMaras?"

Luc stared at me from atop his camel. "No." He shook his head slowly. "That doesn't make sense. First of all, why wouldn't he tell us if he suspected Penelope or Mat? He didn't hold anything back when it came to Duke Marco's parents. And why in the Twelve would the Reverend Mother of Balance leave someone corrupted by the demons or a skinwalker in the position where she could do that much harm . . ." He swallowed hard as he reached the same conclusion I had.

"No." he repeated. "That would mean Reverend Mother Alara's a traitor too, and this mission was truly a set up from the beginning."

But his token denial meant nothing, and we both knew it.

Yar peered at me from the dip of the camel's neck. The grim set of his lips and his abrupt nod said he agreed with my assessment even if his high brother didn't want to.

"What the demon are you two blathering about?" Aduba demanded.

I glanced at Elizabeth riding far ahead of Luc. I'd instructed Tyra to stay by the justice's side on the pretense she needed a warden's assistance more than I did. Nantan walked alongside Elizabeth, obviously speaking to her.

My grandmother had been in the same novice class as the Reverend Mother and Penelope. Maybe the alleged pirate attack wasn't only a pirate attack after all. What better way to assassinate a Temple seat?

Aduba's statement about the best lies rolled through my mind. The Reverend Mother admitted my grandmother was in line to head our order. Thalia's death meant Alara was named Reverend Mother instead and allowed Penelope to assume the Orrin seat when she had been originally destined for a novice training position. And Elizabeth had been Penelope's protégé.

Balance, help me. I'd been tricked again.

Chapter 33

Shi Hua stumbled down the corridor toward Jeremy's quarters, the Reverend Father's pronouncement still ringing in her head. Mateqai had rose from his pallet outside her door and followed her without saying a word.

What would Jeremy say when she told him? How would he react? She wasn't sure how she felt about the Reverend Father's announcement.

This went way beyond the novices. And with the Reverend Father in the link, she hadn't been able to ask Mei Win how Jian had reacted to the news. This wasn't the first time she missed her old friends. When they had been novices, they would have gathered in one of their dormitory rooms with sweets and tea and picked apart the implications of their superiors' decision.

This was the first time since she clutched her mother's skirts she felt so vulnerable and alone.

Warden Tadhg stood guard outside Jeremy's quarters. He gave her a questioning look but said nothing.

Screwing up her courage, Shi Hua knocked on Jeremy's door.

"Enter."

She squelched the urge to run back to her own quarters and pushed his door open. Turning to Mateqai, she said, "We need to speak privately." As much as he had become her shadow over the last few days, the subject she needed to discuss was too embarrassing to do in front of him.

He nodded and pulled the door shut behind her.

Three alabaster globes were lit. Jeremy sat cross-legged in his bed with several books and scrolls spread over his blankets. He was shirtless with the turn of warmer weather though he wore the cotton pants favored by many men in the

Long Continents as sleep garb. It wasn't like she hadn't seen her classmates in various states of undress, but with this news . . .

He glanced up. Concern crossed his face. "Can't sleep?"

She grimaced. No, they definitely didn't need the wardens to hear this particular conversation. "I can't, but not for the reasons you would think."

"So, what could possibly more troubling than murder, demons, and treasonous renegades?" His teasing smile faded. "Shi Hua?"

She walked to his desk, pivoted his chair to face him, and dropped to the wooden surface, but she could no longer look at him. "I received some news from home tonight. You'll be getting confirmation from Standora by courier within a couple of days—"

"They're recalling you? Now?"

She looked up, and his incredulous expression almost made her laugh.

Almost.

"No. Th-the . . ." Her gaze dropped. Spots danced in her eyes, and her lungs reminded her to take a breath. "All the nations' leaders of the Temples of Balance and Light have decided . . ." She swallowed hard. "Have decided to suspend our vows of chastity for the coming Spring Rituals."

Jeremy was silent for so long she finally dared to take a peek. He started laughing. Not just laughing, but roaring.

When he finally calmed down, he wiped the tears from his face. "Oh, that was a good one. You got me." He waggled his forefinger at her.

"I wouldn't joke about something like this," she choked out.

He immediately sobered. "You're serious." His incredulous expression was back.

"Very."

"What? How?"

"I contact one of my best friends in Jing every night," she started softly. "Tonight, when I spoke with Mei Wen—she's a justice, remember?—the Reverend Father joined the link. He told me of the decision so I wouldn't think you were trying to deceive me when you received the confirmation."

"Is it, um, mandatory?"

"Yes." The whole thing was so bizarre she still couldn't quite wrap her mind around it. "For our nation, where woman are admitted to Light, we, uh, are required to bed someone from, um, our own order," she finished in a rush.

"But you're not in Jing—oh!" Red streaks spread across his chest and up his neck until they reached his cheeks. "I . . . understand. They want to increase the odds of a child with Light talents." He stared at the open book in front of him.

She cleared her throat. "While they would prefer the high brother—"

A sharp bark of laughter erupted from Jeremy. "Don't even think about that! If the chief justice finds out—"

His eyes met Shi Hua's, and they both started laughing.

When their humor died, she wiped her eyes. "I don't what's worse—Anthea and Luc thinking they're hiding their affair or the ambassador thinking he can steal her away from the high brother."

"The Spring Rituals are still a couple of weeks away." Jeremy swiped his own face. "And the queen's army will be here soon. There will be more Light priests for you to choose from."

She shook her head. "That is not what I want." She looked down at her fingers folded in her lap. "I mean . . . I would prefer . . ."

"It's kind of hard for two women to conceive a child," he said softly.

She looked up and chuckled even as her face grew warm. "Apparently, the high brother isn't the only one who is terrible at keeping personal secrets."

"No, he isn't."

They were both quiet for a long time before she finally said, "If I must do this, I'd rather do it with a friend."

Jeremy cleared his throat as well. "Are you sure you, um, want . . ."

"Yes."

The awkward silence continued until the bells tolled Second Night.

"I've never—" Jeremy cleared his throat. "Never, um, been with a woman or a man before," he finished lamely.

For some reason, his admission made her feel a bit better about her confusing miasma of emotions. "Neither have I."

A relieved expression filled his features. "Look, if you change your mind before the Spring Rituals come around . . ."

"I won't."

He didn't appear as reassured as she meant her words to be.

"If you don't want to," she rushed on. "I mean, if you don't find me attractive—"

"I do."

"Oh."

"If we weren't sworn to Light, um, and if you liked men, I, uh, I'd probably would have, maybe . . ." His cheeks turned deep scarlet.

"Said something," she finished in a rush. "We could always talk to Sister Dragonfly. She, um . . ."

"Has experience with both genders?" Jeremy finished hopefully.

"Yes."

"Did you want to do it together or separately?"

Spots danced in her sight, and Shi Hua forced her lungs to take a deep breath. "Let's wait until the confirmation comes. I don't want any of the other seats to make assumptions about what we're doing and why."

"All right." He nodded. "We have a plan."

"Yes, a plan."

He scrubbed at his face again before he said, "Any chance you heard from Tandor or the *Unbridled* tonight?"

She shook her head. "I tried to reach them before I spoke with Mei Wen. I-I fear the worst with the Temple of Balance gone."

"The chief justice wouldn't have done anything without good reason," Jeremy said sternly. He almost sounded like High Brother Luc. "And she has a penchant for surviving. She would have dragged everyone to safety, kicking and screaming." He gave Shi Hua a smile. "She's done it before."

"I know." Shi Hua looked down at her entwined fingers. "I'd just feel better if I knew where they were."

Jeremy climbed off his bed and crossed the floor. He knelt before her and covered her hands with his. "Knowledge will come with patience."

She shook her head and laughed. "You're struggling for something to say if you're resorting to Temple mottos."

"Because I don't have the slightest clue of how to make you feel better," he murmured.

He released her, and they both rose to their feet.

"Try to get some sleep," Jeremy said. "Things will be busier than we can imagine when the queen's army arrives." He kissed her lightly on her forehead.

Words clogged her throat at his affectionate gesture. She merely nodded and left his chambers.

She walked back to her own quarters, Mateqai trailing behind her, when reality hit. Istaqa could barely tolerate her presence now. How would he and the rest of the staff and wardens deal with a pregnant priestess, much less a newborn, in their Temple?

Chapter 34

Well before sunrise, we camped in a depression a bit over a league from Tandor, a spot where the Wildlings could keep an eye and ear on the tunnel back into the city without revealing our obvious presence to the renegades. Also, Reverend Father Nizhé'é' didn't want dust from our passage to give away our position during the day.

Our outriders hadn't run into any renegade patrols, which worried me. Why didn't they give chase when we escaped? We were too valuable of assets to simply let us walk into the desert. The skinwalker had barely questioned me before we put a crimp in his plans.

Unless the renegades assumed the other skinwalkers would take care of us as they had the first round of escapees from Tandor.

Those thoughts along with my worry about Elizabeth's true loyalty led to a fitful sleep in the relative coolness of the Reverend Father's tent for the rest of the day.

Aduba's loud, long laugh outside the tent jerked me awake. I was surprised to find myself alone. I dressed and lifted the flap. Clergy, wardens and civilian warriors hurried to and fro, gathering belongings and loading animals.

"It's about time sleepyhead!" The high brother's chuckle carried across the entire camp. A handful of his Diné and Plains brothers gathered around him and Reby to examine the parchment spread across a camp table.

Surprised Luc had let me sleep so long, I glanced at the activity around us before joining them. "Anything from the scouts?"

"Either the renegades don't know, they don't care, or they have a surprise planned for us," Reverend Father Nizhé'é' said as he and Luc joined us with a half a dozen Thief and Light priests. "Other than lookouts on the wall, they've seen nothing. Only your party's scents were detected near the desert tunnel entrance."

"What about the northern entrance?" I asked. The growing sense of unease that had started during last night's march wasn't abating.

"I'm in contact with my Wildlings," the Comanche high brother said in stilted Peaceful Sea trade tongue. He tapped his temple with his forefinger. "Scents there are old. All human."

"Do they know how old?" I asked.

The Reverend Father had to clarify my question.

"Months." The high brother shrugged.

Damn. Long enough the Wildlings couldn't get a good read on them other than the species who left them. Unfortunately, too many of our current foes were human.

"The northern entrance would have been more convenient for the Assassins Guild," Luc remarked as if following my thoughts.

I cocked my head. "What do you mean?"

"As much as they've been running between Tandor and Orrin, why come all the way out here to access the tunnel system?" He gestured in the general direction of the National Road. "Once they had total control of Tandor last summer, they would have used the two city gates for any mounts. You can't take horses or camels through the tunnels."

Whatever Luc suspected, he'd lost me. "So, you're saying they won't be guarding this section?"

"Why take the risk coming this way after you brought down the Balance kitchen ceiling and the porch roof on their heads?" he answered.

Aduba tapped a spot on the parchment. "It would be foolish for them not to station guards within the tunnel. And they could very well be planning to bring the tunnel down on our own heads. The renegades had a measure of Jing flash powder with them."

"How much?" Reverend Father Nizhé'é' asked.

Aduba held up his hands, indicating a space roughly my forearm's length. "I'd guess about five minae based on the size of the sack. They wouldn't let me near it."

"That's not good news." Luc scratched at the stubble on his chin. "All they'd have to do is place small amounts on the ceiling supports."

"What if we turn the same fear on them?" I grinned. "Reverend Father Biming did give me a dozen flash-bangs."

"You used two on Balance, remember?" Luc pointed out.

Aduba stroked his short beard. "You don't want to be tossing flash-bangs around down in the tunnels. We damage the structural supports with one of those things, and we'll do the renegades' job for them. Especially if they've already rigged powder on the supports."

"Hadar!" I whirled around, searching for the Thief priest.

He rushed up to our little group. "Yes, Lady Justice."

I produced one of the flash-bangs from my satchel. "Can you help me with a little surgery?"

He pursed his lips as he took the explosive. "You need something bigger or smaller?"

"Smaller. Like crackers?" Thank goodness, I'd listened when Shi Hua talked about the Jing entertainment uses for flash powder.

"I'll need to scrounge some paper for crackers." He tossed the flash-bang, testing its weight. "I can make thirty to thirty-five from this. Do you need to string them together?"

"No, I want individuals." I fished another flash-bang out of my bag. "Will these two be enough to scare the water out of men in the dark?"

Hadar grinned. "I can see what my fellow Thieves have that could go beyond making the renegades wet their trousers."

At First Evening, I led a contingent of Conflict, Thief, and Light clergy and wardens through the desert opening into the Tandor tunnel system. Reby insisted on accompanying us, as did Tyra.

For a moment, I thought my warden would throw an actual tantrum. Yar saved both our prides when he pulled her aside and relayed our conversation from last night. Tyra's eyes grew wide, then her mouth set in the same grim line as his had.

She marched over to me and bowed. "I beg your forgiveness, Chief Justice. I was out of line." She leaned closer so no one else would hear. "However, if you get yourself killed, I will feed your corpse to the next demon I meet."

I swallowed the laugh that threatened to spill out of me. Instead, I merely nodded and said, "Understood, Warden."

Unlike my mix of humor and annoyance at Tyra's threat, part of me felt terrible for leaving Luc with the supply train, but at least, he didn't even consider throwing a tantrum. In a pitched battle, he would be a liability, and he knew it. However, Aduba hadn't helped my lover's mood by assuring Luc he would watch my back.

On the other hand, Luc could help Tyra keep an eye on Elizabeth. Maybe there was a little part of me that was still human. I didn't want to believe she had played me.

But then, I hadn't wanted to believe Mat had also done so in the middle of our investigation into Sister Gretchen's death either. However, I did my duty then, and I'd do it now.

Elizabeth hadn't blocked the truthspell two days ago, but none of us had known the right questions to ask. However, we needed to deal with the renegades before they discovered the army literally camped outside one of Tandor's entrances. Once the battle was done, I could focus on questioning Elizabeth properly.

Luc had grumbled at my obvious attempt to have him do something useful, especially with my overabundance of flattery. However, I needed people I trusted to make sure she didn't cause trouble while we tried to retake Tandor.

Hadar was just as peeved with me when I told him to stay with Quan and the supply train as well. While the ambassador was recovering nicely from his torture with the attention of a proper healer, I worried about the ramifications should a member of the Jing imperial family die within Issura's borders. The fact that Quan didn't argue with me meant more had been done to him than the obvious surface damage.

At the entrance, Reby removed the simple shift she wore and gave it to me for safekeeping. As I rolled it and stuffed it into my shoulder bag, she melted into her polecat form. She shook out her fur, looked up at me, and nodded.

When our infiltration team entered the tunnel, I took point. Aduba literally breathed down my neck since I'd drawn back my hood for greater range of vision. The high brother rested one large palm on my left shoulder as I led him forward.

"No wonder justices are irritated all the time. Having to rely on others to lead me around pisses me off, too," he muttered.

"Hush," I whispered back, but I couldn't help smiling at his observation.

Behind us, Reby chuffed, the equivalent of a polecat's laughter.

The trio of Light priests kept their distance behind the three of us. Luc assured me they kept their light balls at lower illumination. Low enough not to tip off someone ahead of Aduba, Reby, and me, but high enough, they and the other clergy weren't tripping over each other or the occasional rock on the floor.

I halted when I spotted the symbol for Death Luc had drawn on the wall. We hadn't run into any interference. None at all. Why weren't the renegades guarding the tunnels?

I must have accidentally sent the thought through silent speech because Aduba asked, *Could they have sealed the other entrances to the temples?*

If they have, then this whole exercise was for nothing. I stalked over to the gray symbol and lightly brushed my gloved fingers over it. The tingle of Temple magic was gone. Instead, the same virulent energy that had blasted me when I attempted to open the passage at Light taunted my senses.

I strode to the symbol for Vintner on the other side of the tunnel. The same alien magic greeted me. It made me desperately wish for a good soak in my own bath to wipe away the feeling of contamination. Rejoining Aduba, I took his hand and told him of my discovery.

That confirms were dealing with more than one skinwalker. A mix of his resignation and anger flared along our link.

We'll check the others, but we may have to enter through Balance. I started in that direction, but he jerked me to a halt.

You said the Temple was dead after you and Elizabeth activated its defenses.

It was. The same odd impression of someone looking over my shoulder was followed by an almost physical sensation of being pushed towards the Temple of Balance. *If the renegades think the Temple is dead, they won't be guarding it.*

And how do you plan to get into Balance if it's dead?

We have flash-bangs, and the Temples are made of sandstone. They should crack the stone open to allow us entry. A sense of approval came from my invisible watcher.

Aduba's color shifted to a brighter orange. *If you're wrong, the renegades will still hear the blasts. We'll be trapped down here.*

Would you prefer to retreat and launch a siege on your city, High Brother? You've already seen what they will do to civilian hostages.

Our silent argument gave the rest of our infiltration team time to catch up with us. Aduba glanced at the faces of the others. I wasn't sure if he was looking for support, or calculating the odds of my idea versus the cost of a siege in his head.

I relayed our respective plans to the rest of our contingent.

One of the Diné Thief priestesses reached out and rested her hand on Aduba's upper arm to add her opinion. *There's no harm in trying. If the physical structure of Balance has collapsed, the renegades will assume the explosion is merely the rubble settling, and we won't be able to get through anyway. If the building is relatively intact, they probably aren't guarding it, believing no one can gain entrance without magic.*

We will still check the other Temple entrances as we go, I said. Everyone nodded in agreement.

Everyone except Aduba.

Finally, he murmured, "None of you have seen what one of these skinwalkers can do."

We found your people's bodies in the desert, the Thief priestess said. *We are well aware of how dangerous they can be.*

It's not the same as fighting one, he added silently.

Frankly, I'd rather face one of them instead of a demon. At my words, the group stared at me. Shock roiled from their minds. Had dealing with demons become so common to me I was jaded concerning a skinwalker?

Aduba nodded. *We'll try it your way, Anthea.*

We resumed our trek, stopping at the sigil for each entrance to a Temple. All of them were contaminated with the virulent magic of a skinwalker. My heart sank. If we couldn't infiltrate Tandor, a siege would condemn the civilians trapped in the city.

We reached the section where the tiny creatures on the wall and ceiling of the tunnels had been obliterated by Balance's defenses. Afraid I would miss the correct block, I crossed to the opposite side of the tunnel. Once again, I trailed my gloved fingers along the wall until I reached a contaminated section. The surviving skinwalker didn't even try to hide the trap he or his partner had placed on the Light entrance anymore.

Here's the sabotaged entrance to Light, I said. *Aduba, there should be a block directly across the tunnel from this one. Lay your hand on it.*

I thought you could see in the dark, he protested.

I shook my head. *There's too much damage from Balance's defense spell on the walls in this section for me to make out which block is supposed to be our secret entrance.*

No one questioned my half-truth. I could see my fellow clergy just fine. However, I didn't want to explain the tiny creatures that glowed purple underground. Last thing I wanted was to give the renegades an advantage if one of them managed to infiltrate the nations east of Issura.

Aduba laid his bare hand on a block on the opposite side of the tunnel. I crossed to it, stripped off my right glove, and crouched before the sandstone.

Placing my hand on the block didn't produce the dead sensation I expected and had experienced two days ago. It almost felt like my silent observer was on the other side. The faintest hint of magic tickled my skin.

Over the years, I had my own doubts. About the Twelve. About my role with the Temples. About Balance Herself. But now I wondered exactly what was responding to me, guiding me, whenever I was this close to the walls of a Balance Temple.

"It's not as dead as you said," Aduba whispered.

I noticed. This wasn't the time to chide him about speaking aloud. None of us heard anyone else down here. I hadn't seen anything. And Reby surely would have said something if she smelled anyone beyond those who'd escaped with us.

I continued to probe past the weakened spell for the entrance. No hint of skinwalker magic though. No other layers of Balance magic either. Time to risk speaking out loud. I'd rather trigger a potential trap so we knew who and how many we might be dealing with in the tunnel system. "I'm going to activate the opening. The rest of you retreat to the entrance at Conflict. If the second skinwalker sabotaged the entrance beyond my ability to detect, I want you out of the way."

"And if something happens to you, Justice?" the priestess of Thief asked.

I lifted the strap of my satchel over my head. "Ever use a flash-bang before?"

She grinned as she accepted my bag. "Once or twice."

"This is the stone you want to crack."

"Just so I can find it again." She crouched between Aduba and me and pulled out a dagger. With quick, deft motions, she scratched the symbol for Balance at the center of the block. The pale green carving faded moments after she was done.

She examined her handiwork and nodded. "That'll do. Tap out a signal." She demonstrated with the hilt of her knife. "If someone unfriendly is inside of Balance when you open the entrance, we don't want them hearing your voice."

I inclined my head. "Understood."

The Thief priestess climbed to her feet and followed the rest of our contingent back up the tunnel. Aduba reached over and squeezed my shoulder before he strode after the other clergy and wardens. There was nothing to say, silently or otherwise.

I waited until they were dim blobs of orange in the distance before I removed my left glove and placed both hands on the sandstone. A trickle of magic remained, but not enough for me to simply activate the spell. I would need to charge it first. I ran my fingers over the surrounding blocks and concentrated.

Nothing. Absolutely no Balance magic to draw on besides myself.

Was there some kind of failsafe inherent in the access spell? Or had the skinwalkers managed to hide their signature, and a trap waited to kill me?

"Well, Lady Balance, I hope you actually give a rat's backside about keeping these demons and their allies in check," I muttered.

As usual, She didn't deign to answer me.

Trying to breath deeply and evenly, I fed my own energy into the block. Maybe I should have brought Elizabeth with me, bound and gagged, so I could use her to charge the entrance instead.

A sensation hit me, one akin to the tap of our old swordmaster's wooden practice blade on the back of my head when I made a foolish move during practice. My invisible benefactor was right. The thought was unworthy. I had nothing on which to base my suspicions. Yet.

And if I were wrong, Issura simply couldn't afford to lose both of us. Not with demons running loose.

Because I had no doubt the skinwalkers knew where some of those blasted demons were. It also explained why Brother Jon was abducted and his skin taken. A novice master had leeway in traveling through the queendom, searching and testing for those with talent. No one would have questioned his presence in Tandor. At least, not at first.

Something pushed on my palms, but it wasn't the stone itself. A signal from my mysterious benefactor? Looking over my shoulder back in Orrin was one thing, but the incidences here were truly beginning to unnerve me. Who or what would take such an interest in me, much less try to aid my efforts?

I stopped feeding energy into the block and rose to stretch out my muscles. If the skinwalkers had laid a trap, I couldn't detect it. I sketched the appropriate gesture with my sword hand and muttered the incantation.

The sandstone rolled itself back, just like the one in my bedchambers in Orrin, albeit far more slowly. I released the breath I hadn't realized I held.

I drew my own knife and tapped out the signal with its hilt. The sound echoed through the tunnel. Silently, the Temple personnel returned.

I slipped through the passage, Aduba on my heels as he promised.

Elizabeth's bedchambers looked as if they'd aged centuries, if not millennia, since the last time I was in here two days ago. Piles of dust lay where most of her furniture had sat. Her armoire had collapsed into shards of rotting wood and clumps of decayed clothing. The bookshelves were in similar straits. Bits of leather were all that was left of the books themselves. The stamps we used for our raised writing in Balance and all other metal objects were crumbling with rust. Anything ceramic had smashed when the furniture they sat on had disintegrated.

The door was also a pile of rotting shards and dust. Two skeletons lay across the threshold. I crossed the room and peered around the doorjamb. More bones were scattered down the hallway. With their clothing a part of the dust on the floor, it was hard to tell who we'd killed or how many.

Who I'd killed. I was the one who activated the spell, not Elizabeth. Yet, I couldn't garner much remorse. Not after what the renegades had done to Tandor's cobbler and his family.

The silence of the building was unnerving. Even the morgue below the Temple of Death had some sound. The drip of ice melt. The creak of the wooden shelves as corpses were placed or taken for their last rites. The groan of metal when it heated or cooled. But here and now, it seemed like the noise of my own breathing was muffled.

I don't hear anyone.

I jumped even though Aduba used silent speech. Once my heartbeat returned to normal, I said, *Neither do I. Be careful. There are more bodies in the hallway.*

He ordered the Light priests to extinguish their illumination. With Balance's doors and shutters gone, there must be enough light from outside for the normally sighted folks. I picked my way through the debris and the rest followed.

Sandstone blocked the side corridor toward the kitchen and storage rooms. Our couple of flash-bangs must have worked too well. They hadn't just brought down the ceiling over the porch and kitchen to prevent the renegades' escape.

I took a closer look. No, the flash-bangs did their initial job. The cracks and wear of the stone said the defensive spell brought down the rest of this corner of the temple after the flash-bangs had weakened it.

This was no longer a temple of the Twelve. We crept through the tomb of our enemies. When we reached the courtroom, a single skeleton lay before the dais. My time spell had failed, but the skinwalker possessing High Brother Dav had only made one step or two before the defensive spell hit him. Once again, I silently prayed that Death had been merciful to the priest driven mad by the abuse heaped upon him.

More crumbling bones collected in the temple's reception area. The remnants of one main door hung from an awkward angle. Its rusted hinge squealed as the last panel swung in the night breeze.

Chief Justice? The Thief priestess beckoned me closer to where she crouched next to two of the fallen. With her dagger, she pointed to an embroidered patch and another fragment of cloth with recognizable piping that had survived the Balance defensive spell.

The magistrate of Tandor and his peacekeepers had sided with the renegades. It explained his refusal to investigate the rash of deaths. Yet another reason to question Elizabeth a little more thoroughly. I regretted not bringing her chief warden's journal with us. I could have used it as proof should Elizabeth be tried. However, it would have been destroyed along with everything else in the temple.

My gaze swept the courtroom again. It held the same state of decay as Elizabeth's bedchambers. The wood had decayed, and the glass in the windows was gone. If any of the renegades remained in Tandor, none of them had stepped into Balance in the last two days. Only the wind had stirred the dust near the doors and windows.

A flicker of green fur in a high window caught my eye, and I reached for my sword. Aduba and the clergy with us drew theirs as well, whether from my action or their own glimpse of the creature.

"Sisquoc," Aduba breathed, and he lowered his weapon.

The puma Wildling squeezed through the window and leapt to the floor. He crossed to Tandor's high brother of Conflict and rubbed his head against Aduba's thigh. In return, the high brother scratched behind Sisquoc's ears.

Red teeth glowed against Aduba's orange skin. *The Wildlings know where the dozen remaining renegades and the second skinwalker are.*

It explained why the skinwalker had sealed the Temple accesses and no guards were stationed at the tunnel exits. They didn't have enough personnel left to watch them. I'd killed most of them with Balance's defenses.

Which Temple are they using for their last stand? I asked.

If anything, Aduba's grin became more wicked. *The renegades are split between the Queen's Gate and the Neighbor's Gate, and the skinwalker is hiding in the duke's fortress.*

We relayed Sisquoc's intelligence to the Reverend Father, Luc, and a couple of other clergy with the Diné army. The army would divide further and march for the two gates in Tandor. Meanwhile, the Wildlings and Thieves waiting at each tunnel entrance would meet underground and enter the city through Balance.

Aduba sent half of our team to each gate. If they could quietly take out the renegades manning the city defenses, all the better for the civilians. A pitched battle through the streets, even if we were only dealing with a dozen men and women, would result in civilian casualties no matter how careful we were. The renegades had already shown how much they regarded the people's lives in Tandor.

Meanwhile, Aduba, Sisquoc, Reby, and I had the much harder task of killing the skinwalker. This one was the wilier of the two, the one who'd actually abducted Luc. He wouldn't stand still and let me freeze him as his compatriot had done.

The main gates into the fortress were closed and locked with guards, according to Sisquoc, but he and the clergy who had remained behind could us get past the curtain wall. Getting inside the keep where our foe hid would be the major problem.

That, and preventing the skinwalker from possessing one of us.

The puma led us to the duke's fortress by an indirect route. Every storefront was closed and shuttered. No one was on the streets, not even a few diehards at the taverns. Still, we were sticking to the shadows from the way Sisquoc prowled from building to building.

I could sense people inside their homes and apartments. No one dared to peek out. After what the renegades had done to their fellow citizens, I couldn't blame them.

The two Death priests and the wolf Wildling waited for us in a corner where the granite of the fortress's curtain wall and the clay bricks of a merchant's estate wall met the city's sandstone wall. I immediately understood why they chose this spot. The hand and footholds stood out even to my odd sight.

The Wildlings shifted to their human forms for the ease of the climb. We followed them up and over the wall. The high roof of an outbuilding shielded us from the keep. The Wildlings shifted back once we were safely on the ground.

I peered around the corner of the outbuilding. At a flare of color along the top of the main keep's parapets, I signaled the group to wait, and Sisquoc eased up beside me. Placing a hand on his fur, I asked, *Can you identify the people along the top of the wall?*

The skinwalker is using the duchess's household guard to man the fortress. He had some inkling trouble would be coming when you escaped. The puma coughed, and a tickle of humor came through our link. *I doubt he expects you this soon.*

Quan's reading of the Balance chief warden's journal nagged at me. *Has Duchess Nadine been recruited by the renegades?*

The puma shook his head. *We don't know. Allegedly, she's been in seclusion since the death of Duke Enzo and their son, but she could just as easily be a hostage.*

I grabbed the high brother of Conflict's arm with my other hand. *Have you seen Duchess Nadine lately?*

Aduba shook his head. *Not since midsummer before she delivered her babe. The other skinwalker never mentioned that she was one, but he never said she wasn't either.*

Either way, this is a trap.

I know. His mental voice was grim. *But we need to get you close enough to identify the second skinwalker. We can't let this one escape.*

Obviously, someone didn't listen to the Reverend Father's lecture on how normally sighted people could recognize a skinwalker, but I wasn't about to point it out to Aduba. On the other hand, Luc would be pleased I was learning how to hold my tongue when someone acted idiotic in a crisis.

The portcullis for the main entrance into the keep was raised, furthering my suspicions. Or else they thought the main gates would hold. We needed to get those people off the walls and into the courtyard. All without getting ourselves killed in the process. We needed a distraction.

I reached into my bag and pulled out a handful of the crackers Hadar had made with the assistance of some other Thief clergy.

The tingle of magic behind me and a hand on my sword arm automatically made me reach for my dagger with my left. I whirled to find Reby in human form.

What are you planning?

I pointed at a wagon. *Setting that on fire to entice the staff off the walls in order to deal with it.*

She waved at my handful of spelled paper and flash powder. *If you set off the crackers out here, they'll close the portcullis. Let me get inside first. Trajan? Sling.*

The wolf shifted to human form. One of the Death priests handed him a strap of woven yarn and leather.

Once I'm inside, aim for the guards on the parapet.

I hated to admit it, but her plan was much better. If the girl couldn't shape-shift, she definitely would have ended up in Conflict.

Do you want me to hit them? Trajan asked.

Yes, Reby and I said at the same time.

She gestured at my bag again. I pulled her shift out of my bag. She donned it and wiped a few handfuls of dirt over the material and her exposed skin.

Stay out of sight until I'm inside. Reby winked at me before she started screaming and ran for the raised portcullis.

Chapter 35

After a count of five heartbeats, Trajan stepped from behind our cover and launched five crackers. His speed and accuracy amazed me. Each one exploded as it hit someone on the parapet. Shouts of shock and pain echoed through the small courtyard.

This way, Justice, Sisquoc said. I followed him and one of the Death priests. We stuck to places that must have been shadowed from the watchers on the wall.

Behind us, the sling whistled again. Another series of bangs came from the top of the keep. More shouts and screams.

The wagon I'd wanted to use burst into flames. The blackish silhouette of Aduba stood in front of the white glare.

"Fire!" he roared.

I wasn't sure whether to laugh because he'd stolen my idea, or to be horrified that he was such an obvious target. He made a spectacle of running back and forth from the animals' stone drinking tank to the fire with buckets of water that only partially hit the burning wood.

Sisquoc leaned against my thigh and pressed me against the wall. The Death priest followed suit. More shouts and running footsteps vibrated the stone against my back. People poured from the keep, their attention focused on the flames. I examined each one, but they all had the yellow and orange glow of humans.

When no one else came out, Sisquoc trotted toward the entrance. The Death brother and I raced after him.

A guard standing inside the gatehouse squealed when he spotted the puma, but no one heard him over the commotion outside. The Death priest rushed forward and touched the guard's forehead. I caught the guard's spear before it hit the floor while my fellow clergy dragged the man back to a corner.

In wolf form, Trajan slunk into the gatehouse, the second Death brother right behind him. An instant later, Aduba jogged through the entrance.

Together, he and the second Death priest lowered the portcullis. Yes, we were trapped, but so was the skinwalker as long as he possessed someone inside. I tried not to think about the idea of him slipping into one of the people outside the keep. Hopefully, his desire for my death would kept him motivated enough to remain inside whoever he currently wore.

The keep of the duke of Tandor was far more practical for defense than Duke Marco's estate in Orrin. Murder holes lined the ceiling of the narrow corridor between the guardhouse and the main section of the keep. From my reading after my first encounter with demons, boiling oil and molten metal affected our foes when conventional weapons passed through them.

I had the impression something was watching us through the murder holes though I couldn't spot anything besides stone through the openings. Unfortunately, I also had the impression that whatever watched us wasn't my benefactor from Balance.

The second portcullis remained raised after we pass through it. No guard stood next to the winch. Somewhere ahead of us, Reby spoke through pretend sobs. Another feminine voice answered her.

Aduba's brows drew together. One of the Death priests rested his hand on my arm. *That's Duchess Nadine's voice.*

After seeing the skinwalker wear Brother Jon like a cloak and possess High Brother Dav, I wasn't about to assume this was the real duchess.

"You might as well come in, Aduba," a male voice called out. "And bring the Red Justice with you."

So we were being watched.

Merchant DiSand, the Death priest whispered in my mind.

A squeal that could only have come from Reby pierced my ears.

"If you don't, we'll just have to play with your little Wildling," DiSand said loudly.

Aduba and I exchanged glances. He shrugged. I had to agree. Even if Reby's life wasn't in danger, there was no sense skulking about the keep if DiSand and the duchess knew we were here.

We entered the great hall. I squinted at the fires blazing in the five evenly placed hearths. The flames weren't for warmth or light. My heart sank. The renegades had discerned the secret of my sight. But the painful glow of the fires didn't disguise the green-gray sickly figure who held Reby by the throat.

The other skinwalker. At least the duchess's body carried the yellow-green cast of possession. She hadn't been skinned. But how in the Twelve did I get the skinwalker out of her and destroy it?

I shifted to examine Ural DiSand. He stood maybe a couple of fingerspans taller than me, and his build was quite average, not the heavier form of many other merchants who overindulged in their wares. The magic of a civilian sorcerer danced along my skin, but he showed no signs of the corruption of a skinwalker.

But then neither had Samael DiRoy before I executed him. Or High Brother Dav who'd been broken by repeated possessions.

Ignoring the two renegades, I examined the plaster walls. Nothing unusual met my gaze.

"What are you looking for, my dear Justice?" the skinwalker purred.

Remembering the woods surrounding DiRoy's decrepit manse outside of Orrin, I tilted my head and examined the ceiling. Three spots, blacker than the void from which Balance emerged, clung to the plaster above us.

"Your pet demons," I replied.

My fellow clergy followed my gaze. Gasps of dismay came from the two Death priests. Sisquoc and Trajan growled. Aduba swore in what I assumed was his birth language in the Cradle.

I, however, cursed my own ineptitude. I should have kept the Light priests with me after all.

DiSand barked an order in the guttural speech of the demons. They simply uncurled and dropped from the ceiling. Their claws clicked against the tile floor of the great room.

From their movements, these weren't hatched in our plane of existence. But they hesitated, as if my presence worried them, and they kept themselves planted firmly between me and DiSand.

"So you're the person who's been causing me so much trouble." Humor lay thick in DiSand's voice.

"I could say the same about you." I tilted my head and regarded him. "Exactly what did I do to you? Hiring the Assassins Guild seems to be an excessive waste of money. Money that could be spent on better things."

"In your case, it definitely has been a waste," he said dryly. "The Guild Master doubled the price on your head to be paid out of his own gold. Your continued survival has offended his sensibilities."

I shook my head. "If you and your guild master hadn't tried to assassinate me, more than once I might add, you wouldn't have aroused suspicion, and maybe you would have gained control of Issura by now."

DiSand smiled. "If the former Lady DiMara hadn't become obsessed with her son's paramour, you would never have known about DiRoy's efforts until it was too late. But then, it's already too late for your precious Orrin."

I laughed, and the demons muttered among themselves. "I doubt that. The Orrin alarm bell sounded from Death, not Balance or Light. Unless you decided to change tactics after you failed to poison that particular Temple here?"

"Maybe we did—"

"Shut up!" the skinwalker screeched.

The demons grumbled among themselves, but I wasn't sure if it were me or the skinwalker who irritated them.

Damn. DiSand had been about to reveal something important. Time to try a different tactic.

I managed to hold on to the smile I wore. "If the Temple of Death worried you renegades, Sister Shi Hua wouldn't be at the top of your guild master's list."

DiSand shrugged. "She was merely an annoyance to our efforts to control the imperial family."

Something didn't feel right. The renegades targeted Light because their magic could destroy demons. The only person they were concerned about in Balance was me because I could see demons. Maybe Elizabeth's survival was truly happenstance over her distaste for her cook's goat stew. And when the renegades truthspelled her, they discovered her relationship to me and my secret.

But Death . . .

The demons needed to stop Death before any of the Temples launched their last resort defenses.

Bertrice.

No. She wouldn't have destroyed the entire duchy of Orrin, killed all of its people, and cut Tandor off from the rest of Issura. Not unless she didn't have any other choice.

Luc's words taunted me. *Even if I don't trust Shi Hua, I do trust Jeremy and Yanaba to do whatever they must to keep Orrin safe.*

Despite Shi Hua's mishandling of what truths to tell Luc and me, I trusted her to help Jeremy keep the city safe as she had before.

As long as she were alive.

As would Bertrice.

Balance, please let Quan be correct about why he hadn't heard from Shi Hua for the last two nights.

But DiSand, like Samael DiRoy, was merely a tool for the invaders. Their loyalty to their summoner only lasted as long as it took to ally themselves with someone more malleable.

Or someone they already had an alliance with.

I turned my attention from DiSand to the demons and flicked my fingers in a particular pattern. "You shouldn't have been so obvious about who you needed to protect."

At my signal, Reby's bones shifted, and she slipped from the skinwalker's hold. Bright green fur sprouted from her skin. She winked at me and lifted her tail. A yellowish cloud enveloped the skinwalker.

An unearthly scream erupted from the greenish-yellow figure, and she began clawing at her eyes. The demons raced to protect their summoner, only to choke on the polecat spray themselves.

The duchess is still alive. We need to force the skinwalker into DiSand. Out loud, I yelled, "Don't let anything out of this room!"

Aduba and the younger priests followed my orders and focused their efforts on the skinwalker. Nothing major. Little cuts with knives. Scratches and bites.

Every time the demons tried to engage one of them, I'd toss a cracker at them and light it. The Light ignition spells were probably nothing more than mosquito bites to them, but my efforts kept them irritated and off balance.

Reby's second spray of the skinwalker though was his last straw. A green-tinged black mist poured from the duchess's mouth and nose, and she collapsed to the flagstones. The cloud hovered a moment over her fallen body before it darted for Aduba.

The high brother raised his left hand and muttered a spell. The cloud swirled around him, but his wards acted as a layer of armor.

DiSand darted for the fallen duchess and drew his sword. Sisquoc pounced on the merchant, but barely avoided a knife-slash to his unprotected belly.

Unfortunately, the demons decided since we couldn't harm the skinwalker when it was incorporeal, they would focus their efforts on me.

I knew from bitter experience steel had no effect on these creatures. And they were fast. Too fast. I closed my eyes and felt the flow of time in the great hall.

One of the Death priests launched a spell at the back of a demon. The creature would dodge the spell, but I sped the timing of the spell and slowed time around the demon.

It screamed in outrage at the injury.

The second Death priest launched his own spell. I yanked his magic to me and redirected it into the face of the demon in front of me. It couldn't shriek in outrage without the equivalent of a mouth.

The third demon leapt at me. Trajan met it in mid-air. I opened my eyes as they both cried out when talons and claws cut. Black and hot pink blood sprayed across the flagstones. They tumbled over the floor, each seeking purchase.

When possessing Aduba failed, the dark cloud of the skinwalker flowed in Reby's direction. The Wildling had shifted back to her human shape and dragged the duchess toward the largest fireplace. With a gesture and a muttered word, the flames flowed out of the hearth and cocooned the two women.

The miasma coming from the skinwalker tasted of rage and hate. Those emotions arrowed at the downed merchant, and the awful cloud surrounded him. Penetrated him. I reached into my cloak pocket, pulled out a bottle, and flung it at the rising DiSand.

Demon claws intercepted the tiny piece of glass. It turned and glared at me while making the awful sound that was their laughter.

I smiled in return. "You think you're the only one who can learn new tricks?"

Aduba threw his bottle. Glass shattered next to DiSand, and my spell enveloped him and the skinwalker. Behind the time-frozen forms, the high brother drew his sword.

"Farewell, demons." The huge priest grinned and with one stroke of his equally huge sword, DiSand's head separated from his shoulders and bounced once on the flagstones before it settled to stare at me with an outraged expression.

The demons howled. Three muffled pops took them back to their plane of existence.

The flames receded from around Reby and the still unconscious duchess. Soot covered nearly every inch of the Wildling's skin. She propped her fists on her hips and surveyed the scene.

"If you don't mind, Chief Justice, I think I'm going back to being a mountain bandit. It's a much easier way of making a living."

Chapter 36

The other two teams did their best to capture a live renegade, but once again, self-inflicted poison took the lives of the ones who survived the brief skirmishes at each of Tandor's gates. Poor Duchess Nadine did her best to answer our questions, but the experience of being possessed and witnessing her own hands take the lives of her son and husband took their toll on her mind and emotions.

By morning, the citizens found themselves with a Diné and Plains Nations army occupying their city. For some reason, they found this situation far more satisfactory than their previous overlords.

Slowly, Reverend Father Nizhé'é' and I put together the events Aduba, Nantan, and Elizabeth were unaware of. The second skinwalker, as Duchess Nadine, had called together the handful of nobles in the duchy, claiming to be seeking a marital arrangement after the duke's murder. He poisoned them and their families to keep them from interfering with the renegades' plans.

That left the duchess, the three surviving Temple seats, and a handful of guild masters as the only local leadership left in Tandor. Frankly, I wasn't sure how much help the duchess and the justice would be without care from the clergy of Child. Nor could I blame the Reverend Father for being unwilling to send his eagle Wildling north.

Not until we heard from Shi Hua anyway.

Elizabeth's assessment of the fate of most sea-faring delegations had been correct. Nantan and Hadar had gone out with a surviving ship captain Nantan trusted and found evidence of the sunken caravels.

Why the renegades let the Sea Peoples' fleet continue to Orrin was the question that confounded me. They would be long gone by the time we returned home. I just prayed to Balance they didn't have any demon eggs onboard as they headed back to their islands.

Once the Reverend Father was assured we had rooted out all the actual renegades, he summoned his supply train. I liked him even more for not risking his support staff.

Or for risking my lover's life.

Tyra and I readied for bed in the unoccupied quarters of one of Tandor's murdered junior Light priests. Neither of us felt comfortable sleeping in the dead temple, even if it's structural integrity weren't questionable. I wanted nothing more than a dreamless sleep after being awake from sunset to sunset.

"If I didn't say so earlier, thank you for not getting yourself killed last night." She struggled to pull off her uniform shirt. The one I'd found for her was a bit snug, but it couldn't be helped. Reverend Father Biming had sailed away with our own clothing.

"I delegated just like you, Gina, and Little Bear keep insisting." I grinned at her as I yanked off the ridiculous sand boots I'd been forced to wear.

"I just never dreamed you'd delegate the killing."

Before I could summon a rejoinder, pounding on the door brought steel immediately to both our hands.

"Chief Justice! We have word from Orrin!" Hadar's voice.

Tyra and I glanced at each other. She motioned me to say something before I opened the door.

"One moment!" At her nod, I yanked on the latch.

Hadar turned bright red, but I wasn't sure if it was due to the swordpoint at his throat or Tyra's nude bosom. He swallowed hard. "I swear by Thief the ambassador is in contact with Sister Shi Hua at this moment. He sent me to request your presence along with High Brother Luc."

"Have you given the message to the high brother?"

Hadar gulped, but he couldn't tear his gaze from Tyra. "Not yet, m'lady."

"Then stop staring at my warden, and go!" I shut the door and turned to her. "I think you have an admirer."

She snickered and reached for her uniform shirt. "Not my taste."

"Well, it's good to know you're not cheating on me."

When her head popped through the opening of her shirt, she sniffed in derision. "Don't you dare use me to make someone else jealous."

"That's 'Don't you dare use me to make someone else jealous, m'lady,'" I corrected.

"Don't you dare use me to make someone else jealous, Chief Justice." Her look dared me to correct her again.

I shook my head at her impertinence. Maybe we both needed the byplay after the stress of the last six days.

Once we were adequately dressed and armed, we jogged down to the junior priest's quarters Quan was using. Luc and Yar rushed from the other direction. The Diné Conflict warden standing watch acknowledged us all with a nod before he knocked and opened the door.

I was a little surprised to find Reverend Father Nizhé'é' already here. He held the ambassador's hand while Quan sat cross-legged on the bed with his eyes closed.

The Reverend Father gestured sharply. "Hurry! Sister Shi Hua can't keep the link going forever even with High Sister Bertrice's help."

Luc swung on his crutches to the bed, sat beside the ambassador, and took his other hand. I stood between him and the Reverend Father and clasped his and Luc's palms. The familiar presence of Shi Hua and Bertrice filled my mind.

Thank Balance you're both alive, I said.

We could say the same about you, Bertrice said. The two priestesses' relief was as palpable as my own.

Bertrice laid out the events in Orrin, including what had really been done to Dante and his family. Bile coated the back of my throat over my own failure at sensing the demon eggs within the peacekeeper, his wife, and children. And my fists clenched when Shi Hua said that Yanaba had been forced to trigger Balance's defensive spells in Orrin as well.

However, since my protégé was linked with the spell and inside the protective stone of the statue of Balance, it hadn't drained all the magic from the Temple. The explanation made me feel slightly guilty I hadn't suffered as Yanaba had. At some point, Balance Herself would settle my account one way or another.

Luc relayed our own experiences since our arrival in Tandor, and the Reverend Father added the decisions made by the Diné, the Cliffdwellers, and the Plains Nations civilian and Temple leaders.

So those damn demons tried the same stunt they pulled with the Chumash and Apache centuries ago. Bertrice's sour tone carried through the link. *A courier from Standora has already arrived. The queen's army and a Temple contingent are marching south.*

Can you two send a message to all the home Temples? I asked. *Death and Wildling have been the only Temples in Tandor to come out of this mess relatively intact. The rest will need all new staffs in every position. And can you petition for me that Sister Reby of Wildling should be promoted to Tandor's seat. She has acted with exemplary courage and fortitude in this crisis.*

Of course, Bertrice replied.

Have you heard from Biming? Quan's only comment during the entire conversation.

No, Your Highness. Shi Hua's voice sounded small and sad. *I've been trying during our scheduled contact times.*

And the poor girl is about to pass out, Bertrice added. *We'll contact you tomorrow night.*

With those words, the link faded abruptly.

Quan blinked and yanked his hands out of the Reverend Father and Luc's hold, but not before I caught a hint of his grief. He feared the worst for Biming, and the emotion was breaking the ambassador's heart.

I reluctantly released the hands I held. "Thank you for sending Hadar to fetch us, Ambassador. Good eventide." I whirled and left the bedchambers before I became the conduit of his tears.

Chapter 37

Reby and I surveyed the mess of what had been the Tandor Temple of Balance. She had left Sisquoc in charge of cleaning out their own Temple, claiming I had no one to help me put things right here.

I tried not to think about Elizabeth. Nantan assured me he would keep her at Death until I came back to question her later. I simply didn't have the energy for a truthspell, much less an intensive interrogation, right now.

Nor did I try to think about Yanaba's recovery in Orrin. From Bertrice's information last night, my second could be permanently incapacitated. A thread of dread climbed up my spine at the thought of Tandor with no justice at all.

Or that's what I told myself. My brief experience with foresight while taking the duchess's fortress had thrown off my sense of stability. A tiny part of me wondered if I'd latched onto something worse coming for us in the future. Something not clearly seen, but there nonetheless.

With one hand on her hip and the other holding a borrowed broom, Reby surveyed the wreckage. "I feel like I'm a little girl again, sweeping up my mother's workshop."

"Cleaning would go much faster if you had actual supplies."

We turned at the female voice behind us. The woman who'd argued recipes with Luc entered the courtroom. Behind her was Tandor's master weaver and several other people. They all carried buckets, rags, brooms, and in a few cases, shovels.

"I never really introduced myself before." The woman gave me a slight smile. "I'm Bathilda."

"I'm Anthea."

Bathilda's smile turned rueful. "We know who you are."

"Then you can just call me Red." I grinned. The group of civilians stared at me with varying degrees of shock and horror.

A sharp bark of a laugh burst out of Reby. We all looked at her.

She shook her head. "When did you develop a sense of humor?"

"About the same time you stopped robbing travelers in eastern Orrin," I shot back.

"You really aren't going to let that go, are you?" She threw her hand in the air. "I was a stupid child who'd lost her mother."

I cocked my head. "Ah, I see. You couldn't rebel against your own mother, so you decided to use me as a surrogate."

Reby's mouth opened, but whatever she was about to say was interrupted by Hadar's shouts.

"Justice! Chief Justice Anthea!" The young Thief priest burst into the courtroom. His skin glowed bright orange, and he bent over to catch his breath. "High Brother Luc and the Reverend Father need you at the lookout for the Neighbor's Gate right now."

A chill ran through me.

Reby muttered an imprecation under her breath. "An army?"

Hadar nodded. "They think. A large group is headed this way from Cant."

There was only one reason Luc would be on the lookout tower. Only one reason he'd want my opinion when Aduba and Hadar had distance-view glasses up there.

I raced out of the dead temple and down Tandor's main thoroughfare. Reby ran beside me. Panic flowed from her mind. We'd been lucky with the three demons the second skinwalker had summoned. We'd taken the bastards by surprise.

The crowds on the street parted as I screamed at them to get out of my way. Enough fear of the renegades remained. They darted into entryways and alleys as Reby and I raced for Tandor's southern gate.

Wardens were barring the massive iron doors as we approached. I scrambled up the ladder to the lookout.

And the sight of Luc peering through a distance glass at the edge of the wall finally struck me. "How did you manage to get up here?" I said between gasping breaths.

He lowered the distance glass. "Supply basket."

Normally, he would make some joke or bitter comment about adapting to the loss of his foot, but his seriousness scared me. As did the bright orange glow of Reverend Father Nizhé'é' and Aduba's faces when they hadn't been running as I had.

"What do you make of that?"

In the distance, sand glowed white, but the glare didn't totally block out the yellowish dust plumes. It was the line of absolute black between the sand and dust that chilled my very marrow. I tried to control the urge to vomit over the side of the wall.

"What is it?" Reby whispered from beside me.

"Demons."

Turn the page for a sneak peek of the next Justice novel, *A Matter of Death!*

A Matter of Death

Excerpt © 2018, Suzan Harden

The queen's army arrived in Orrin at First Morning on Fifth Day, exactly a week after the awful day demons were discovered and destroyed inside Balance and Death. Everyone at the Temple of Light, except the wardens on duty, had been at morning prayers when the peacekeeper arrived with the news regarding their visitors from the capital.

Shi Hua watched as Magistrate DiCook's messenger whispered to Brother Jeremy, the acting seat of the Temple. Chief Warden Nicholas rose and joined the two men, probably more out of worry that a priest he was charged with protecting might be harmed rather than curiosity.

Once the peacekeeper scurried out of the main sanctuary, Jeremy bowed to the civilians attending the dawn services. "Forgive me for our abbreviated worship, but Sister Shi Hua and I have been called to other duties."

She scrambled to her feet, sketched the requisite gesture of respect to the statue of Light, and crossed the sanctuary to join Jeremy. *Are you sure the queen requested my presence?* she asked silently.

Amusement filled his eyes. *The crown princess is leading the army, and yes, she specifically asked for you. She's with Duke Marco and Prince Alika at the duke's estate along with Reverend Father Farrell.*

Of course. It would not do for the crown princess to ignore the local nobility. She would need their vassals to augment her forces. Nor could she meet with one Temple alone without arousing the ire of the other eleven. Unfortunately, the queen, the duke of Orrin and the chief justice of Balance were too entwined in their personal relationships to totally avoid all questions.

To add to the complications, half of the Sea Peoples fleet still anchored in Orrin's harbor. Prince Alika and several of his captains refused to leave Issura after the discovery of the demons and their eggs in the city. While captains and sailors of the departing ships had been truthspelled, no one could guarantee the ships weren't carrying demons or eggs without the odd sight of Orrin's chief justice to search people, ships, and all property for demon contamination.

However, Prince Alika didn't have a distance speaker with him, and it would be nigh impossible for Shi Hua to contact someone in the islands she didn't know. So he sent half his fleet home on the chance they could successfully raise the alarm.

I still don't know why the crown princess would want to speak to me, Shi Hua protested silently while she jogged alongside Jeremy to the stables, their wardens following as shadows. It didn't help matters that she was not an Issuran citizen, though both her own Reverend Father of Light in Jing and the Reverend Father of Light here in Issura had agreed to the temporary transfer. But with the spate of demon activity over the last month and a half, Shi Hua wondered if she'd ever see home again.

Because right now, you are our primary contact with Tandor, Jeremy chided. *And our sister city is under a demon attack.*

Shi Hua swallowed a groan. She'd only talked with High Brother Luc, Chief Justice Anthea, and Ambassador Quan twice, once before the demon army arrived at Tandor's doorstep and once after. Since then, she hadn't been able to penetrate the demon's magic, not even with assistance from other priests and priestesses. All she knew for sure was those loyal to the queendom of Issura still held the city of Tandor. Otherwise, the demons would already be hammering at Orrin's gates.

This was not going to be an enjoyable meeting at the duke's estate. And she hadn't broken her fast yet.

Who else will be there? she asked silently as she and Jeremy saddled their mounts. Chief Warden Nicholas and Warden Mateqai did the same. There had been too many assassination attempts in Orrin over the month and a half. And after last week, not one of the Temple wardens allowed any of the clergy to attend the privy without a guard.

High Brother Han and High Sister Bertrice are already there.

Of course, the seat of Conflict was responsible for organizing the city's defenses in the case of an attack. And demons had managed to have themselves delivered to the Temple of Death by wearing the bodies of a murdered peace-keeper and his family.

"What about Justice Yanaba?" Shi Hua asked.

Jeremy looked down at her from atop his horse. "You're the one visiting her every day. What do you think?"

Jeremy's gentle question was an answer in itself. Shi Hua climbed onto her own mount. Yanaba had nearly killed herself defending the city from the demons who'd snuck into Orrin wearing human skins. She shuddered. They'd come so close to losing the city, and its defense had been costly.

"You know High Sister Bianca will find a way to insert herself into this meeting," Mateqai said.

Nicholas shot his junior warden a dirty look, but Jeremy merely nodded.

"If she is there, fine." Jeremy sounded far older than his twenty-one winters. "All of the Temples need to let go of our petty differences. We have demons on our border, and we must work together."

"Yes, sir," Mateqai said.

Nothing more was said on the ride to Duke Marco's estate.

Loud voices and tension thickened the air in Duke Marco's great hall when Shi Hua and the rest of the party from Light arrived. A huge map of Issura covered most of a large table. Whatever argument was happening died as the duke's steward announced their presence.

At the sight of High Mother Bianca seated next to Duke Marco, Shi Hua glanced at Mateqai. The corner of her warden's mouth quirked, but otherwise, he kept a solemn mien, which the situation warranted.

However, Mother Bianca sat on the duke's left. His sister, Lady Alessa, sat on his right. Shi Hua wondered if she'd be allowed to extend felicitations to Lady Katarina before they left. If the duke's wife weren't so close to her delivery, she would no doubt make sure Mother Bianca wasn't anywhere near her husband.

Reverend Father Farrell's face lit up with a huge grin. "Just the people we need to speak with!"

The head of the Issuran order of Light sat at the opposite end of the table to the left of an imposing woman. Shi Hua sucked in her breath when Crown Princess Chiara turned to appraise the newcomers.

Not even Emperor Bao Chengwu of Jing gave off such an intimidating air. The crown princess didn't bother with any accoutrements or insignia of her rank, other than her own gray-streaked blue-black braids wrapped and pinned in the shape of a coronet. She dressed in plain black leather and steel chainmail. Her dark eyes were piercing, and Shi Hua had no doubt the crown princess missed little of what happened around her.

Following Jeremy's lead, Shi Hua bowed.

"We come to serve, Your Highness," Jeremy murmured.

A wry smile lightened the crown princess's face. "From what your colleagues have said, it sounds to me like you and your Temple have been doing more than your fair share of service, Brother Jeremy." She gestured at the two people on the other side of the Reverend Father.

To his left was High Brother Han of Conflict. The normally jovial priest was especially somber behind his bushy red beard.

Beside Han sat High Sister Bertrice of Death. Her short hair gleamed silver in the morning light from the manse's high windows. She didn't look any happier than Han.

The crown princess pointed at two empty chairs between Orrin's magistrate, Malven DiCook and another man dressed in the same military garb as the crown princess. "Please take a seat, Brother Jeremy. I'd like to ask both you and Sister Shi Hua some questions about the events in Orrin over the last two months."

Worry wormed its way through Shi Hua, and not just because the heir to the throne of Issura knew her name. She'd never feared the people here before, but Ambassador Quan had always been with her at these types of meetings. As his bodyguard, her attention had been consumed with watching for dangers to him.

But then came the discovery of renegades infiltrating Issura's Temple of Light and her temporary transfer to Orrin. High Brother Luc's irritation with her performance as a priestess would be a mosquito bite compared to the displeasure and consequences should she incur Crown Princess Chiara's wrath.

For the next candlemark, Shi Hua and Jeremy were questioned. About their first encounter with a demon egg. The discovery of demons wearing human skins. Justice Yanaba's spell to freeze and destroy the demons, the one that nearly killed her. The demon eggs hidden in the corpses of Peacekeeper Dante and his family.

But when Crown Princess Chiara questioned the wisdom of Chief Justice Anthea and High Brother Luc's absence at such a crucial time, everyone from Orrin erupted in protest.

Everyone except High Mother Bianca.

"Enough." The crown princess slapped the table hard enough that goblets, wine decanters, and even the parchment jumped and shivered.

Everyone went silent until Reverend Father Farrell cleared his throat. "It was mine and Reverend Mother Alara's decision to send the two of them to Tandor—"

The crown princess held up her forefinger.

His face flushed. "I will not be silent when you question—"

"I will not tell you again, Reverend Father," she said coldly before she turned her intimidating gaze on Shi Hua. "Why aren't you defending them, Sister?"

Shi Hua swallowed hard. "It's not my place—"

"No, your place is in a Temple in Jing." The crown princess's eyes narrowed. "But you're here, and I'll use whatever resources are at hand. Now, why aren't you defending them?"

Shi Hua dug her nails into her palms to keep from retorting in kind. Quan had never been this rude, even when he had been the crown prince of the empire. She lifted her chin. "Because Chief Justice Anthea and High Brother Luc don't need to be defended. They know their duty, and they have served to the best of their abilities."

Something thawed in the crown princess's icy demeanor. "Even if such service means the ultimate sacrifice?"

Shi Hua worked to keep her face impassive, but her gut clenched. Maybe it was a good thing she hadn't broken her fast after all. "Yes, Your Highness."

Crown Princess Chiara faced High Mother Bianca. "You were the only one from Orrin who didn't take umbrage at my words. Why?"

The priestess cast a sly look in Reverend Father Farrell's direction. "It's not my place to question the instructions from another order." She turned to the crown princess. "But as Sister Shi Hua has stated, our seats of Balance and Light will defend the queendom from demons with their very lives if need be."

The crown princess blew out a deep breath. "Since we've lost contact with our clergy in Tandor, we must assume the worst." Her gaze bore into Bertrice. "High Sister, can you activate the defense spells at your sister Temple in Tandor from here?"

Bertrice's face paled to nearly the color of her hair. "Your Majesty, you cannot be serious!"

Crown Princess Chiara leaned her elbows on the scarred wood, her palms pressed together, and her chin resting on her fingertips. "I fear High Mother Bianca is right, albeit indirectly. Destroying the Duchy of Tandor may be the only way to stop the demon army."

Glossary

Words and Phrases Specific to the Justice Series

Apprentice – lowest rank of a trade or craft guild

Berda – a person whose appearance or behavior when it comes to gender/ sexuality is flexible

Britannia – Toscan name for a series of islands off the western coast of the Old Continent. The two largest are Eire and Albion. Four hundred years before Anthea's time, the queens of Eire and Albion were losing their battle against the demons. They ordered the islands evacuated and the Temples of Death to launch their last resort spells. The islands are now barren, and no one who steps on them lives for long.

Briton Diaspora – refers to the survivors and their descendants of the evacuation of Britannia who are now scattered around the world

Brother – title for any fully ordained priest of any Temple that accepts men, except for the Temple of Father

Cant – Issura's neighboring nation-state to the south

Chengzhou – the capital of Jing, a nation-state in the eastern shore of the Old Continent

Chief Justice – title of the highest ranked priestess at a Temple of Balance

Chief [name of trade] – the highest ranking master guild member of a trade in a city or region

The Cliffdwellers – loosely aligned city-states on the southeastern border of Issura

The Cradle – according to legend, the continent where Child created the first members of the human race

Duke/Duchess – highest ranking noble of a region

Father – title for any fully ordained priest of the Temple of Father

Gray Mountains – a mountain range that runs the entire length of the western side of the Long Continents

The Grand Canal – a human-built canal that passes through the isthmus connecting the Long Continents

Guild – a civil organization for a trade or craft

Healer – a person with the magical ability to heal illness and repair wounds

High Brother – title of the chief priest of a city Temple, except the Temple of Father

High Father – title of the chief priest of a city Temple of Father

High Mother – title of the chief priestess of a city Temple of Mother

High Sister – title of the chief priestess of a city Temple, except the Temples of Balance or Mother

Iberia – nation-state on the southwestern corner of the Old Continent

Issura – queendom on the western coast of the Northern Long Continent; the Peaceful Sea forms its western border with the nation of Pagonia to the north, the nation of Cant to the south, the nations of the Cliffdwellers and Diné to the southeast and the Gray Mountains to the east

Jing – nation-state on the eastern side of the Old Continent

Journeyman/Journeywoman – middle rank of a trade or craft guild

Justice – title for any fully ordained priestess of the Temple of Balance; alternate term of address is Lady Justice

Kemet – nation-state on the northeast corner of the Cradle

The Long Continents – the two continents separating the Peaceful Sea from the Panthalassa Sea, they are connected by a narrow isthmus

The Lost Continent – southern continent between the Peaceful Sea and the Storm Sea. By Anthea's time, the original inhabitants were believed to be slaughtered by demons 500 years before. Sailors from the Sea Peoples and Maurya who landed there after the inhabitants' disappearance reported screams but found no one. Those with magic talents went mad. Not even the priests and priestesses from Child could save them. Those who tried went mad themselves.

Magistrate – elected official of a city or town in Issura who is responsible for civil and criminal law enforcement and the city or town's defense/care in an emergency

Master – senior member of a trade or craft guild based on analysis of his/her peers; the clergyperson who is primarily responsible for the training of a novice class

Maurya – the southern-most nation of the Old Continent

Middle Sea – shallow sea that separates The Cradle from the Old Continent

Mother – title for any fully ordained priestess of the Temple of Mother

National Road – main, paved road through the nation of Issura. It roughly parallels the western coastline.

New Thenos – an island city/state on the eastern coast of the Northern Long Continent

Novice – a person in training to become a priest/priestess of the Twelve

Orrin – third largest city in the queendom of Issura with the second largest port

Pagonia – Issura's neighboring nation to the north

Panthalassa Sea – ocean that separates the Long Continents from the western part of the Old Continent and the Cradle

Peaceful Sea – ocean that separates the Long Continents from the eastern part of the Old Continent, the islands and archipelagos of the Sea Peoples, and the Lost Continent

Peacekeepers – men and women who act as a city's police force. They report to the city's magistrate. They also act as an auxiliary defense force if their city or nation is attacked.

Reverend Father – senior-most priest of a Temple order, the leader of that sect in the nation in which he resides

Reverend Mother – senior-most priestess of a Temple order, the leader of that sect in the nation in which she resides

Seat – person holding the highest ranking position of a Temple

Shakya – nation-state in the western portion of the Old Continent, southwest of Jing and northeast of Maurya

Sister – title for any fully ordained priestess of any Temple that accepts women, except for the Temples of Mother and Balance

Standora – capital and largest city of Issura

Storm Sea – ocean bordered by the eastern part of the Cradle, the southern part of the Old Continent, and the western part of the Lost Continent

Talent – a person attuned to magic; active talents can cast spells, passive talents can only trigger spells that an active talent has primed

Tandor – Issuran city that guards the border with Cant and Diné

Temple – a collection of people dedicated to the service of one of the twelve gods; a building that houses such people; the primary place of worship for one of the twelve gods

Tianjin – Jing's largest seaport

Tiwan – the capital of Cant

Toscana – nation-state on the southwest section of the Old Continent; location of the first battle against the demons

The Twelve – the collective name for the twelve deities of the Justice universe

Valencia – duchy in the nation-state of Iberia; known for their innovative shipbuilding designs

Warden – security guard of a Temple, they act as supplementary military personnel in the event of a demon invasion

THE TWELVE TEMPLES

Mother

Cloak Color – Light blue

Motto – "To give without thought; to forgive with love."

The Temple of Mother is responsible for the teaching of household arts, such as spinning, weaving, food storage and preparation. The order is also responsible for caring for those who have lost their families.

Father

Cloak Color – Dark blue

Motto – "All tools are weapons, and weapons tools."

The Temple of Father is responsible for the constructive arts, such as carpentry and smithing.

Balance

Cloak Color – Black

Motto – "Balance in all things."

The Temple of Balance runs the judicial system. A justice is the judge in criminal and civil cases.

Light

Cloak Color – Medium brown

Motto – "Light brings truth, for without truth, there can be no justice."

The Temple of Light is responsible for codifying contracts and mediating contract disputes. A Light priest also acts as the bailiff for a justice, and is often the one to truthspell a witness or the accused. The Temple of Light also provides military support to a nation's civilian army.

Knowledge

Cloak Color – Gold

Motto – "With patience, knowledge comes."

The Temple of Knowledge is responsible for education and for recording historical events. They essentially act as the library system for the Justice universe.

Thief

Cloak Color – Grey

Motto – "Hiding in plain sight."

The Temple of Thief acts as the intelligence-gathering arm of both the Temples and the civilian leaders. They finance their efforts through gambling dens.

Conflict

Cloak Color – Dark Red

Motto – "Destruction is the necessary evil, for it clears the way for new growth."

The Temple of Conflict focuses on strategy and all martial arts. They are the primary support and teachers of a nation's army.

Love

Cloak Color – Medium Red

Motto – "Pleasure is life."

The Temple of Love are the holy prostitutes. They also deal with sex education and lead the Spring Rituals, the annual fertility rites which were first used to breed as many humans with magical talent as possible. Don't underestimate them. They fight just as hard and as nasty as their fellow clergy in Conflict.

Child

Cloak Color – Light green

Motto – "All things are new once."

The Temple of Child is responsible for the emotional health of citizens. They also develop and teach agriculture and animal husbandry techniques.

Wilding

Cloak Color – Dark green

Motto – "All creatures return to us."

The Temple of the Wildling God deals with management of wild animal populations, forestry, and the protection of ecosystems. They are the only clergy who can shift into a secondary animal form.

Vintner

Cloak Color – Purple

Motto – "The line between wisdom and madness is one sip."

The Temple of Vintner not only deals with the cultivation of grapes and the production of wine, but they also promote the gathering, cultivation and processing of all medicinal herbs.

Death

Cloak Color – Black

Motto – "For every life, there is a death."

The Temple of Death takes care of the gathering of the dead, the last rites, and disposal of corpses. They also act as a repository for the last wills and testaments of all citizens.

CHARACTERS

QUEENDOM OF ISURRA
ORRIN

Temple of Balance

Chief Justice Anthea – a circuit justice for ten years until her appointment/ sentence as Chief Justice at the age of thirty winters ("Justice")

Chief Justice Penelope – deceased, predecessor to Anthea as Chief Justice

Chief Justice Thalia - deceased, predecessor to Penelope as Chief Justice, maternal grandmother to Anthea

Justice Yanaba – junior justice after the events of *A Question of Balance*

Sivan – personal assistant to Chief Justice Anthea and head of the household staff

Donella – senior clerk

Lailani – junior clerk

Chief Warden Little Bear – head of the wardens

Warden Tyra – junior warden

Warden Gina – junior warden

Warden Aglaia – junior warden, died in the battle to retake the Temple of
     Love (*A Question of Balance*)

Warden Daniel – junior warden

Warden Noko – junior warden

Warden Jonata – junior warden, Aglaia's replacement from the Standora
     Wardens' Academy

Warden Dezba – junior warden

Hogarth – former chief warden under Justices Thalia and Penelope, now
     stablemaster, husband of Deborah

Deborah – Head cook, wife of Hogarth

Nathan – squire to Chief Justice Anthea after he was sentenced to pay
     reparations for stealing bread, an orphan, age ten winters at the time of his
     sentencing in *A Question of Balance*

Ming Wei – squire to Justice Yanaba, nine winters old at the end of *A Question
     of Balance*. Originally from Jing, she was sold by her parents to a Jing
     noble as a sex slave and brought to Issura. When the noble's crimes were
     discovered, he immolated himself and his slaves. Ming Wei was the only
     survivor and has severe scar tissue on her face, back and arms.

Temple of Light

High Brother Luc – a circuit priest for twelve winters until his appointment as
     chief priest at the age of thirty-two winters between the events of "Justice"
     and "Diplomacy in the Dark"

High Brother Kam – semi-retired, predecessor to Luc as chief priest, poisoned
     and died during the events of *A Question of Balance*

Brother Mat – Second to Luc. His birth name is Micah. He murdered the real
     Mat on his way to Orrin from Standora. Died under Anthea's truthspell
     questioning in *A Question of Balance*.

Brother Jeremy – youngest junior priest

Istaqa – personal assistant to High Brother Luc and head of the household
staff

Edberth – former personal assistant to High Brother Kam, he now acts as
evening assistant to High Brother Luc

Chief Warden Nicholas – head of the wardens

Warden Gibb – junior warden, died shortly after the renegades' kidnapping of
High Brother Luc in *A Question of Balance*

Warden Mateqai – junior warden, a passive talent, becomes Sister Shi Hua's
personal bodyguard during the events of *A Modicum of Truth*

Warden Tadhg – junior warden

Temple of Love

High Sister Gerd – chief priestess, biological daughter of Thalia and Kam,
biological mother of Anthea. She was removed from office on charges
of fraud, bribery of a public official, unlawful magic, and conspiracy to
commit murder. Later, the charges of dealing in demon artifacts and
treason were added.

Sister Dragonfly – Gerd's second, is acting High Sister after the events in *A
Question of Balance*, becomes High Sister after the events in *A Modicum of
Truth*

Sister Gretchen – priestess, deceased. The discovery of her body in one of
Duke Marco's wine barrels precipitates the event in *A Question of Balance.*

Temple of Conflict

High Brother Han – chief priest

Temple of Death

High Sister Bertrice – chief priestess

High Brother Kai – deceased, predecessor of Bertrice, retired in Bertrice's
favor as the temple seat and became a teaching brother in Standora until his
death

Brother Xander – Bertrice's second

Chief Warden Axton – head of the wardens

Temple of Vintner
High Brother Ben – chief priest

Temple of Mother
High Mother Bianca – chief priestess

Temple of Father
High Father Jerrod – chief priest

Temple of Child
High Sister Mya – chief priestess

Temple of Wildling
High Brother Jax – chief priest, second form is a wolf
Sister Farrah – Jax's second, second form is a fox

Temple of Thief
High Brother Talbert – chief priest

Temple of Knowledge
High Sister Mariana – chief priestess

Nobility and their retainers
Lord Samael DiRoy – distant cousin of the queen, executed for summoning
   demons in "Justice"
Duke Benedetto DiMara – father of Marco, Alessa, and Isabella, husband of
   Cora, convicted of conspiracy to use illegal magic to mind wipe his son
   Marco during the events of "Justice", imprisoned at Standora for life
Lady Cora DiMara – mother of Marco, Alessa, and Isabella, convicted of
   treason and demon dealing, executed by the Reverend Mother Alara of
   Balance during the events of "Justice"

Duke Marco DiMara – duke of Orrin, inherited his post at the age of eighteen winters after his parents were found guilty of numerous offenses and stripped of their titles and property

Lady Katarina DiMara (nee' DiLove) – Temple-born wife of Marco, animal healer, her mother was a priestess of Love and died of the wasting sickness shortly before Katarina's eighteenth winter.

Lady Alessa DiMara – sister of Marco, a passive talent, lover of Sister Gretchen of Love

Lady Isabella DiMara – sister of Marco, attends the University of Standora

Bartholomew – retainer of Duke Marco's until it was learned he'd assaulted Lady Alessa and Sister Gretchen. Lady Alessa subsequently asked Chief Justice Anthea for clemency and hired him to manage the estates Sister Gretchen willed to her.

William – retainer of Duke Marco's

Julian – retainer of Duke Marco's

Titus – captain of Duke Marco's flagship, the *Mar Tranquilus*

Citizens

Malven DiCook – duly elected magistrate of Orrin

Dante – one of DiCook's peacekeepers, dies at the beginning of *A Modicum of Truth*

Barbora – wife of Dante, dies at the beginning of *A Modicum of Truth*

Jaime – one of DiCook's peacekeepers

Guilds

Chief Healer Aaron – head of the Healers' Guild

Master Healer Devin – second to Aaron in the Orrin Healer's Guild, originally from New Thenos

Journeywoman Bly – a junior healer, often assists Master Devin at autopsies

TANDOR

High Brother Dav – chief priest of the Temple of Light

Chief Justice Elizabeth – chief justice of the Temple of Balance

Minerva – the new clerk with the Temple of Balance, a renegade

High Brother Aduba – chief priest of the Temple of Conflict

Brother Tighan – second of the Temple of Conflict, a renegade, killed by Aduba during the fall of Tandor

Sister Rabit Runs – priestess of the Temple of Conflict, killed by a skinwalker while escaping to Diné in *A Modicum of Truth*

High Brother Nantan – chief priest of the Temple of Death

Sister Reby – second of the Temple of the Wildling God, first introduced as a shapeshifting thief in "The Perfect Partner", second form is a polecat

Brother Sisquoc – priest of the Temple of the Wildling God, second form is a puma

Brother Trajan – priest of the Temple of the Wilding God, second form is a wolf

Duke Enzo DiToscana – Duke of Tandor, murdered by a skinwalker possessing his wife

Duchess Nadine DiToscana – the widow of Duke Enzo of Tandor

Ural DiSand – merchant from Tandor, implicated in the Assassins Guild plots in Orrin

Amarantha DiRoma – Tandorian merchant, rival of Ural DiSan, murdered by renegades shortly before they poisoned most of the personnel of the Tandorian Temples

STANDORA – capital city of Issura

Reverend Mother Alara – head of Issura's Temple of Balance

Reverend Father Farrell – head of Issura's Temple of Light

Brother Jon – novice training priest at the main Temple of Light in Standora, murdered by the skinwalker at Samael DiRoy's abandoned manse prior to *A Question of Balance*

Justice Rose – novice training priestess of the main Temple of Balance in Standora when Anthea was a novice

Crown Princess Chiara – eldest child and heir of Queen Teodora of Issura; lady general of the queen's army

PANA VALLEY

Lord Aleister DeGrove – noble noted for his vineyards

JING EMPIRE

CHENGZHOU

Empress Bao De – ruler of Jing a century before Bao Yu, she sacrificed herself to stop a demon army

Empress Bao Yu – ruler of Jing until her death from natural causes during "Courting Trouble"

Emperor Bao Chengwu – current ruler of Jing, succeeded his mother Bao Yu during "Courting Trouble"

Ambassador Quan Po – half-brother of the current Jing emperor Bao Chengwu; was heir to the throne until his nephew was born

Reverend Father Jin – head of Jing's Temple of Light

Sister Shi Hua – a priestess of Light, who was tapped as Po's bodyguard. She received additional training from Conflict, Thief, and Love. Originally from the town of Yintze in the southern province of Chu.

Brother Lin – novice master of Light

Brother Jian – a priest of Light, classmate of Shi Hua during their novice years

Brother Fa – a Wildling priest, his second form is a tiger, a friend of Shi Hua and Jian during their novice years

Justice Mei Wen – a priestess of Balance, Shi Hua's closest friend other than Jian during their novice years

Sister Yin Li – a priestess of Love, Shi Hua's maternal aunt

Reverend Father Chen – head of Jing's Temple of Conflict

Brother Shang – a priest of Conflict, Shi Hua's instructor when she was a novice

Reverend Father Biming – head of Jing's Temple of Thief

The Unbridled – spy ship used by the Temple of Thief, a four-masted carrack built in the Iberian duchy of Valencia, captained by Reverend Father Biming during *A Modicum of Truth*

Brother Hadar – a priest of Thief from the Kingdom of Hejaz, serving on board *The Unbridled*

ISLANDS OF THE SEA PEOPLES

Kingdom of O'ahu

Prince Alika – youngest son of the king of the Sea Peoples, one of Sister
Gretchen's worshippers, the father of her unborn child

Captain Iakepa – senior captain of the O'ahu trading fleet

DINÉ NATION

Reverend Father Nizhé'é' – head of the Diné Temple of Conflict

Acknowledgments

There's a lot of people who made this book possible. Thank you to . . .

Elaina Lee of For the Muse Design for creating such marvelous covers.

Jaye Manus of QA Productions for making the inside look as beautiful as the outside and for tolerating my perfectionist tendencies.

Gretchen Reise Kelly and Rebecca Babb, my soul sisters who have been my cheerleaders.

Darling Husband and Genius Kid for doing an inordinate amount of cooking for the last several months. Taco Tuesdays for everyone!

And most of all, the readers who demanded this story.

Suzan Harden is a recovering attorney who writes fiction to regain her sanity. She currently lives in the Great Lakes region with a husband who believes writing is a practical career option and a kid who thinks she's too enamored with zombies.